The Upstart Crow

An Introduction to Shakespeare's Plays

Gareth Lloyd Evans

Edited and Revised by Barbara Lloyd Evans

J M Dent & Sons Ltd
London   Melbourne   Toronto

First published 1982
© Gareth Lloyd Evans 1982

This book is set in 11/13pt Garamond (Stempel) by
Tradespools Ltd, Frome, Somerset
Printed in Great Britain by
Richard Clay (The Chaucer Press) Ltd, Bungay, Suffolk for
J. M. Dent & Sons Ltd
Aldine House, 33 Welbeck Street, London W1

British Library Cataloguing in Publication Data

Lloyd Evans, Gareth
   The upstart crow: an introduction to
Shakespeare's plays.
   1. Shakespeare, William – Criticism and
interpretation
   I. Title
   822.3'3   PR2976

ISBN 0-460-10256-7
ISBN 0-460-11256-2 Pbk

Contents

Introduction

In 1592 Robert Greene, a dissolute but prolific writer of plays and pamphlets, wrote an attack on stage players which included what has generally been taken as a reference to William Shakespeare:

> Yes trust them not: for there is an upstart Crow, beautified with our feathers, but with his *Tygers hart wrapt in a Players hyde*, supposes he is as well able to bombast out a blank verse as the best of you: and being an absolute *Johannes Fac totum*, is in his own conceit the only Shake-scene in a country.

Greene was an unpredictable, neurotic man, with many chips on his shoulder. His envy, malice and jealousy turned itself on any real or imagined rival, and by 1592 Shakespeare had done more than enough to attract his baleful attention. He castigated Shakespeare for copying the ways of the fashionable dramatists of the time – the 'University Wits', a group of which Greene was a member – and for dabbling in all kinds of theatrical endeavour.

Some of Greene's colleagues may privately have concluded that he may well have had a point. By 1592 Shakespeare was revealing an astonishing imaginative versatility and a flowering of dramatic language, but, above all, he had what some might deem the not over-endearing ability to take up any dramatic genre and form used by his colleagues and turn it into something noticeably superior to anything they could achieve. Greene's use of 'upstart' may well have been echoed on a good many lips.

In a sense, this image has remained. No one has ever excelled Shakespeare in the writing of dramatic poetry, no one has challenged his mastery of dramatic form, his depth of characterization, his versatility in plot, theme and expression. But, whatever phrase is chosen to describe him, Shakespeare's quality and pre-eminence, in an age when unique superiority is regarded with suspicion and the strictest clamours of egalitarianism threaten to drown the claims of individual endeavour, need re-asserting. Late twentieth-century comment on and presentation of Shakespeare's plays is dominated by the so-called principle of making them 'speak to the twentieth century'. This is an easy-on-the-eye proposition. Justification for it – citing the historical record that each generation has tended to see and express Shakespeare in its own way – is strengthened by the claim that not only is this inevitable, but that the plays would atrophy were they not subjected to this constant process of 'renewal'. While there is much force and truth in this argument, it ignores the inherent dangers of an over-conscious addiction to making Shakespeare speak in the cultural mores, modes and manners of a time not his own, and, in any case, where does 'renewal' end and 'reconstruction' begin?

The latter half of the twentieth century has concentrated to a remarkable extent on reconstructing Shakespeare in terms of its own sense of itself – often to a degree which makes some of the transmutations of previous eras seem, by comparison, mild and merely cosmetic. The sickening coils of modern racism, the frantic amoralities of permissiveness, the mordancy of existentialism, the intellectual and emotional impoverishment of political egalitarianism are examples of only the most prevalent concerns of our century to have been offloaded into interpretations of Shakespeare's plays. In the process, the plays' shapes have been manipulated, manhandled, and their language pauperized. As a result, instead of fulfilling the laudable and natural urge of each generation to see Shakespeare from its own standpoint, it has distorted and almost inevitably diminished the inherent qualities which constitute his genius.

Some scholars, certainly, and not a few directors, seem overconcerned with the idea that only by inflicting huge changes on his plays, is it possible to 'make Shakespeare speak to the twentieth century'. Here, they say, is a sixteenth-century play. I am a twentieth-century man. What can I do to it to make it speak to my century? The assumptions and arrogances of this are obvious but the practice continues.

On the other hand, there is the other director, in the minority, alas, who says – Here is a sixteenth-century play. I am a twentieth-century man. What can it do to me to enable me to make it speak to my century? Such an approach acknowledges Shakespeare's quality, rather then parading creative parity with him. It accepts that the director's imagination (already sensitized by contact with modernity) should be prepared to accept not the images that it creates itself, but those which step out from the play. The finest modern productions and modern commentaries of Shakespeare acknowledge that he makes his most vital impact when the Elizabethan reality of the plays is not expunged, but held in some kind of creative tension with modern sensibilities. This is, in fact, not to make Shakespeare speak to the twentieth century on its own terms, but rather to cause the twentieth century to listen to Shakespeare with its own ears.

This book, which in effect, amounts to a collection of essay-introductions, varying in length, to each of Shakespeare's plays, is written from that point of view, for while I acknowledge the inevitable process by which each generation brings its own unique experience into its interpretation of Shakespeare's plays, I have, so far as is possible, tried to display the innate 'Shakespearian' uniqueness of them. The reader will, it is hoped, find that each play is interpreted, perhaps illuminated, by a process which has given as much weight to historical reality as to modern sensibility. The book has no thesis to deploy or prove except that of affirming the astonishing 'oneness', the cohesiveness of the playwright's imagination. If the book has a continuing theme, then it is provided by Shakespeare's own imaginative integrity.

It will soon become obvious to the reader that the critical appraisals of each play are usually based on two criteria – one, scholarly, the other, experience of stage-performance. The scholarly basis is, so to speak, nearer the surface; the amount of theatre-going that has contributed to these critical appraisals is, however, not always so evident. Indeed the very premise on which the book was written – the necessity of combining historical reality with modern experience – could not have been upheld without my continuing exposure to Shakespeare on the stage – for it is through theatre that modern sensitivities reveal themselves at their most intense and exciting.

It seems only logical, therefore, that the experiences of theatre should also be noted – although strangely, this is hardly ever done. One reason which might inhibit their inclusion is that the experience of Shakespeare on the stage is seldom a single influence confined to the complete effect of a whole production. One often remembers details, moments, of a production which, in the context of the whole, may be deemed small, even personal, for, indeed, one is often deeply stirred by a happening, a tone of voice, a gesture, a pause which has left others unmoved.

An experience of theatre which extends from the Second World War to the present day is bound to have left a rich cluster of memories both large and small. Each one of them has influenced the critical appraisals which are made in this book. To name only a few is not only to acknowledge a debt but also to pay profound respect to the men and women of theatre who have helped to make this present century listen to Shakespeare on his own terms and in his own tongue.

At the small but potent repertory theatre in Birmingham (1951), Douglas Seale virtually discovered the *Henry VI* trio and revealed their potential if somewhat inchoate qualities; Peter Hall and John Barton (Royal Shakespeare Theatre, 1964), even though they subjected the English history plays to intensive editing, triumphantly retained their geographical and political stature as well as their piercing human detail. Peter Brook, with Paul Scofield, displayed with almost painful clarity Shakespeare's ironic amalgam of domestic and cosmic, in *King Lear* (Royal Shakespeare Theatre, 1962), while a virtually unknown actor, David Ryall, again at Birmingham, in 1979, achieved the virtually impossible task Shakespeare has set for the player of Lear – to combine absurdity with dignity. Laurence Olivier's *Macbeth* at Stratford in 1955 blazes still in the memory – not only for the huge dimension of its quality, the frightening inevitability of its interpretation, but also for moments of perception which still quicken the pulse – hearing, for example, the despairing gruffness of tone and recalling the head shaking like a wounded bear, as Olivier spoke ''twas a rough night', is not only emotionally disturbing but a reminder of Shakespeare's intention and of Olivier's ability to employ even the smallest image to sum up large meaning. One recalls, too, Ian McKellen's strained white-faced beauty as Richard II, the clatter of the daggers in his hands as he returned from Duncan's chamber in *Macbeth* and the chasms of dark pausing in his speaking of 'Tomorrow and tomorrow . . .' In the same production (The Other Place, Stratford-upon-Avon, 1976) Judi Dench for the first time in living memory got rid of the female devil, which had become customary, and gave us Shakespeare's devilish female.

Perhaps no production of *Hamlet* can satisfy completely, but the play can inspire unexpected conclusions. The American film and television actor, Richard Chamberlain, laden with liabilities, in England, of his nationality, his accent and his record, created (Birmingham Repertory Theatre, 1969) the most vulnerably young, passionately-spoken Prince the English stage had seen since Gielgud in the 1930s. The Ophelia of this production (the then unknown Gemma Jones) is the only one, in my experience, whose madness was convincing, unembarrassing, and poignantly true to the text.

Other productions still illuminate the critical imagination less specifically, but rather by their insight into Shakespeare's world and the control with which that world was vivified for a modern audience. Franco Zeffirelli's *Romeo and Juliet* (Old Vic, 1960) was, in some respects, less notable than blameworthy, yet, despite its most culpable aberration (vicious cutting), its visual appropriateness, its mood, its astonishing evocation of the bitter-sweetness of the lovers' plight, reached closer to the heart of the play than other more faithful plods through the full text. Trevor Nunn's production of *A Comedy of Errors* (Royal Shakespeare Theatre, 1976), poised with superb balance between stage-farce and musical, caught accurately the play's own crazy logic and its swoops from farce to lyricism. John Barton's *Twelfth Night* (Royal Shakespeare Theatre, 1969) did more than any production of one of Shakespeare's romantic comedies to emphasise the 'oneness' of Shakespeare's imagination. The emotional temperature, the visual tones, the shape and colour of acting and interpretation all confirmed how the playwright's romantic comedy looked as much forward to the graver issues of the later plays as backward to the happy permissiveness of the early comedies.

Many fecund memories clamour for attention – Brook's *A Midsummer Night's Dream* (Royal Shakespeare Theatre, 1970), his *Titus Andronicus* (Royal Shakespeare Theatre, 1955), Ron Daniels's *Pericles* (The Other Place, Stratford-upon-Avon, 1979) and a *Cymbeline* of unbroken magic at Stratford, Ontario. Gielgud's Angelo and Benedick, Patrick Wymark's Launce, Michael Hordern's Caliban, and Richard Griffiths's Bottom at this moment of writing may well be masking other memories of individual performances. And, ironically, there are some memories of Shakespeare in performance which crave attention in which his genius was more honoured in the breach than in the observance. Even a 'bad' production, however, can stimulate the critical imagination – every garden needs its weeds.

This book is intended to be neither solely the record of scholarly investigation, study-bound, nor solely of theatrical experience, but an amalgam of both. Perhaps, indeed, my background – a family of actors – conditioned me from an early age unconsciously to adopt a way of reading a play which always, for good or evil, gives that play, in my imagination, the elbow room to move in and out of its literary reality and into its theatrical life. I cannot merely see speeches on the page, I hear them: characters do not remain embedded in the text, I see them, even, am inclined to become them.

This has its problems. The disposition to be scholarly does not always sit easily with the urge to experience theatrically, and, indeed, it is not always conducive to peace of mind and soul to be at times denounced by the world of theatre as an upstart thespian, and by the chambers of scholarship as an upstart reviewer. If either be true, however, one can take comfort, if only adjectivally, in being in the best possible company.

Gareth Lloyd Evans

1 The Early Histories

Almightie God hath created and appoyncted all thynges, in heaven, yearth, and waters, in a most excellent and perfect ordre. In heaven he hath appoynted distincte Orders and states of Archagelles and Angelles. In the yearth he hath assigned Kynges, princes, with other gouerners under them, all in good and necessarie ordre.

For where there is no right ordre, there reigneth all abuse, carnall libertie, enormitie, synne, and Babilonical confusion. Take awaie Kynges, Princes, Rulers, Magistrates, Judges, and suche states of God's ordre, no man shall ride or go by the high way unrobbed, no man shal slepe in his awnes house or bed unkilled, no man shal kepe his wife, children, and possessions in quietnesse, all thynges shall be common, and there muste nedes followe all mischief and utter destruccion, bothe of soules, bodies, goodes and common wealthes.[1]

That is the burden of Shakespeare's history plays, with different degrees of emphasis, from the beginning to the end. The great idea of order, degree, pattern, as the natural ordained force in all creation, and the consequent perils if it is shaken or broken, informs all his history plays and is also the matrix in which he has set his tragedies and comedies.

Indeed, in a very significant sense, it may be said that there is no real separation between Shakespeare's historic, tragic and comic vision. The direction in theme and plot taken by certain groups of plays may be categorized by those labels, but the idea of order remains the chief informing spirit of them all. The history plays explore the political implications of order – and its opposite; the tragedies explore the human and political results of a retreat from the principle and fact of order; the comedies affirm, sometimes joyously, the human benefits which an acceptance of natural order can achieve.

Shakespeare's obsession with order was no theatrical or intellectual exercise. Like many of his contemporaries, he had reason to fear, on realistic grounds, the palpable results of a collapse of natural order. It is difficult for us to realize the nature of the fears with which the Elizabethans lived, because we have not lived in this country through a time when the religious and political status quo was consciously overthrown.

Henry VIII's secession from Rome was a political act, but its ramifications affected the deepest reaches of men's minds and souls.

1

Luther's stark comment on Henry puts the case with rigid exactness – 'What Squire Harry wills must be an article of faith for Englishmen, for life and death'. In plain terms Henry's breakaway and the subsequent reformation of the Church in England was a major surgical operation. He caused the personality of England's religion to change, ruthlessly cutting out the material power of the old Church and in so doing he created, painfully, a nation which, miraculously in his daughter's time, thrived, despite sedition, fear, doubt, bewilderment and blood-spilling. In the pursuit of his own conception of nationhood Henry caused 57,000 subjects to perish during his reign. Their heirs in the following reign had cause to know what happened when an order which had lasted a thousand years was broken.

Religious and political arguments that the end justified the means often obscure the fact that the means employed by Henry, and only to a lesser extent by his daughter, to bring about a new order, created a state of tension, bewilderment and fear. People found that the palpable grounds of their faith were snatched from them. The determined ones continued in the old Catholic faith in a covert and dangerous atmosphere. The less determined accepted the new dispensation with perhaps a nostalgic look backward to more familiar usages. Elizabeth brilliantly turned peril into a sense of glorious opportunity, but her own reign was wracked by the effects of what her country had inherited from her father. Many things – rebellion in the North of England, the Spanish Armada, the fiery ambition of Essex, the worries about her marriage – gave her subjects a practical demonstration of what happens when an old order is rudely forced. Not one of them realized the import more clearly than Shakespeare.

This does not necessarily mean that Shakespeare wished a return to the specifics of the old Holy Roman Empire – with all that it meant in religious terms. Shakespeare is concerned with examples of disorder certainly, but equally with the principles that lie behind. He is, in his history plays, not a political historian but a moralistic statesman; in a sense he may be said to be concerned less with the facts of history than with the pride, prejudice and pity of it.

His attitude to historical events was nurtured by his education and by his absorption of the contemporary scene about him. As a plain historian he exhibits all the faults common to his contemporaries either literate or illiterate. We go neither to him nor his contemporaries for historical accuracy; like them his conception of the flow of history was governed by the idea of great events manipulated by great individuals; he, like his fellows, learned his

2

history from the flawed narratives of such chroniclers as Hall[2] and Holinshed;[3] he is careless about details; he will invent when invention can be made dramatically impressive; he will always sacrifice apparent historical actuality to psychological and dramatic truth. In one respect he is unique – in the comprehensiveness of his vision of the human element in history. His times, his education, prompted him naturally to turn to the great event and the great individual for his plots and themes, but his own equally natural disposition was to encompass the story of the little known as well as the famous. His common citizenry, his unnamed soldiery, his gallery of petty rogues and unsung heroes do not occupy, quantitatively, as large a part of his actions as do the high-born, but, in terms of their value as created creatures, they occupy a high place.

The chief lessons Shakespeare learned from history were, first, that order must be maintained or discord follows, and, second, that the history of a nation is the history of all its citizens. Many of his contemporaries also shared these conceptions but to the Elizabethan illiterate, history was an attractive mêlée of fact and fancy; in his imagination myth and fact rubbed shoulders. History, to those who lacked enchantment, in fact, became a story, a chronicle, where the familiar and fanciful combined.

The insatiable greed for historical chronicle was, however, in the early years of Elizabeth's reign, given a sharpness by the intermittent but growing patriotic sense of Englishmen. England's dangerous isolation as a result of her secession from Rome, the consequent threats of invasion, the slow build-up of middle-class economic strength – these were the frameworks upon which was hung that delicate fabric by which patriotism is recognized as a national, emotional emblem.

If palpable event and circumstances drove the English towards a sense of themselves, the bizarre reality of a Queen upon the throne caused them to celebrate themselves as Englishmen. Elizabeth shrewdly played upon her femininity to induce romantic responses, some of which had a reckless but fine adventurousness, some a flippant bravado, while others were either modishly ridiculous and vaunting or imperishably magnificent. Voyages, ambuscadoes, piracy, discovery, the plumage air of fashion, the meticulous artistry of words and of music – all these, sometimes subtly, sometimes blatantly, seemed, by some alchemy, to consort to celebrate Elizabeth and through her, England. She taught the English a subtle and fecund narcissism behind which her own image glowed. Yet she induced a patriotic spirit at all levels and her common touch was as firm as her regal patronage. It is this atmosphere which Shakespeare catches and plays upon in Henry V's speech before Harfleur.

A third lesson that Shakespeare learned from his view of history and his experience of his own times was that the healthy commonwealth is one in which an emotional rapport between the leader and the led exists in a condition of mutual respect. He lived through times when the lessons of history were frequently subject to practical testing. It is because of this that his history plays, though they explore the often agonizing processes by which order and disorder appear and disappear, never fail to mirror the movements of the present tense in the eternal dance.

For the mass of Elizabethans history was, certainly, as much a story as a fact and their thirst for the story was intensified by the growing patriotic spirit of their own age. Their own conception of the idea of order and pattern was in-built and pragmatic. They accepted the fact of class distinction, of allegiance to those above them and responsibility to those below:

> 'In the Universal order of things the top of the inferior class touches
> the bottom of a superior: as for instance oysters, which, occupying as
> it were the lowest position in the class of animals, scarcely rise above
> the life of plants, because they cling to the earth without motion and
> possess the sense of touch alone.
> .... So also the noblest entity in the category of bodies, the human
> body, when its humours are evenly balanced, touches the fringe of
> the next class above it, namely the human soul, which occupies the
> lowest rank in the spiritual order.'[4]

Behind this workaday acceptance there was a vast body of theory in Elizabethan writings which explored the nature and implications of the universal order. Shakespeare undoubtedly had access to some of them like Hall's Chronicle, Church Homilies and, most particularly, *A Mirror for Magistrates*,[5] an imaginary series of monologues on the theme of political and social ethics. In contemporary political and religious terms the order is simply expressed – God, the archangels, the angels, the Pope, the monarch, the nobles and clergy, the common people in descending social order; in this simple chain of existence allegiance and duty flow upwards and responsibilities flow downwards. The pre-eminence of the theme of order in Elizabethan writings need not be surprising in view of Henry VIII's action with regard to one element in that natural order, for it is obvious that when, in his religious policy, he, *mutatis mutandis*, removed the

4

Pope from the series, there would be much heart-searching and intellectual questioning. It is not without significance that the title page of the Great Bible[6] of 1539 has an illustration which simply and directly implies not a breaking of the old order but a slight (though profound) redisposition of its upper links. Henry is shown seated on a throne, his left hand holding out a Bible (verbum dei) to his nobles, his right hand presenting the same book to his bishops. Below the throne in descending order, the verbum dei is dispersed by clergy to people who cry out, while looking upwards, 'vivat rex' and, at the lowest point, 'God save the king'. Immediately above Henry, God leans beneficently from a clouded heaven. The Pope is absent. This important illustration makes two stark points: first it implies the Tudor doctrine of the Divine right of Kings – that very English solution of the problem of what happened when the former interceder (Pope) between monarch and God was removed; second, it implies the monarch's position as head of both Church and State. These two matters lie at the root of what is called the Reformation in England.

Shakespeare's exploration of history must be seen against these contexts. His panorama of English history holds within it considerations about and images of political order and disorder, about the duty of monarchs and the responsibilities of subjects, about the sin of usurpation and of rebellion, about faction and alliance, about honour, bravery and chivalry. English history provided him with his material and his own times implemented it actually and in intellectual and moral terms.

The dramatic use which he made of his knowledge and experience was nurtured by his acquaintance with the most popular of early Elizabethan dramatic forms – the chronicle play. It is a formidable task to disentangle the ingredients and varieties of theme and form of this staple diet of audiences in the 1570s and 1580s. A comprehensive definition of chronicle play would involve so many qualifications as to be meaningless. This much, however, may be said – the chronicle play synthesized in dramatic form those notions of and attitudes towards history which we have noted. They appealed to the thirst for narrative by detailed and often tedious depictions of areas of English history (*The True Tragedy of Richard III*); they celebrated the greatness of great men (*The Famous Victories of Henry V*); they concerned themselves with dramatic discussions of the pressing themes of the duties and responsibilities of kingship, and of the sin of rebellion (*The Troublesome Reign of King John*); they exploited the new-found patriotic English fervour (*Locrine*); they frequently imply or state directly the concern with the idea of order and disorder (*Woodstock*); the best of them (Marlowe's *Edward II*) tragically and vividly personalized, by concentrating on the weakness of the single individual, the abstractions about kingship which deadened most of the other examples of chronicle. Except for Marlowe's plays and for certain isolated scenes in the plays of others, the chronicle plays hold within themselves, in a very crude state, almost all the ingredients which Shakespeare refined in his own history plays. It may be emphasized that Shakespeare's history plays, particularly the mature ones, exemplify clearly the truth that a significant part of his genius lay in an unerring ability to improve and refine the grosser matter of other men. But these grosser things were very popular, and there can be no surprise, though at the time there must have been much professional envy, at the fact that Shakespeare quickly became dominant among his contemporaries – he made strong ale for audiences who already had a large capacity for small beer.

The theatre in which Shakespeare served his apprenticeship in the late 1570s and early 1580s was essentially one in which corporate effort was the norm and the opportunity for individual achievement the exception. Greene's angry and envious remarks about Shakespeare – 'the upstart Crow, beautified with our feathers that with his Tygers hart wrapt in a players hyde, supposes he is as able to bombast out a blanke verse as the best of you . . .' – express his own feelings, but it may be inferred that more may lie behind them.[7] The emergence of Shakespeare as individual dramatist out of the ruck and reel of co-operative authorship, theatrical apprenticeship, was no mean feat in a world dominated by the idea of multiplicity of talent and activity. Greene's remarks bring us face to face not only with the harsh realities of the world of Elizabethan theatre but with one of the great critical problems connected with Shakespeare's early histories. In the twentieth century at least forty plays not included in the first folio have been ascribed in whole or part to Shakespeare. Conversely, multiple authorship of a number of plays, included in the first folio, (notably the three parts of *Henry VI*) has been claimed by a formidable array of critics. No conclusion, however, particularly about the authorship of the early histories, is within sight, and one may welcome the possibility of minute contention while regretting the fact that a winter of speculation can chill a springtime of appreciation. One essential element remains after the arguments about authorship of the *Henry VI* plays. It is simply that whatever, for example, the truth or untruth may be of Dover Wilson's meticulous allocations of acts and scenes in *Henry VI(I)* to Peele, Greene, Nashe and Shakespeare himself,[8] the play itself is Elizabethan – it is, in that sense, of a piece, even though it may be a flawed piece from an immature hand.

Doubts about authorship are matched by doubts about the chronology of writing of the trilogy. Up to recent times a majority of scholarly opinion argued that parts two and three were written before part one; latterly the tendency has been to believe they were written in the correct historical order and that they were all in existence by the summer of 1592. The matter is complicated by the existence of a play *Harey the VI* described in Henslowe's diary as 'new' on 3 March 1592.[9] Dover Wilson and others believe that this play was a revision by Shakespeare of a play originally written by Greene or Nashe.[10] Yet another body of opinion argues that Part I as we have it is a revision by Shakespeare of an early play by himself, and that the revision was undertaken after he had decided to make the trilogy and *Richard III* into a connected epic-chronicle of English history. This theory is given some cogency by the undoubted impression that is given at the end of Part 1 of a serial intention. Suffolk ends part one with the words:

> Margaret shall now be Queen, and rule the King;
> But I rule both her, the King, and realm.   [I.H.VI.V.5.108]

And Suffolk begins Part II in a position of honour and potential power:

> In sight of England and her lordly peers,
> Deliver up my title in the Queen
> To your most gracious hands, that are the substance
> Of that great shadow I did represent: [II.H.VI.I.1.12–15]

Similarly Part II ends with Warwick's threat:

> Sound drums and trumpets, and to London all:
> And more such days as these to us befall.   [II.H.VI.V.2.32–3]

and Part III begins with his:

> I wonder how the king escaped our hands.   [III.H.VI.1.1]

This close inter-relationship gives a very strong impression of serial intention – at least as we have the plays today. Whether the intention was there from the beginning remains a matter for conjecture.

Henry VI Part I

Within the span of time covered by this play the needs of dramatic compression have caused some manipulation of history. The most notable example is the retention of La Pucelle at the battle of 1451 in which Talbot was killed: Joan, in fact, was burned in 1431. In every such case the dramatic result justifies the historical manoeuvring, and this instance is a good example of Shakespeare's theatrical sensitivity. Talbot is the hero of this play, Joan the villain – they are kept in tense opposition to the end of their lives.

Part 1 stands alone in the trilogy in that it has a distinct hero in the strict sense of the word. Talbot is brave, honourable, selfless, untainted with the guiles of faction and political manoeuvring – he is 'noble-minded', a 'renowned noble gentleman', 'his fame lives in the world'. The effect of his presence in the play, for the Elizabethan audience, might, without fancy, be compared to that of the heroes of Western films. Not only does he possess all the virtues of the professional man of arms, and is presented in an individual radiance which illuminates him, but he exhibits a romantic guile in his handling of female deviousness. He baulks the wicked plot of the Countess of Auvergne with a foresighted insouciance which would do credit to a latter-day range-rider trapped by a hot-blooded Mexican beauty. She says, in defeat, 'Victorious Talbot! pardon my abuse'. He replies, 'Be not dismayed, fair lady,' and they go off together.

Unsophisticated audience taste in these matters never changes. Strictly in theatrical terms Talbot's character ministers to that audience need for the dashing, brave man. Added to this he dies a death of immense poignancy having fought to the last and been forsaken by treacherous allies.

Yet, within the thematic texture of the play, Talbot is much more than this. He stands for certain positive virtues against a background of negative chaos. He is the leader of an English army tackling the hated French. He is also, therefore, a kind of folk-hero of English chronicle – it is not fortuitous that the battle cries, 'St. George' and 'A Talbot, A Talbot' become synonymous in the play. For the Elizabethans his presence became a rallying point for their own intense patriotism.

In his capacity as hero and symbol he is opposed by a female villain who also occupies a symbolic position. To the Elizabethans

Joan was a despicable figure with Rome-ish affiliations – a tricksy woman warrior, one who claimed high birth but was of peasant stock, claiming control from the Almighty but calling upon evil spirits in time of need. Shakespeare completes a picture which, in the main, is repulsive, by clearly implying that she is also a harlot. The brave Talbot shines in virtue even more against this dank background.

Yet, like him, she is more than she seems. She stands for the supreme enemy – the French – regarded by all true Englishmen as treacherous in friendship and vicious in war. The opposition of Talbot and Joan would have been regarded as one between Good and Evil. The colours of black and white are painted broadly in the depictions of their opposition but it is a measure of the hand of Shakespeare in the play that his own characteristic humanism highlights a few features which make these two characters something more than obvious abstractions. Talbot's death, as he cradles the body of his own son, has that peculiar Shakespearean touch which always proves the validity of emotional generalization in the truth of individual experience. Talbot, as a character, steps out of the mist of romantic pathos into the keener air of actual individual tragedy as he speaks words over his dead son:

> O thou whose wounds become hard – favoured Death,
> Speak to thy father ere thou yield thy breath!
> Brave Death by speaking, whether he will or no;
> Imagine him a Frenchman and thy foe.
> Poor boy! he smiles, methinks, as who should say,
> Had Death been French, then Death had died today.
> Come, come, and lay him in his father's arms.
> My spirit can no longer bear these harms.
> Soldiers, adieu! I have what I would have,
> Now my old arms are young John Talbot's grave. [IV.7.23–32]

In the whole canon of Shakespeare's plays this is the first example of that characteristic poetic quality which creates a sense of truth to common human experience by combining general emotion and concrete individual example.

Similarly, but with quite different results, Joan is humanized. In the twentieth century, which is far more prepared to ignore both her nationalistic symbolism and her supernatural solicitings, her character, as it is written, still has a hard reality. Indeed what seemed despicable to the Elizabethans has, to us, much that is wryly attractive. One of her asides has a superb double-effect. When the Duke of

Burgundy, having listened to her emotional blandishments, decides to turn coat and follow the Dauphin, she says:

'Done like a Frenchman – (*Aside*) turn, and turn again'   [III.3.85]

This ironically clinches the English view of the French but it also implies her own sardonic wit – of which there are several other examples. Indeed, for a modern audience there is more wit than menace in this character and what, in the more sensitive Elizabethan political air, would have been deemed gross is, for us, a kind of feminine bluntness.

Indeed a measure of the change in attitude between the sixteenth and the twentieth centuries is clearly shown in the treatment of Joan in successive modern productions. A. C. Sprague records that in Benson's production of 1906 Joan 'was played unexceptionably as a brave warrior'. In 1959 at the Hovenden Theatre Club she was played 'with obvious sincerity by a charming young actress . . . so unwitch-like that one was almost persuaded of her innocence.'[11] In 1964 she appeared at the Royal Shakespeare theatre as a charming but coquettish exemplar of feminine emancipation, claiming the right to make war on the basis of a precedence established by centuries of male example. In both Talbot and Joan there is much energy of that kind which can create not only theatrical excitement but induce theatrical experimentation – as modern productions testify.

However, whatever opportunities are given to and taken by modern interpretation, for the Elizabethans these two characters are deeply committed to yet another role in the action. Talbot is the one vital repository of order in an environment which is almost totally disordered. The picture of England is the most despondent of any in the history plays. Almost the whole of the first act emphasizes a condition of national decadence. This takes several forms.

First, it appears, right at the beginning, as a kind of inertia due to shock at the death of Henry V, 'whose deeds exceed all speech'. The shock produces an unproductive nostalgia and, at the same time, disintegrates the unity, the order, which that great king had created. Exeter irritatedly reacts to the nostalgia:

'We mourn in black; why mourn we not in blood?
Henry is dead and never shall revive.'   [I.1.17–18]

Only a few lines later the disintegrative forces have begun to work, expressed in Gloucester's answer to the Bishop of Winchester's pious requiem on Henry V:

'The Church! Where is it? Had not churchmen pray'd,
His thread of life had not so soon decay'd.'   [I.1.33–4]

Second, national decadence is shown in the speed by which
faction establishes its hydra-headed presence. Gloucester opposes
Winchester, dissension arises between Richard Plantagenet and
Somerset; their rose-plucking quarrel ranges others severally on
opposite sides. 'Base and envious discord' rapidly becomes the motto
of the play's action.

Third, it appears in the way in which individual vice grows out of
general disorder. The hand of Shakespeare seems, in this respect, to
reveal itself strongly again. As he humanizes Joan and Talbot so he
individualizes the frailties of other characters who, together, are a
mere generalization of a sick kingdom. Typically, he is economical in
this process – a line, a phrase, a word, rightly placed, make these men
move into a single spotlight. Winchester's vaulting, arrogant ambition appears like a child's petulance when, alone, he speaks to
himself:

'Each hath his place and function to attend:
I am left out; for me nothing remains.
But long I will not be Jack out of office.'   [I.1.173–5]

Gloucester is shown as a well-meaning, small-minded, hot-tempered
man with too little political guile to match his times. He consistently
backs, with the best intention, the wrong political horse, not least in
his reaction to Suffolk after the news that Margaret has agreed to
marry Henry VI:

'Her father is no better than an earl,
Although in glorious titles he excel.'   [V.5.37–8]

He is immediately steamrollered into silence by Suffolk's crushing
and unctuous statement of the title, wealth and influence that
Margaret will bring with her.

Fourth, the sense of decadence and disorder is demonstrated with
keen irony by the self-destructive actions of the English. This is
evident enough in the senseless weakness of fighting a war while
engaged in mutual quarrelling, but it also has a sharper, more
poignant and, at the same time, more bitter focus. Somerset and York
bicker about who should send reinforcements to the hard-pressed
Talbot. Neither does, and their vacillation is the direct cause of Talbot's
death. It is, however, of greater significance than this. Talbot's
death is the final quenching of that spirit which inhabited Henry V.
Both as man and symbolically he is the heir of that creative

spirit of unity and order which Henry bequeathed to England. With Talbot's death Henry V truly 'never shall revive'.

It is with this consideration of Talbot, which is somewhat below the theatrical surface of the play, that a greater depth can be perceived, which not only mirrors a stronger thematic relationship between Joan and Talbot but in which moves the true historical complex of the play's meaning in Elizabethan terms.

Act II.5 offers a clue to this deeper consideration. It is one of little dramatic merit, relying for effect on the emotional vibrancy gener-ated always in the theatre when venerable age is on its death-bed, attended by sympathetic youth. Old Mortimer, speaking to Richard Plantagenet, refers to the usurpation of Richard II by Bolingbroke, who then established himself as Henry IV, fathered Henry V, and grandsired the present king, Henry VI. Mortimer speaks bitterly of his own right to the throne, as great-grandson of Edward III, next in line to Richard II:

'I was the next by birth and parentage;
For by my mother I derived am
From Lionel Duke of Clarence, third son
To King Edward the Third . . .'   [II.5.73–76]

What he says incites Plantagenet to think of his own claim to the throne. He leaves Mortimer, determined:

'Either to be restored to my blood,
Or make my ill th'advantage of my good'.   [II.5.128–29]

England is cursed by the crime of usurpation, which implies a disturbance by violence of the natural order of being. No matter how weak the king or how virtuous the possible successor, usurpation, by single act or by rebellion, is a sin which, in a kingdom, must be expiated before the health returns to it. As O. J. Campbell comments:

'Talbot is made the scapegoat for the sins of the royal house. The
direst of these was Bolingbroke's contrivance of the deposition and
death of Richard II, God's deputy on earth. His punishment through
the wildness of Prince Hal was only a partial expiation. During
Henry V's reign, because of the king's piety, God held in abeyance
the retribution still due, but the curse, operative again at his early
death, falls upon Talbot.'[12]

Fate is a potent motivator of Part I and its palpable servant is Joan of Arc who declares – 'Assign'd am I to be the English scourge'. She claims to be directed by God, but she makes appeals to witchcraft, and to the English she is a witch. There is no incompatibility here. As Tillyard says, 'God was ultimately in control' using both 'stars and evil spirits to forward his own ends'. The evil spirit is Joan, the stars are those cold silent harbingers which, if ill disposed in the cosmos, foretell disaster:

> 'What! shall we curse the planets of mishap
> That plotted thus our glory's overthrow?'   [I.1.23–4]

If well disposed, as they are for the French, the prognosis is good:

> 'Mars his true moving, even as in the heavens
> So in the earth, to this day is not known.
> Late did he shine upon the English side;
> Now we are victors, upon us he smiles.'   [I.I.1–4]

Such evocations were not academic exercises for the Elizabethans – they lived in the everyday presence of witchcraft, and watched the patterns of the stars with anxious hearts:

> 'And Mars being placed near unto the sun sheweth that there shall be a great death among people. Old women that can live no longer shall die for age: and young men that have userers for their fathers shall this year have great cause to laugh, for the devil hath made a decree, that after they are once in hell, they shall never rise again to trouble their executors.'[13]

Within the depths of the play's meaning Talbot and Joan meet in an allegorical dance – she executes him – he becomes a sacrifice in the agonizing movement towards expiation of England's sin. The main thematic movements of all of Shakespeare's history plays are indicated in this play – order and disorder, faction, rebellion, the sin of usurpation, honour, cowardice, deceit, the thirst for power, the gigantic force of a sense of right and blood. In the midst of these motifs and themes which are later to be developed and deepened by maturity there sits one other lonely form – the figure of kingship. All these thematic elements in the long run bear down upon the solitary figure who, both actually and symbolically, is twisted and turned in their dangerous currents. Henry VI is a shadowy figure in Part I. What we most remember of him is his ineffectuality amidst his quarrelsome nobles, his piety, his indecisiveness, but above all, a sense that, with all his weakness, it is he better than anyone else who knows the meaning of the events as they swirl about him. It is he who says,

'Civil dissension is a viperous worm
That gnaws the bowels of the commonwealth.'   [III.1.72–3]

In Part I he is, and is regarded, as a mere pawn in a game which has far from run its course. He is not yet important enough to be destroyed but, as he is unwittingly part of the great crime, the expiation of it will engulf him eventually. Theatrically, Talbot is the hero; politically (in E. M. Tillyard's words), Res Publica, the State, is hero. Yet, this play has, as all Shakespeare's histories have, a silent, dead hero, whose long arm reaches across the decades, and touches State, brave men and kings. The arm is that of Richard II. It is the crime against his kingship that Shakespeare's histories relate and expatiate upon..

Henry VI Part II

If 'allegorical' suits as a general description of Part I, then 'naturalistic' may be used of Part II. The King, the Queen, the nobles who, in Part I are, as characters, subservient to the working out of the thematic movement, now come starkly into the foreground. We are face to face with actual event and, at times, made deeply aware of the motives of individuals.

Shakespeare is still concerned with his basic themes of order, disorder, rebellion, faction and the sin of usurpation, but we are now nearer to the human actions, thoughts and feelings which those themes generate. The King, too, is more critically placed in the dramatic action. In Part I the lining up of opposing factions under the rose emblems did not, though dangerous, immediately threaten his crown but was the result of Richard Plantagenet's bid to regain the Dukedom of York – now, Plantagenet does not hide ambition to obtain what he considers to be his by right, the throne of England.

One of the most absorbing aspects of Part II is the depth and skill of Shakespeare's depiction of political manoeuvring. It has a grim human truth and encompasses ambition, deceit, expediency, cruelty and a rare example of ineffective political honesty. This, combined with the growing danger to Henry's throne, results in an atmosphere of relentless inevitability. There is no hero to mitigate, by bravery or nobility, the working-out of the curse on England which took root by the usurpation of Richard II. Malevolent fate itself seems attached to the day-to-day acts of treachery and deceit which abound in the play – Gloucester's wife is no witch-like La Pucelle, but she employs a witch; Richard, the young son of the ambitious Duke of York is no devil come from hell, but there is that about him which suggests unnatural evil. He is 'a heap of wrath, foul indigested lump ... as crooked in thy manners as thy shape.'

Yet it is the deeds of men which push the play on its dark course, and there is a remarkable example at the outset of Shakespeare's skill in quickly indicating the deviousness of political iniquity. Suffolk has returned, his mission to obtain Margaret's hand in marriage successfully accomplished. Gloucester, the Protector, is incensed at the unfavourable terms of the marriage settlement, and calls upon the memory of Henry V to try to spur his noble confrères to agree with him. He gets a dusty answer from the erstwhile Bishop of Winchester, now newly made into a Cardinal:

15

'My lord of Gloucester, now ye grow too hot:
It was the pleasure of my lord the King'.   [I.1.131–2]

Gloucester leaves, prophesying that 'France will be lost ere long'. It is
at this point, in an episode of little more than two hundred lines, that
a morass of intrigue is revealed and the individual mud-stained hand
of each participant shown for what it is. The scene is completely
convincing largely because of two qualities in its construction. First,
the atmosphere is argumentative, changing from cold reason to hot
passion; second, the language has a naturalistic bite to it. Short
statements give a sense of amazing actuality to the scene, 'For France,
'tis ours; and we will keep it still', 'But wherefore weeps Warwick,
my valiant son?', 'This weighty business will not brook delay',
'Uncle, how now?'. Starkly, the audience is given the illusion of
being present at a conference which, after its official business is over,
falls into a quarrelsome argument.

It is important to stress the qualities of this early scene, since it
sets a standard of naturalistic writing and atmosphere which is
maintained throughout the play. There is no other history play of
Shakespeare's which maintains such a sense of factual chronicle, and
which so clearly distinguishes the various forms of political intrigue
in individual characters. This, in itself, is absorbing for the audience,
giving the play a newsreel intensity which is in sharp contrast to the
more ritualistic movement of Part I. But more than this, it points to
future developments in Shakespeare's handling of certain character
types, charting the lineaments of those characters which he is later to
develop with full imaginative power.

There are five such – Gloucester, Margaret, Warwick, Richard,
Duke of York and Jack Cade.

Gloucester is doomed from the start. His second speech in the
play – a fiery but slightly pathetic harking back to the glories of
Henry V – is greeted with impatience and dismissiveness. His blood
ties with Henry VI, his position as Regent, his own outspoken
honesty, avail nothing against the pressures of the forces of disorder.
The play is, to a large extent, concerned with his fall. It is an actual
fall brought about by intrigue, but it is also symbolic: he represents
the last vestiges of the spirit of order which, having been created by
Henry V, is now in swift dissolution. He has no allies, not even his
wife, and he is, in a sense, an ineffective man knowing, in his heart,
the truth of his situation:

'My Lord of Winchester, I know your mind;

'Tis not my speeches that you do mislike,
But 'tis my presence that doth trouble ye.'   [I.1.134–9]

Yet Gloucester's ineffectiveness is less one of character than a result of his psychological and political inappropriateness in this new sombre England. Shakespeare does not make the mistake of inducing mere pity for a representative of a decency that has passed away. Gloucester's shrewdness also is strongly revealed, and his ability to see the truth behind the mask. He plays an important part in one of those strange scenes, characteristic of Shakespeare, which, at first sight, seem irrelevant to the play's dramatic movement, and yet are closely interwoven in the thematic meaning. There is one such in *Henry IV* Part I (the scene of Francis the drawer) and in *Julius Caesar* (The assassination of Cinna the poet). Here, it is the scene at St. Albans where an alleged miracle has occurred involving one Simpcox whose sight is said to have been miraculously restored. The episode does not occur in the main chroniclers, Hall and Holinshed, though Sir Thomas More has an account of it in the *Dialogue of Comfort*. It is more likely, however, to have been derived from the chronicler Grafton.[14] It occupies one hundred lines and its apparent irrelevance would seem to qualify it as a certain victim for modern cutting. Yet, apart from the fact that the mature Shakespeare occasionally makes use of such scenes to make particular points, there is no reason to dismiss it on the grounds that he was immaturely and mechanically sticking to his source chronicler. Even the young Shakespeare shows a shrewd selectivity with his sources.

The nature of Shakespeare's use of this scene may be described as oblique naturalism. It is a proof of the reality of the relationship of Gloucester to the rest, using indirect means whose effects are powerful and evocative. After Cardinal Winchester's unctuous introduction, Gloucester takes complete control of the affair and, step by step, reveals this poor man for what he is – an out-and-out fraud. He has not been blind from birth, therefore he has not recovered his sight; he is not lame; he is, in Gloucester's words, 'the lyingest knave in Christendom'.

What does this scene show? – that men may lie and seek benefit from the lie; that men may be deceived and suffer from the deceit; and, more specifically, Gloucester's shrewd ability to detect the false from the true. The various reactions to the scene are very telling. Henry cries in a kind of despairing anguish, 'O God, seest thou this, and bearest so long?' The deceiver's wife shouts, 'Alas, sir, we did it for pure need.' Margaret, the Queen, says, 'It made me laugh to see the villain run.' It is a strange little allegory of the state of the kingdom, that men may deceive, that others may excuse it for need, that one may laugh at it, and one despair that God allows it to continue.

This is the indirect meaning of the scene, but its naturalism clinches its importance. The Cardinal's reaction is to say, 'Duke Humphrey has done a miracle today', with an obvious sneer; Suffolk increases the implied denigration with his words, 'True, made the lame to leap and fly away'. Gloucester ironically stitches the scene's implications to the present tense reality of England's low fortunes when he turns on Suffolk, reminds him of the marriage settlement with Margaret's father, and cries:

'But you have done more miracles than I:
You made in a day, my lord, whole towns to fly.'   [II.1.158–9]

The scene is multi-layered in its effects. It symbolizes the state of England; by implications it spreads the crime of deceit from high to low, and it underlines the difference between the honest Gloucester and those who seek his downfall. One further point is noteworthy. Simpcox's wife's claim that it was done for need links the scene with the Jack Cade episodes. In naturalistic terms England is led to deceit and is ripe for disintegration not only from the top but also from below.

Gloucester is assassinated for political reasons, but before his end, Shakespeare deepens the poignant effect of his character on the audience by personalizing his situation. Gloucester's wife has a naked ambition to be Queen. She is as incapable of listening to the disavowals of her husband as is Lady Macbeth, yet she has one quality which the Lady of Glamis lacks. She reveals a simple tender love for Gloucester, as indeed he has for her. It is her action in invoking a puerile necromancy to achieve her ambitions which sets the seal on her husband's fate. Shakespeare movingly domesticates the extremes of unreasoned ambition and pure honesty by applying an uncomplicated love – the result is ironic and pathetic disaster:

DUCHESS: What, gone, my lord, and bid me not farewell!
GLOUCESTER: Witness my tears, I cannot stay to speak.   [II.4.85–6]

The Duke of Gloucester is the first portrait in a gallery of good and worthy political men who are constantly frustrated by their own virtues in a political world whose game they cannot play. There are several versions of the character, some less defeated than others, some less sympathetic to the audience than others. What they have in

common is a goodness of spirit and mind which, in some way, is
baulked by the realities of the world they have to inhabit – the Duke
in *Measure for Measure*, Polonius, Antigonus, and another Gloucester in a greater play who speaks words so apt to this play:

> '. . . love cools, friendship falls off, brothers divide; in cities,
> mutinies; in countries, discord; in palaces, treason. . . .
> We have seen the best of our time:'   [*King Lear*.I.2.101–108]

Shakespeare's mind and heart never lost the imaginative sense of
the ironic status of good and great men who suddenly find the best of
their time is gone.

In direct opposition to Gloucester are three characters – the
Cardinal, Suffolk and York. From the point of view of Shakespeare's
later development the last is the most important. He has all the
qualities, including title, for strong kingship, except for one thing –
relentless, self-seeking ambition. He is an astute diplomat, knowing
how and when to play his hand. After some argument with Suffolk
and Somerset he agrees to go to Ireland with troops supplied by
Suffolk to quell a rebellion. The last thing he wants is to be absent
from England, but he turns all to advantage:

> '. . . Yet be well assur'd
> You put sharp weapons in a madman's hands.
> Whiles I in Ireland nourish a mighty band,
> I will stir up in England some black storm,
> Shall blow ten thousand souls to heaven or hell;'   [III.1.347–51]

He has undoubted courage and warlike strength, and he is true to his
supporters. Yet, in his soul, there is a hot reckless ambition which is
not only of obvious danger to others but has a quality of sinister self-
regard – a kind of doting on self-aggrandisement:

> 'Let pale-fac'd fear keep with the mean-born man,
> And find no habour in a royal heart.
> Faster than spring-time show'rs comes thought on thought,
> And not a thought but thinks on dignity.
> My brain, more busy than the labouring spider,
> Weaves tedious snares to trap mine enemies.
>
>   . . . . .
> I fear me you but warm the starved snake,
> Who, cherish'd in your breasts, will sting your hearts'. [III.1.335–44]

There is more of this to come, in even darker hue, from Shakespeare,
in the words of self-looking villains like Iago, but ironically, and
more to the point here, is its next appearance in York's own son,

Richard of Gloucester, suggesting that, in evil, the child is father to the man:

> . . . . .
> 'Why, I can smile, and murder whiles I smile,
> And cry "Content!" to that which grieves my heart,
> And wet my cheeks with artificial tears,
> And frame my face to all occasions'.   [3HVI.III.2.182–5]

A singular quality of men, in Shakespeare's plays, destined to crime and resourceful in execution, is this quality of self-regarding, but there is also one other attribute, of which York is the first example. It is simply that such men, once steeped in crime, stain everything that they touch. Iago stains the whole society around Othello, England is poisoned into despaired rebellion by Richard III, the commonalty, led by the mad Jack Cade, are incited to rebellion by York. Like all murderers such men have to prove, in deeds, the intoxicating implications of words that they have spoken only to themselves.

The chosen instrument of York, Jack Cade, is the first of Shakespeare's lower-class rogues, though in him there is a dangerous incalculable quality which sharply individualizes his presence. This is in contrast to Bardolph, Nym and Pistol of Shakespeare's later histories who share the quality of brash, cheeky knavery which conquers our sympathies in all their appearances. Until his bleak death in Iden's garden, however, Cade has nothing of this, although the surface of his character and his language superficially resembles his later colleagues. Shakespeare is unable to give him the blessing of his own or our sympathy because what he represents is completely inimical. It is a cliché of Shakespearean criticism that he hates mobs because they are the most stark and obvious examples of disorder in a commonwealth, and because they exhibit most of those qualities in man which dehumanize him – unreason, unbridled passion, hatred, violence, indiscipline and insensitivity of mind and feeling. There is no sympathetically presented mob in the whole of Shakespeare. But more than this is the effect of the corporate identity of the mob on those individuals whom Shakespeare chooses to isolate from the mass. The identified citizens of *Julius Caesar* and *Coriolanus*, the two tribunes of the people in the latter play, and Jack Cade in this play have most of the loathed characteristics of the mob. Cade exemplifies them all. He is boastful – 'valiant I am'; he seeks popularity by fulsome promises – 'there shall be in England seven halfpenny loaves sold for a penny'; his sense of inferiority in the face of anything of superior quality – 'Away with him, I say! hang him with his pens and ink-horn about his neck'; he is cruel – 'Go, take him away, I say, and strike off his head presently; and then break into his son-in-law's house, Sir James Cromer, and strike off his head, and bring them both upon two poles hither'. He is all these things, and he is fickle, ignorant and sly.

In this play, more than in any other history, the personality of the mob is filtered into one man – as character he cannot escape this destiny. Pistol in *Henry IV* has some of his characteristics – slyness, undependability, fickleness, bravado – yet he remains curiously endearing. Shakespeare, it seems, is always prepared to make allowances for the single rogue, the lonely low criminal, the knave unconnected with his society – the Autolycus – but his abhorrence of the law of political misrule is so strong that the allowance is withdrawn from people like Cade. It is tempting to suspect that a Cade unconnected with mob violence would have entered into the audience's sensibilities favourably.

Yet, having withheld sympathy so conspicuously and having created a character as powerful as Cade, Shakespeare cannot allow him to slip into limbo completely without a touch of pity. There is perhaps only one character in Shakespeare (Iago) who goes to perdition unaneled by his author. Cade's death, in Iden's garden, has a brutal pathos about it, and his last words burn the underlying meaning of his rebellion in our minds:

'Tell Kent from me she hath lost her best man, and exhort
all the world to be cowards; for I, that never feared any,
am vanquished by famine, not by valour'.   [IV.10.72–4]

Iden's garden is England, Iden is an almost anonymous relic of the spirit of order, Cade is disorder – Shakespeare has taken us through the crazy perils of Cade's rebellion and returned us to his proper theme, the disintegration of the commonwealth.

Warwick is one of Shakespeare's great noble rebels – a more worthy ally of York than Cade. Shakespeare's picture of him is exactly that of kingmaker. He is militarily powerful, he is faithful, he is an obvious but effective diplomat, in his own lights he is honourable. He does all things for what he believes to be the best possible reasons and, of all the forces of disintegration, he is the most honest. He gives the inescapable impression of the kind of rich business man who achieves his satisfaction from sponsorship and patronage rather than from the ultimate possession of power. He is

Shakespeare's first noble rebel and, as character, has strong affinities with the elder Northumberland of *Henry IV*, although he is never 'crafty sick'. In both there is an establishment quality – they are reluctant to upset the status quo but their limited imaginations force them to it; they stand for certain standards of honourable behaviour; only reluctantly do they accept any action which involves duplicity.

Margaret of Anjou, who becomes England's Queen, has no respect for any status quo which does not minister to her own ambitious desires. She is the most feminine of all Shakespeare's female villains – her femininity is sexually expressed and her villainy is practical but she has nothing of Cleopatra's sexual deviousness and no whisper of supernatural solicitings inform her ruthlessness. Already in Part I in the scene with Suffolk who is magnetized by her charms there has been more than a hint of her physical attractiveness. In Part II the emphasis is on her consuming ambition to be unquestioned queen of an unquestioned king, and on the strange fidelity of her love for Suffolk. The relationship with Suffolk displays both elements in her character. He promises her that she herself 'shall steer the happy realm' missing Henry out of the equation, but his own place in it is implicit throughout the play. Suffolk is little without Margaret, but she finds in him material which she can use. In contrast with Henry to whom she pays but lip service, Suffolk has ambition which chimes with hers, and she works upon it. If Warwick is a kingmaker so is Margaret – by temperament. Where, in Lady Macbeth, the urge to create greatness in a man and to cohabit with it is secretive and private, in Margaret it is more open and more practical. She plays masterfully with her tongue in maligning Gloucester, keeping a wary eye on all the fractious impediments to her desires. Sprague records a description of a modern actress's depiction of Margaret at the Old Vic: 'Once Gloucester had crossed her. ... one knew from the mere flash of her eye, the tightening of her mouth, that he was doomed',[15] and he also reports a remark by Douglas Seale, the director of a notable production of the trilogy, of 'Margaret's quick look of disappointment at first sight of the pious young king'. These two comments are the two extremes between which Margaret's character develops – determination and disappointment. Her presence in the play gives a tense intimacy to the underlying theme of order and disorder, for she is nearest to the King and the nearest to one of his potential successors. It is through her that we learn the personal connotations of what deceit, intrigue, ambition in the hierarchy of the commonwealth mean.

Once more the play bears down upon the solitary possessor of the throne of England. Henry is a much less shadowy figure here than in Part I. Because of York's ambition, Suffolk's ambition and the Queen's ambition, Henry is now more vulnerable and Shakespeare makes this poignant by concentrating not on the abstraction but on the personal realities of kingship. Margaret describes him accurately:

> 'Henry my lord is cold in great affairs,
> Too full of foolish pity;'   [III.1.224–5]

and nothing that we see of him disclaims this judgment of his wife. His character is put in sharp perspective by a scene in *Richard III*, when Richard in a sardonic attempt to win favour from his subjects appears before two bishops reading a bible. This is a calculated impersonation of the dead Henry VI. Henry is too good for kingship. As we see him in Part II, he is a man of justice, of kindness, of conscience, of religious piety, but all of these virtues droop into ineffectuality by a malaise of the soul. The wickedness of men is too much for him to bear; all he desires is to meditate upon the goodness of God. Shakespeare, however, shows great skill in preventing the character of Henry from falling into inconsequence. Each movement in the direction of his eventual death brings a twist of the knife to Henry's tortured soul and a man, not a cypher, is seen to be crucified. Line after line and scene after scene exemplifies this. He wants to have no truck with Suffolk's marriage settlement: after a council meeting to decide the regency of France he says 'For my part, noble lords, I care not which:/Or Somerset or York, all's one to me'; he is completely deceived by the alleged miracle at St. Albans and naively utters 'Poor soul, God's goodness hath been great to thee'; when the deception is revealed he is almost in despair – 'O God, seest Thou this, and bearest so long'. On two occasions only does he seem capable of exercising will – the first is in his demanding Gloucester to give up his staff of regency, the second is in the midst of his anger at the death of Gloucester. Yet, the first is done despite himself, and the second leads him only to a tearful calling for God's justice – 'For judgment only doth belong to Thee', an unconscious denial of kingship in the harsh realities of mediaeval politics. His reaction to Cade's rebellion is altruistic:

> 'For God forbid so many simple souls
> Should perish by the sword! And I myself,
> Rather than bloody war shall cut them short,
> Will parley with Jack Cade their general'   [IV.4.10–13]

23

which is a heartrendingly true but politically naive reading of the situation. When a greater rebellion stares him in the face, his appeal is correct – 'O, where is faith? O, where is loyalty?' – but there is no will in him to enforce them. He is an example of the irony that to rule well does not require absolute goodness, and he suffers as man because he is unqualified as king.

Henry VI – Part III

In 1923 Logan Pearsall Smith wrote of the trilogy that 'they are woven of the stuff of the common Elizabethan drama, and whether Shakespeare really wrote them has often been debated.'[16] This represents the major critical opinion of the twentieth century. Critics have either teased at them minutely to separate out authorship, or quickly raced through them with slight nods of approval at bits and pieces. It is only recently that opinion has veered to a belief that the plays, though flawed and immature, have a far greater dramatic and theatrical strength than they were previously allowed. The reason for the change is significant. It began with the success of Barry Jackson's very full production at the Birmingham Repertory theatre in 1953,[17] and has gained strength through the Royal Shakespeare's adapted version of 1963, when many were astounded by the riches which these stage-realizations uncovered.[18]

This refurbishing is a cypher of a larger movement which has gained pace since the last war. The long and wide gulf between academic perception and theatrical appreciation has begun to narrow, partly because the scholar has begun to show himself more amenable to the effects of theatre, while it, in turn, has begun to lose something of its terrified suspicion of scholarly work, and proper appreciation is now seen to come from a creative balance between scholarly investigation and theatrical practice.

Part III has been the greatest victim of past critical comdemnation, but no play that is entirely crude in construction, characterization and language can survive the stage. In the reading it seems at times chaotic, its language varying from the extremes of awkward naturalism to mechanical lyricism. Yet even a production which has not attempted to tidy it reveals that, on the whole, the language suits its speakers and the situation, and one may point to several examples of an exciting architecture of form. The killing of the young Rutland is echoed with fierce irony in the death of young Edward, the emptiness of the paper crown York is forced to wear is pathetically underlined by the crown that Henry wishes to discard, the actual genocide of England achieves a moving symbolism in the scene of the father who has killed his son, and the son who has killed his father. The hot bickering of angry nobility, expressed with a fierce economy of words:

RICHARD: Are you there, butcher? O, I cannot speak!

25

CLIFFORD: Ay, crook-back, here I stand to answer thee,
  Or any he the proudest of thy sort.
RICHARD: 'Twas you that killed young Rutland, was it not?
CLIFFORD: Ay, and old York, and yet not satisfied.
RICHARD: For God's sake, lords, give signal to the fight.

[II.2.95–100]

which actualizes the immense cruelty of these civil wars, is contrasted sharply by the incantatory, lamenting comment on that actuality:

HENRY: How will the country for these woeful chances
  Misthink the King and not be satisfied!
SON: Was ever son so rued a father's death?
FATHER: Was ever father so bemoan'd his son?
HENRY: Was ever king so griev'd for subjects' woe?
  Much is your sorrow: mine ten times so much.
SON: I'll bear thee hence, where I may weep my fill. [II.5.107–13]

That so much artistic order can be discerned in a play which covers so immense a canvas and has so many characters of moment, is itself a kind of triumph, but that is not all. The hand of a very cunning man who was sensitive to theatrical suspense and climax is also present. In Act I, for example, Henry, Warwick, York, Northumberland, Clifford and Exeter are wrangling about Henry's right to kingship, an episode punctuated with such phrases as 'Peace, thou!'; 'What then?', 'Why whisper you?', 'What mutter you?' – which induce in an audience a sense of excited expectation – who will come out best? Who is on whose side? More than this, however, we may see the scene as an example of a dramatist who, even in his younger years, keeps in his mind the visual realization of a scene. The short phrases, suggesting that behind the heard dialogue silent conspiracy is going on, picture a stage in which small groups form and reform, glances are passed, lips silently move – the activities of dissension.

Then there is the scene, which Tillyard calls dull and routine, in which Margaret, with her son, is pleading help from Lewis of France. She has almost succeeded when Warwick is announced. Margaret's cry: 'Ay, now begins a second storm to rise' is certainly true, for the scene rises to a swirl of argument, acrimony and passion, given an extra sharp piquancy by the spectacle of stealthy womanhood at odds with Warwick's stolid power. Dramatic curiosity is increased when Lewis and Warwick draw aside to talk, and tension between characters re-emerges when they return to Margaret, and Lewis announces that he has withdrawn his promised aid. The dramatist, however, has not even yet finished manipulating audience emotion. At the moment of Warwick's triumph a post from England arrives to announce Edward's treachery in having already married the Lady Elizabeth, despite Warwick's commission to win the hand of Lewis's sister for him. Warwick's triumph dissolves, his position is difficult – the desperate Margaret breathes success again. On the level of pure theatricality this scene is impressive, but it also allows for a strongly dramatic clash of character.

In Part III Shakespeare had three major problems which, unsolved, could have produced a disastrous failure, for, in themselves, they are mutually exclusive. He had to show in naturalistic detail the deviousness, cruelty and waste of the Wars of the Roses; he had to maintain the non-naturalistic theme of order and disorder; and he had to contend, one suspects, with a compulsion to move away from broad chronicle into the deeper shoals of individual character – becoming more interested in Richard, Duke of Gloucester than in anything else as the writing proceeded.

He largely succeeded in reconciling the three problems by accepting that their common denominator was the dramatic and theatrical potency of individual characterization. Each of the three elements has its own pattern, but the basic grain, maintained by Shakespeare, is the reality of character. Because of his recognition and manipulation of this common quality the transitions between the three modes is achieved.

The depiction of the Wars of the Roses is characterized by a sense of violent skirmish, uncertain loyalties, physical weariness, and utter brutality. The overall impression is entirely true to the reality of war – the heroics, where they occur, are found in individuals, but the base note is of the senselessness of conflict and of man's overweening self-deception. The illusions and pathetically bombastic emotions kindled by war are sharply focused by occasional concentration on personal reactions; at the very outset three young men come bravely in to announce their bloody spoils:

> EDWARD: I cleft his beaver with a downright blow.
>   That this is true, father, behold his blood.
> MONTAGUE: And, brother, here's the Earl of Wiltshire's blood,
>   Whom I encountered as the battles joined.   [I.1.12–15]

and Richard of Gloucester, not to be outdone, throws down the Duke of Somerset's head and shouts to it – 'Speak thou for me and tell them what I did.'

Shakespeare's fidelity to the actuality of war is precise, even to the frequent, mindless ridiculousness of it. There is something of the ludicrous in the way the throne keeps changing hands in this play, and in Edward's self-deceiving pomposity each time he climbs into its wobbling seat. The main emphasis, however, is on the brutality of war, and the deceit which it engenders. This is achieved by a method which has the added result of laying bare, to an extent not seen in Parts I and II, the basic traits of certain characters, almost as if Shakespeare, having shown certain characters almost as figures in a ritual in Part I, established their general individuality in Part II, now relentlessly uncovers their black souls. The implication is obvious – a kingdom rushes to anarchy not only because of a curse, not only because of the configurations of the stars or the rhythm of history, but also because of the acts of men. The curse, the fate and the human figures become consanguineous.

Warwick dies with words which incontestably show what has lain beneath his power-hungry life – a conceit of the spirit:

'For who lived king, but I could dig his grave?
And who durst smile when Warwick bent his brow?'   [V.2.21–2]

Edward clambers into kingship and the quality of his coming reign is prefigured in the lascivious hedonism, the weakness at the core, of his wooing of Lady Elizabeth and his double-dealing with Lewis of France. Margaret's fierce womanhood and insatiable ambition is shown in its true essence – inordinate cruelty. Her half-insane taunting of the captured York and the sickening refinement of the paper crown and blood-soaked handkerchief gives some true measure of her soul:

'Off with the crown; and, with the crown, his head;
And, whilst we breathe, take time to do him dead.'   [I.4.107–8]

In these ways Shakespeare brings together the actualities of war and the stark facts of individual human responsibility for them.

In sharp, but welcome contrast, is the mode in which Henry is presented. At the beginning he is seen, as king, against the confused background of war and intrigue, as naturalistically presented as the rest with an emphasis on his will-sapping inability to deal with the gross realities of the times. His mood wavers from a resigned, 'Be patient, gentle Earl of Westmorland', to an empty, powerless anger, 'What title hast thou, traitor to the crown?'. Shakespeare increases the poignancy of his weakness by showing that it leads him into actions which are totally and pathetically inimical to his saintly personality. Even his desperate attempt to stop bloodshed by making the compromise that his dynasty's claim to the throne should cease with his own death kicks back at him – in trying to stop war he is denying his own son the heirloom of the crown. He dithers about attempting solutions that are doomed at their inception.

There are, however, three points in the play which suggest that Henry's dramatic role has been conceived in a different context – outside the present-tense events of the play – even making a comment upon them. The first is when Clifford speaks before Towton:

'I would your Highness would depart the field:
The Queen hath best success when you are absent.'   [II.2.73–4]

The irony is obvious, the implications are pitiful – the ruler for whom Margaret and Clifford are to fight is a liability. Yet his removal from the action prepares us also for the scene when Henry, alone, above the battlefield, muses to himself, and witnesses the scene of the sons and fathers. Henry's speech is the first of several set-pieces spoken by Shakespeare's kings in which the condition of kingship is contrasted with that of simple men. Moreover the whole scene gives a strange impression partly created by the ritual language and the antiphonic structure of the speeches being on a different time-scale from its context. The war has brought about the situation, but the meaning goes beyond the mere present tense.

Henry VI, *Richard II* and *Henry V* all have soliloquies which go to the heart of the ironies, the loneliness, the awesome responsibilities of kingship, and the last play has also a scene in which common soldiery are used to broaden the implications of the King's private musings. Henry VI and the sons and fathers and Henry V with Bates and his colleagues acquire a symbolic status, shut out briefly from the relentless pressures of the present tense, and representing the unchanging realities of the human condition behind the ceaseless flow of events in particular times and places.

The scene's meaning is further extended by the emblematic quality of Henry's later meeting with young Richmond. The defeated Lancastrian lays his hand upon the head of a Tudor. He touches a future when the curse will have been removed from England, when history will have turned yet another corner:

'Make much of him, my lords; for this is he
Must help you more than you are hurt by me.'   [IV.6.75–6]

Henry VI is victim, commentator and prophet of the historical process, but the triumph of Part III lies in Shakespeare's ability to make Henry also a suffering man – a poignant victim of events and conditions for which he is completely unsuited.

Part III represents more than the final act in the Wars of the Roses; it is the last of Shakespeare's chronicle plays. The one stark indication that his fecund imagination had begun to grow beyond the restricting form of historical narrative and broad characterization is shown in the character of Richard of Gloucester. In him the nature of a more mature conception of characterization is immediately apparent and is simply explained, but its implications are profound and complex. They are well signified in some lines he speaks before he drags off Henry's body, whom he has murdered. He says:

'I have no brother, I am like no brother;
And this word "love", which greybeards call divine,
Be resident in men like one another,
And not in me! I am myself alone.'   [V.6.80–3]

At once we seem to have entered another country of dramatic conception, and we, as audience, enter into Richard's personality to an extent that is impossible with York, Warwick, Henry and Margaret. They wear their personalities upon their sleeves, and they are the slaves of action and event, make calculable responses to situation, and rarely give any clue to their inner selves. Shakespeare, with Richard, had learned the difference between the appearance and reality of character, understanding that what a man does and says may not correspond to what he thinks and feels. Shakespeare begins to be able to communicate both elements in this paradox simultaneously. It is a process of creation out of which, later, were born Hamlet, Macbeth and, most notably, Iago, and is the beginning of total character-creation in which what is and what seems are given equal force. In Part III Richard stands out as a new type of dramatic character and as a theatrical force. Neither as individuals nor as dramatis personae are the many participants in the trilogy able to stand up to this new power, and as their rabid political morality displaces Henry's ineffective graciousness, so they themselves are soon to be replaced by something altogether more sophisticated:

'And, that I love the tree from whence thou sprang'st,
Witness the loving kiss I give the fruit.
(*Aside*) To say the truth, so Judas kissed his master,
And cried "All hail!" when as he meant all harm.'   [V.7.31–4]

'This shoulder was ordain'd so thick to heave;
And heave it shall some weight or break my back.
Work thou the way – and that shalt execute.'   [V.7.23–5]

This is the note on which the trilogy really ends. Edward's final words, 'For here, I hope, begins our lasting joy' are a pathetic irony in view of what we have already learned of Richard of Gloucester's character and intentions.

It would be idle to pretend that this trilogy is a work of the highest artistic merit, but its faults lie more in the execution than in the intention. At times the construction of scenes is amateurish; at times the characterization fades into indistinctness; the language veers, sometimes violently, between correct poise and gauche lack of control. The virtues of the plays lie, indeed, more in intermittent parts than in the whole. Yet a grand design can be discerned beneath the broken surface, its details emerging at times with astonishing power and effect.

Because the majority of criticism has concentrated on the trilogy's flaws one is perhaps emboldened to try and demonstrate its fitful virtues, and there can be no more valid justification for doing this than the proof of the plays' tremendous theatrical force as revealed in modern production. Academic dismissal of them sometimes tends to forget the hugeness of the canvas that a young dramatist was trying to cover. Shakespeare was working towards a unity of three intransigent elements – chronicle history, political morality and, above all, his own surging and growing inclination towards a drama of individual character. Failure, in such an attempt, is relative both to that attempt and to the power of theatrical experience which the plays on stage generate. ·

Richard III

The hypnotic presence of Richard, Duke of Gloucester, lures critical discussion of this play away from the dramatic context which he dominates. The twentieth century, spurred by its sometimes obsessive interest in morbid psychology, is particularly inclined to concentrate on his character, especially since the other historical events and personages are irretrievably remote from the modern imagination. Furthermore, since Richard III is Shakespeare's first great villain hero, the desire to find his dramatic origins – be they in his affinities with medieval Vice, Senecan villain or Machiavellian political principles – have served to increase his importance.

There can be little doubt that Elizabethan audiences, already whetted by Marlowe's *Tamburlaine*,[19] had a strong appetite for characters of extraordinary evil. The evidence of the publication of *Richard III* is unarguable in its implications. Quartos appeared in 1597, 1598, 1602, 1605, 1612 and 1622. This is a remarkable testimony of popularity in an age where the life-span of plays was commonly very short, but naturally in Elizabethan times, as in ours, a single character, realized by a good actor, proved very attractive with the audience, and the appearance of the great Richard Burbage in the title part doubtless clinched its success. In any case the appetite for chronicle history was very strong and this play would have had a particular attraction for reasons not directly connected with Richard. The time-gap between the battle of Bosworth and 1597 (the date of first performance) approximates fairly nearly to that between ourselves and the ending of the Crimean war. This comparison brings into stark relief the emotional effects that Shakespeare's depiction of Richard's times would have incited.

Balaclava, Florence Nightingale, the courageous inanities of the Light Brigade, still have a power to reverberate in the historically sensitive; Bosworth Field, the princes in the tower, and Crookback Richard could not have been less evocative to the Elizabethans. True, the evocations were not, as ours have been, nurtured by detailed historical narrative and reconstruction in film, book and television; but word-of-mouth transmissions across the generations, which the Elizabethans largely relied upon, are no less, perhaps more, powerful chroniclers. Henry VI was a remote monarch, but Richard III ambled sinuously through the Elizabethan imagination. Moreover there was a particular connection with their own time. The end of

Richard coincided with the appearance of Henry Richmond, the harbinger of the Tudors, grandfather of Elizabeth I. Richmond ends his exhortation to his troops at Bosworth with the words:

'Now civil wounds are stopp'd, peace lives again –
That she may long live here, God say amen!'   [V.5.40–1]

O. J. Campbell comments, 'This was a petition that every Elizabethan audience in the 1590s must have joined in with a sevenfold amen.'[20]

Shakespeare's continuation, then, of the long saga which began with the lamentations over the dead Henry V, had a very sharp focus for his contemporaries. In strictly dramatic terms the focus is double; it is the ultimate example (and the most bleak) of the workings of the curse upon the commonwealth, yet it is also a looking forward to the removal of that curse. The play is both an end and a beginning.

Dramatically, too, the play is marked off from its predecessors in that the curse is embodied less in the total society of the play than in one man. Indeed, the curious isolation which this gives to Richard increases, by compression, the sense of evil which is his personal *raison d'être* and the curse of his kingdom. The relationship of the other characters – some of them scarred, tired relics of earlier broils - to Richard, is depicted less in naturalistic terms than in a choric mode. It is as if the Queens, in particular, recognized this man as the embodied result of iniquities in which, innocent or culpable, they had all been closely involved in the past. But Richard is not only a specific embodiment of England's curse, he is also a kind of black judgment on the rest:

'I had an Edward, till a Richard kill'd him;
I had a husband, till a Richard kill'd him;
Thou hadst an Edward, till a Richard kill'd him;
Thou hadst a Richard, till a Richard kill'd him'   [IV.4.38–42]

There is a wry self-indulgence in the curses and recriminations which these relics of female royalty hurl at Richard and each other. Margaret, in particular, has no element of self-reproach for her bloody part in the events which have brought Richard to power. Margaret is no longer the character she was in *Henry VI*. She is a choric figure, giving all the right responses, expressing all the regrets, sorrows and acrimonies without really acquiring an individual reality. The choric element is inimical to the realism called for by the modern audience, for it increases, by contrast, the sense of the melodramatic we feel in Richard's character. A notable example of this effect is the scene where Margaret curses him. The ritual movement of her lines and Richard's fiercely terse replies conspire to produce a sense of unreality.

The play's chief weakness is the dramatic imbalance between Richard and what surrounds him. Apart from the chanting Queens the male nobility lack, as a whole, the sharply observed qualities which are noticeable (if intermittently) in the early trilogy. Neither Buckingham nor Hastings, the most personalized of them, have much dramatic potency. Thematically these nobles are tired relics of old strife and warfare, dramatically they serve merely to emphasize the fierce presence of Gloucester. While this has its positive side, in that Richard's evil is given a stark isolation, it also makes that very evil difficult to believe. The Queens and nobles seem utterly defenceless, and even the active opposition of Henry Richmond is no more, dramatically speaking, than a conventional assertion of the final triumph of good.

The isolation of Richard creates a crucial problem of interpretation for the director and actor. Is Richard to be depicted as monster so that 'the violent volition of this monster still carries us along'?[21] The rhodomontade actor would find it difficult to resist finding in Richard some undefined supernatural evil force and to make him *grand guignol*. But this has its risks – when, for example, Barry Sullivan acted the part in 1876, 'mirth, on this occasion, gradually descended upon the audience who "grew at last to treat the play as a burlesque and greeted each successive activity of Richard with a laugh".'[22]

Is he to be depicted as a renaissance version of a stock figure of the mediaeval morality play – the Vice – who was, in thematic terms, less a character than a representative of a spirit of mischief, not so much a human embodiment of evil, but of the amoral, conscienceless side of man?[23] He jested rather than uttered curses, he pranked rather than committed heinous crimes, he tended to the likeable but he was unpredictable. He was, indeed, a twister – which is precisely what Richard calls himself:

> 'Thus, like the formal vice, Iniquity,
> I moralise two meanings in one word.'   [III.1.82–3]

Do the other, more subtle, ingredients in his character come from Shakespeare's reading of the popular *Il Principe* by Niccolo Machiavelli? The popular Elizabethan conception of Machiavellianism was a simple rationalization of a work of serious political thought. One aspect of this book was seized upon – where Machiavelli argues for the amoral nature of political acts. This gradually filtered into the notion that ends justify means. It was then only a simple step to charge Machiavelli with advocating completely unprincipled diabolic thought and action in political matters, making his name synonymous with human *diablerie*, evil action, subterfuge. Shakespeare's Richard is as explicit about his Machiavellian antecedents as he is about the Vice:

'I will set the modern Machiavel to school.'

However, without minimizing them, these affinities in Richard's acts and character to this notion of Machiavelli do not, of themselves, or in consort with the Vice elements, seem to add up to the whole character. Some aspects are missing.

Some critics have suggested that these may be found in the result of Shakespeare's knowledge of Senecan drama which exercised a tremendous influence upon Elizabethan writing (particularly *Titus Andronicus*). Seneca, in the first century AD, wrote tragedies in which – a villain-hero is provoked to bloody revenge for some act perpetrated upon him; he is often incited to this by a ghost; there is an implacable stoicism in the posture of the villain-hero as he proceeds to his revenge; the plays are written in an enveloping rhetorical style; there is a huge sensationalism of plot and incident, much of which is reported, most bloody and unnatural deeds of violence are present; there is a strong choric element; ritual curses are a marked (and tedious) feature of the plays' writing. The ritual curses, with more than a suggestion of the choric mode, declaimed by the Queens in *Richard III* certainly seem Senecan in origin. Clarence's death is testimony to the blood-spilling; the appearance of the ghosts (who do not, of course, incite Richard to revenge) suggest, too, the way in which Seneca used the supernatural.

However, as I have written elsewhere:

In Seneca, and the typical Elizabethan counterpart like *The Spanish Tragedy*, the avenging figure has, however thin, a precise fact to work upon. The typical 'hero' is determined to do to another or others that which has been practised upon him. He has always, according to his own lights, a reason for what he does. Richard has no particular reason. . . . he avenges himself upon the idea of opposition, and not upon a particular deed done to him. Richard's malevolent playfulness is indeed another of the characteristics which

marks him off from the Senecan villain. There is something dull
about the Senecan avenger – a kind of stolid dedication to the mere
act of revenge, a dedication which steamrollers out of him any
deviousness of character. But Richard of Gloucester makes a wit out
of villainy, and the proof of this lies in many scenes of the play, most
notably in the wooing of Anne.[24]

When one adds to these dissimilarities the strange charm of Richard,
his subtle dissembling, his wry self-regarding and his total lack of
stoicism, it is clear that, only in the most general terms, as avenger, as
instigator of most bloody deeds, is this man a Senecan villain.

Richard III is perhaps the first example of a process of character
creation which came to fruition in Hamlet, Prince Hal and Iago. A
clue to its nature is in Richard's musing about the way to attain the
crown:

'Why, I can smile, and murder whiles I smile,
And cry "Content!" to that which grieves my heart,
And wet my cheeks with artificial tears,
And frame my face to all occasions.
. . . . . .
I can add colours to the chameleon,
Change shapes with Proteus for advantages,
And set the murderous Machiavel to school.
Can I do this, and cannot get a crown?
Tut, were it further off, I'll pluck it down.'   [3H. VI. III. 2. 182–195]

To dissemble and gain a desired result by so doing is the source of
Richard's power and this ability he shares not only in genre, but also
in practice, with the actor. Richard has both the narcissism and the
dissembling instincts that make the actor.

Richard, having killed her husband, 'becomes' (as an actor
'becomes' his role) an honest regretful lover to the hypnotized Anne.
He woos her cynically in a spirit of villainous scheming wit, but it is
his actor's skill which wins her. No one who has experienced the
extraordinary double-focus that an actor can exert on his role – being
(on stage) King Lear in all his power, while simultaneously cracking
sotto voce jokes with supernumaries unheard by the audience – can
be surprised at Richard's success. This brilliant actor successively
becomes a sympathetic brother to the Clarence he has already
doomed, in the court of dying Edward, with breathtaking skill, a
man of injured innocence, full of outraged susceptibilities, then
(perhaps his greatest performance of all) an unworldly monarch
sibillanting the Bible in his twisted lips, flanked by two Bishops. He

is actor all through and he knows it:

'I can add colours to the chameleon
Change shapes with Proteus for advantages.'

By the time he came to write this play Shakespeare was a firm inhabitant of the actors' world where illusion dances with reality in a rhythm which is intoxicating. The actor's function is, paradoxically, to find himself by not being himself and to convince unwitting victims that what they see is true. And the extra ingredient in the character of Richard comes from Shakespeare's growing recognition of the potency of the theatrical possibilities that are present in the equivocal figure who walks the line where what is and what seems merge. Later, Hamlet is to put on 'an antic disposition', Hal is to feign for his own purposes and Iago to dissemble because 'I am not what I am'. Those creatures of the half-world between illusion and reality – the Fools, Feste and Touchstone, and notably Lear's unnamed Fool – are perhaps the ultimate point to which Shakespeare's obsession with the world of the actor could go and still prove a viable instrument for communicating thoughts and feelings which lie beyond spoken words and the ordinary areas of characterization.

Richard of Gloucester is one of the most actable characters in Shakespeare, not because he is Vice, Senecan, or Machiavellian, but because he is actor. Those other elements helped, but what makes him hypnotic, credible and an obsession to an audience is the extent to which he embodies the characteristics of the actors with whom Shakespeare worked and who so caught and fired his imagination.

The one obvious testimony to the strong possibility that in *Richard III* Shakespeare had begun to utilize the inner compulsions of his own imaginative world, giving them precedence over the formalized themes of history, is that, as an audience, we are only minimally conscious that these themes are present. In the three parts of *Henry VI* we can hardly escape divine right, usurpation, guilt, bravery and honour; in *Richard III*, however, we can derive tremendous theatrical experience merely from watching the deviousness of Richard alone. It is true that Richmond's speech before Bosworth seems to place Richard within the framework of the historical process, as revealed in the *Henry VI* plays:

'A bloody tyrant and a homicide;
One rais'd in blood, and one in blood estblish'd;

. . . . .

One that hath ever been God's enemy.'   [V.3.246–252]

Yet this is not all that we, as audience, have known of this man. We do not think of usurper, or mere bloody tyrant, but of a man who has immensely intrigued us, claiming from us a reluctant but inevitable admiration for sheer audacity. When Richard is absent from the stage, we yearn for his return, not as representative of disorder, or as part of an historical process, but as a thrilling dramatic entity. We require, as audience, a little touch of Richard in the night because, as character, he has more magnetism than anyone else.

Shakespeare, in this play, had begun to see behind the monumental formalities of the great historical themes into the complexities of individual character. The play's imbalance, which has been commented on, is a result of this. It is an unsatisfactory historical conclusion to the trilogy because it is such a satisfactory introduction to the drama of individual character.

Titus Andronicus

Shakespeare's school education, his acquaintance with contemporary dramatists and growing knowledge of audience taste account, in large part, for the obvious influence of the Latin dramatist Seneca on his work. This influence, dispersed and modified in the early histories, can be clearly seen in his first tragedy – *Titus Andronicus*. The gentle-minded, fearful of believing that Shakespeare could have written this mass of horror, have questioned its authorship. The facts are that it is included in the first Folio and that it was referred to by Francis Meres in 1598 as one of Shakespeare's 'excellent tragedies'.[25] Those who find this insufficient evidence for Shakespeare's authorship, may consult Dover Wilson's[26] and J. M. Roberston's[27] differing claims for collaborative authorship. The dangerous quicksands of internal evidence do little but assure us that there is a common quality of rhetorical high-flown verse in the three parts of *Henry VI* and in this play. Considering, however, the authorship problems of that trilogy and the fact that the rhetorical mode itself was common property, it is as well not to stand upon these grounds. Contemporary scholarly opinion generally has the view that the play is wholly Shakespeare's.

Its date of composition is unknown. Henslowe's Diary, a fecund but treacherous source of information, records a performance of 'Titus and Ondronicas' in January 1594 and calls it 'ne' (new), although this may well refer to an old play newly refurbished. An earlier entry of April 1593 referring to a 'ne' play *'Titus and Vespacia'* is held by some to refer to *Titus Andronicus*. Finally, Ben Jonson in the Induction of his *Bartholomew Fair* 1614 refers to a play, *Andronicus*, written some twenty-five or thirty years before, with some asperity.

This play, although Shakespeare's first venture into tragedy, is of a kind very different from that usually associated with him. It is frequently forgotten that he began his career in an intellectual atmosphere in which medieval and the new Renaissance precepts of thought were in collision. The medieval influence is readily seen in many of the conceptions of history which inform his early trilogy, though, as has been seen, these were already being mutated by Renaissance/Tudor beliefs. *Titus Andronicus* is a straightforward example of the influence of Renaissance classicism.

Seneca exerted a strong attraction on literate Elizabethans. His

long-held reputation was given renewed impetus by the fast developing growth of interest in the classics of Greece and Rome, and their
establishment as final standards in the matter of content and
technique. Seneca, pushed to the forefront of the educational and,
eventually, of the theatre world, was the only Latin tragic dramatist
to be studied and copied, with imitations of his plays being
performed at the universities, the Inns of Court and, eventually, the
more public theatres.

Shakespeare may have read Seneca in the original, but more likely
in the popular translation of his plays which appeared in 1581 entitled
Seneca His Tenne Tragedies. Alexander Nevile, in his translation of
Seneca's *Oedipus* in 1591, wrote that it was meant: 'only to satisfy the
constant demands and requests of a very few familiar friends, who
thought to have put it to the same use that Seneca himself in his
Invention pretended; which was by the tragical and pompous show
upon stage to admonish all men...' Sir Philip Sidney writing in his
Apologie for Poesie of poetry as aiming at 'the winning of the mind
from wickedness to virtue', gives some explanation of how a Senecan
play with all its horrors might have commended itself even to the
most morally prurient when he says: 'shall the abuse of a thing make
the right use odious? Nay truly, though I yield that Poesy may not
only be abused, but that being abused, by the reason of his sweet
charming force, it can do more hurt than any other army of words,
yet ... being rightly used (and upon the right use each thing
conceiveth his title), doth most good.'

The attraction of the Senecan type of play can thus be explained
by its slaking of two almost paradoxical thirsts – the first, an
unsophisticated desire to see sensational events on stage, and the
second, to justify the pleasure gained by believing that thereby the
mind is won from wickedness to virtue.

So far as is known Seneca's plays were originally performed for
small private upper-class Roman audiences and were more of an
animated reading than a full-scale theatrical performance. All the
plays have a claustrophobic atmosphere – dark deeds are done, or
lengthily reported, in locations which seem walled-up, secretive,
private. Although *Titus Andronicus* is set in various parts of Rome, it
still gives a strong feeling of a closely-confined environment, where
we eavesdrop into a dank world of people who lack the light, the air
and the sky. Again, as in Seneca, the play is concerned exclusively
with the affairs of the high-born in which political and social life is
conditioned entirely by lust, greed, cruelty, ambition and above all

revenge. We learn little about the Emperor, Tamora, her sons, and Titus himself, other than that their swift and angry disposition is quick to take offence and to avenge with most bloody resolution.

The concentration upon single motivation gives a ritualistic quality to the characters, as each does his solo act in a drama where the music never changes, a quality intensified by the kind of language and the heavily episodic construction. Muriel Bradbrook says it is 'more like a pageant than a play'.[28] This is true and a faint but sinister rhythmical music would seem to be an essential background to the procession of lurid images. Peter Brook's famous Stratford production of 1955 emphasized this with its processive inevitability and eerie *musique concrète*. The success of this production has done much to entitle us to question the many scholarly strictures hurled at the play, typified in J. C. Maxwell's comment, 'It is, I think, the one play of Shakespeare which would have left an intelligent contemporary in some doubt whether the author's truest bent was for the stage.'[29]

It is true that the play has many faults. The characterization, in general, lacks depth and subtlety of motivation. There is an overabundance of violent climaxes, so that we become sated with sensation. There are scenes whose purpose can be divined but whose execution is faulty. There is, frequently, a separation between the realities of character and the verse they speak – at times they orate 'poetry' without giving the sense of speaking from within themselves. For the modern audience the author is sometimes dangerously close to crossing the line that separates horror from the ridiculous.

The main culprit, perhaps, is the play's language which is fundamentally that of a young poet reeling intoxicatedly from the effects of his own verbosity and the influence of his peers – notably Marlowe. The most striking example of the separation of poetic utterance from character-reality is in the scene where Lavinia appears mutilated and ravaged by Chiron and Demetrius. The scene has no need of embroidery, but that is what it receives. Lavinia stands before us, despoiled, and we have a speech of forty-seven lines of rhetorical force, but with little dramatic relevance:

> 'Alas, a crimson river of warm blood,
> Like to a bubbling fountain stirr'd with wind,
> Doth rise and fall between thy rosed lips,
> Coming and going with thy honey breath.
> But sure some Tereus hath deflowered thee,
> And, lest thou should detect him, cut thy tongue.'   [II.4.22–7]

The speech proceeds in this rhetorical vein, making the whole matter embarrassingly incredible. Lavinia stands raped, and is addressed and commented upon with second-rate Marlovian sweet sonorities and references to myth and legend. Quite simply, we cannot believe that the man who makes the speech is outraged and grief-torn.

The speech also contains (as do others in the play) the mark of the immature dramatic poet – the use of question marks, always a telltale sign of rhetoric unrelated to psychological truth of character or situation.

Yet it still has much dramatic and theatrical validity, which, far from casting doubts on its author's future as a dramatist, should rather raise excited speculation about the nature of his development. Of the positive qualities (which Brook seized upon), some are embryonic in appearance, others more mature, but all clearly point the way in certain directions.

First, there are moments when the flow of rhetoric suddenly, and with great effect, checks itself and clenches around character, and reality replaces, if only fleetingly, the incredible. Titus's separate lines, 'These words are razors to my wounded heart' when the ingrate Saturninus turns on him; his wry comment about an erstwhile friend who has married one of Titus's enemies – 'I am not bid to wait upon this bride'; the pitiful rebuke he addresses to Marcus after he first sees his ravished daughter:

TITUS: Why, I have not another tear to shed.

These, with their swift glimpses into character, have the effect of giving some justification and dramatic potency to some of the longer, less muscular speeches.

Second, in the character of Titus and Aaron two later characters are foreshadowed. Titus, the man of stupid pride, courage, inflexible determination, in whom even love is subservient to a high but destructive self-will, is a first limning of King Lear. Such men are heirs of pain and grief which they accept with stoic fortitude – it is in this acceptance that Titus approaches the tragic frontier which Lear was to cross. Aaron the Moor is 'portentous and diabolic: his blackness an outward symbol of his diabolic nature, recognized by all.'[30] Like Richard III and Iago his lineage is mixed with the medieval Vice and with Machiavellianism. He is a chuckling despoiler of whatever is good and worthy in the human spirit. Yet he cannot, any more than Richard or Iago, finally be regarded as mere dramatic cypher. All three characters have had injected into them that characteristically Shakespearean element of the humanly possible – in their wit, their weaknesses and their fears. In this they exhibit something which is vulnerable and therefore more human than supernatural. Aaron is the first of a group of characters through which it might be said that Shakespeare tested the truth of his prevailing optimism about the redemptive ability of the human race, which often proves the better by being subjected, from time to time, to the worst.

Third, the dramatist in Shakespeare shows, if only occasionally, how intractable material may be made viable by the exercise of imaginative discipline. The infamous banquet scene in which Chiron and Demetrius are brought on in a pie, are unwittingly tasted by their mother who then, in company with Lavinia, is killed by Titus, would tax the sensibility of most people. In its source (Seneca's *Thyestes*) the event is prolonged and related in ponderously rhetorical verse. In its intermittent attempts to be naturalistic it becomes sickening comic. Shakespeare's intuition is, however, finer. His scene is only thirty-eight lines in length, there is lingering neither on the pie nor, more importantly, on Tamora's realization of her ghastly meal. She is despatched immediately she knows. The scene is full of short sharp exchanges in which Lavinia's death is a pathetic sudden detail, but given poignancy by her father's anguished cry – 'Killed her for whom my tears have made me blind.' The audience has little chance to lapse into incredulity or laughter. Shakespeare's dramatic skill, raw as it is, makes it all short, sharp and final.

Titus Andronicus, then, is the play of a young man caught between the extremes of an exuberant imagination and the dictates of fashion, its faults being a direct result of his inability to make either call the other's tune. Modern production has shown that, apart from its surprising viability as a theatrical piece, it contains undeniable indications of future development. It is, in many ways, the excited lab work of a developing genius.

NOTES

1 From the 'Sermon of Obedience, or An Exhortation concerning good Ordre and Obedience to Rules and Magistrates', from a *Book of Homilies* of 1547.

2 Edward Hall (or Halle) c.1498–1547. Historian. His chronicles were published posthumously 1548 as *The Union of the Two Noble and Ilustre Famelies of Lancastre and York*.

3 Raphael Holinshed died c.1580. His *Chronicles* (1st volume, published in 1577) was reprinted and enlarged in 1587 – which edition Shakespeare used.

4 Higden's *Polychronicon*, 2nd Book.

5 *A Mirror for Magistrates*, first printed 1559. The 1563 edition contained an introduction by Sackville. Further editions appeared in 1578, 1587, and 1610. It was a collection of verse biographies of tragical historical personages.

6 The *Great Bible*, 1539, prepared by Coverdale for Henry VIII. Part of it supplied the text for the *Book of Common Prayer* (1549).

7 Robert Greene, 1558–92. Pamphleteer and playwright. It was in *Groatsworth of Wit* (1592) that he attacked Shakespeare as an 'upstart crow'.

8 J. Dover Wilson, Introduction to New Cambridge Edition of *Henry VI* (1952).

9 Philip Henslowe, died 1616. Theatre owner and manager; kept a memorandum account book – the so-called Diary – from 1593 to 1603.

10 Thomas Nashe, 1567–c.1601. Dramatist and pamphleteer. He wrote the first picaresque novel, *The Unfortunate Traveller* (1594).

11 A. C. Sprague, *Shakespeare's Histories* (1964), p. 115.

12 O. J. Campbell and E. G. Quinn, *A Shakespeare Encyclopaedia* (1966).

13 Thomas Nashe, *A Wonderful Astrological Prognostication* (1591).

14 Richard Grafton, c.1513–c.1572. Printer and chronicler. His *Chronicle*, 1543, from the time of Edward IV: in 1548 added the history of the years 1532–47 to Hall's *Chronicles*.

15 Sprague, op. cit., p. 118.

16 Logan Pearsall Smith, *On Reading Shakespeare* (1933), p. 140.

17 See J. C. Trewin, *Shakespeare on the English Stage 1900–1964* (1964).

18 In the Royal Shakespeare Theatre's production of 1965, John Barton compressed the three Parts into two, the first called Henry VI, the second Edward IV.

19 Christopher Marlowe, 1564–93. Poet and playwright. *Tamburlaine the Great* was written c.1587 and published in 1590.

20 O. J. Campbell and E. G. Quinn, op. cit., p. 700.

21 Sprague, op. cit., p. 131.

22 Ibid.

23 See B. Spivack, *Shakespeare and the Allegory of Evil* (1598).

24 Gareth Lloyd Evans – 'Seneca and the Kingdom of Violence' in *Studies in Latin Literature and its Influence (Roman Drama)*, edited by D. R. Dudley and T. A. Dorey (1965), pp. 141–2.

25 Francis Meres, 1565–1647. Author of *Palladis Tamia* (1598).

26 J. Dover Wilson, Introduction to New Cambridge edition of *Titus*

Andronicus (1948).

27 J. M. Robertson, *Did Shakespeare write Titus Andronicus? A Study in English Literature* (1905).

28 Muriel Bradbrook, *Shakespeare and Elizabethan Poetry* (1951), p. 110.

29 J. C. Maxwell, Introduction to New Arden edition of *Titus Andronicus*, (1953).

30 Bradbrook, op. cit., p. 107.

2 The Early Comedies

It is in the nature of young artists to experiment in mode, form, and content – an essential and often uncontrolled flexing of the imaginative muscles. The danger, however, is that the critic may isolate the author from such a context. No writer, least of all the dramatist, is generated solely by the inner workings of his mind. He is conditioned very much by his cultural environment. The fact, for example, that Shakespeare wrote, in a short period, several history plays, a Senecan revenge tragedy and a number of comedies in a variety of modes is, of course, a measure of excited, young versatility, but it also indicates the nature of the varied context in which he, as man and artist, lived. He shows in his history plays that he is capable of transcending the conventional with individual sensibility in form and content. The comedies reveal the extent to which he was governed by theatre fashion and the examples of his contemporaries.

The Comedy of Errors, *The Taming of the Shrew* and *Love's Labour's Lost* are modish comedies. They are the product of Shakespeare's reading of Latin literature, his manipulation of the form and content of the Roman dramatists, Terence[1] and Plautus[2], and his susceptibility to the influence of the group of contemporary, academically-trained dramatists known as the University Wits.[3] Although we can gain rich delight from these plays of his (particularly *The Shrew*) with no knowledge of the work of the University Wits – Lyly, Peele, Greene or Gascoigne – this interweaving of influence is so complex that scholarly claims have been made for the authorship or part-authorship of several of Shakespeare's plays by one or other (or even several collectively) of this group.

Artifice is the keynote of plays like Greene's *James IV* (1591), Lyly's *Campaspe* (1584) and *Mother Bombie* (1587), elements from which Shakespeare later refined and modified in his maturer comedies. In the 1580s, however, what he found in them led his own pen in the direction of conscious contrivance in plot, character and language, for his early comedies, to one degree or another, have an apparently conscious fastidiousness of technique and imagination. The measure of his superiority, however, is less in his technique than in the gradual emergence of an individuality of vision. His contemporaries remained largely within convention of all kinds; he gradually either made use of or rejected the same conventions to communicate a vision of existence which extended beyond them. Consideration of

47

Shakespeare's early comedies therefore demands a balance between critical appreciation of his handling of conventions and a sensitivity to his unique if, as yet, limited vision.

The nature of the conventions is simply stated: plots derived from classical sources, often complicated or devious in form; stock characters, almost folk figures of Latin drama – crafty servants, bombastic soldiery, ageing but affluent lovers, duped parents; highly artificed language. This is exemplified in its English counterpart in Lyly's style – ostentatious imagery full of classical allusion, verbal conceits, rhetoric, self-conscious wit, aphorisms, alliteration – a paraphernalia of artifice which, like some rich fruit, delights with its first tasting but palls as it becomes habitual. The setting, particularly in Lyly, is often pastoral, with young shepherds and shepherdesses, baulked swains and disguised amorata playing out a love story. From Robert Greene he learned much about the way to complicate these plots, interweaving main and sub plot; from the Commedia dell'arte he took stock low-life characters – the braggart, the lowly priest, the clown and the cheeky boy – and the sophisticates like the pedantic scholar and the bombastic soldier; from Terence and Plautus he learned how to manipulate such stock figures within the five-act form, how to capitalize on mistaken identity, how to manoeuvre intrigue. He came to realize from reading, either the original or a translation or an adaptation, that where Plautus uses ridicule Terence uses irony, that where the one is coarse the other leans towards refinement, where the one is given to idiomatic vernacular speech the other is more elegantly literary in verbal tone and form.

However, although it is easy to enumerate the general and particular qualities which Shakespeare inherited from these various sources, it is difficult to pin down the particular source of any individual influence. For example there are many adaptations from Plautus in the fifteenth and sixteenth centuries, for use on the Italian stage. Arisosto's *I Suppositi* of 1509,[4] itself an adaptation of Plautus's *Amphitruo*, in its turn formed the basis for George Gascoigne's *Supposes* in 1566. This Shakespeare took over as the Bianca subplot in *The Taming of the Shrew*.

The complicated weaving and interweaving of literary modes and influences, involving matter both ancient and contemporary, writers both long dead and ambitiously still alive, may engage the researcher in unravelling to a point where the threads break. The truth is that the young Shakespeare showed himself as capable as any of using modes which were common stock, and, what was more to the point for him, of keeping his name in the forefront of the young dramatists, combating by sheer virtuosity the tense envies and jealousies which undoubtedly crowed and grunted in that small theatre world. Greene's attack on Shakespeare in which he refers to him as an 'upstart crow' is commonly held to be a good example of the tensions which inhabited the Elizabethan literary world, and it certainly has a sneering envy about it. However, a lesser-known attack by Nashe on dramatists whose learning is faulty gives a more direct impression of the temper of the times.[5] Such men, he says, are:

> 'a sort of shifting companions, that runne through every arte and thrive by none . . . that could scarce latinize their neckeverse if they should have neede.'

He was not, presumably, referring directly to Shakespeare, but his words suggest an atmosphere in which no one was likely to be immune from calumny. Shakespeare would have been particularly vulnerable, not only because of his achievements, and because he was not a member of the University Wits, but also because the discerning, with no axe to grind, were beginning to laud him:

> 'As Plautus and Seneca are accounted the best for Comedy and Tragedy among the Latines: so Shakespeare among the English is the most excellent in both kinds for the stage; for Comedy, witnes his Gentlemen of Verona, his Errors; his Love labours lost, his Love labours wonne, his Midsummers night dreame, and his Merchant of Venice . . .'[6]

This comment by Francis Meres offers a tacit recognition of Shakespeare's pre-eminence in those very forms and modes of comedy and tragedy which were part of the common stock and style.

There can be no doubt that Shakespeare, in his early comedies, showed evidence of being captivated by accepted modes and his language, quite apart from his dramaturgy, echoes the courtly forms of his contemporaries. It is his point of view, which grows into comprehensive vision as he matures, which clinches the evidences of individuality. He may be said to be creator where his contemporaries are artificers; he comes to write with imaginative purpose where his contemporaries exercise nimble fancy; he begins to find individual characters where they rest happy with types. Above all, he moves inexorably in the direction of a fairness of judgment of the human world which is his most unique quality, towards the correct compassion of Art, rather than the agile self-regard of Artifice.

The Two Gentlemen of Verona

The Two Gentlemen of Verona is probably the least popular of all Shakespeare's plays. The combination of a complicated plot, a remote world, insufficient characterization and a good deal of highly-wrought, dramatically unviable verse account, to a large extent, for its neglect, which, it is tempting to conclude, is justifiable. Its general effect is curiously unpleasant. Of the two heroes Proteus is a faithless libertine whose redemption seems artificial, and even Valentine's romantic attractiveness has a thin and superficial glitter – a combination sufficient in itself to produce an irritation of the sensibilities. Paradoxically this is increased because its heroine, Julia, with her charm and strength of will, is too good for the situation in which she is placed and the priggish companions she is laboured with. She belongs, in essence, to the company of Rosalind and Viola.

There are, however, some fugitive pieces of gold. Apart from Julia herself, the character of Launce attracts the delighted approval of any audience. Admittedly he has the advantage of acquiring a certain status since he is accompanied by a dog, and the English mania for the animal that accompanies a master and seems imbued with human characteristics is well-known. The result, as Shakespeare exploits it, to immortalize the dog and, by association, the master as well.

Yet, if we can set aside any predisposition towards a compulsive love for the dog, it is possible to see that Launce has qualities admirable and important in themselves and, though he may have affiliation with the typical bumpkin characters of the Commedia dell'Arte,[7] is, in fact, one of the first of Shakespeare's great natural comics. The line is rich through Bottom and his crew Gobbo, to the gravedigger in Hamlet. The chief characteristics of these naturals are simple to enumerate but complex in their significance and meaning.

They have reached the page of Shakespeare's manuscript largely out of direct experience which has been sifted through the dramatic imagination, having no place in any literary source; even where, as in the case of Launce, the character-type may be found in foreign places, their essence is characteristically Shakespearean. Their true source is the Warwickshire country population he had known as a child and which, doubtless, he continued to know, from time to time, in his adulthood. They are lower class; they usually have a slow cunning of mind; they treat language like reckless, slightly pompous, but endearing libertines. To the men of more sophisticated caste with whom they have to deal, they seem witless and exasperating but, in fact, they have a remarkable (if paradoxical) ability to live, with a secretive joy, on their wits. They always seem to have something in reserve – a piece of basic knowledge, a secret, a crushing anecdote, an ability to wear down the bright rapiers of sophisticated speech with the broadsword of relentless talk, for they are rarely conquered.

Their essential quality is their actuality, their down-to-earthness. Like the soil and the seasons, which are their true context, they have an underlying rhythm of spirit, and it is this basic reality which Shakespeare has captured. Launce's famous speech to his dog is one of the classic set-pieces of naturalistic prose in the canon. It has all the knowing, extrovert, confiding and gossipy mind-wandering which is typical, even now, of the Warwickshire countryman (especially if he knows there are townsmen to treat with). Launce is anxious to give all the evidence for the resolution of some point which eventually gets lost in his dissociated advocacy, and his speech becomes a kind of social document – social trivia, but in depth. We learn the character of the mother, the father, the maid, even, while he expatiates upon a dog that, unaccountably to him, has no human feelings.

There are two features of the speech that require special emphasis. The first is its superb dramatic value. It would be very difficult for an actor not to make a success of it, not only because of its verbal humour, but because of its charting of the visual comedy which should accompany it. The cat 'wringing her hands', the shoe, representing, variously, the mother and father, the staff being 'my sister'. It shows Shakespeare's total awareness of an actor's requirements, both verbal and visual. Secondly, the speech affects not only the experience we have of the play, but implies something of the nature of Shakespeare's expanding vision of life. The presence of Launce and, to an extent, of Speed (the more sophisticated, clownish character) provide a welcome antidote to the cloying unsatisfying romanticism of the world which they serve. It is a pleasure to encounter these wide-eyed realists just as those points where the complicated blindness of the sophisticates becomes irritating. We are drawn back to the practicalities of love and life by such words as these –

> ... 'He lives not now that knows me to be in love; yet I am in love;
> but a team of horse shall not pluck that from me; nor who 'tis I love;
> and yet 'tis a woman ...'   [III.1.264–7]

– after we have shared the wallowing of:

> 'She is my essence, and I leave to be
> If I be not by her fair influence
> Foster'd, illumined, cherish'd, kept alive.
> I fly not death, to fly his deadly doom:
> Tarry I here, I but attend on death;
> But fly I hence, I fly away from life.'   [III.1.182–7]

Yet this directness is more than welcome contrast, and more than comic relief. It suggests a deeper kind of relationship between the natural, more practical attitude, and the romantic way of love and life. Within this relationship lies the beginning of the unique Shakespearean vision of the meaning and value of love and life.

The theme of the play is the power of love and the way in which the power affects, both for good and evil, the will and judgment of those who fall under its spell. Both Valentine and Proteus quite literally spend the entire action involved in nothing else but the pursuit of love's dream. They are completely under a spell, as Valentine admits:

> 'For, in revenge of my contempt of love,
> Love hath chas'd sleep from my enthralled eyes,
> And made them watchers of mine own heart's sorrow.'
>   [II.4.129–131]

If Valentine is passive, a victim of Love's power, Proteus more actively challenges and contests its influence, attempting to bend it to his own desires:

> 'If I can check my erring love, I will;
> If not, to compass her I'll use my skill.'   [II.4.209–10]

Love acts as catalyst, showing Valentine to be right-minded, honourable, tactlessly generous, and Proteus to be cunning, dishonourable and selfish. Between these two extremes Silvia, and particularly Julia, are caught. The former, with something of Bianca's disposition in *The Taming of the Shrew*, quiescently drifts on the tides of happiness and unhappiness which approach her, making little attempt to strike out for either shore. The latter not content to drift takes a bearing:

> 'Then let me go, and hinder not my course;'

If Valentine represents Love's passion, Proteus Love's duplicity, then Julia is Love's truth. Like Rosalind and Viola she knows there is no

easy way to true love. She is capable of being deceived by Proteus –
'His words are bonds, his oaths are oracles'. She is capable of lyrical
and sentimentality, and can bridle at a rival, but she is incapable of
merely waiting to let love have its way with her. By comparison with
her and her compeers in the later romantic comedies, the male
counterparts lack a sense of being in control of their own destinies.
They may, like Proteus, indulge in sharp activity to fulfil their ends,
but the means and the ends are unworthy. They may, like Valentine,
have a shrewd theoretical knowledge of the ways of women –
'woman sometimes scorns what best contents her' – but this
knowlege seems merely academic.

For Shakespeare the essence of true love is that it is romantic,
faithful and finds ultimate validation and fulfilment in the order of
marriage, but it cannot achieve its fullness without the existence of
obstacles and the operations of practicality and activity. Shakespeare
finds romantic and faithful love among both men and women – in
Valentine, Berowne, Benedick, in Julia, Rosalind, Viola, but only in
the women does he seem to find the ability to prove, to test, to
activate and make practical what the heart cries for. Julia's speech
when she discovers Proteus's duplicity expresses the Shakespearean
heroine's superior usages and knowledge of the ways of Love –

> 'Alas, poor fool, why do I pity him
> That with his very heart despiseth me?
> Because he loves her, he despiseth me;
> Because I love him, I must pity him.
>
> . . . . .
>
> I am my master's true-confirmed love,
> But cannot be true servant to my master
> Unless I prove false traitor to myself.'   [IV.4.89–101]

In the more general context the 'natural' posture of Launce and Speed
acquires a greater meaning. Speed says to Valentine – 'Ay, but
hearken sir; though the chameleon love can feed on the air, I am one
that am nourish'd by my victuals, and would fain have meat', harshly
and crudely distinguishing between appetites. Julia, however, recon-
ciles the appetites which true love activates – she, like the naturals,
knows the value of accepting 'commodity' as a part of the truth of
life, but unlike them she also knows that neither life nor love is
fulfilled unless commodity is graced by fidelity, in the giving vein.

The Comedy of Errors

On 28 December 1594, the gentlemen of Gray's Inn saw a play under rather unusual circumstances. Its presentation followed a near riot from which the Ambassador (the representative) from the Inner Temple escaped with his colleagues, presumably in a hurry: 'After their Departure the Throngs and Tumults did somewhat cease, although so much of them continued as was able to disorder and confound any good Inventions whatsoever'. One can imagine the organizers, frantic to stop the brawling, calling quickly upon the actors to begin their piece – 'a Comedy of Errors (like to Plautus his Menechmus) was played by the Players. So that Night was begun, and continued to the end, in nothing but Confusion and Errors; whereupon it was ever afterwards called, The Night of Errors'.[8]

The play concerned was undoubtedly Shakespeare's *The Comedy of Errors* and the account somewhat tartly implies that it did little to mitigate the confusion which dominated the evening festivities. However, the play's own confusion is beautifully organized, its errors are enchanting to speculate upon, and its comedy ranges easily between farce and fantasy, ending upon an affirmative note of total contentment.

In the right circumstances it would have been an appropriate choice for Gray's Inn and its classically learned scholars. The eye-witness account, more concerned with strife than with Art, still has time to recognize the affinity between the play and the Latin play *Menaechmi* of Plautus. If the writer had had time he might have mentioned that there are also affinities with Plautus's *Amphitruo*, for the outlines of Shakespeare's plot, the dispositions he makes of the couples, the element of farce, are all derived from the popular Roman dramatist.

It is impossible to say with any certainty when it was written. Reasons, though not conclusive, can be given for dating it as early as 1589 or as late as 1594. It has particular affinities with *The Two Gentlemen of Verona*, which is sometimes regarded as Shakespeare's first comedy, but also with *Love's Labour's Lost*, now generally regarded as being the latest of the early group of comedies. These affinities are both in the language and the characterization. There are, as R.A. Foakes has pointed out,[9] relatively unusual words common to this play and *The Two Gentlemen of Verona* – 'hapless', 'peevish', 'overshoo' – and the dialogue of Launce and Speed has much of the mixture of punning artifice and simple naturalism to be found in the mouths of the Dromio brothers.

Yet, even more certainly than with *The Two Gentlemen of Verona*, Shakespeare has put his own handprint firmly on this play. There is an assurance in both dramatic construction and in the writing. The complicated plot is handled with great dexterity, and the language has fewer moments when it takes heedless wing, losing all contact with the groundwork of character and situation. Moreover, Shakespeare displays a characteristic ability to deal with a bewildering plot. The position of Ægeon, the sudden transformation of his wife from nun to rediscovered wife and mother, the potential sourness of the relationship of Adriana with her sister and with her husband, could, in less blessed hands, lead to unsweetened tartness of the kind that mars *The Two Gentlemen of Verona* and leaves our experience of *The Merchant of Venice* somewhat bitter to the taste.

It is the more remarkable that Shakespeare was able to unify the tastes and tones of the play when the atmosphere of the first two scenes is closely considered. It is a solemn, almost sombre situation which we encounter, where an ageing man, already laden with the grief of loss, is faced with the final dispossession – his own life – upon an edict which even a sympathetic ruler cannot rescind:

'Hopeless and helpless doth Ægeon wend,
But to procrastinate his lifeless end'.   [1.1.158–9]

This atmosphere is scarcely relieved by the opening remarks of his lost son, Antipholus of Syracuse:

'He that commends me to mine own content
Commends me to the thing I cannot get'.   [1.2.33–4]

Admittedly it is a characteristic of Shakespeare's comedies to make the dark light enough – eventually – and there are sufficient examples in both early and more mature comedies to confirm this – the early scenes of *As You Like It* are notable for the cruelty which surrounds Orlando and the faithful Adam. Yet there is no other romantic play which, at its beginning, so relentlessly emphasizes an unrelieved sombreness, unmitigated by any comic overtone or under-tone. However, the play moves, after the first two scenes, very quickly in the direction of romantic farce and the memory of the early darkness does not blight either our affection for the comedy that we witness or our readiness to accept the final and complete resolution.

This Shakespeare brings about in two ways. First, simply by

'losing' Ægeon from the dramatic action for the major part of the comedy when the farce of action has its head. He rediscovers him only at that correct point when we realize that the old man's tribulations are about to come to a happy conclusion. He is not allowed to wander throughout the play, an irritant to the comedy and a tiresome jabber at our moral susceptibilities.

Second, the play is a comedy very largely written in terms of situation rather than of character or even, in a sense, of theme. With the exception of Pinch (a fantastic), no character, including the Dromio twins, is allowed to be excessively comic in itself; the comedy is a result of what happens rather than what is. The result is that the audience is put in the comforting position of being able to laugh at situation while, if they wish, continuing to realize the 'seriousness' of the underlying theme. In this sense, Ægeon, both Antipholuses and Dromios and Adriana, occupy a similar position. They all have suffered or do suffer real or imagined loss – loss of children, of parents, of husband, of identity. The play, thematically, is a series of interwoven variations on the theme of loss. Every character is in the same boat. No one is isolated, and so no one jars either our enjoyment of the plot or our speculations about what lies beneath the plot.

The simplest testimony to Shakespeare's dexterity with the plot line in the fact that, at no point, is there any reason why the audience should be confused as to who is whom or what is what. This clarity is considerably aided by Shakespeare's deployment of three devices – a rope, a gold chain and, less mechanically, by the reactions of the bewildered Dromios. There is no more certain way of establishing comic identity than by the use of cuffs and blows and the individual reactions thereto. The kind of skill which we applaud in modern thriller and farcical dramatists by which identity is either established or confused by simple devices (like J.B. Priestley's cigarette box in his *A Dangerous Corner*) is used dextrously in this play.

The comic effect of the confusion of identity is given an extra piquancy by the impression that the confusion is capable of infinite reduplication – like an image seen in a succession of mirrors. One becomes delighted both by ingenuity and the possibility of infinite comic progression. The dangers that, overdone, it will pall, and relax into mere comic device, Shakespeare avoids by controlling the extent and nature of his variations, so maintaining the comic tension and, at the same time, personalizing, to some extent, characterization which is otherwise thin and underdeveloped. It is the reaction of the characters to the fog growing about them that personalizes them. Antipholus of Ephesus, a precipitate young man, is quick to anger, in love with his wife, but quite prepared to play tit for tat for her imagined infidelity -- a Petruchio whose taming has not quite succeeded:

> 'Good Signior Angelo, you must excuse us all;
> My wife is shrewish when I keep not hours.
> Say that I linger'd with you at your shop
> To see the making of her carcanet...'   [III.1.1–4]

Antipholus of Syracuse, a quieter young man, is a little saddened by his lot, romantically inclined, responding to the situations, not outraged like his brother but as in a dream (at first the place seems like hell-mouth then like fairyland then like hell-mouth again), a Romeo with a touch of Shylock's Antonio about him:

> 'Because that I familiarly sometimes
> Do use you for my fool, and chat with you,
> Your sauciness will jest upon my love,
> And make a common of my serious hours'.   [II.2.26–9]

Adriana, a dutiful wife, is capable, naturally, of jealousy, but preserving an anxious and, at times, tearful fidelity to the end. She is the stuff of which Shakespeare's later wronged beauties will be made:

> 'I see the jewel best enamelled
> Will lose his beauty; yet the gold bides still
> That others touch and, often touching, will
> Where gold; and no man hath a name
> By falsehood and corruption doth it shame.
> Since that my beauty cannot please his eye,
> I'll weep what's left away, and weeping die.'   [II.1.109–15]

Not only, however, does Shakespeare keep a firm hold on the comic chaos, he introduces an episode which presents a point of rest for the audience's racing involvement and deepens the meaning of the tensions which are so judiciously created. This is the Luciana/ Antipholus of Syracuse confrontation in which, for a short but significant space, the potential results of mistaken identity seem more poignant, less comically resolvable. Luciana believes him to be her sister's husband and his professions of love to her thus seem particularly despicable. She pleads with him to be loving to his wife: 'Comfort my sister, cheer her, call her wife.' Antipholus's reaction is to declare his love for Luciana: 'Sing, siren for thyself, and I will dote'. Luciana desperately tries to direct his thoughts to the one she believes to be his wife – her sister. His reaction is to redouble his protestations of love for her and Luciana, stricken, despite herself, replies with a winsome pathos:

'O soft, sir, hold you still;
I'll fetch my sister to get her good will'.   [III.2.69–70]

She is caught in love and, ironically, what she believes to be illicit is, in fact, legitimate. Confusion of identity here hides an affirmative true love mistaken by one of the participants for its opposite. Luciana tells her sister of her alleged husband's protestations, in words that are ironic; for he wooed her 'with words that in an honest suit might move'.

Luciana is a sad and honourable woman, brought to the point of suffering for a love which seems false but is true. What happens to her calls our attention, as an audience, back to the underlying theme of the play. Foakes expresses it thus:

Our concern for the Antipholus twins, for Adriana and Luciana, and our sense of disorder are deepened in the context of suffering provided by the enveloping action. The comedy proves, after all, to be more than a temporary and hilarious abrogation of normality. It is, at the same time, a process in which the main characters are in some sense purged, before harmony and the responsibility of normal relationships are restored at the end.[10]

What is lost, or apparently lost, by each character, is restored, because order is restored. The result is that every character seems a more ordered person, and every relationship a firmer one.

It is well to emphasize that in the comic interaction of true and false, illusion and reality, what is and what seems, by which these characters are comically tested we are seeing the beginnings of one of the great themes of Shakespeare's plays. It would be endowing this play with far too much importance to say more than that the theme is announced, but the announcement is clear. What is equally clear is that the interactions of illusion and reality forced upon him by the story are closely associated even at this early stage in Shakespeare's development, with his preoccupation with the idea of order and disorder, whose existence as a dominant in his imagination is manifest in the history plays. What the *Comedy of Errors* implies is that love must be tested, and what *is* and what *seems* are part of that testing, and that order, represented by true love within the formalization of marriage, is the ideal and successful outcome of an honest and faithful submission to the testing:

'Why, headstrong liberty is lash'd with woe.
There's nothing situate under heaven's eye
But hath his bound, in earth, in sea, in sky.
The beasts, the fishes, and the winged fowls
Are their males' subjects, and at their controls.
Man, more divine, the master of all these,
Lord of the wide world and wild wat'ry seas,
Indu'd with intellectual sense and souls,
Of more pre-eminence than fish and fowls,
Are masters to their females, and their lords;
Then let your will attend on their accords.' [II.1.15–25]

Love's Labour's Lost

'*Love's Labour's Lost* was a battle in a private war between court factions.' This statement by Richard David neatly and clearly underlines the uniqueness of the play.[11] No other play shows so much consistent evidence of Shakespeare's involving himself so closely in one of the many vituperative literary quarrels of the day, for there are many both obvious and hidden verbal references to it, and it is certain that some of the characters are intended to satirize some of the actual participants in a now long-dead literary row. It is, in modern parlance, an 'in-play' whose full impact no modern audience will ever experience because the events to which it is attached, and the allusions which it employs, are defunct. Some scholars, commenting upon the fact that it is the only play of Shakespeare's with no known literary source, combine caution with incredulity and believe still that a source may be found.

In this play Shakespeare deploys satire using contemporary events as his material, and the nature of both suggests that the play was not intended, initially at least, for public performance. Its logical setting was private performance for afficionados, either at Court or at some noble household, possibly Southampton's.[12] Richard David suggests that the large number of boy players required in the play argues for a household which had a resident troupe of choristers. Wherever the place, the audience would have been literate, noble, and doubtless well primed to enjoy the 'in-jokes'.

Its relationship to the literary coteries of the time helps, though not precisely, to date its writing to about 1593. Contemporary satire soon stales, and the iron of the particular quarrel to which the play relates was hot in 1592–3. This creates a problem since construction and comparative maturity of execution suggest that the play might well be the last of the four early comedies, so placing it not before 1598 – too late to catch the heat of the controversy. There is some evidence to suggest a revision of the play around 1597 but the nature of this (variant speech-headings, conflicting allusions, alternative versions of the same speech) are largely technical, and do not alter the play's overall literary status.

What is certain is that the verbal style, the characterization, and the plot (what there is of it) put the play firmly in the context of the mid 1590s – courtly comedy influenced in style by the University Wits and in plot and character by Latin and Italian models; while the evidence of the growth of a characteristically individual vision of the meaning of Love links it particularly with *The Comedy of Errors* and, to some extent, with *The Two Gentlemen of Verona*.

The events are based with remarkable fidelity on certain actualities. In 1578 the Princess of France (Marguerite de Valois) was an ambassador from her mother (Catherine de Medici) to the court of the King of Navarre, when one of the issues discussed was Marguerite's dowry which involved the suzerainty of Acquitaine. Catherine herself visited the King in 1586 and on both occasions the opportunity was taken for much junketing, doubtless given an extra piquancy by the presence of the young ladies who accompanied Marguerite.

The academy of the opening scenes of the play also has an historical basis. In the 1580s the King of Navarre, perhaps fired by the example of the Medicis, somewhat self-consciously made himself a patron of the Arts but, more to the point, '... furnished the court with principal gentlemen of the Religion and reformed his house', so creating a sophisticated salon or academy in which the favoured discussed artistic matters. Shakespeare may well have heard first-hand accounts of this, but more likely got his detailed knowledge from a book – '*L'Académie Française*'[13] – translated into English in 1586, and very popular.

The actual existence of such an academy must have fallen like manna into Shakespeare's imagination, hungry at this time for sustenance to strengthen his comments upon a domestic literary quarrel. It is a marriage between factual material and his satirical usage of it that gives *Love's Labour's Lost* its peculiar style and tone.

The Elizabethan literary world was a ferment of talent, genius, envy, love, jealousy and hatred. Its intellectual and emotional temper was increased by the very smallness of that literary world. Shakespeare seems, on the evidence we have, not to have been so bitterly involved in its darker pursuits as many of his contemporaries – Marlowe, Greene, Nashe and Ben Jonson. The impression is that he was generally admired, though the very sharpness of Greene's attack makes it clear that he was not immune from the attentions of the envious. The quarrels and arguments, conducted in speech and written word, were many and varied in subject and style, and any attempt to sort out issues and personalities is complicated by the fact that participants often changed sides.

A detailed account of the bewildering circumstances of the contextual events of *Love's Labour's Lost* appears in Richard David's introduction to the New Arden Edition. What is apposite to an appreciation of the play's dramatic and theatrical realisation may be summarized as follows:

1 There was a prolonged quarrel between Gabriel Harvey, Cambridge scholar, friend of Edmund Spenser and Thomas Nashe, also a Cambridge man, dramatist and phamphleteer, friend of Greene and Lyly.

2 The quarrel followed upon the publication of the famous Martin Marprelate tracts,[14] Puritan pamphlets attacking the episcopal organization of the established Church. Whitgift, the Archbishop of Canterbury, attempted by guile and physical force to suppress them and to discover their authors, and after vainly attempting to answer them, and failing to match their intellectual energy and vituperative brilliance, the Bishops employed professional writers for the task.

3 One of these was Thomas Nashe, whose most effective answer, in play form, was his *An Almond for a Parrat* (1590).

4 The arguments, now involving both lay artists and clergy, became more personal, spreading in subject and theme beyond their original context.

5 Having published a contribution to the Marprelate affair which said, in effect, 'a pox on both your houses', Harvey, in two pamphlets – *Plaine Percevall* and *The Lambe of God* – included an attack on Greene and Nashe.

6 To this, in 1592, Nashe in his *Perce Pennilesse, his Supplication to the Divell*, furiously replied.

7 In the following two years the two men engaged in attack and counter-attack, reconciliations being attempted and refused.

By 1594 the original grounds of controversy – which were religious – had changed, and the quarrel between Nashe and Harvey, largely personal, showed tensions and disagreements which involved basic literary attitudes. Peter Alexander writes:

'Gabriel Harvey, the Cambridge scholar, stood for Learning, and also, Nashe declared, for pedantry and conceit: Nashe, the Cambridge graduate and satirist, regarded himself as the man of worldly experience as opposed to the mere plodder in books. The opposing parties fought under names that now require some translating: those who stood for scholarship were known as the Artists; those who preferred experience as their teacher called themselves Villainists, Nashe the protagonist of the Villainists professing to regard the debtors' prison, which he had known, as a more instructive centre for an author than a college. Worldly experience was, of course, incomplete without love'.[15]

The connection between Shakespeare's plays and this bizarre contretemps of Artists versus Villains can be seen in specific verbal allusions and in terms of character. In Nashe's pamphlet, in which he first replied to Harvey, there is constant playing on the words 'purse' and 'penny'; in the famous verbal gymnastics between Armado and Moth in Act I of *Love's Labour's Lost* the latter is referred to as 'tender juvenal' generally regarded as being a nickname for Nashe. Moth is almost undoubtedly, in his quipping mockery of the learned, intended to be Nashe. Harvey is less easy to identify, for his style – affected and allusive – is to be found mocked in both Holofernes and Armado. Even though positive identifications may be difficult, however, the play itself demonstrates the ridiculousness both of self-conscious learning and nimble, often empty, sniping at it from opposition. Although the play does not seem to take sides on any particular issue, it can be regarded as a general rebuke, first, of dissension, which is profitless, in that it does not lead to any sense of order or unity, and second, of attitudes to life which confuse fact with truth, learning with wisdom, dalliance for true love and theory with experience. To suggest that Shakespeare, not being a man of formal learning himself, was making a case for the truth of experience as superior to the sophisticated posturing of learning, is too narrow a view of the play. In any case, even at this early stage in his career, Shakespeare's tendency is towards reconciliation of opposed forces, not the taking up of sides, and this reconciliatory grasp can be clearly seen at the end of the play by modern audiences who may miss much of the topical background which is its context. However, it is not easy to take Moth, Armado and Holofernes, for example, at their face value by deliberately forgetting their possible reference to actual people, for if we forget the ghosts that lie behind them we are left with fantastic characters, and a modern audience will accept such characters, such artifice, only if two conditions are satisfied – first that they are interesting in themselves, and second, that they are involved in an ingenious plot. On neither score do these characters satisfy, though this is not to deny that a nimble-pated actor can use them for creating a sort of comic pantomimic display of technique. Their remoteness is considerably increased by the simple fact that they are the chief wanderers in a verbal maze whose entrances and exits are covered up in thickets of Elizabethan allusion.

ARM: (to Hol.) 'Monsieur, are you not lett'red?
MOTH: Yes, yes; he teaches boys the hornbook. What is a, b, spelt
   backward with the horn on his head?
HOL: Ba, pueritia, with a horn added.
MOTH: Ba! most silly sheep with a horn. You hear his learning.
HOL: Quis, quis, thou consonant?   [V.1.39–46]

To a modern audience then, the plot line lacks theatrical surprise or
interest; the characterization, with the exception of Berowne and, to
some extent, of the princess, is lank – the cynic might call it an
ineffectual clash of Debs and Blades.

The only mood in which the modern audience can approach this play
with hope of delight is one of relaxation, in which one is prepared to
spend time with a frivolity which provides the kind of intellectual teasing we associate with the crossword puzzle. Muriel Bradbrook writes –
'nowhere else does Shakespeare display so consistent a linguistic interest
as here. The varieties of speech set off each other, and are more sharply
differentiated than elsewhere: style is a garment indeed, and each
character dresses in his own fashion'.[16] This is true – in this play verbal
hue has taken the place of psychological truth.

The King of Navarre is known to us as formal and courtly, being
every inch the glass of fashion and the mould of form, and thus is
entirely figured in his language which always seems on the point of
moving into sonnet – neatly balanced in argument, musical and
flourishingly conclusive. Yet, in everything he says, which is to say,
everything he is, he always mistakes the elegance of form for the truth
of content:

'Therefore, brave conquerors – for so you are,
That war against your own affections
And the huge army of the world's desires
Our late edict shall strongly stand in force.'   [I.1.8–11]

His courtiers, with the exception of Berowne, are mirrors of their
leader. They, like him, are trapped within a golden cage of language,
protected by its symmetry from any real engagements with the facts
of life.

The language of the lovers when they appear together is that of
love's self-conscious combating – defensively bright, ostentatiously
fashionable in the courtly manner, delicately allusive, making points
not wounds in its childlike playfulness:

KING: 'All hail, sweet madam, and fair time of day!
PRIN: 'Fair' in 'all hail' is foul, as I conceive.

KING: Construe my speeches better, if you may.
PRIN: Then wish me better; I will give you leave.'   [V.2.339–43]

Holofernes is a victim of language because he is a victim of his own conceit to be a man of the moment and consort with learned and fashionable people – like Armado. He cannot go directly to a point for that is too ordinary; he skirts around meaning, fearful of seeming put down by mere clarity:

'The posterior of the day, most generous sir, is liable, congruent, and measurable, for the afternoon'.   [V.1.78–9]

Armado created, like the rest, out of his own speech, is almost all wind. He is high-minded about words, but neither his mind nor his tongue can quite match the grandeur of his pretensions. His rhetoric has the effectiveness of air that slowly escapes from a pricked balloon. He is a Malvolio whose ambitions have not yet been touched with rancour:

Sir, the King is a noble gentleman, and my familiar, I do assure ye, very good friend. For what is inward between us, let it pass . . . for I must tell thee it will please his Grace, by the world, sometime to lean upon my poor shoulder, and with his royal finger thus dally with my excrement, with my mustachio: but, sweet heart, let that pass.
     [V.1.82–94]

Moth flies towards words with an unerring skill, but is too quick to allow them to burn him. His pert language, matching obscure allusion with downright comment, isolates him and makes him a solo performer in the complex dance of words:

ARM: Is there not a ballad, boy, of the King and the Beggar?
MOTH: The world was very guilty of a ballad some three ages since; but I think now 'tis not to be found; or if it were, it would neither serve for the writing nor the tune.
ARM: I will have that subject newly writ o'er, that I may example my digression by some mighty precedent. Boy, I do love that country girl that I took in the park with the rational hind Costard; she deserves well.
MOTH: (aside) To be whipt; and yet a better love than my master.
ARM: Sing, boy; my spirit grows heavy in love.
MOTH: And that's great marvel, loving a light wench.   [I.2.105–18]

Berowne's character, however, seems more robustly constructed because, as Muriel Bradbrook comments,[17] he speaks 'with more than one voice', he is 'both guilty of courtly artifice and critical of it'.

He, like his colleagues, plays at dalliance with language but he gives evidence of realizing at times some substance behind the shadows. Like Mercutio he has reached that mid-point of development where the delights of verbal play and the realities of meaning are beginning to have equal validity in his mind, where, in fact, verbal play is used to reveal the realities not ornament them. He is as capable of dalliance as the rest, but never lets it dominate him:

> 'Now, for not looking on a woman's face,
> You have in that forsworn the use of eyes,
> And study too, the causer of your vow;
> For where is any author in the world
> Teaches such beauty as a woman's eye?
> Learning is but an adjunct to ourself,
> And where we are our learning likewise is;'   [IV.3.305–11]

Thus each plays his part in a larger pattern of extraordinary device and virtuosity, and in the final analysis they demonstrate the paradox that it takes fine language to mock fine language. Shakespeare can play verbal games with far greater power and deeper interest than those literary ghosts who lie behind this play's action, and in the long run he demonstrates in this play the delicious ineffectiveness of verbal contention. The last scene, however, clearly implies that a deeper intent lay elsewhere – fed and conditioned by the particular cast of his own imagination.

An extraordinary change of pace and mood occurs with the appearance of the messenger – Mercade. The play, up to this point, has been almost entirely playful. The lovers, particularly the men, have had their fun, the ladies have enjoyed themselves with judicious coquetry. Only Berowne, in his satirical mocking words about the impossibility of the academy, has hitherto given some hint of the ridiculousness of the gaming. Now it is he (and as late as Act IV.3) who announces the possibility that the play's theme will, quite unexpectedly take a different course:

> 'For wisdom's sake, a word that all men love;
> Or for Love's sake, a word that loves all men;
> Or for men's sake, the authors of these women;
> Or women's sake, by whom we men are men –
> Let us once lose our oaths to find ourselves,
> Or else we lose ourselves to keep our oaths.
> It is religion to be thus forsworn;
> For charity itself fulfils the law,
> And who can sever love from charity?'   [IV.3.353–61]

Even now, the king and his lords, shifting their ground with mindless ease mistake his words for a declaration of just another move in the great game. 'Saint Cupid, then! and, soldiers, to the field'.

Berowne is, intellectually, the audience's key to the play's change of mood, and it is not necessary to agree explicitly with the critic, Walter Pater, that there is something of self-portraiture in Shakespeare's handling of him, to feel that there is nevertheless some truth in Pater's conclusion:

> In this character, which is never quite in touch, never quite on a
> perfect level of understanding, with the other persons of the play,
> we see, perhaps, a reflex of Shakespeare himself, when he has just
> been able to stand aside from and estimate the first period of his
> poetry.[18]

There is a connection between the way this character is presented and the mood-shift of the play. Berowne, having made his gamesome points and shown that he is as capable as the next of tripping a light fantastic, becomes aware of the necessity not to compromise the realities inside his own imagination. In him, this awareness – intermittent but sharp, is summed up in his words after the entry of Mercade:

> 'Honest plain words best pierce the ear of grief'.   [V.2.741]

which is as much as to say, there is a time to stop the nonsense. Shakespeare's own awareness of this dominates the last scene where Mercade brings a notice of death – the catalyst that dissolves illusions. Shakespeare has already shown through Navarre and his lords that love cannot be pushed aside – even flippantly. Now he proceeds to show that an acceptance of love must involve more than striking one colour and hoisting another, and it is Berowne who sees clearest. He comments on 'What in us hath seemed ridiculous' asking for love's grace by which the former dalliance may be purified, for all have to earn that grace, and prove that present oaths are not empty like past ones.

This is the only comedy of Shakespeare's which ends with lovers on probation, as it were. Games must be paid for by penances which will prove fidelity – but we do not see the result. What we witness at the end is a cooling of morning sunlight – the academy, the muscovites, the nine worthies – all shadows – are dissolved, replaced by a natural imagery:

'This side is Hiems, Winter, this Ver, the Spring; the one maintained
by the owl, the other by the cuckoo.'   [V.2.878–80]

The lesson is that men and women must have a care – life, like the
natural world, has its seasons, and none lasts for ever.

The Taming of the Shrew

This play is involved in one of those teasing puzzles whose solution at present is impossible but whose existence throws a diffused light on the complicated world of Elizabethan theatre. In 1594 there was published a play entitled *The Taming of A Shrew*,[19] an untidy but recognizably obvious twin of the play printed in the 1623 Folio of Shakespeare's plays as *The Taming of The Shrew*. Suggestions as to the relationship between the two are as follows:

1 *A Shrew* is a clumsy pirating by someone else of Shakespeare's *The Shrew*, for although the only published version extant is that of the 1623 Folio, the play was obviously written early in Shakespeare's career.

or 2 Both plays, one by an unknown hand, the other by Shakespeare, are separate versions of an earlier, now lost, source play.

or 3 Shakespeare took over *A Shrew* from another dramatist, refurbished it and produced *The Shrew*.

Within this framework, speculation and subtle exegesis is rife.

There is only one instance in which it may be said that *A Shrew* is superior to *The Shrew* – it includes, at the end, the return of Sly, the tinker, waking from his dream, which is omitted from *The Shrew*. This return is dramatically logical and his disappearance in *The Shrew* warps the design of the play. Some critics believe that Sly's absence from the text of *The Shrew* in the Folio is, as Alexander suggests,[20] 'due to carelessness or some error in the handling of the copy' and it is, even allowing for Shakespeare's relative immaturity when he wrote the play, difficult not to accept this scholarly opinion for the absence of Sly is an elementary fault. Those modern productions which have transplanted him from the end of *A Shrew* have conclusively demonstrated the logic of his return and, by implication, underlined the theory that Shakespeare in all probability had a hand in *A Shrew*, and that there may well have been carelessness in the handling of the folio copy by the printer.

The Bianca sub-plot is taken, either directly from Ariosto's comedy *I Suppositi*, or from the English version by George Gascoigne – *The Supposes*. Shakespeare grafts on to this the Petruchio/Katharina plot and, in so doing, turns what was in the original source a main plot into a sub-plot. In reading, the transpositions from one plot to another leave much to be desired, but, on the stage, the play has a strong unity which comes more from its spirit than from its construction. To the reader the whole affair seems footling, slightly irritating, with little motivation to Kate's behaviour, and little realism in Petruchio's reactions. The parade of servants and suitors is tedious and the play's morality seems equivocal – Petruchio seems merely a fortune hunter, hell-bent for a dowry, Kate's capitulation seems false and time-serving.

On stage, however, all these seeming flaws resolve into a delightful, romping series of escapades, and good players can, with some justification from the text, mitigate the uneasy speculations about Kate's and Petruchio's notions and antics. The reasons for its success and popularity are varied. In the first place the stories are basically simple and well-defined, and gain piquancy from being stories within a story. The play does not tax the intelligence, but it teases the imagination. More than this, however, the content is quite simply an archetype – the war between man and woman, a theme, a staple of music hall and cartoon, which is one of mankind's most comic-serious exercises in flippant narcissism. And when the basic ingredient of sex warfare is mixed with a particular brand of romanticism, the result, for audiences, is irresistible. In *The Taming of The Shrew* the romantic element is Petruchio. He is, we may think, every woman's dream of a kind of ideal lover – coming to take her by storm, to club her to his cave, and then to become gentle, and, possibly, her slave. He is the secret man they hope inhabits all men – particularly their husbands. To a lesser extent Kate represents the kind of challenge that many men imagine they wish to be confronted with in love – involving beauty, passion, resistance and eventual surrender. Love caps all in the end. Perhaps, too, Katharine administers to every woman's innate desire to be won, to seem (but only to seem) to lose the final battle, and yet to emerge, finally, as equal.

The attraction of the play is thus concentrated on this archetypal status of the two main characters, but it maintains its popularity for two other reasons – first, because of the bitter-sweet status of Sly in the action; there is a wry sadness in watching him tussle with illusion, but a comic joy in witnessing his robust vulgarity. Second, the main comic figures – Gremio, Grumio, and Baptista – are rich in theatrical possibility. To some extent they are near to the Jonsonian 'humour' characters, but their comic potency is of that kind which is attractive without being offensive because it is general rather than particular. It is from their reaction to each other rather than from their individual characteristics that comedy emerges – mocking, half-satirical, half-farcical – rather in the manner of the Keystone Cops of the silent films.

It has, however, been persuasively argued that it is wrong to regard the play as a mere comic or farcical piece, that in George Hibbard's words 'it is about marriage, and about marriage in Elizabethan England'.[21] He claims that the play is designed to show and contrast two opposed Elizabethan attitudes to marriage – the idea of marriage as a purely business arrangement, and as a true union of hearts and minds. He concludes:

> It portrays the marriage situation, not as it appeared in the romances of the day, but as it was in Shakespeare's England. And the criticism it brings to bear on it is constructive as well as destructive. Baptista, the foolish father who knows nothing about his daughters yet seeks to order their lives, is defeated all along the line. So is Gremio, the old pantaloon, who thinks he can buy a wife. The play's disapproval of the arranged match, in which no account is taken of the feelings of the principals, could not be plainer.[22]

These well-documented claims should not be lost sight of, yet at the same time it is quite clear that the comedy of the play is more theatrically durable than the contemporary particularities which are embedded in it.

This comedy is in the hands of the barely individualized characters – types whom we laugh at not because we do not know what they will do next but because we know only too well. As a group they have strong connections with Commedia d'ell Arte. The nuisance father, the raddled old lover (Gremio the Pantaloon), the romantic young lover and his tricksy servant. Perhaps the most affecting is Gremio. His comedy induces sympathy even while we laugh at him, a mixed reaction conditioned by a balance of qualities inside the character. We laugh because his age makes his romantic pretensions ridiculous, but sympathize because he knows the perils of age – 'and may not young men die as well as old?' We laugh because he is so reckless in his attempts to find a wife, but sympathize because he knows and accepts that his chances are meagre:

> 'Nay, I have off'red all; I have no more;
> And she can have no more than all I have!'   [II.1.373–4]

We laugh because of the contrast between his dying embers and the fiery desire of Lucentio, but sympathize because there are no ashes in his shrewd mind:

71

'Sirrah young gamester, your father were a fool
To give thee all, and in his waning age
Set foot under thy table. Tut, a toy!
An old Italian fox is not so kind, my boy'   [II.1.392–5]

- words that Lear might have heeded in another time and place.
Gremio's self-knowledge raises him out of absurdity into comic
realism. Not so Baptista. He is all farce – he knows, sees and really
hears nothing. He flounders through the action with, he thinks, the
reins of power in his hands but it is an ass that he rides – himself.

Lucentio is, in a comic sense, to Petruchio what Hotspur later,
and in a deeper sense, is to Hal. The former is romantic, blind to
anything but the immediate object, governed by passion, shallow in
intelligence; the latter – apparently wayward, governed by hidden
will, by shrewd intelligence – gradually finding a direct path to the
objective from which nothing will cause him to swerve. Hotspur,
however, has no equivalent to Lucentio's servant – Tranio – the
brains of the outfit, and it is largely through watching his nimble
dexterity that we are able to suffer the incipient boredom of watching
the self-indulgent Bianca being wooed by the thickly romantic
Lucentio.

These characters create one world in the play, which Shakespeare
skilfully contrasts with another, a world which is mercantile to the
end; bargaining is its element, and, even at the conclusion of its
biggest transaction (the marriage of Bianca), the gambling element
remains in the final wager. We see it in action in Act II when Gremio,
Baptista and Tranio argue about who has most to give as a dowry.
Even the slightly more romantic Hortensio expresses his feelings for
Bianca in material terms. She is, to him, a 'treasure', 'a jewel' and he
consoles his disappointment with a rich widow. Because of the comic
spirit which hangs about this world, it seems less sour and mean than
limited in intelligence and emotional responses. For this reason
Bianca herself, the prize in the lottery, is less attractive than her fiery
sister, for Bianca belongs to this world of commodity and in all
probability her whole future married life will be based on the stocks
and shares of wedlock, not on the realities of true love.

Significantly, Kate does not seem a part of all this. It is not just
that she is set apart because of her temper, but because of her implied
attitude to this materialistic world – in itself a cause of her impatience.
Even in her wilder moments she has a more refined conception of
love. When she physically attacks and berates Bianca, it is not mere
shrewishness, but a desire for truth that emerges:

'Of all thy suitors here I charge thee tell
Whom thou lov'st best. See thou dissemble not.'   [II.1.8–9]

When she gets an equivocal answer, she says:

'O then, belike, you fancy riches more.'   [II.1.16]

She is set apart from this profit and loss world, not just because she is less marketable than Bianca but because she rejects it, by losing her temper with its ways. She is, as it were, in a limbo – not having found a world with values which will enable it to love her for what she is.

At first, the auguries are bad. Petruchio seems even more mercantile than the rest – 'Why, nothing comes amiss so money come withal'. He is bland about his intentions:

'I come to wive it wealthily in Padua;
If wealthily, then happily in Padua'.   [I.2.73–4]

Indeed Shakespeare so emphasizes this aspect of Petruchio (he is even more efficient at bargaining than the rest) that one's suspicions are aroused that a deep purpose lies behind. Its nature is not long delayed. As soon as he meets Kate his references to the mercantile aspects of marriage have a different tone. When he speaks now of 'bargain' it is to a secret one between her and him – alone. When he arrives, tattered, at the wedding, he shouts – 'to me she's married not unto my clothes'. Most significantly, before he bears her away he returns to commodity, but the tone is mocking and dismissive:

'She is my goods, my chattels, she is my house,
My household stuff, my field, my barn,
My horse, my ox, my ass, my any thing,
And here she stands; touch her whoever dare;'   [III.2.226–9]

but he adds – 'fear not, sweet wench, they shall not touch thee, Kate.' Love makes him mock what is merely material. In his determination to win Kate the means he uses amount to a denial of the values of commodity. He deprives her and himself in order to win her from any lingering affiliations with the trappings of the other world. When they are stripped away, nothing is left – save love:

'And where two raging fires meet together,
They do consume the thing that feeds their fury.'   [II.1.131–2]

Kate resists, partly because she believes she has been traded to this man – and at a knock-down price. She is shrewish for this reason, certainly, but also because she cannot believe that this one is any different from others. Her experience on her wedding night begins to convince her that he is, and she too begins to change, as they both begin to move into their own mutually acceptable world. Shakespeare emphasizes the difference between their world and the one they have left, through the great comic scene which precedes their arrival at Petruchio's house. Petruchio has his plans laid, but it is a desperate lot he casts. Derek Traversi puts it thus:

> Petruchio's entire attitude . . . reflects a commonsense which is the
> necessary counterpart of idealism, saving it from the dangers of
> empty posturing and self-gratifying excess. Repeating a device
> already used in *The Comedy of Errors*, the lesson is driven home by
> the attitude of his servant, Grumio, in whom, at his better moments,
> a similar sense of reality prevails.[23]

and we are given the account of the journey home – no romantic idyll but a slogging match in the mud. Grumio ends his account, in its way as trenchant as the account of Gadshill, with the words:

> '. . . winter tames man, woman, and beast; for it hath tam'd my
> old master, and my new mistress, and myself, fellow Curtis.'
> [IV.1.19–22]

The scene with the tailor equally fulfils a double role. It is fine, broad, visual comedy but it suggests more – it represents the final committal of both of them, after a hard fight, to naked love as opposed to mere partnership:

> 'For 'tis the mind that makes the body rich;'   [IV.3.168]

The scene [IV.2] of their return journey is as important in emphasizing the change that has occurred in Kate as the wedding scene is in what it tells us about Petruchio. She has, by now, been 'tamed', and the 'taming' involves a recognition that the reality of love is more important than outward word or show. In their new-found but still cautious delight in one another they play a game which is a smiling impersonation of the old confusion they had both made between illusion and reality. They can now afford, in delighted consort, to make it a game, because neither is any longer alone – they have found their world. On its comic level this scene is one of the most affirmative of love's truth in the whole of the early plays.

Yet one thing remains to do – they have to conquer the world of commodity which they left. They return to prove to us, and to Padua, the truth of their metamorphosis, achieving that proof in the terms of that mercantile world – by a wager, so making its validity all the more relevant for having made use of the rules of that world. Kate's last speech puts the case for the natural correctness of woman's submitting to man. This would have been understood and applauded by the Elizabethans. Yet if any other wife in the play had made this speech it would have been a mere formality. We know, Kate knows, Petruchio knows, and Shakespeare knows that, behind the formal words, there is a deeper meaning. Kate and her husband have won each other by love, and within its total truth such things as honour, obey, and submit, are not bits and snaffles but wings. It is a celebration of the mystery of love's wealth – where 'property was thus appalled' and 'Either was the other's mine'.[24]

NOTES

1 Publius Terentius Afer (Terence), c.190–159 B.C. A slave, educated and emancipated by his master, who wrote six plays.

2 Titus Maccius Plautus, c.254–184 B.C. Soldier, merchant and playwright – author of *Menaechmi* and *Amphitruo*.

3 The group included Christopher Marlowe, Robert Greene, George Peele, Thomas Nashe, Thomas Lodge and John Lyly.

4 Ludovico Ariosto, 1444–1533. Poet and playwright. *I Suppositi* was the most famous of his prose comedies, *Orlando Furioso* his influential epic poem.

5 Thomas Nashe's preface to Greene's *Menaphon* (1589).

6 Meres, op. cit.

7 Commedia dell'Arte – the popular Italian drama of the sixteenth and seventeenth centuries, with stock characters and improvised dialogue.

8 *Gesta Grayorum*, the records of Gray's Inn, printed 1688.

9 R. A. Foakes, *Introduction* to New Arden edition of *The Comedy of Errors* (1962).

10 Ibid.

11 R. David, *Introduction* to Arden edition of *Love's Labour's Lost* (1951).

12 Henry Wriothesley, 3rd Earl of Southampton (1573–1624) – to whom Shakespeare dedicated his poems *Venus and Adonis* and *The Rape of Lucrece*.

13 Shakespeare may have learned about such academies from this popular account by Pierre de la Primaudaye.

14 Martin Marprelate was a pseudonym used by the writers of the Marprelate pamphlets, Puritan tracts attacking the Episcopal structure of the Church of England. 1588–9.

15 Peter Alexander, *Introductions to Shakespeare* (1964), p. 65.
16 Muriel Bradbrook, op. cit., p. 213.
17 Ibid., p. 215.
18 Walter Pater, *Appreciations* (1889).
19 For a discussion of the relationship between the two, see Hardin Craig, 'The Shrew and A Shrew', in *Elizabethan Studies in Honour of George Reynolds* (1945).
20 Peter Alexander, op. cit.
21 George Hibbard, 'The Taming of the Shrew, a Social Comedy', in *Shakespeare's Essays*, eds. Thaler and Sanders (1964).
22 Ibid.
23 Derek Traversi, 'Shakespeare, The Early Comedies', in *Writers and their Work*, no. 129 (1960).
24 Shakespeare, *The Phoenix and the Turtle*.

3 The Years of Consolidation

The effects of environment on a writer are not always obvious but they are crucial. The Warwickshire countryside, the small-town activities of Stratford, the friendships of youth and its hates and loves, all found their way into the imagination, thence into the plays and poems, of Shakespeare. Sometimes their presence is plain, at others, it is fugitive – a kind of gentle pressure rather than a sharp reality.

But, in whatever form, the influence of another environment – that of London and the world of theatre – was no less strong. The evidence is myriad – in the plays, in the reading he indulged in, in the different human types he was enabled to meet, in the sophistications of politics, law, public and private morality that he encountered. These early days of his life in London led to a large expansion of both his imaginative and actual experience.

By 1595, when he was thirty-one, Shakespeare was almost certainly a 'sharer' (shareholder) in the famous Lord Chamberlain's Company of players and found himself in the company of both a great comedian – Will Kempe – and a great tragedian – Richard Burbage.[1] This, in itself, would have been sufficient spur to his imagination, and he obviously made full use of the presence of these two men and others in his creation of a variety of leading male heroic and tragic roles, and comic parts, to be found in his plays. Indeed he found more and more that what his imagination conceived was capable of realization in practice by a talented group of players who gave spirit and body to an amazing collection of characters – Henry V, Hotspur, Henry IV, Falstaff, Richard II, Romeo, Mercutio, Juliet, Bottom, Oberon, Titania, Gobbo and Shylock.

London itself – even then an exciting metropolis – fed his imagination and memory. Seeing the citizens of Windsor, perhaps witnessing the Garter ceremony, mixed with memories of Sir Thomas Lucy's Charlecote Park, near Stratford, helping to bring about *The Merry Wives of Windsor*; rugged, perhaps fond, recollections of the Whitsuntide festivities in Stratford hobnobbing with the smooth affluence of royal and noble behaviour, gave a comic wryness to *A Midsummer Night's Dream*;[2] noisy pub nights, possibly in dangerous Southwark, gave raucous life to Henry IV's Boar's Head Tavern, to Doll Tearsheet and Mistress Quickly, while images from the Cotswolds rose up with kind comedy and sharp pathos; a recent

London scandal – the alleged attempt on the Queen's life by a Jewish doctor[3] – which Marlowe had earlier fictionalized, stirred his pen to write *The Merchant of Venice* – and indeed many other examples could be instanced. Certainly it was only an astonishing capacity to listen, select and recreate that enabled him to run the gamut of verbal communication from the vernacular prose of *The Merry Wives of Windsor* to the heart-piercing poetry of *Romeo and Juliet*. In so many ways Shakespeare was not only laying strong foundations, but beginning to show, with some authority, the potential power of his architecture.

The years from the early 1590s to the opening of the Globe Theatre in 1599, where the Lord Chamberlain's Men acted, were very much years of consolidation – both of his status in the uncertain world of his profession and of his own creative talents. His membership of one of the leading acting companies of the day gave him not only the chance to rub shoulders with his peers, to benefit financially, socially and professionally, but also the opportunity to flex his creative muscles. This was precisely, and, seemingly restlessly, what he did, for this period is characterized by what would be expected from a young writer anxious to ensure his future in the theatre – constant variety, a trying-out of abilities in as many directions as possible. In *A Midsummer Night's Dream* he essayed fantasy, farce and romance; in *The Merry Wives of Windsor*, perhaps by commission, he made his one and only attempt at writing middle-class citizen farce; in *Henry V* he outdid other historical/chronicle writers with his passion, patriotism and the sweep of his dramatic narrative; in *Romeo and Juliet* he achieved one of the greatest romantic tragedies of young love; and in *The Merchant of Venice*, in the character of Shylock, he revealed a subtlety he could now bring to the presentation of complex personalities.

It is, however, in the two parts of *Henry IV* that he most surely justifies the assumption that these were the years of consolidation. Here, he shows, for the first time, how naive it is to think of his imagination as divided neatly into separate areas of activity – tragic, comic, historical, with sub-compartments like romantic, farcical, melodramatic. The two *Henry IV* plays are a huge distillation of an imaginative unity and coherence in which these disparate elements are held in the solution of his vision of existence.

In these years, then, Shakespeare learned of the multi-dimensioned, multi-faceted reality of life and how to communicate it in his plays with increasing assurance and authority.

Richard II

Two of Shakespeare's plays written in close proximity to one another share a strange status in the canon of plays devoted to the unfolding of the story of Kings, nobles and commen men with which the playwright was concerned for the greater part of his working life. Neither *Richard II* nor *King John* sits very easily in the complicated pattern which binds the other histories together. *Richard II* particularly seems cast in different dramatic mould. Although it directly and starkly shows the actions of conspiracy, the cares of kingship and the mêlée of faction which generate the main themes of all the histories, it is not for these that we remember or admire the play. It is a sad and lonely play largely because its king is a sad and lonely figure.

However, it must be noted that in the case of *Richard II* there is a very large and demonstrable gap between its original and its present impact. The play was written soon after the beginning of 1596. On 7 February 1601 it was revived and performed by the Lord Chamberlain's Men on the afternoon before Essex's abortive rebellion. The circumstances of the play would have immediately found a strong echo in the contemporary scene. On 10 February Augustine Phillips, one of the Lord Chamberlain's Men, was questioned under oath about the play's performance, and the record affirms the connection between the play and contemporary events:

> '. . . Sr Charles Percy Sr Josclyne Percy and the L. Montegle with some thre more spak to some of the players . . . to have the play of the deposyng and kyllyng of Kyng Richard the second to be played on Saterday next promysyng to get them xls. more than their ordynary to play yt.' The players 'were determyned to have played some other play, holding that play of Kyng Richard to be so old & so long out of use as that they shold have small or no Company at yt.' But at their request they 'were content to play yt the Saterday and had their xls. more than their ordynary for yt and so played yt accordyngly.'[4]

There is also strong evidence that, even before this time, the play had been regarded as a dangerous comment on political matters, for the deposition scene was omitted from the first published quarto of 1597. Its inclusion would have been likely to arouse the Queen's anger. Throughout her reign she was conscious of an ever-present threat of deposition and, as she grew older, her lack of an heir only served to increase her sensitivity to plots and stratagems. She does not, however, seem to have blamed the actors or the playwright for the use made of the play as a piece of political propaganda. Yet all this is whirled away in the winds of time and although the political elements in it are strong they do not, in themselves, excite us today. It is more their effect upon this isolated king that affects the modern audience.

Two sides of Richard are presented and a measure of Shakespeare's skill is the way in which he makes them compatible although they differ considerably in essentials. Richard is off-stage for eight lines in Act II.i, for the whole of Act II.11.ii, iii, and also iv, and Act III.i. In the earlier scene Shakespeare seems to have deliberately sought to show Richard in the worst possible light. He is incapable of listening to other's arguments; he seems unaware of the potential danger to his throne in his banishment of Bolingbroke; he is indecisive and rash in his action; he is totally reckless in agreeing to the levying of taxes which not only will be resented but are to be collected by an unpopular favourite of his own. All these faults may be judged as indicative of a weak kingship and Shakespeare is relentless in keeping them before our attention. Yet this weakness, mixed with haughty arrogance, is not the whole of the picture. Further flaws are revealed and these point less to kingly insufficiency than to personal viciousness. Richard's behaviour to the dying Gaunt is insensitive, then arrogant, then cruel. He stabs Gaunt with short wounding phrases:

'Can sick men play so nicely with their names?'	[II.1.84]
'Should dying men flatter with those that live?'	[II.1.88]
'I am in health, I breathe, and see thee ill.'	[II.1.92]

His cutting reply to York which catalogues the wrongs Richard has committed – Gloucester's death, Bolingbroke's banishment – is simply:

'Why, uncle, what's the matter?'

His final act, the seizure of Gaunt's lands and goods, completes the dark portrait Shakespeare gives of him in the first part of the play. During the interim, when he is not on stage, his kingdom begins to fall to pieces – rebellion is rife, disaffection appears in every corner. It seems it must be beyond the bounds of credence for us to be stirred to any sympathy for the despicable king who has been presented to us. Yet it is within this interim that our attitude is worked upon and prepared for a change. Ironically it is York (the man most aware of the mistakes that Richard has made) who leads us to a point where the revaluation of our attitude towards this king is made possible. York, throughout the play, is a representative of the status quo, he is a man whose principles are founded on the acceptance of the rule of law and order. He says to Bolingbroke:

'Thou art a banish'd man, and here art come,
Before the expiration of thy time,
In braving arms against thy sovereign.'   [II.3.110–12]

The implications are clear – rebellion is a sin and, in rebelling, even against such a king, Bolingbroke cannot be excused.

When we next see Richard, another dimension has therefore been added to the background of his character. Personally condemnable as he is, Shakespeare has not put him inalienably in a position of moral right. He *is* annointed king. Our awareness of this creates a tension between our knowledge of him as person and as victim of an illegal rebellion. We may never forget the Richard we saw at the lists or at the deathbed of Gaunt, but our condemnation of him now has conditions to it. Shakespeare does not pause to ease us into this new dimension – its implications are apparent in both the meaning and the manner of Richard's words at Berkeley:

'Dear earth, I do salute thee with my hand,
Though rebels wound thee with their horses' hoofs.
As a long parted mother with her child
Plays fondly with her tears and smiles in meeting,
So, weeping – smiling greet I thee, my earth,
And so thee favours with my royal hands.'   [III.2.6–11]

Here, for the first time, Richard the poet speaks. From this point onwards he has to be judged on the exquisite composition of his words. We may remember the insufficient man but we are forced now to witness one who celebrates through words the realities of his kingship. Richard, through adversity, has moved from petulant man into beleagured king. He has become aware of the awesome fact of kingship and though, when he speaks, he still involves his personal feelings in his words, it is largely the articulate symbol of majesty that we hear. He is both the poem and the poet.

His thoughts and feelings are almost entirely inward-looking; practically his whole preoccupation is with himself as the theme of his poetic speculations upon kingship. As the play advances, these speculations move from the general to the particular. When he first

realizes the extent of the rebellion it is the sanctity of kingship that
concerns him:

> 'Not all the water in the rough rude sea
> Can wash the balm off from an annointed king;
>
> . . . . .
>
> The deputy elected by the Lord.' [III.2.54–7]

The subsequent success of the rebellion causes him more and more to
identify his own person with the attributes of kingship. The process
begins when he is told of the deaths of Bushy, Bagot and Green. He
indulges in a superb paean of grief about the cares of kingship and the
vulnerability of that condition, in the speech which begins:

> 'No matter where – of comfort no man speak.
> Let's talk of graves, of worms, and epitaphs;' [III.2.144–5]

Here the word 'king' and the personal 'I' become one in the form of a
begging question:

> 'I live with bread like you, feel want,
> Taste grief, need friends; subjected thus,
> How can you say to me I am a king?' [III.2.175–7]

This process of identification is rich in implications within Richard's
mind. In his new-found consciousness of himself he not only begins
to make 'king' and 'I' one flesh, but adds Christ – the ultimate
symbol of rejected kingship on earth – to the reckoning. The slightest
indication of treachery will push Richard into a Christ-like posture.
Believing, wrongly, that Bushy, Bagot and Green are traitors, he
cries:

> 'Three Judases, each one thrice worse than Judas!' [III.2.132]

His frequent iteration of the divine right of kingship has, for him, an
additional potency in his role of Christ:

> 'If we be not, show us the hand of God
> That hath dismiss'd us from our stewardship;' [III.3.77–8]

The words he has given to express his chosen identification with
Christ are explicit:

> 'Do they not sometime cry "All Hail!" to me?
> So Judas did to Christ . . .' [IV.1.169–70]

and in a superb display of self-dramatization he plots the way whereby the earthly kingdom is abandoned for the kingdom of heaven:

> 'And my large kingdom for a little grave,
> A little little grave, an obscure grave'   [III.3.153–4]

Towards the end his self-dramatizing imagery reaches a climax of grandeur. He pushes the drama of self that he has created to a conclusion. Only he himself is able to denude himself of the solemn splendour that he has, by his imagination and words, encrusted about him. Bolingbroke stands curiously powerless while the great actor/poet dominates the stage. At this point Richard has achieved the maximum effect his imagination can gain. The poet has created his masterpiece:

> 'I give this heavy weight from off my head,
> And this unwieldy sceptre from my hand,
> The pride of kingly sway from out my heart;
> With mine own tears I wash away my balm,
> With mine own hands I give away my crown,
> With mine own tongue deny my sacred state,
> With mine own breath release all duteous oaths;
> All pomp and majesty I do forswear;   [IV.1.204–11]

Yet neither Shakespeare nor, through him, Richard, has finished with our emotions. Having satisfied, with grief-stricken hedonism, his own imagination, Richard still has a trump to play. After stripping himself as person and king, becoming a nothing, he abandons his verbal voyaging with Christ, and plays upon the simple fact that he has now become a nothing. Bolingbroke can merely abide while Richard dominates and makes his final assault upon the world. He acts out, in a scene of dazzling and, in every sense, theatrical power, the meaning of what has happened to him. He has hypnotized us with words and now he taunts Bolingbroke with one single histrionic deed:

> 'Good king, great king, and yet not greatly good,
> An if my name be sterling yet in England,
> Let it command a mirror hither straight,
> That it may show me what a face I have
> Since it is bankrupt of his majesty.'   [IV.1.263–7]

The mirror is obtained and Richard continues:

> 'Is this the face which fac'd so many follies,
> That was at last out-fac'd by Bolingbroke?

A brittle glory shineth in this face;
As brittle as the glory is the face;'   [IV.1.285-8]

It is left to the Bishop of Carlisle to utter the stark meaning of the events that have led to this scene:

'The woe's to come; the children yet unborn
Shall feel this day as sharp to them as thorn.'   [IV.1.322-3]

These lines restore the play to its larger historical meaning. Richard has taken us, for a time, out of the historical process and bent our minds towards his individual grief and deprivation.

Yet the fuller meaning is clear. The curse has fallen upon England. From this point onwards Shakespeare uses Richard himself to stress the historical meaning of what has happened. Though we do not lose sight of the suffering man, we are aware always of the grief to come to a whole kingdom:

'And some will mourn in ashes, some coal black,
For the deposing of a rightful king.'   [V.1.49-50]

While it may be that, for the twentieth century, the emphasis on Richard supplies the greater dramatic potency, the broader historical meanings of this play should not be underrated. At many points the external equivalents of Richard's inner torments are affirmed. York, having berated Richard for his shortcomings, is no less severe on Bolingbroke for his rebellion. Even Bolingbroke himself cannot forbear to see the grandeur of majesty in Richard. He expresses himself in words which echo Richard's own elevating of himself into a god-figure:

'See, see King Richard doth himself appear,
As doth the blushing discontented sun
From out the fiery portal of the east . . .'   [III.3.62-4]

Bolingbroke's crime and sinfulness are not ignored. They receive oblique but effective utterance in Bolingbroke's own words at the end of the play:

'Lords, I protest my soul is full of woe
That blood should sprinkle me to make me grow.'   [V.6.45-6]

The point where the inward-turning imagery of Richard and the outer meaning of the events meet at flashpoint is the scene where the crown goes to Bolingbroke. Nowhere is the validity of Richard's status as annointed king more directly stated. Bolingbroke is invited to 'seize' the crown; it is held before him and mused upon by Richard. Bolingbroke is unable to take it, and lamely reminds Richard that he thought Richard had been willing to resign it. At the very moment of obtaining the crown of England Bolingbroke enters into that characteristic inertia of will which dominates his character as Henry IV. It is achieved by Richard's demonstration not so much of personal grief as of the awesome reality of usurpation.

Indeed a kind of inertia is also characteristic of the whole opposition to Richard. The rebellion itself has nothing of the direct and bloody activity of the Wars of the Roses or the later rebellion which, in turn, was to threaten Bolingbroke's throne. The first scene at the lists and the gage-throwing scene have a curiously statuesque and merely ceremonial quality. No battle is seen in the play. There is an air of apology about the whole matter, and a strong sense of incipient guilt. Only in theoretical terms is Bolingbroke shown as capable of being a stronger, better king than Richard – we are mainly led to assume this will be so. In fact Shakespeare does not go out of his way to prove Bolingbroke's superiority – he remains no more than an illegal alternative to a demonstrably weak monarch. The play is held fast in an atmosphere of grief, doubt and guilt. It never asserts in action that might will triumph over weakness and right.

Richard II is the source play out of which later historical themes take their material. It initiates the curse that must be expiated. However, it is also very different in kind from the later histories. It is deficient in action; its 'demonstration' of history is subservient to the emphasis on the protagonist; certain scenes seem conceived less towards forwarding the action than to presenting ritual or symbolic pictures. The scene at the lists, for example, although it may be said to serve the purpose of introducing the plot and revealing something of Richard, its construction and movement rigidly and mechanically imitate the actual formalities of the medieval tourney. Shakespeare has leaned heavily and slavishly on Holinshed:

> When he heard what they had answered, he commanded that they should be brought forthwith before his presence, to hear what they would say. Herewith an herald in the king's name with loud voice commanded the dukes to come before the king, either of them to show his reason, or else to make peace together without more delay. When they were come before the king and lords, the king spake himself to them, willing them to agree, and make peace together: 'for it is' (said he) the best way ye can take.' The duke of Norfolk with

due reverence hereunto answered, it could not so be brought to pass, his honour saved . . . [5]

This scene, on stage, unless produced carefully, becomes a slightly ludicrous panoply of antiquated ritual, and its dramatic purpose can easily be lost. A more extreme example of a scene which does not take wing out of mere ritual is the gage scene. Modern producers have been known to cut it and it is difficult not to sympathize with them. Its presence can be theoretically justified by claiming that it shows how the act of rebellion brings with it internal dissension – rebellion doomed to self-destruction. In theatrical terms, however, it is difficult to produce the scene without inducing a comic response from the audience. The repetitive throwing down of gages by a circle of noble lords irresistibly conjures up a kind of musical-chairs behaviour, and as recent productions have shown, this effect cannot be removed even by concentrating the production on evoking a sense of great and elaborate ceremonial. The difficulty arises from the fact that there is no variety in the ceremonial ingredients of the scene and, more important, nothing in its verbal pattern can lure the mind away from its mechanical superficiality of construction and movement. Once again it is undigested Holinshed:

'I say' (quoth he) 'that he was *the* very *cause* of his death'; and so he appealed him of treason, offering by throwing down his hood as a gage to prove it with his body. There were twenty other lords also that threw down their hoods, as pledges to prove the like matter against the duke of Aumerle. [6]

Another scene that is often cut is the garden scene. This is in a different category. It is a characteristic example of Shakespeare's method, in the early histories, of allegorizing the meaning of historical events. The garden is England; the message is simple. All plants in the garden must be kept in due order; what is weed must be destroyed; what grows in too much profusion must be pruned; what is weak must be tended. The result must be order and due proportion. The scene is often cut on the grounds that it interrupts the action and is too obvious an image of England's condition. If the scene were merely that then cutting it might be justifiable. However, it performs another and most important function. It is largely through this scene that the character of Richard's Queen is given some substance. Up to this point she has been a shadowy creature, faithful but neglected. In this scene the agony of being Queen is brought home in a far more telling way than in, for example, *Richard*

III. In that play there is something unbelievable about the collection of weeping ex-consorts who hold a prolonged wake on their grief. Here, however, a pathetic individual tragedy is sharply outlined.

It is also a well-unified scene. The garden is, as it were, real; the gardeners are real, the Queen is real. Yet both garden and gardeners are also symbolic and the scene proceeds on two levels – the one direct, the other implicit. In the end neither level dominates. They merge into one complete and unified effect clinched by the gardeners' inclusion of the Queen within the symbolic pattern of the garden:

> 'Here did she fall a tear; here in this place
> I'll set a bank of rue, sour herb of grace.
> Rue, even for ruth, here shortly shall be seen,
> In the remembrance of a weeping queen.'   [III.4.104–7]

It is, however, not only the presence of such scenes of ritual and symbolism that serve to intensify the distinctiveness of *Richard II* as a history play. The primal curse, which long affects England as the result of Bolingbroke's usurpation, is shown in its working out as vicious and brutal. As he had done in *Henry VI* and *Richard III*, Shakespeare shows the active results of the curse, but all the ingredients of history as Shakespeare saw them – rebellion, usurpation, divine right, honour, duty, patriotism – are curiously abstract in this play. Gaunt's speech on England celebrates an abstraction; Bolingbroke's rebellion stands back, as it were, from the forefront of the action – a cypher of disaffection rather than the thing itself; the jealousy of the nobles is not shown in fierce stark brutality but as a formal testy ritual; the realities of usurpation are talked about rather than shown in action. The play's motto might well be, in Aumerle's words:

> 'No good my lord, let's fight with gentle words.'

There is a withdrawal from the active facts of historical events. It is as if the whole play is a series of arranged tableaux conveying, but not embodying, the great and abiding themes which are developed in the other histories.

But what, more than anything else, distinguished this play and gives it the status of a lyrical poem is the nature of the language. A.C. Sprague has truly written: 'On Richard's lips the poetry of the young Shakespeare seems wholly natural.'[7] The important words are 'young' and 'poetry'. The play is shaped on the same velvet anvil that created the Sonnets, *Venus and Adonis*, and *Romeo and Juliet*. The result is a rhythmical celebration of, and rumination on, action – not action itself. Indeed any movement towards action is stifled by the overwhelming interference of lyrical speech. It is noticeable how often Richard starts speeches with words that are a kind of lyrical evocation:

'Mine ear is open and my heart prepar'd.'   [III.2.93]
'No mater where – of comfort no man speak.
Let's talk of graves, of worms, and epithaphs.'   [III.2.145]
'Now mark me how I will undo myself:'   [IV.1.203]

These lyrical passages aspire to the condition of music. It is as if Richard is making a pathetic substitution for an order which his kingdom is losing, by ordering his thoughts and feelings in a musical pattern. In the end he finds that this is not enough. He hears music outside his cell and says:

'Music I do hear?
Ha, ha! keep time. How sour sweet music is
When time is broke, and no proportion kept!'   [V.5.41]

The music continues, but only to remind him of his approaching end. He shouts:

'This music made me. Let it sound no more;'   [V.5.61]

But, at last, with a curious indication of self-knowledge, he relents:

'Yet blessing on his heart that gives it me!
For 'tis a sign of love; and love to Richard
Is a strange brooch in this all-hating world.'   [V.5.64–6]

The music he creates through his words is not only an attempt to hold fast to an order, a pattern, but an obligation to his own love of himself. The tragedy of Richard II is that of the poet, who, taking himself as his subject and theme, falls in love with what he creates. He has no qualifications whatsoever for the kind of kingship demanded and the actualities of political life, except for one thing – a sense of the grandeur of kingship. His tragedy, personally as it is expressed, has a certain irony in it. Like a poet, he knows and can communicate the truth of his own experience; unlike a poet he has been called upon, as king, to be, and do, more than this. He is completely unequal to the task, being both poet and monarch.

King John

Doubts about the date of composition of this play tend to isolate it from the other histories. There is no quarto version and there is a considerable body of opinion which claims that the folio text comes from Shakespeare's 'foul' papers.[8] If this is so, then it means we are face to face with a very early draft of the play. The date of composition is unknown. Internal evidence presents the customary difficulties of weighing possibility against instinct. *Richard II*, by reason of its lyrical power and the strength of characterization of the protagonist, would seem to be a later play; on the other hand, there are scenes in *King John* which display a mastery of dramatic and theatrical technique which seem superior to those shown in *Richard II*.

A consensus would probably show that a majority of scholars accept 1594 as the most likely date of composition.[9] This, however, has been strongly challenged, largely on the basis of an anonymous play called *The Troublesome Reign of King John of England* which bears striking similarities with Shakespeare's play, and which, published in 1591, was obviously popular. The argument for an earlier date for *King John* than 1594 hinges on the possibility that *The Troublesome Reign* was an early version by Shakespeare of *King John*, but proof positive that this is so has never appeared.

It also stands apart from Shakespeare's other history plays for thematic reasons. In the first place, although the status of kingship:

'What earthy name to interrogatories
Can take the free breath of a sacred king?'

is part of the groundswell of the play, it is not a dominant theme. Secondly, although the fate of England is obviously involved in the action, it is not presented against the direct or implied background of the pattern of history, as in Shakespeare's other histories. This difference is reinforced by the nature of the Bastard's character, which affects our acceptance of the whole story and of the historical issues behind it.

It is difficult to account for its comparative neglect in the theatre. It gives the director much scope for diversity of action, set and pace; its characters, both male and female, are, in several cases, strongly written. At least three of them (Constance, Blanche and the Bastard) ought to prove irresistible to the acting profession. Yet, when it appears in the repertory of any theatre, it somehow seems surprising that it should be there. Perhaps there is an irremovable psychological blockage to its acceptance by audiences. King John is the Demon King, after all, of our island story. His reputation as predator of the people's rights has given him a quasi-mythological status of the one really obvious tyrant that English history has produced. Richard II is attractive in his villainy, but John is beyond the pale.

The main theme of the play, which concerns the concept of right and succession, is given different interpretations by different characters. King John stands for sovereign right in terms of kingly rule, and Philip of France is in much the same camp. Then there is the Bastard's claim to be recognized – that he has a right to an identity. Thirdly there is the conception of right as seen and promulgated by the representative of the Holy See, Pandulph. Fourthly there is the strident, emotionally-based sense of threatened right in Constance. And lastly there are the claims to the throne on behalf of the pathetic Arthur.

This persistent and all-enveloping theme of 'rights' is announced at the very beginning of the play with Chatillon's statement that Philip of France's claims on behalf of John's nephew are sound. The atmosphere, generated by the exchanges that follow, pervades the whole action with a bickering and reasonless conceit. A superficial view might conclude that this treatment is of the same nature as that of the *Henry VI* plays, for, at first glance, it looks like the relentless pride and empty egotism that characterizes the warring nobility in those plays. There is, however, a subtle difference in *King John*, in the much stronger implied condemnation of the bickering feuds, which comes to the surface as a kind of mockery of the various assertions of right, might and succession. The depiction of John, for example, contains at times all the boastful blimpery of a great war:

> 'Be thou as lightning in the eyes of France;
> For ere thou canst report, I will be there,
> The thunder of my cannon shall be heard.' [I.1.24–6]

The protestations of Arthur's supporters ring a little artificially. They protest their disinterestedness too much, and condemn themselves out of their own mouths with a holier-than-thou emphasis which arouses suspicion:

> 'Upon thy cheek I lay this zealous kiss
> As seal to this indenture of my love:
> That to my home I will no more return
> Till Angiers and the right thou hast in France, ...' [II.1.19–22]

And King Philip's remark to John:

> 'England we love and for that England's sake
> With burden of our armour here we sweat.'   [II.1.91–2]

is as ironic in effect as Henry V's celebrated remark to Kate that he loves France so much he will not part with a village of it!

If there is any doubt that Shakespeare's intention is to make these contestants condemn themselves, Act II.1. should remove them. The bickering which, for a time is carried on in blustering rhetoric, suddenly becomes personal, reducing the scene to the proportions of a family squabble:

> K.JOHN: Alack, thou dost usurp authority.
> K.PHILIP: Excuse it is to beat usurping down.
> ELEANOR: Who is it thou dost call usurper, France?
> CONSTANCE: Let me make answer: thy usurping son.'   [II.1.117–110]

The rhetoric eventually returns. This time, however, the contestants are ridiculed by the reluctance of the people of Angiers to open their gates to either army and the play is pushed very near to comic frontiers when the rival kings bombast their pride, right and might, only to be told, coolly, that neither of them adds up to anything unless they can prove it. The sense of the ridiculous is increased by the interjections of the Bastard:

> 'O, tremble, for you hear the lion roar!'   [II.1.294]

The roar is only as 'gentle as any sucking dove'.

The Bastard's presence governs one part of our reactions to these events. It is through him that we are really convinced of the overblown pointlessness of it all. It is, however, the unwitting cause of all this bombast – Arthur, John's nephew – who governs another part of our reactions. In the long scene of direct confrontation at Angiers he is present, an almost silent witness of events he has unwittingly set in motion simply by existing. He speaks twice only – once at the opening of the scene, and, later on, makes a telling, moving interjection to his mother:

> 'Good my mother, peace!
> I would that I were laid low in my grave,
> I am not worth this coil that's made for me,'   [II.1.164–5]

If the Bastard offers something of an ironically comic focus on events, then Arthur provides their inherent pathos.

The statement and demonstration of the kind of right and might asserted by John and the King of France move, in the first part of the play, relentlessly forward, unsubtle, even boring, were it not for the presence of the Bastard and Arthur. In Act III, however, another version of right and might is introduced in the person of Pandulph, the papal legate, and his appearance coincides with a change in John's character. Till now John has been little more than an example of a monarch who, cognisant of his station, shouts his claims to the air. Pandulph stands for the right of the church through the Pope, as head of the Holy Roman Empire. What results is a direct argument between one authority, come to emphasize its power, and another, which does not accept that authority. In terms of true history, Shakespeare has ignored the actual facts of John's relationship with the papacy – John did, in fact, submit to Innocent III, and was compelled to surrender his crown to Pandulph and have it returned to him as vassal. The scene with Pandulph, indeed, expresses clearly the fundamental conflict between Rome and the English reformation and swerves away from a depiction of medieval power politics to an unequivocal statement of the Tudor position and the opposition to it. In doing so Shakespeare has placed John, if only for a time, in an entirely different light, for here John is seen as embodying the new-found patriotism of England itself. For the more discerning members of an Elizabethan audience, his reply to Pandulph would represent an affirmation of the Tudor concept of the Divine Right of Kings. In the speech:

'Tell him this tale, and from the mouth of England
Add thus much more, that no Italian priest
Shall tithe or toil in our dominions;
So under Him that great supremacy,
Where we do reign we will alone uphold,
Without th' assistance of a mortal hand.'   [III.1.152–8]

John is presented as King in Tudor terms and he benefits from the translation. He is shown to be within his rights, and, for a brief time, he, the Tudor concept of Kingship, and Elizabethan patriotism become one.

One must not, however, while appreciating the political implications of the play, ignore the examples of dramatic skill that are displayed. Pandulph is a powerfully drawn character, arrogant, meticulously certain of his argument, assured in his status and in what he represents. Quite apart from his fluent command of the subtleties of polemical argument, he has a wry sense of timing. The whole scene (III.1.) is notable for dramatic irony. Pandulph's arrival, for example, has come at a time when apparent amity has been achieved – breaches seem to have been closed, wounds licked, and a marriage arranged. Constance's fierce agony of spirit alone infects the atmosphere. Hearing of Blanche's political betrothal, she cries out:

'Hast thou not spoke like thunder on my side,
Been sworn my soldier . . .
And dost thou now fall ever to my foes?'   [III.1.124–7]

Pandulph's intervention reinforces what Constance's outcry has revealed – the weak expediency of these people. And at a point in the play when we are becoming bored with the parade of ineffectualness, Shakespeare introduces this character who has sufficient dramatic power to restore the balance and interest of the play.

The theme of right has yet another form and colour, in which pathos plays some part. It is embodied in Constance. When one contemplates Queen Margaret and Constance (and, also, for example, Volumnia and Lady Macbeth) it is not easy to dismiss the idea that Shakespeare has two quite distinct conceptions of womanhood. One is best represented by Rosalind and Viola; they are ideal and the more precious in being rare. The other, at the opposite extreme, is represented by four regal women. They are the embodiment of female assertiveness, displaying something of the animal which, when cornered or denied what it believes to be its right, fights with the tooth and claw of anger, grief, and cruelty. Such women are not loved, but feared, admired and respected for their strength of will. They dispose to the full a range of devices to achieve their ends – persuasion, seduction, threat, subversion and self-indulgent emotionalism. Constance is of this breed. She has authority:

'Stay for an answer to your embassy,
Lest unadvis'd you stain your swords with blood;'   [II.1.44–5]

She is mistress of a goading mockery:

'Do, child, go to it grandam, child;
Give grandam kingdom, and it grandam will
Give it a plum, a cherry, and a fig,
There's good grandam!'   [II.1.160–3]

She can make grief speak on her behalf

'I will instruct my sorrows to be proud,
For grief is proud, and make his owner stoop.'   [III.1.68–9]

She falls, a figure of vulnerable distress, before Lewis, and shakes his conscience with a well-timed use of the word 'honour':

'His honour. O, thine honour, Lewis, thine honour!'   [III.1.316]

She does not have Richard III's coldly calculated ability to emulate the chameleon, but her part in this play, like his, has histrionic motivations, and one aspect of the theme of right – a primitive, totally acquisitive and fierce one – flourishes in her character.

In the midst of these variations upon the basic theme, stands the Bastard, preserving our interest and patience throughout the whole affair. He would, one feels, be much better remembered were he in a better play. Examined in isolation, he is a character created with much more depth than the others. He is, like the rest, an ambitious man, and he gets what he wants – recognition. He delights in status, in being recognized, courted for favours. he is a conceited young man, delighting in what his audacity gains, yet he is also, as he himself claims, one who will:

'. . . deliver
Sweet, sweet, sweet poison for the age's tooth.'

The 'sweetness' of it is the delight he experiences watching his poison at work, and never is it more sweet than when he makes the kings and warriors look foolish before the walls of Angiers. He manipulates them in their stupid war game:

'O prudent discipline! From north to south,
Austria and France shoot in each other's mouth.
I'll stir them to it . . .'   [II.1.413–5]

There is, in fact, a dangerous mischief-making element in his character, but there is more too. He despises those whom he can cheat and fool, eyeing their actions cynically and satirically:

'Mad world! mad kings! mad composition!
John, to stop Arthur's title in the whole,
Hath willingly departed with a part;
And France, whose armour conscience buckled on,
Whom zeal and charity brought to the field
As God's own soldier, rounded in the ear
With that same purpose-changer, that sly devil,
That broker that still breaks the pate of faith . . .'   [II.1.561–8]

With the audacious frankness of a realist, the Bastard is prepared to capitalize, for his own good, upon the way of the world as he sees it.

94

It is impossible, throughout most of the play, not to see in him something of Thersites in *Troilus and Cressida*. On a simply theatrical level, both characters occupy a similar position, by reason of their soliloquies, for, from time to time, they very conspicuously stand apart and comment, or rail, alone, and their general tone is similar. Although Thersites expresses himself more venomously, both he and the Bastard are cynics, satirists and despisers. They are both in pursuit of self-satisfaction; they both despise their victims; they both have a kind of honesty. Perhaps, more important, they both act as *agents-provocateurs* to the meaning and action of their respective contexts. The essential difference between them is that whereas Thersites's whole function is to rail without commitment, the Bastard is more involved in the actions upon which he looks with such quizzical gaze. Thersites wants the world to end, so to speak, on his own terms; the Bastard wants it to continue – on his own terms.

Shakespeare, when dealing with themes involving disorder, human deceit, vanity and cupidity, seems to have reacted, with different degrees of force, against his own depiction of the world, expressing that reaction through the medium of certain characters. It is variously expressed – loathsomely as in Thersites, with cynical witty candour as in the Bastard, with piquant roguery as in Autolycus, or with profound mockery as in the Fool in *King Lear*. Such characters are no better than the world they prey or rail upon, but, in their different ways, each has a candid and realistic view of that world. It seems as if Shakespeare, when confronted with some of the worlds of disorder he has created, cannot prevent himself from embodying some part of his own intermittent feeling that the life of man and his ways can only be regarded with a sardonic eye – that mankind deserves no more.

The Bastard offers, however, additional grounds for speculation. There occurs a seemingly complete reversal of his character in the last part of the play. It requires much suspension of incredulity to equate his earlier speeches of invective and raillery with this last speech about England. If, in the first three acts, he has affiliations with Thersistes, by Act V the affirming patriotic glow of Talbot and Henry V begins to shine in his words. It might be suggested that with the coming death of John, the Bastard sees before his eyes a final crown of recognition – the assumption of the leadership of a stricken country; or even argued that the Bastard is all of one piece, and that the cynic has bided his time, and, now, like those he has earlier condemned, he is prepared to play the rhetorical patriotic game for his own ends. Nevertheless, it is still difficult to put together the man who treats Lewis and Pandulph with such scorn, and makes fools of warriors, with the man who makes a declaration that is a set-piece of the patriot:

> '... Naught shall make us rue,
> If England to itself do rest but true.' [V.7.116–7]

If the function of the Bastard seems ambiguous, that of King John seems, to say the least, unattractive. He is the least dramatically magnetic of all Shakespeare's kings. Henry VI has a piteous and compelling dignity in his weakness; Richard II has a curious beauty in his vacillation; Henry IV excites undiminishing curiosity by his displays of conscience and his grief; Henry V is spectacular in his self-conscious majesty: and, of all the weak or evil monarchs, Richard III is the most compulsively attractive. King John, however, almost sidles his way through the play. Shakespeare's attempt, at one point, to use him as an emblem of Tudor patriotism and challenging power is quite unconvincing, for there is no convincing sense of kingliness in him. He lacks that one quality which all the rest of Shakespeare's monarchs, whatever their vices or virtues, have in abundance, the ability fully to engage our interest. John's major trait, in fact, is a meanness of spirit.

John is politically reckless, unctuously cruel, sanctimoniously hypocritical and dangerously fickle.

> 'We cannot hold mortality's strong hand.
> Good lords, although my will to give, is living,
> The suit which you demand is gone and dead:
> He tells us Arthur is deceas'd to-night.' [IV.2.82–5]

His very death, which Shakespeare attempts to dignify by putting in his mouth words of high lyrical pathos, succeeds only in seeming a kind of petulant self-indulgence. It is as if Shakespeare found King John not only uninteresting but incapable of striking fire from his imagination. There is a sense in which one can say that Shakespeare seems to have 'liked' even his most villainous king – Richard III – possibly for his astonishing audacity, but that King John left him cold. John is a coward, unfaithful even to villainy, and everything about him goes off at half-cock.

So the play lacks a central force. In vain Shakespeare tries belatedly to fill the gap by raising the thematic status of the Bastard, but the attempt fails because, interesting as he is, the Bastard's character is dramatically fractured, and no dramatist can create a national emblem out of a convinced and convincing cynic.

It is remarkable that this play, which displays a relatively jaundiced and tired view of historical events and personages, should have been written so closely in time to *Henry IV*. Although the play has many excellent theatrical moments – it is far more viable in the theatre than is commonly supposed – it has an uncharacteristic untidiness and fragmentation which suggests not only haste in writing, but a preoccupation with other matters. We may perhaps hazard a guess that Shakespeare was busily tending the growing seeds of Hal and Falstaff, and lost patience with this weedy plot of English history.

Henry IV – Parts I and II

The two parts of *Henry IV* represent one of Shakespeare's highest achievements.[10] They have a richness of plot and theme, a grand variety of language, an exciting versatility of characterization which at no point lose hold on our imaginations, making them among the most consistently exciting of Shakespeare's plays. They are also much more. They represent the first absolute confirmation in the canon that the mechanical critical divisions of Shakespeare's mind and art into the categories of comedy, tragedy and history are superficial, misleading and irrelevant, for in these two plays the tragic, comic, and historical visions are combined to create a many-dimensioned view of the human scene. The reality of the plays lies in the interaction of historical narrative with the tragic figure of the conscience-stricken King and the gigantic comic presence of Falstaff. None of them is an isolated or insulated dramatic element, and it is partly because of this unity of vision that modern critics claim that Shakespeare conceived of his history plays as a vast epic of English history. Dover Wilson summarizes it:

> When Shakespeare set forth along the road which began with Richard II, he had the whole journey in view; had indeed already traversed the second half of it; and envisaged the road before him, which stretched from the usurpation of Bolingbroke, through the troubles of his reign, to the final triumph of his son over the French, as a great upward sweep in the history of England and the chapter of that history which the men of his age found more interesting than any other.[11]

It is claimed by adherents to this view that the earlier history plays (*Henry VI*, *Richard II*, *King John*) find their logical fulfilment in the two parts of *Henry IV*. The emphasis in the earlier plays is on the development of certain themes, certain types of character, and on a gradually widening and deepening conception of patriotism and of what constitutes a nation. Similarly, in the Henry IV plays he seems not so much concerned with a connected historical account as with a demonstration of the lessons of history – the undertow beneath the chronology. In its length and depth *Henry IV* has, of itself, something of the epic. In its picking up and developing of earlier themes and issues, it is, in the last analysis, an epic within an epic.

If it has certain and very obvious connections with the earlier histories, it goes far beyond them in its dramatic scope. Although it is, like *Henry VI*, to a degree, a chronicle play designed to show great actions performed by great men, it is far from confined to the great. In both *Henry VI* and *Richard II* areas of society below those of royalty and nobility (Jack Cade's rebellion, the citizenry of London duped by Richard of Gloucester) are depicted, often with sharp observation, but there is a strong separation between the different layers of society. There the respective inhabitants of high and low merely 'visit', so to speak, those areas which are not their own. Here is little co-mingling – royalty descends, looks and commands and what lives below is summoned, listens and is dismissed. In both parts of *Henry IV*, however, the kingdom is not depicted as a set of separate social groups. Each group knows its place certainly – there is no breaking of the eternal law of class and position – but there is a far greater intercourse between one class and another. This opening of doors between high and low distinguishes this play from its predecessors, giving it a greater sense of human richness and reality. Furthermore, there is no longer an overwhelming sense that what is called the commonwealth consists almost exclusively of royalty and nobility. The England of *Henry IV* Parts I and II is a rich amalgam of all its citizens, high and low. The earlier themes – divine right, rebellion, the trials of kingship, the complex of usurpation, the curse upon England – are all there, but the individual human experiences of both nobility and low commoner – experiences which have to be endured inside the historical context – are given far greater prominence.

This richness of imagination and detail invigorating the characterization, is also present in Shakespeare's handling of the 'isms' and issues of history. In the earlier plays, martial honour, chivalry, even treachery itself, seem part of a mere ceremonial of human behaviour. In this play they become more vitally real by being subject to an acid test which corrodes their conventionality – the test of practicability at the hands of the time-serving Falstaff. No concept, no convention, no tired image nor ritual is allowed to remain in a state where its abstract presence overrides its practical validity.

Any enumeration of the separate elements which enrich these plays, however, should not be allowed to obscure the amazing width of canvas upon which Shakespeare worked. Although the two plays have a broad historical sweep, they are, uniquely, what may be described as 'geographical' plays. England is no mere stage upon which ignorant armies clash by night. *Henry VI* could well be played upon a bare stage. So could *Henry IV*, but *Henry IV* demands precise indications of location. There is a greater sense of 'place' about this king's court than any other's; the Boar's Head Tavern is no mere piece of vague generalization; and even the clearer air of the Cotswold country demands more than a distant cyclorama and a front apron – there is cot and orchard here. In fact the play might well suffer more in production from a slavish adherence to the scholar's concept of Elizabethan staging than from the modern set-designer's judicious use of his sources. On the other hand the play itself does not inhibit spectacle by the kind of verbal/visual indications of the Chorus in *Henry V*, even though its rich variety of human beings are so much part of the woof and warp of their surroundings that they invite visual evocations of that which is their environment.

The plot line is simple; it is its total length together with the variety of characterization which deceive the audience into believing that it is winding and complex. A king, enthroned through usurpation, is threatened with rebellion, which is met and overcome. The king dies and his son assumes the crown. In so far as Hal's adventures in the world of Falstaff can be described as a sub-plot, this consists of his meeting with Falstaff, his protection of him and his rejection of him. The play's human richness misleads one into believing that Hal's engagement with Falstaff is long as well as close, but, in fact, the intimacy of their relationship is over and done with by the end of The Boar's Head scene in the middle of Part 1. Hal sees Falstaff intermittently afterwards but with no more (for Hal) than nostalgic remembrance and (for Falstaff) misplaced hope.

There are two great thematic catalysts which by their actions deepen and enrich the sparse plot line. The first is the fact that Henry IV is a usurper and the true history of this king is less that of his overcoming a rebellion than that of his agony of his ever-present guilt about what he has done to get the crown. Henry moves between an inertia brought about by conscience and a tired activity goaded by threats to the security of what he has done. He is a study in the pathetic irony that power, ill got, corrodes the strength and will of the begetter. Bolingbroke took the crown reluctantly, the dazzle of gold overpowering a certain stolid virtuousness in the man. As Henry IV, he learns the consequences of his actions in the form of a personal cross he has to bear, but he also knows them in an external historical sense, and he believes that his errant son is the punishment visited on him:

'I know not whether God will have it so,
For some displeasing service I have done,

That, in his secret doom, out of my blood
He'll breed revengement and a scourge for me;'   [1H.III.2.4–7]

He lives trapped, first by his guilt and second by the suffocating ceremony of kingship. Henry VI, a rightful king, grieves abstractedly about the cares of the throne, Richard II creates a poetic elegy about it, Henry IV feels the cares in a physical sense:

'How many thousand of my poorest subjects
Are at this hour asleep! O sleep, O gentle sleep,
Nature's soft nurse, how hath I frighted thee,
That thou no more wilt weigh my eyelids down.'   [2H.III.1.4–7]

Henry's response to his position as usurping king gives a poignant dimension to the events which conspired to remove him from the throne. He himself was in Northumberland's rebellious position after Berkeley (*Richard II*), and Northumberland recognizes the personal dimensions behind the covering generalities of rebellion:

'. . . Let order die!
And let this world no longer be a stage
To feed contention in a ling'ring act;
But let one spirit of the first-born Cain
Reign in all bosoms, that, each heart being set
On bloody courses, the rude scene may end
And darkness be the burier of the dead!'   [2H.I.1.154–9]

The second catalyst is closely related to the first. Simply stated it has its existence in the irony that the heir to the usurper is considered, with apparent justification, to be feckless. Because of his personal reaction to his own guilt, Henry IV's response to his son's apparent insufficiency becomes deeply personal. He is not merely a tired king but a father grieving over his son's dissaffections. Hal himself is a very clear expression of a recurring Shakespearean theme, the opposition of illusion and reality. The audience knows more about Hal and his intentions than his father knows, and this induces a classical theatrical irony, the effect of which is sharpened by the way in which the king/prince relationship enlarges in the father/son one.

Thus the historical focus (the epic quality) and the tragic focus merge. The 'tragedy' of the play is in the keenly-felt guilt of Henry representing loyalty, and of Northumberland representing rebellion, and it is also present in the dramatic implications of the father/son relationship. All these elements are bound together by something which casts a dark and elegiac shadow, for both parts of the play demonstrate the outmoded nature both of Henry's kind of kingship and his (as Bolingbroke) kind of rebellion. Both the kingship and rebellion are consanguineous in the sense that they have their being in old familiars of convention, honour, chivalry, right, even treachery. They both have about them a weary inertia. In no other play is there such an impression of old and medieval concepts dying before the assaults of new concepts and ideas. In Henry IV, I & II, King, Hotspur, Prince John, Northumberland, represent an older age, subsisting upon thought and behaviour which Hal is to change. Falstaff acts as catalyst. He cynically demonstrates how untrue to the new age these patterns are, and Hal, having learnt much from him, sets about making kingship into a new and positive reality.

Hal is purposeful. He determines to show one face, an illusory one, and at the chosen time to replace it by the real one, so that his 'reformation' will seem the more spectacular. This decision is a mixture of young arrogance, vanity, and serious creative intent and it is part of his charm that it is so. There is much of the actor in him, revelling in the effects he will have when he has taken off his make-up:

> 'My reformation, glitt'ring o'er my fault,
> Shall show more goodly and attract more eyes
> Than which hath no foil to set it off.'   [1.H.I.2.206–8]

He exults in disguise; for him the best part of Gadshill is that Falstaff should not have recognized him, and when he returns to the 'Old Frank' after Shrewsbury with Poins, his boyish delight in dressing up shows itself once again.

Yet he is actor only in part of his personality. He wishes to be total king, and to do this he has to make two rejections, both of them, in different degrees, poignant to him – his own father, as king, and Falstaff, his 'adopted' father, and his 'rejection' of his father is by far the more poignant. It is forced upon Hal, not by personal animosity, but by the demands of his determination to disguise his purposes from the world. In no other play of Shakespeare's is there such an evocative portrayal of a father/son relationship. It involves love, suspicion, misunderstanding, and deception, and, as it unfolds, it probes benath the surface of the play's main theme – the secret ambitions of Prince Hal. Hal's conception of the meaning of kingship and the ceremony which surrounds it is changed by his experiences, and is emphatically coloured by his relationships with Henry IV. When Hal addresses the crown at his father's bedside, he looks at it with the eyes of a realist, for he has already learnt of the duplicities of gold from Falstaff ('Never call a true piece of gold a counterfeit'). He speculates not upon its symbolic glory but upon the care it brings to its wearer. All Shakespeare's kings do this, but none makes such a personal identification between the abstract idea of care and the personal experience of it. 'Care' and 'father' become inextricably entwined for Hal:

> '... The care on thee depending
> Hath fed upon the body of my father;'   [2H.IV.5.159–60]

Hal's form of address in this scene alternates between 'thee', 'majesty', 'father'. For him, the crown is a repository of majesty, or/ and power, but the pain it brings with it forces Hal to personalize its implications:

> '... I put it on my head,
> To try with it – as with an enemy
> That hath before my face murd'red my father'   [2H.IV.5.166–8]

The King's responses to his son maintain the level of the personal:

> 'Oh my son,
> God put it in thy mind to take it hence,
> That thou might win the more thy father's love,'   [2H.IV.5.178–80]

Hal's rejection of his father involves a paradox, paralleled by the contradiction he sees in the crown itself. The crown, to Hal, is two things: it is 'the best of gold', 'fine, most honoured, most renowned', but it is also the 'worst of gold' in that it destroys he who wears it. Henry IV, as king, corresponds to the first notion, but, as father, he is in truth a thing of pain, grief and conscience. Hal responds to both, but he is torn in two, because his love for his father is as strong as his determination to reject the kind of kingship which his father represents. As the action of the play progresses, Hal does much to allay Henry's doubts about his fitness to succeed him, yet a shadow remains between the two men which prevents the personal bond from even being completely and unbreakably connected.

The rejection of Falstaff is less deeply poignant, though the specific act is often regarded by critics and many theatregoers as being more affecting. To understand the nature of and need for this rejection, it is necessary to understand Falstaff himself. He has been made into a giant by the encrustation of the sentiment of successive generations of critics and theatregoers. He has become an English monument like the Albert Memorial, whose associativeness is more countenanced than its actuality. There are indeed two Falstaffs – the character in Shakespeare's play and an image in the national imagination.

The English are characteristically drawn to show affection for men whose outward life is extrovert, hard-headed, and bonhomous, and which appears to be anchored to a shrewd, no-nonsense practicality of thought and feeling. John Bull perhaps best sums up, for the English, the values of uncomplicated opulence and simple shrewdness – the results of a steady application of good sense. He is a sort of ideal businessman, arriving, through astuteness, at a position where he can hobnob with all-comers without losing a down-to-earth grasp of the facts of existence. If you substitute Falstaff for John Bull, all you need to add is an amazing way with words. Such a man has irresistible attractions for a race that prides itself in calling a spade a spade. He has a cunning penchant for self-preservation, a habit of always turning up on the leeward side of the law, an ability to collect satellite minions about him, immense in appetite and with an enviable verbal dexterity. He epitomizes the ideal material man, exciting sympathy, because his personality seems a pattern for all material men, and reverence, because it is displayed with such largesse. He is an embodiment of that curious optimism by which material men live – wit, audacity, cheek, and expediency will see them through, they believe, anything. They do not have to be like Macawber and wait for things to turn up: while they remain cheerful and confident they make things turn up.

But such men are vulnerable and liable to self-pity. They try to obliterate age, mutability and death by a constant use of all their powers. Intimations of these enemies make them immediately pathetic:

> 'Peace good Doll! Do not speak like a death's head; do not bid me
> remember mine end.'   [2H.II.4.224–5]

Hal's rejection of Falstaff has become symbolic of the kind of treachery which material men feel is likely to be inflicted by an ingrate world. It is called inexcusable, but often for reasons unconnected with the play itself. The logic of history means nothing to the Falstaff-idolator. They see his dismissal as a cowardly removal of 'a great guy'. For them it is as if the boss has sacked the life and soul of the party for spite; it does not matter that he is capable of wrecking not only the party but the firm as well.

If Falstaff has become the embodiment of what is called the English comic spirit, it is because, to the English, he represents, in an exaggerated way, the best of the English character. J.B. Priestley's masterly essay 'In Praise of Falstaff' typifies the English attitude to this archetypal god.[12] Hal, to Priestley, is no gentleman; his heart and mind are smaller than Falstaff's. The fat knight loves Hal but gets nothing in return. The prince goes on to Agincourt, becomes a 'popular hero', a 'figure for patriots in a noisy mood'. Falstaff, also, goes to his own Olympus:

> Whenever the choice spirits of this world have put the day's work out of their minds and have seated themselves at the table of good fellowship and humour, there has been an honoured place at the board for Sir John Falstaff, in whose gigantic shadow we can laugh at this life and laugh at ourselves, and so, divinely careless, sit like gods for an hour.

The Falstaff who exists as a character in the play of *Henry IV*, however, requires a less emotional approach. The most significant thing about him is that he has many acquaintances but no real friends. His minions, Bardolph, Nym, Pistol, Quickly and Tearsheet, are his victims rather than anything else. They are attracted to him like moths to a flame, circling about him in the hope of advancement. Pistol's quick gallop to Shallow's place in Gloucestershire with the news of Hal's accession is the action of a man who does not want to lose the main chance. Mistress Quickly's access of tears upon the departure of Falstaff to the wars is the action of a sentimental woman. Falstaff's presence in her tavern house, at least, gives it a rowdy status. His departure is the end of a shoddy glory and, in any case, she is disposed, being what she is, to weep upon departures. Shallow swells like a greedy sparrow in Falstaff's presence, not through affection but, first, because of that pride in association (Sir John Falstaff, hobnobber with royalty, and London man to boot) and second, like the rest, in hope of advancement. Falstaff dislikes Prince John and is disliked by him. The Lord Chief Justice knows him for what he is – king of a world of commodity. The relationships of such a man depend more on head and pocket than on blood and heart.

It is the much maligned (by the critics) Hal who, alone, shows most warmth and affection to Falstaff. Priestley says that Falstaff loves Hal and that his heart is 'fractured and corroborate' because of the rejection of that love. Wherein, however, does Falstaff's love lie? At no point in the play is there any truth or firm suggestion that Falstaff's relationship with Hal is, on his side, based on more than pride and avaricious expectation. When we first see them together Falstaff is in great good humour and harps about what changes, to his advantage, will occur when Hal becomes king:

> 'Marry then, sweet wag, when thou art king, let not us that are
> squires of the night's body be called thieves of the day's beauty;'
> [1H.I.2.22–4]

The phrase (or its equivalent) 'when thou art king' rings through the early scenes of Part I like hard cash. He eagerly accepts acting Hal's father in the joking game, but in order to ingratiate himself:

> '. . . there is virtue in that Falstaff; him keep with, the rest banish.'
> [1H.II.4.414–5]

If it seems critically fastidious thus to judge a speech in a scene which has much comic atmosphere and intention, it is well to recall that Falstaff himself is not merely playing a game. When Falstaff says at the end of Act II Scene 4:

> 'Banish not him thy Harry's company. Banish plump Jack, and
> banish all the world.'

Hal replies:

> 'I do, I will.' [1H.II.4.461–4]

Despite the fact that the Sheriff's men are at the door, and everyone else is preparing to leave, Falstaff will not let go. He cries:

> 'I have much to say on behalf of that Falstaff.'

Even when the hostess announces that the Sheriff is come to search the place, Falstaff does not hear her. He is too concerned to get a satisfactory answer from Hal:

> 'Dost thou hear, Hal? Never call a true piece of gold a counterfeit.'
> [1H.II.4.474–5]

Throughout the play self-aggrandisement, commodity, dominate both his relationship with Hal and that with his minions. He is at his height of apparent triumph when visiting Shallow. Preferment is just around the corner but he still has eyes upon any material chance that presents itself, and he has a clear idea of what he can do with Master Shallow:

> 'I have him already temp'ring between my finger and my thumb, and
> shortly will I seal with him.' [2H.IV.3.127–8]

In contrast to Falstaff's sense of human relationship is Hal's hard but honest procedure. On the strictly personal level, he displays a far greater unselfishness than does his giant acquaintance. He sees that the stolen money from Gadshill is returned; he protects Falstaff from the authorities; he is tolerant to Falstaff's assumption of the responsibility for Hotspur's death; his speech over the apparently dead Falstaff has a direct honesty in it:

'What old acquaintance! Could not all this flesh
Keep in a little life? Poor Jack, farewell!
I could have better spar'd a better man:'   [1H.V.4.102–4]

He does not pretend more than he says and takes Falstaff as he is, matching trickery with harmless fun and, in doing so, displays a remarkable tolerance and affection. Hazlitt's comment: 'The truth is, that we could never forgive the Prince's treatment of Falstaff' speaks for multitudes. Yet within the world of the play there are two factors concerning this that must be noted. The first is that Hal has not only made it clear to Falstaff that rejection will come, but it should be clear to the audience that it is necessary in order to fulfil a purpose which, whether one likes it or not, goes beyond his own or Falstaff's mere personal status. The second is that Falstaff as close intimate of King Henry V would have been disastrous. We must in this respect read the play in the Elizabethan context, which was sensitive about anarchy, chaos and order. William Empson makes this point: 'Falstaff's expectations were enormous ... the terrible sentence "The laws of England are at my commandment, and woe to my Lord Chief Justice" meant something so practical to the audience that they may actually have stopped cracking nuts to hear what happened next ...'[13] This remains true whether one accepts Falstaff on a realistic or a symbolic level. Whether he be mere Fat Knight or Vice or Lord of Misrule, somewhere he has to end; even a Lord of Misrule must have a stop to his reign, for it is nature's law that carnivals must end.

Yet, however much a cool summation of the fat knight reduces him from national mythology to not altogether likeable old codger (and there are a few who find him just that), even his detractors find this man, whom reason can minimize, growing in the mind as if by some mysterious process of self-generation. If you do not stay to praise him, at the very least you are compelled to laugh with him. The truth of the matter is that Falstaff, as he exists in the play, hardly has a character at all. It is possible, certainly, to summarize what he does, and it is justifiable to say that he does such and such because he is a man of commodity. Yet this does not take us very far, and one realizes that in terms of the psychology of character, there is very little further that one can go. Falstaff changes only his mood; for the rest he is the same at the end as he is at the beginning. We do not receive even those darting little insights into the inside of character that we are given of some of the minor characters. His wit is a superb series of generalizations; his cowardice is a plain fact; his lying is an inevitable foible, his very pathos is predictable. What, indeed, makes even his detractors pause, is something that comes from outside Falstaff, something over which he has no control, for when one tries to turn him loose into the real world, Falstaff trundles away, fugitive. His status, as a kind of national emblem, is dependent on the fact that he is an image – for some an ideal one. He represents what many audacious men might wish to be. However often one might be inclined, at a robust party, to see Falstaff in the fat extrovert across the room, the inclination fades, not because Falstaff is larger than life – for all great dramatic creations are that – but because none of Falstaff's characteristics add up to a sense of reality. Even those critics disposed to see Falstaff as real are prone to slip into their appraisals intimations of unreality. Thus Priestley refers to him as 'a test of our sense of humour'. Bradley writes of him as 'the bliss of freedom gained in humour'.[14] The truth is that Falstaff is not so much witty as the embodiment of Wit, not so much cowardly as the embodiment of Cowardice, not so much a liar as the embodiment of Falsehood. Situations are set up for him. If quick-wittedness is to be displayed, we have:

> 'By the lord, I knew ye as well as he that made ye. Why hear you, my masters: was it for me to kill the heir apparent?'   [1H.II.4.259–61]

Expedient cowardice is to hide its face –

> '... Give you a reason on compulsion! If reasons were as plentiful as blackberries, I would give no man a reason upon compulsion, I.'
> [1H.II.4.231–3]

If the slippery talent of lying is to have its say, Falstaff is there, the large puppet of his creator's limitless deviousness of invention, pat upon his cue:

> What, art thou mad? art thou mad? Is not truth the truth?
> [1H.II.4.222–3]

Falstaff's position in these plays, however, is also important for thematic reasons. He embodies all the undoubtedly attractive qualities which the material world offers. In fulfilling this role he enables Hal to learn that kingship and commonwealth do not exist upon abstractions, upon ceremony alone. Falstaff represents the vitality of day-to-day existence, the unruly comedy of its activities, the curious pathos of its desperate attempts to be more than temporary. This was the world in which many Elizabethan Londoners had to live – responding to the calls of appetite with weapons of native wit. Falstaff, the fat knight, became in Shakespeare's lifetime a popular figure, not because he bestrode the stage as a recognizable actuality, but because he summed up the audacious principles and practice by which the deprived, the expedient, and the eternally optimistic sought to live.

There is a danger that the immensity of Falstaff's presence may lure the mind from the dramatic richness of context. For the modern audience, not much concerned with the themes of honour, duty, treachery, usurpation, and divine right, Falstaff has become more important than the issues and themes behind the actions in which he is involved. John Wain puts it thus: 'He is the man we are always hoping to meet in the bar'.[15]

Yet there comes a point in every critical assessment of these plays when the critic realizes with amazement that the tremendous comic inventiveness of the dramatist is far from exhausted by the creation of Falstaff. In their different ways, the Cotswold scenes are as powerfully achieved as the Boar's Head episodes. The stark demi-monde of London life is balanced by the shrewd parochialism of the Cotswolds. In their realism lies proof of Shakespeare's intimate knowledge of country ways. He brings the essential, almost paradoxical, qualities of the countryman's way of thought and feeling to the surface. The sense of generation, of the slow and changing fundamentals of life are here:

> 'Certain, 'tis certain, very sure, very sure; death, as the Psalmist
> saith, is certain to all, all shall die. How a good yoke of bullocks at
> Stamford fair?'   [2H.III.2.35–8]

Here commodity mixes with mutability, and together they induce a sense of pathos which, if it were not mitigated, might become maudlin. The hardening element is the shrewd philosophy of the countryman which, in itself, has two aspects. The first is the eye-to-the-main-chance materialism, an indestructible and sly cupidity, seen, for example, in Justice Shallow's dealings with Falstaff. The second is a kind of pride in status and the presence of apparent status. Shallow is as full of jabbering conceit about his own position as he is about the chance of hobnobbing with the great Sir John – did they not hear the chimes of midnight together? Shallow's comic richness comes from an aspiration for equality with 'greatness' which is at odds with his doddering senility:

> 'The same Sir John, the very same . . . Jesu, Jesu the mad days that I
> have spent! and to see how many of my old acquaintances are
> dead!' [2H.III.2.27–33]

There is even greater depth, however, to the superb realism of these scenes. Behind Shallow and Silence stand their social inferiors – servants and small tenants. They are not entirely allowed to become the victims of Sir John's gigantic interruption of the even tenor of their lives. The reluctant recruits to his troop have all the deviousness of mind which characterizes the so-called 'simple' peasant when he is confronted with a sophistication which thinks it can triumph over them. Shakespeare does not allow his countrymen to be bested. Falstaff's rugged army is not composed of oafs:

> 'A whoreson cold, sir, a cough, sir, which I caught with ringing in
> the King's affairs upon his coronation day, sir. [2H.III.2.177–9]

Although Falstaff may lord it over the Boar's Head he is not, in the final analysis, the lord of the Cotswolds. He may be fawned upon by Shallow, but his measure is taken by the humble uncommitted servant who comments on Sir John and his company:

> No worse than they are back bitten, sir; for they have marvellous
> foul linen. [2H.V.1.32–4]

Shakespeare's sensitivity to human truth is remarkably displayed here. He does not allow Falstaff to steamroller these people. He preserves on the one hand the largeness of Falstaff's presence but, on the other, allows for the shrewd good sense of these country folk.

This kind of balance is indeed the hallmark of these two histories. It is the balance between general precept and individual practice, between the large vista and the small detail. Falstaff's thematic function is made gloriously credible by his dealings with his fellows; the emblematic significance of Hal, the new order, and Hotspur, the old, is vitalized by their foibles and follies as men. The dark issues separating king and prince finds expression in the poignancy and intimacy of the father/son relationship; and even as a political concept – *Res Publica* – is quickened into reality by the individuals who hobnob in its towns or countryside. *Henry IV*, Parts I and II, certainly constitutes the most comprehensive political and sociological study of a country ever undertaken, not with academic sobriety but with full-blooded and superbly controlled artistry.

Henry V

Henry V,[16] the most optimistic of Shakespeare's history plays, is popular with audiences and regarded with suspicion by some scholars. Its optimistic atmosphere is, to a very large extent, a logical outcome of Shakespeare's treatment of the themes introduced in the two plays of *Henry IV*. In those plays, the curse under which England had lain since the usurpation of Richard II is still in operation. The accession of Hal, untouched by the personal guilt his father feels, put the curse in abeyance, and his reign is allowed to be productive and glorious. We witness the other side of the dark fortunes which had attended England throughout the previous reign. Where rebellion existed there is now amity; where guilt flourished there is now a pious assumption of strong kingship; where the commonweal lacked a sense of identity and unity, all is now one, and kingship freed, if only temporarily, from its bonds of guilt now discovers an almost ideal status. Henry V is a model for a Christian monarch, kind but just, a repository of honour, aware of his duties and responsibilities to his people. He has both a regal colouring and that common touch which allows him easy commerce with high and low. The measure of his assured status is proved by the relationship which his contemporaries are shown to have with him. The church gives spiritual sanction to his military intentions; his nobility join with him in common purpose; the common soldiery find, in him, one who knows them and whom they will trust.

Thus the play is a kind of processional, with the lineaments of a well-designed frieze, which has come to life. The monarch, resplendent in perfection, leads a willing people towards the gates of success, pride, power, and patriotic fervour. It is the atmosphere of a national epic which accounts for its popularity with audiences, making no great intellectual demands, merely asking us to watch and applaud events which strike easily into our hearts. Dover Wilson has caught well the nature of the play's appeal:

> But happening to witness a performance by Frank Benson and his company at Stratford in August or September, 1914, I discovered for the first time what it was all about. The epic drama of Agincourt matched the temper of the moment...[17]

It is not without significance that towards the end of the Second World War the play was successfully filmed by Laurence Olivier. Its success was not entirely due to Olivier's brilliant solution of the many problems attached to translation from stage to celluloid. It appeared at a penultimate time in the war, when, after sacrifice and deprivation, there was an overwhelming sense in the Western world that evil forces were near defeat. In England there was a strong sense that duty and patriotic determination had, once again, achieved victory and glory. The common soldier of the play – Bates – and his confrères were easily identifiable with what the English take to be typical of their common soldiery – men given to complaint, argumentative, no respectors of persons, but with stout hearts of oak; and the victory of the rugged few at Agincourt was easily identified with that classic tradition that England always fights best against odds. The ageing politician and leader, Churchill, knew, as did Henry, that leadership must have style. He couched his sentiments in words that crossed the boundaries of age and class:

> This is no war of chieftains or of princes, of dynasties or national
> ambition; it is a war of peoples and of causes. There are vast
> numbers, not only in this island, who will render faithful service in
> this war but whose names will never be known, whose deeds will
> never be recorded. This is a war of the Unknown Warriors; but let all
> strive without failing in faith or in duty, and the dark curse of Hitler
> will be lifted from our age.[18]

A similar spirit pervades many of Henry's speeches:

> '... And you, good yeomen,
> Whose limbs were made in England, show us here
> The mettle of your pasture; let us swear
> That you are worth your breeding – which I doubt not;
> For there is none of you so mean and base
> That hath not noble lustre in your eyes.'　　　　　　[III.2.25–30]

Both speeches are rhetorical in the grand manner. They are self-consciously stylish. They eschew particulars and make simple but potent emotional demands upon their audiences. Each has the voice of the individual who speaks, and of the collective, usually inarticulate, spirit of a whole people.

The atmosphere of this play and the style of its protagonist, has led some scholars, however, to disapprove of it. Barrett Wendell's comment well represents the basis of this scholarly attitude:[19]

> In the honestly canting moods which we of America inherit with our
> British blood we gravely admire *Henry V* because we feel sure that

we ought to. In more normally human moods, most of us would be forced to confess that, at least as a play, *Henry V* is tiresome.

The play has been called jingoistic and its hero priggish; its lack of intellectual depth has made it to be compared unfavourably with other, less popular, plays by Shakespeare. It appears, however, that judgment of it depends to a large extent on factors external to it, particularly individual political and social beliefs. The internationalist finds it reactionary, contemplative men find it superficial, socialists find it élitist, pacifists find it disgusting. In fact, *Henry V* celebrates the events and the feelings which embrace a nation in one of those moments of history when a nation feels it natural to think proudly of itself as a corporate whole – any jingoism it has is more the result of spontaneous pride than of calculated principle. The preparation for the kind of king Henry V is to be has been carefully made and presented to us:

'The breath no sooner left his father's body
But that his wildness, mortified in him,
Seem'd to die too; yea, at that very moment,
Consideration like an angel came
And whipped th' offending Adam out of him,
Leaving his body as a paradise,
T' envelop and contain celestial spirits.'   [1.1.25–31]

Certainly when we see Henry at the beginning of this play all doubts have gone – he is in unquestioned majesty. What now remains is the palpable proof of his status as great king which the play is to unfold, and which will confirm Hal's melodramatically-expressed intention at the beginning of *Henry IV, Part I* to surprise by reform. There is an air of relaxed and confident expectation at the play's beginning which is given some piquancy by the long speeches of the two ecclesiastics. Nowadays it is difficult to accept their long essays into legal niceties without a smile, yet it is essential that what they have to say about Henry's claims and the Sallic law should be taken seriously, as indeed the Elizabethans did. For them, the speeches would not have been taken as semi-comic pedantics, muttered and sipped by two ageing clerics. The Elizabethans were sensitive to matters concerning right and succession, and less impatient of listening to the rolling logic of unquestioned authorities than we are. More important, Henry's claim was regarded as historically justified. If the clerics' speeches are disregarded then Henry's adventures in France must be seen as an illegal act and, as a result, the play's patriotism and pride, its picture of a unified nation, can only be seen as a bad and cynical joke. As Arthur Humphreys says:[20]

> The Archbishop's prominence and Henry's earnest injunctions to him 'justly and religiously' to state the case are meant as proof that the claim is lawful and French resistance to it unlawful, so that by contumacy France provokes an 'impious war' not only against her rightful sovereign but against God, the source of royal authority.

In short, for Shakespeare's dramatic and thematic purpose, Henry must not only be, but be seen to be, the true image of a Christian king.

Throughout the play a sense of ordered legality about actions that are taken is emphasized. The judgment on the three traitors at Southampton cannot be regarded merely as an emblematic clearing up of one dark corner in an otherwise consenting kingdom. It has other implications. The story of Henry V was well known, and the conspiracy of Cambridge, Scroop, and Grey was accepted as having happened in fact. For many in the audience knowing this history this episode would have a special meaning. For those who did not the scene would have the general effect of reminding them of the frequent threats by traitors to their own monarch's life and it is worth remembering that Shakespeare emphasizes that the judgment on them is the result of the application of a severe but fair law which the traitors themselves had appealed to.

The sense of an utter correctness of behaviour by this royal Henry is intensified by his Christian piety. His decision to enter France is approved by law, and furthered by invoking the blessing of God. The intercession and approval of the Almighty is sought many times in the play, not least in those speeches where Henry questions himself and speculates upon the duties and responsibilities of kingship. The scene with the common soldiers before Agincourt gives us perhaps the most intimate and warm experience of this, when Henry steps out of the image of Christian king and is revealed in confrontation with his maker:

> 'O, not today, think not upon the fault
> My father made in compassing the crown!'   [IV.1.289–90]

This king's piety is not a simple dedication to the will of God nor a jingoistic assumption of God's blessing, for it has within it a powerful penitential motive – Henry is not, as some critics would have him, the cold hero who, by military prowess, restores England's fortunes;

his actions are a conscious penance – he leads his people to glory and, he hopes, expiation:

> '. . . More will I do:
> Though all that I can do is nothing worth,
> Since that my penitence comes after all,
> Imploring pardon.'   [IV.1.298–301]

The play, in its concentration on the legal correctitude of royal action and on the sanction of the Almighty, mirrors an order encompassing both the kingdom of heaven and of earth. It sharply contrasts with disorder in *Henry VI*, *Richard III* and, to a lesser extent, *Henry IV*. In this play there are no references to malevolent stars, no hints that the planets wander in disarray. Such references would be superfluous, almost blasphemous, since God now smiling upon England has chosen to direct her path towards order and unity. The play takes its place in the continuing design of Shakespeare's history plays:

> 'Oh God, thy arm was here!
> And not to us, but to thy arm alone,
> Ascribe we all.'   [IV.7.104–6]

It is also a logical continuation of the *Henry IV* plays in another respect. Quite clearly, Henry V is an older and wiser Prince Hal. The prince's education into kingship, self-imposed, is now complete, the play being, so to speak, his graduation ceremony. One of its most certain aspects is the emphasis on the fact of Hal's 'reformation' from wild boy to glorious king which emerges, not only in the general celebrative atmosphere of the play, but in the references made to the King himself. The completeness of his reformation is affirmed by both speeches and imagery:

> 'A largess universal, like the sun.'   [4.Prol.43]
> 'Never was monarch better fear'd and lov'd
> than is your Majesty.'   [II.2.25–6]
> 'A little touch of Harry in the night.'   [4.Prol.47]

Hal's education in *Henry IV* had involved the rejection of two mentors, his father and Falstaff. His succession involves a return to a royal status different from that inhabited by his father or envisaged by Falstaff. His occupancy of the throne is based on a knowledge which he has learned from both, and it necessarily involves the rejection of both. The play of *Henry V* offers ample evidence of the 'knowing' which Hal has achieved. It is conveyed, for example, with telling force in the speech:

> '... And I know
> 'Tis not the balm, the sceptre, and the ball,
> The sword, the mace, the crown imperial,
> The intertissued row of gold and pearl,
> The farced title running fore the king,
> The throne he sits on, nor the tide of pomp
> That beats upon the high shore of this world –
> No, not all these, thrice gorgeous ceremony,
> Not all these, laid in bed majestical,
> Can sleep so soundly as the wretched slave
> Who, with a body fill'd and vacant mind,
> Gets him to rest, cramm'd with distressful bread.'   [IV.1.255–66]

The 'I know' in these lines is no empty remark. Its existence, taken in conjunction with our knowledge of the Hal of the previous plays, radiates the whole meaning of Hal's words about kingship. Without these words, and our experience of Hal, it is a mere set-piece, typical of those uttered by Shakespeare's kings about the cares of the throne. The 'I know' makes all Hal's words simply but profoundly factual.

The comprehensiveness of this new kind of kingship is proved by Henry's ability to talk naturally with his common soldiers. Words like 'honour', and 'duty', which exist in the previous histories as mere abstractions, have a different status in this play because they are proved by experience and action. Henry's duties as king are not merely clearly defined but shown in action. Honour emerges in the depiction of Henry's high standard of honesty, right judgment, and nobility of mind, when dealing equally with high and low born. Duty and responsibility are embodied in the care which Henry has for his subjects and in his ability to question his own motives for action.

Yet Henry is not merely a flawless embodiment of the ideal king for there seems to be a calculating quality in the man. The first scene of the play is the best example of this. It is implicit that Henry is determined to go to France whatever the legal conclusions of the bishops. It is true also, as Derek Traversi says, that 'he has a willingness to shift the responsibility upon others, to use their connivance to obtain the justification which he continually, insistent-ly requires'.[21]

For the actor, however, there is sufficient textual justification to interpret Henry as something of a young *eminence grise* who bends (as in the wooing of Kate) only with difficulty towards a relaxation of will and purpose. There are elements in his character, however, which mitigate this impression of inflexibility, and although Henry may be

117

an older and wiser Hal, there is still something of the younger man left in him. Naturally in *Henry V* Shakespeare took care to disperse the long shadows from *Henry IV*. Falstaff in *Henry V* is mere nostalgia and when the master goes, the rest very quickly become expendable. It is important, however, to note how they are despatched. Bardolph is hanged, Nym disappears, Poins never appears, and Pistol, though more sharply characterized, is relegated from bombast to cutpurse, for without the presence of Falstaff the comedy in him cannot swell – it is thin and circumscribed. The conclusion cannot be escaped that the remnants of the Boar's Head are deliberately cleared away, and are seen to be cleared away, so that no suspicion of a connection of the old order with the new Hal may be entertained.

But the assumption that it is Henry V himself who clears away these remnants of the old life is wrong. It is Shakespeare who wills them away for his own dramatic purposes. And, lest what is left seems unremittingly perfect, Shakespeare replaces the attractive but corruptive comedy of the Boar's Head by the affirmative comedy of Fluellen. This kind of comedy, based on generalizations – the stock Welshman, and his stock Welsh accent – is safe, warm and, in the long run, good-natured.

Even more important, however, is Henry's response to Fluellen's presence. In all Hal's dealings with his countrymen, we are made aware of a playfulness of spirit and in Henry V we recognize something of the younger prince still lurking in the older king. In fact, both the wooing of Kate and the relationship with Fluellen are so contrived as to humanize Henry, and if in performance they are minimized or distorted, the charge of priggishness may stand. Their very existence and the emphasis on them not only negates that charge but positively affirms the kind of king Hal educated himself to be – total king – not merely in all the appurtenances of kingship and majesty but in human response as well.

Concentration on Shakespeare's working out of a pattern which has its genesis in *Henry IV* tends to bend the mind towards the English world of the play to the exclusion of the French. There is, however, remarkable dramatic balance in the overall design of the play. The French scenes and the French characters are among some of his best creations of this period in his working life, and his main achievement was to satisfy his audience's contempt for the hated and decadent French without losing a hold on credibility. The French are individualized with remarkable and economic skill. The Dauphin is dangerous and self-indulgent, the Constable a cynical realist, the King fearful and feeble. Even the French Herald is strongly outlined. He is a model of duty and courtesy and is also a wry emblem of an old order which is to receive its death blow at Agincourt. Together these men create a picture in depth. The French world is not set up as a mere 'Aunt Sally' for the glorification of England; it exists as a dramatic entity in its own right; its posture as victim has an intensely real as well as a thematically inevitable quality. Shakespeare's manipulation of the French and English worlds goes beyond simple contrast. There is nothing mechanical about the manner in which he depicts the virtues of the one and the weakness of the other, and the two scenes before the battle of Agincourt are a telling example of subtlety of dramatic grasp. What deepens the general contrast between the atmosphere of the two camps is the absence of French common soldiery. This places the French nobility in a position of curious isolation whereas Henry is seen as gathering about him a small but affirmative fellowship. This not only heightens the dramatic effect but also emphasizes the difference between a complete and an incomplete Commonwealth. In the long run what we are shown in the juxtaposition of English and French worlds before the battle is the difference between virile youth and crabbed age, between a new dynamic politico-military order and one that is old and outworn.

Henry V was the last (save for the doubted *Henry VIII*) English history play to be written by Shakespeare. His long committal to English history ends with such a grand flourish that it is tempting to believe that he had decided that it was time to cease his wrestlings with a mode that had occupied him for so long. By comparison with the other histories the play lacks dramatic abrasiveness, irony, and tragic implications. The cynic might observe that for Shakespeare English history, having gone through hell, ends not in heaven so much as at a mighty fête. But within the large series, its themes have a logical and natural place and that, in itself, suggests a far greater dramatic completeness than perhaps its detractors allow.

The Merry Wives of Windsor

A ghost of Falstaff appears in *The Merry Wives of Windsor*. General critical opinion of the play – that it is a happy trifle – is bedevilled by the nature of this ghost. The Falstaff of Windsor Park is not the Falstaff of Gadshill, the Boar's Head, and Shrewsbury clock. By comparison, he is 'bated' and has dwindled away. Commentators seem reluctant to accept the play at its face value – a clever piece of light entertainment – because they seem nostalgic for a man who once reigned like an emperor and now does not. Others seem put off by the fact that this is the only comedy in the canon whose action takes place specifically in England, and concerns itself almost exclusively with virile middle-class tradespeople. It is as if there is a reluctance to believe that Shakespeare was capable of 'stepping down', both in his depiction of Falstaff and in his use of a social class which is conspicuously absent from the rest of his plays. Georg Brandes, writing of the necessity to entertain the Queen and her court at Windsor, refers, somewhat haughtily, to the amused pleasure the monarch had in catching a glimpse of a class so remote from her own, adding that as a result it 'became more prosaic and bourgeois than any other play of Shakespeare's'.[22] He does, however, draw attention to the fairy dance and song at the end of the play and suggests that Shakespeare 'found it impossible to content himself with thus dwelling on the common earth'.

But there are other intriguing facets to this play. One is the occasion of its first performance; another is the possibility of hidden biographical details, and a third is the depiction of the Welshman, Sir Hugh Evans.

Not only does Peter Alexander write that 'the date 23rd April, 1597 for the first performance of The Merry Wives is probably one of the few dates in the chronology we can be confident about'[23] but Leslie Hotson has also convincingly suggested that it was written for a performance to celebrate the Garter Feast of St George's Day (23 April).[24] On this occasion new knights were inducted into the Garter Order and, following a banquet at Greenwich, their installation took place at Windsor Castle. He further suggests that there is a specific reference to the preparations for the installation in the Fairy Queen's words:

'Each fair instalment, coat, and several crest,
With loyal blazon, ever more be blest!'

120

There may have been a special reason for commissioning Shakespeare to write for the occasion because the patron of his company, The Lord Chamberlain's, was himself received into the Order in 1597. Considerable evidence points to Shakespeare having been asked to write a special play for the occasion.

> 'This comedy was written at her command (the Queen's) and by her direction, and she was so eager to see it acted, that she commanded it to be finished in fourteen days and was afterwards, as tradition tells us, very pleased at the representation.'[25]

As for the possible biographical details it is very tempting to accept the idea that Shakespeare, having been asked to recall Sir John, and casting around for a plot, allowed his mind to wander around the actual place where the celebrations were to take place. The fat knight had to be brought back from his grave to please a Queen, but there were other knights to hand – those to be installed in St George's Chapel. One, in particular, whose graceful estate at Charlecote was a few miles from Henley Street, Stratford-upon-Avon, might very well have come into his memory – Sir Thomas Lucy. In the first scene of the play Shallow enters, says that Falstaff has poached his deer, and refers to his ancestors who bore 'a dozen white luces in their coat'. To which Evans replies:

> 'The dozen white louses do become an old coat well.'   [1.1.16–17]

The pun on 'luce' and 'louse' is obvious enough, the reference to Sir Thomas Lucy, who actually bore Lucy's (pike fish) on his armorial insignia, indirect. And if the story of Shakespeare's deer poaching at Charlecote is true (and though it is unauthenticated, it is feasible) then, in his mind, an association between 'louse' and 'Lucy' would be natural.

The other possible biographical matter centres on Sir Hugh Evans. He has been linked with a Thomas Jenkins who was appointed to the mastership (headship) of the grammar school at Stratford-upon-Avon in 1575. He left the school in 1579 under something of a cloud, and the nineteenth century conjectured that his departure was the result of certain tactless characteristics which Shakespeare memorializes, but mellows, in Sir Hugh. However, little is known of Jenkins, except that he was educated at St John's College, Oxford, and more disappointing to those who wish to perpetuate the connection is the probability that Jenkins was a Londoner.

What can be said with confidence is that the scenes in which Sir Hugh appears are very sharply observed, very like actual memories of a schoolmaster – Welsh or not. Sir Hugh is, without doubt, a pedantic pedagogue. His Welshness, however, may well derive from popular Elizabethan notions of what Welshmen were like. They were regarded as Bible thumpers, shrewd, not to say devious, unless they were watched; they could be conceited in their knowledge (Fluellen gives evidence of this) and were marvellous in their use and misuse of the English language.

The dignified and extrovert religiosity of Sir Hugh, and his disingenuous worldly shrewdness are well drawn in the first scene. Like the important Divine that he believes himself to be, he assumes the status of uncommitted arbiter; like the shrewd Welshman that he is, he keeps his eye on worldly chances:

'I am of the church, and will be glad to do my benevolence, to make atonements and compromises between you.'   [1.1.27–30]

'Ay, and her father is make her a petter penny.'   [1.1.53–4]

He is also given to melancholy and song, two attributes long considered to be inhabitants of the Welsh soul, whilst he never forgets his dignity:

'Pray you, let us not be laughing stocks to other men's humours.'

But the finest of Sir Hugh is seen in the education of his pupil, William. Here, Shakespeare has seized upon the conceit of learning and turned it into superb comic usage:

EVANS: ... What is 'lapis', William?
WILL: A stone.
EVANS: And what is 'a stone', William?
WILL: A pebble.
EVANS: No, it is 'lapis' ...   [IV.1.28–31]

The interplay between Quickly and Sir Hugh in this scene is a fine example of Shakespeare's sharpness of eye for human foibles. Quickly's outraged sensibilities do, in fact, protest themselves too much; overtly she is shown as being no better than she is. Evans's ripostes bespeak the large, flimsy dignity of one who wears his status on his sleeve.

Shakespeare probably did not know the Welsh language, but his ear for the south Welshman speaking English is acute and precise. The tendency to use words for their dramatic effects he seizes upon;

the tendency to drop the initial 'w' is unerringly shown; the absence of the letter 'v' and the occasional habit of using a noun instead of a verb or an adjective – all these, too, he pinpoints, making Evans's speech perhaps nearer actuality than caricature.

Although this play fascinates for its contiguity to Shakespeare's own life and experience of people, in the end, it is the appearance of Falstaff which arouses the deepest interest. He is, in every way, a diminished man and character. The thematic and actual worlds he inhabits seem smaller; his relationship to his surroundings and to others is significant only as a cog in the mechanics of the whole play; his wit lacks the enormous variety, subtlety and point which the old Falstaff commanded. Above all there is no Prince Hal against which he can measure himself, and, in so doing, swell into his own ego. The rag-tag remnants of his former court – Shallow, Bardolph, Pistol, Nym, and Quickly are with him but his relationship to them is now quite put down. His status in the world of *Henry IV* depended on his own large, if fragile, expectations of plenty and some position in the new kingdom. Here those expectations are completely confounded, and this Falstaff is the result. The sycophancy and patience shown by his followers once depended on their hope that he would pull them all into glory and money behind him, but the very first lines of this play show starkly what happens when the star they hitched themselves to declined:

> '. . . if he were twenty Sir John Falstaffs, he shall not abuse Robert
> Shallow, esquire.'   [1.1.3–4]

His first appearance gives some hope that the ghost has something of the old substance left in him:

SHALLOW: Knight, you have beaten my men, kill'd my deer, and
  broke open my lodge.
FLASTAFF: But not kiss'd your keeper's daughter.   [1.1.100–101]

But this is no more than a flash. He cannot control events or people as he used to. The scene at the Garter Inn is small beer compared to the great days at the Boar's Head – the bragadoccio language has a tired edge. What is significant about this scene is Falstaff's open decision to woo Ford's wife so as to get her husband's money. The old Falstaff would, one is assured, have been no less ready to enter a strategem for profit, but he would never have committed himself so explicitly to it; he would have hedged about his intentions, and deployed all the forces of his language, imagination and devious intelligence to make a subterfuge. This ghost, desperate for money, puts his cards upon the table, to be picked up by, of all people, Pistol. Falstaff is become a mere character in a comic intrigue and, as if to emphasize this diminution, Pistol and Nym decide to reveal his plans.

The whole history of Falstaff in this play is of how he is revenged *upon*. This we never see in *Henry IV* (even Hal's revelations about what really happened at Gadshill are turned by Falstaff to advantage), for until the final rejection, Falstaff reigns supreme, precisely because he is not brought to any final challenge. He seems the bigger for this; in this play he seems the smaller, because other people 'consult together against this greasy knight'.

There is no more telling comment on this than Falstaff's own words to Pistol:

> '. . . I myself sometimes, leaving the fear of God on the left hand, and hiding my honour in my necessity, am fain to shuffle, to hedge, and to lurch . . .' [II.2.21–4]

Yet his diminution has another aspect to it. Tremendous visual emphasis is put on his physical discomfiture and he is given no verbal resources to redress the balance. He is placed in a basket, dunked in a river, becoming a figure to whom things are done, a mere agent in a plot line:

> 'I am not able to answer the Welsh flannel . . . use me as you will.' [V.5.155–7]

He *is* used as they will, absorbed mechanically in the play's devious plot and happy resolution. The ghost of the man who 'larded the earth' is invited by Page to 'eat a posset' at his house, to 'laugh at my home, where I will desire thee to laugh at my wife that now laughs at thee'. All are invited 'to laugh this sport o'er by a country fire' by Mrs Page, and she adds 'Sir John and all'. It is as if Shylock had accepted a stern invitation to become a Christian. Like Falstaff, he would have been out of his element.

The iron political and thematic necessities of Shakespeare's *Henry IV* require Falstaff's annihilation; the demands of the plot in *The Merry Wives* require a comic scapegoat. He is, in modern parlance, an all-time loser. In a sense the real death of Falstaff happens when he is asked to sit by the fire and join in laughter and this domestic procedure is mocked by memories of what the other Falstaff would have done with such laughter.

The trading class which defeats Falstaff is one which Shakespeare had never before exploited, on this scale, in his plays. Their reality as a contemporary class in Elizabethan society is more shrewdly revealed by Thomas Dekker and Ben Jonson than by Shakespeare, who avoids any close analysis and concentrates on supplying generalities necessary for the furtherance of the plot. Their morality is straightforward, their humour limited and broad, their intelligence circumscribed, their threshold of tolerance of human foibles not large. The individuals who constitute this class do not give the actor or actress much opportunity for more than broad comic playing, and the situations that surround them are patterned on the quick to-ing and fro-ing of farce. Doors open and close quickly, the arras hides anxious men, swift and ludicrous decisions are constantly being made. All this indeed points to very swift preparation and writing – Shakespeare had no time for niceties of characterization or incident, the main requirement being that the play should be merry.

It is on this point of merriment that one's experience of the play turns. Taken per se, it is a farcical series of episodes in which a biter (Sir John) is bit. It has a mellow and pleasing theatrical conclusion. The 'villain' is brought to heel and finally joins the happy dance and it is not difficult to imagine that first-night audience applauding the antics, hissing the villain, and delighting in the reconciliatory ending, with its acceptable touch of the supernatural world. At the same time one wonders whether there might not have been some, perhaps the Queen among them, who found it difficult to detach the play from their recent memories of the past. Towards the end, Falstaff, shrived of his misdemeanours, is surrounded by those who have defeated him. He turns to Evans and says:

'Have I liv'd to stand at the taunt of one that makes fritters of
English? This is enough to be the decay of lust and late-walking
through the realm.'   [V.5.138–40]

Falstaff, in other days, demolished anyone with his own inspired frittering of the language; he may have lusted for the rewards of commodity, thrived on expectation but, more than anything, he late walked through the realm of England and an heir apparent walked at his side. Any member of any audience who has known and enjoyed that other Falstaff cannot wholeheartedly join in the merriment that this play offers. It may seem heavy-handed when one is faced with a pleasing trifle like this play, to think of richer matters, yet Shakespeare's mind was of a piece, and his creation of Falstaff so strong that we cannot help but see Falstaff all of a piece. He responded to the Queen's demand for a play and diminished Falstaff for her pleasure. She would have been uncharacteristically insensitive if her merriment had not been tinged with sadness.

A Midsummer Night's Dream

If any confirmation were needed of the versatility of Shakespeare's genius in his early days in the London theatre, *A Midsummer Night's Dream* would provide it. It not only stands in sharp thematic and stylistic contrast to the early histories, *The Merchant of Venice* and *The Merry Wives of Windsor*, but it has, within itself, an amazingly disciplined variety of characterization, language, and atmosphere. The realistic eye which informs the creation of the rude mechanicals is matched by the romantic gaze which produces the lyric fantasy of the world of Oberon and Titania, and the inconsequentialities of the two pairs of lovers. Yet the play is all of a piece – the changes of pace, style, and character types are all held within a tender and sensitive grasp; it is a play of love, lovingly written.

Like others of Shakespeare's plays (notably *The Merchant of Venice* and *The Tempest*) its popularity with audiences seems to depend upon a simplification of what, on closer study, seems to be relatively complicated, both structurally and thematically. It has, for example, certain obvious affinities with a fairy story, a fantasy-fable, whose function is simply to lure the mind and affections away from the tribulations of ordinary existence into a world where all will be well and where, by magic, anything is possible.

This is, of course, a simplified image of the play, but its stage history proves the tenacity of an uncomplicated audience-acceptance. Thomas Betterton's version in 1692 retitled it *The Fairy Queen* and added music by Purcell. David Garrick vamped it into a 'new English opera' in 1755, called it *The Fairies* and introduced twenty-eight songs. When Ellen Terry (1847–1928) was eight years old she appeared as Puck, and made her first entrance from a trapdoor while seated on an artificial mushroom. In 1929 Harcourt Williams's production at The Old Vic introduced specially written folk tunes and dressed its fairies in imitation seaweed. Robert Helpmann danced his way through the character of Oberon and, as late at 1959, Peter Hall, though he attempted to modernize the lovers' comedy, somehow contrived to imitate nineteenth-century opulence with his gauze-shrouded set and woodland. Moreover, through the centuries, versions have threaded golden notes of sound to complete the fantastic pattern. Mendelssohn who, over seventeen years, was captivated by the play and wrote, in that period, various parts of his incidental music, is perhaps the most celebrated of many who have embroidered the play. John Smith wrote incidental music in 1755; Louis Spohr made an opera of it in 1826; Hugo Wolf wrote songs for it in 1881 and in 1960 Benjamin Britten was inspired to compose his celebrated operatic version.

The play has held, then, for audiences, the status of fantasy and magic, spiced, but never drenched, with the comedy of the very English mechanicals. There has, however, recently been evidence of a reaction to this traditional treatment of the play typified, perhaps, by Peter Brook's sensational employment of it as a theatrical exercise for the exploration of the relationship of illusion and reality (R.S.T. 1970). The mode for what was termed 'sharp satire' in both television and stage entertainment in the mid-1960s affected other productions. The fairy world became mocking, the lovers were 'modernized' by a studied avoidance of cadence in speaking, and by a glib assumption of contemporary gestures. In varying degrees, the play was used, as it were, to guy itself. This production would, in itself, merit much notice were it not for the fact that it was indicative, first, of the general movement towards the 'contemporising' of Shakespeare in the 1960s and, second, of the vulnerability of this particular play to mockery. *A Midsummer Night's Dream* requires a most sensitive style of interpretation and acting to preserve the quite fragile thematic balance. The Director who decides to 'style' it from any single one of its apparently separate ingredients (the court or the fairy world or Bottom's world) is doomed to fracture its delicacy of structure. The problem is to apprehend and to hold on to its persistent thematic tone which has different appearances and emphases in the various revealed worlds of the play, informing them all and, in the end, unifying them. And the basis of any claim that the play is more than mere fairy tale stuff lies in the nature of this unifying force.

Indeed, some modern critics have sought to identify the thematic heart of the play in terms which might seem to neglect the Elizabethan reality of the work. Jan Kott, for example, finds a hideous and dark symbolism in it: 'The Dream is the most erotic of Shakespeare's plays. In no other tragedy or comedy of his, except Troilus and Cressida, is the eroticism expressed so brutally.'[26] With a ferocious sincerity he has allowed a twentieth-century partisan outlook to denude the play of the one quality which commends it – its ability to please, to content.

The occasion considered as most likely for the play's first performance is generally accepted as either the wedding of Elizabeth Vere, the daughter of the Earl of Oxford, to the Earl of Derby, in

January, 1595 or the marriage of Thomas Berkeley and Elizabeth Carey at Blackfriars, 19 February, 1596. Its creation for a particular ceremony would seem to justify the conclusion that it was intended as no more than light entertainment. Indeed the narrative line and the ending, where the world of lovers is blessed by a fairy world whose own master and mistress have themselves rediscovered their own love for each other, could be taken to reflect the style and atmosphere of its first audience. There is also a strong element of ceremonial, both in the action and in the self-conscious ritual of some of the language. Some commentators, however, believe firmly that it was always intended for public performance, and instance, to support their belief, the presence of Bottom and his fellows.

The nub, as so often in these matters, is the date of composition. Its place in the canon is uncertain, though it is generally regarded as being later than the early comedies but predating *Romeo and Juliet*. A quarto version appeared in 1600 but the consensus of opinion is that it was completed in 1594. No direct source has been discovered; this might be taken to support the idea that Shakespeare, faced with a special occasion, relied on his own invention. The play bears little signs of haste in the writing, though there is stylistic unevenness, which, however, suggests rewriting rather than hasty composition.

Although no direct source has been discovered, Shakespeare certainly drew on his knowledge of a number of books. The complicated wooing tale was a convention of Italian comedy; the story of Theseus and Hippolyta is found in Chaucer's *The Knight's Tale*; there is a version of the life of Theseus in North's translation of Plutarch; Shakespeare's memory of school textbooks may have recalled the story of Pyramus and Thisbe in Ovid's *Metamorphoses*; J. Dover Wilson believes that Bottom's affair with Titania owes something to the story of Cupid and Psyche in Apuleius' *The Golden Ass*.[27] For the rest – the mechanicals and fairies – he need have looked no further than his experience and imagination. All the mechanicals have trade names that Shakespeare could have come across in his native Warwickshire. All the attendant faires are, in their simple functions, closely related to country lore, but it should be emphasized that, in temperament, they are not in line with the commonly accepted beliefs of the time. Fairies were mischievous beings who interfered in human activities, usually to embarrass or to set those activities in disarray, and were often vicious and spiteful. The best known was Robin Goodfellow (Puck) – perhaps more mischievous than evil. Shakespeare has stuck very closely to the conventional and traditional characteristics of Puck but, as if to enhance the happy tenor of his play, has made the lesser fairies if not positively benevolent, at least innocently inoffensive.

The nature and size raises problems about the way in which they were originally staged, and how, nowadays, they should be staged. If the play were written for a private performance at a wedding ceremony, the parts may well have been taken by pages or by children of the nobility. But if the first performance were public, then it is possible that the actors were recruited from the children of the Chapel Royal.[28] The Chapel was officially part of the royal household and consisted, in the 1590s, of twelve children under the supervision of a chaplain as their master and mentor. As early as Henry VI's reign the children had become noted for their singing abilities and, by the sixteenth century, achieved fame for their performing talent in Christmas plays. In the 1570s and 1580s they gave plays in an old converted building at Blackfriars and, at court, are known to have presented Lyly's *Campaspe* (1584) and other of his plays under royal command. Their appearance as fairies in *A Midsummer Night's Dream* would doubtless have delighted an Elizabethan audience; and indeed on those occasions when modern directors have used children, the result has usually been successful.

We are introduced to the play's three worlds in strict order: first, Theseus' Court, then the lower orders, finally Oberon's kingdom. The order is important and seems deliberate. The centre of the action is the court of Theseus; his marriage has priority and it is right that we should be introduced to this centre at the outset. What occurs there gives a hint of darkness to the action – Hermia and Lysander are placed under a threat. The threat is stated simply and anyone accustomed to the conventions of pastoral comedy knows that the threat will be lifted. However, Shakespeare makes doubly sure that the atmosphere of comedy prevails by following the court scene with a glimpse of the uninhibited earthiness of the amateur theatricals. The direction of the play is established, and, more than that, a pleasing and necessary contrast is achieved between conventional sophistication and unconventional realism. Then comes the first fairy scene serving a double purpose. It is both a piquant reflection of the earthly world – even Oberon and Titania have their marital problems – and it implies a happy conclusion by involving the possibility of magic intervention.

These three themes are also remarkable for the fact that there is no sense of sudden and incredible transition from one to another. This natural flow is achieved several ways. Firstly, the forest itself makes a focal point for the action. We learn that the lovers will go to the forest; arriving there before them, we meet the actors, and we remain there to meet the fairies. Secondly, there is a natural connection, between the events we have seen in scene one and what we see in the subsequent two scenes. It is right that we should meet the actors for they 'are thought fit through all Athens to play our interlude before the Duke and the Duchess on his wedding day at night'; it is equally right that we should meet the fairies in this part of the forest for one of the accusations that Oberon hurls at Titania is:

'How canst thou thus, for shame, Titania,
Glance at my credit with Hippolyta,
Knowing I know thy love to Theseus?'   [II.1.74–7]

The situation grows in piquancy as the connections are established – a piquancy that is both delightful and a part of Shakespeare's subtle unifying of the three areas of activity to which we have been severally introduced. A marriage has been arranged, entertainments are planned, and the king and queen of the fairies mutually accuse each other of being in love with the mortals.

It is idle to search the play for depth of characterization; the four lovers are of a piece, with slight variations. They are courtly, well bred, reasonably attractive in personality. Helena, created in the mould of the typical rejected maiden of pastoral romance, is always within reach of tears; Hermia, with more individuality and a stronger will, is a little pert, and is always within reach of a tart remark, having something of Rosalind's independence and a touch of Maria's tongue; Demetrius would sort well with Orlando at his most self indulgent – always within reach of the sighing romantic phrase; Lysander, who knows his own mind and heart, has more spunk and will reach for a conclusion with both hands. Hippolyta, almost all mythological, a true Amazon regal beauty, only just tamed, and still not completely, is eventually humanized by her expression of feminine irritability with Theseus' patience towards the amateur actors.

Bottom is likeable, not merely because he is put in a position with an ass's head where we can laugh at him, but simply because his followers adore him. Without him they are lost; he is the prop and staff of their dithery journey towards the limelight; the acknowledged star-turn of their society. When he returns from his strange adventure, it is like the return of the prodigal – a total triumph. He has come back to his people who need and love him.

131

There can be no doubts about Shakespeare's knowledge of amateur theatricals. The nervous prompter, the star, the confuser of cues, the reluctant heroine, the Armageddon of temperament, are all there. Some commentators have seen in Bottom a satirical portrait of the professional actor, with all his self-indulgences. This may be so but satire in its truest sense involves an element of condemnation and no condemnation is made of these rough and ready men, nor of their leader. They are presented for us to laugh at, but with warmth and affection. The comedy that emerges from their scenes is affirmative in the richest sense of the word – it affirms honest toil, a desire to please, and a horny-handed kind of dignity.

The theatrical episodes are not mere incidents in a story of romantic and supernatural love, for the tender touch which makes all things well for the lovers is also present in Bottom's kingdom. He and his fellows are an inexplicable part of the happy unity.

If the events of Theseus' Court are the focal point of the plot, the meaning of the unity which radiates from the plot is implicit in Theseus' character. He uses such phrases as :

'... everlasting bond of fellowship ...'   [1.1.85]
'How comes this gentle concord in the world
That hatred is so far from jealousy
To sleep by hate, and fear no enmity?'   [IV.1.140–2]
'For never anything can be amiss
When simpleness and duty tender it.'   [V.1.83–4]
'Our sport shall be to take what they mistake;
And what poor duty cannot do, noble respect
Takes it in might, not merit.'   [V.1.90–92]
'If we imagine no worse of them than they of themselves, they may
pass for excellent men.'   [V.1.212–14]

This man is by way of being a philosopher and his thought is all bent actively towards one purpose – to achieve an honest conjunction of hearts and minds in his domain. He is a true law-giver abiding by law in saying that Hermia must accept her father's wishes or suffer the penalty. But he is benevolent and although surprised to find former enmities have dissipated he is content when he sees the four lovers together and knows that amity has been achieved. He chides Hippolyta's impatience at what are for her the longeurs of the Pyramus and Thisbe play:

The best in this kind are but shadows; and the worst are no worse, if
imagination amend them.   [V.1.209–11]

If one were to search for an image to embody the meaning of Theseus' presence in the play, it might be found in some stage business in the Royal Shakespeare Theatre production of 1961. Bottom, as Pyramus, had given his greatest performance; the entertainment was ended; Bottom stood triumphant and flushed. In his ecstasy he dropped his ludicrous wooden sword; it lay between him and Theseus. There was a pause. The duke bent, picked it up, laid it in a graceful and chivalrous gesture across his left arm and, with a bow, presented it to Bottom. Their eyes met for a moment. In that moment there was a 'gentle concord in the world' so that class, status, even occasion was forgotten. Two people met and understood. It was a kind of loving.

If there is one generalization, which few would deny, about Shakespeare's dramatic work, it is that it was written by a man who had a detestation of disorder and chaos and a consequent obsession for bringing together dissident people and attitudes. 'Only connect' is a useful phrase to describe what seems to be Shakespeare's personal aspiration for mankind. At times this aspiration is specifically embodied in characters who, in varying degrees, seem to see more, understand more, than is seen or understood by those around them. The duke in *Measure for Measure* is such a man, Ulysses in *Troilus and Cressida* (explicitly lauding the virtues of order) is another. Prospero, above all, fits so closely that there have been persistent attempts to identify the character with Shakespeare himself – as if the image finally merged with reality. To an extent Theseus belongs to this company, embodying and making more explicit the play's drive towards a sense of unity and reconciliation. His mind is open to be convinced and persuaded – to this extent he is a rational man. He gives the impression of possessing a wisdom denied to others – to this extent he is a civilized man. he is a kind of statesman of the human heart and his 'philosophical' comments, his stern but fair conception of legality, and his treatment of the mechanicals, all underline the play's quest for a happy unity. Through Theseus the play's meaning is made clear. Human happiness can only be achieved by vigilance, to see that people's imaginations and intelligences are open, charitably, towards others. The lovers learn that to achieve happiness they need mutual understanding and tolerance; the mechanicals achieve their hearts' desire – to be successful before their duke – because he is willing to accept them for the goodness of their intentions. The transfiguration of all concerned is completed in the last scene, when the house and its occupants are blessed by the fairy world. Oberon's speech celebrates the new found concord:

'Now, until the break of day,
Through this house each fairy stray.
To the best bride-bed will we,
Which by us shall blessed be;
And the issue there create
Ever shall be fortunate.
So shall all the couples three
Ever true in loving be;
And the blots of Nature's hand
Shall not in their issue stand;'   [V.1.390-9]

The language of the play is a further expression of the aspiration for concord. It is useless to search for a single style in the play, and yet the final impression is that a single style is present. The word 'lyrical' covers a multitude of effects – both laudable and unworthy – and it has been employed over and over again to describe the language. The truth is that so potent is the play's drive towards concord that we believe its language to be all of a piece – a kind of rhythmic singing – this is not so. Bottom, Puck, Hermia, Oberon, for example, all speak very differently. Bottom's words invoke the unflighted prose of his mind and status; Puck's tinkling rhyme embodies the staccato magic of his existence; Hermia's insistent and mechanical liturgy bespeaks the conventional behaviour of the modest romantic heroine; Oberon's wide-ranging music takes us out of time, charms us to accept the magic world. All are examples of the amazing variety of style in the language of the play. What gives us the sense of one single style is the theme itself, and the insistent charm of the language (whatever form it may take in different speakers) which contains one basic element – a patina of happy optimism. In the long run, *A Midsummer Night's Dream*, written at a time when his career was beginning to glow with success, is perhaps Shakespeare's happiest, most concordant, play.

Romeo and Juliet

The popularity of *Romeo and Juliet* is easily explained – it is a tragedy of love. Romantic love, whether it be in the comic or tragic mode, is a constant attraction to the playgoer. The theme of this play which relates the defiance, by two young people, of accepted conventions of behaviour and of the animosity between their elders, makes a direct appeal to a natural human desire to break out of the constrictions of centuries of accepted behaviour. It matters little to audiences whether, in plays of romantic love, the relationship between the lovers is finally successfully achieved (a comic affirmation) or if it be consummated only to be finally broken (the tragic pathos); the actual process of love and loving under conditions of stress and opposition induces a strong sense of identification between the audience and the fictional participants. The comic version produces a state of happy nostalgia for personal opportunities that may not have been taken; the tragic version raises up the pathetic feeling: 'There, but for the grace of God, go I'.

Romantic tragedy, in particular, incites identification because its ingredients can be easily correlated with basic human imaginative experience. Love is celebrated (certainly in this play) through words which are worthy of the subject but, more important, those words give expression to passions which are common to human experience, voicing what most have felt but have found inexpressible. Moreover, the play catches the heart of love at that time of life when its effects are felt most keenly. Adolescent love is self-indulgent, reckless and, to the onlooker, frequently poignant. Those who experience it find it totally absorbing, and any bar to its full expression overwhelmingly great and unbearable. It is experienced at such a pitch of involvement that both its joys and despairs are immense – one kiss describes eternal joy, one slight signals total disaster. *Romeo and Juliet* has all this, but it carries the matter one stage further, for here the odds against young love are too high; what is a melodramatic possibility becomes a reality and these two lovers become, for the sympathetic beholder, sacrifices whose memories are constantly to be worshipped. Despite, perhaps because of, the doom which descends upon Romeo and Juliet, the very intensity of their discovery of each other is an affirmation of love itself:

> Though lovers be lost, love shall not,
> And Death shall have no dominion.[29]

However, this play is very different from Shakespeare's four major plays in this mode and perhaps does not measure up to what is tacitly accepted as the ultimate tragic experience as presented there. Those four plays (*Hamlet, Othello, King Lear* and *Macbeth*) invite us to associate the highest tragic experience with the working-out of the destiny of one dominant hero protagonist. This play is not dominated by the hero. It does not present in either of its main characters a flaw of personality which is played upon to incite the final catastrophe; and, although Fate is present, it emerges too mechanistically, making the catastrophe seem less inevitable than avoidable. Of these ingredients, the existence and status of a major male protagonist is of vital importance. The loneliness, the fight against fate, the descent towards ruin are the factors which, above all, create the fabric of great tragedy. Romeo and Juliet share a destiny – although they die they are, like Juliet's beauty, not conquered. They lie for ever together in a silent but total love and tragic tension is, as it were, loosened *because* they are allowed to share eternity with each other. They lose, in being together, that final crown of loneliness which makes the great tragic protagonists at one and the same time pitiably small and defiantly large. It has often been said that Mercutio's virile presence in the play is curtailed (necessarily so) by Shakespeare, since his vivacity and realism of outlook threatens any sympathies we may have for Romeo. What is most striking about Mercutio is, however, the effect of his solitary death upon us in the audience for it strikes more shockingly into our hearts than does that of the two lovers. Their death gives us a long regret, his wounds with savage intensity. More to the point, their death is romantically logistical, his seems an ironic waste. Mercutio is early established as a credible, active personality (more so perhaps than Romeo), but, more important, there is a curious quality of isolation about him. He is a loner. It becomes fitting, in the end, that Romeo and Juliet should die together; it is altogether unfitting that Mercutio should die at all. His departure is nearer the high tragic status which involves irony and a sense of waste and it is he, and he alone, who takes us anywhere near those frontiers beyond which lie the immensities of tragic experience of King Lear and Hamlet.

The plot is derived from a poem by Arthur Brooke – *The Tragical History of Romeus and Juliet* – which appeared in 1562. Brooke's poem was, however, only one version of the very popular basic story of the love and death of two young lovers which is found in many forms, particularly in Italy in the fifteenth and sixteenth centuries.[30]

Shakespeare may have known other versions, including a lost play to which Brooke refers in the preface to his poem,[31] but this cannot be taken for granted. The important point is that the basic story was immensely popular and that many of the versions have certain common denominators. The operations of fate, the opposition of parents, the effect of the stars on the lovers are some of the abiding features of the story. The romantic cast of Shakespeare's play is, indeed, an indigenous part of the basic story. It must be stressed, however, that the play has certain particular qualities exclusive to Shakespeare himself. The first may be readily understood when it is recalled that the play is the first tragedy he wrote after the early and immature *Titus Andronicus*. There is much in the play to show that he had not yet freed himself from the influence of the Senecan mode of tragedy shown in that early play with such lack of inhibition. The general air of violence about to break out, the bloodshed, the scene in the graveyard and the emphasis on Tybalt in his bloody shroud all derive from the Roman dramatist.

The second demonstrates Shakespeare's skill as dramatist. Brooke makes the action last over several months, Shakespeare reduces it to a few days, so increasing the tragic poignancy of events. Brooke leans heavily towards moralizing, making the tale into an awful warning to youth against promiscuity and parental disobedience; Shakespeare avoids explicit didacticism, being more concerned with the human reality of the story. Brooke's Juliet is a flighty miss, revelling in her deception of her lover; Shakespeare's Juliet is vulnerable, unsophisticated, and torn between her duties to her parents and her love for Romeo.

The third concerns the language of the play. Its distinctiveness lies not only in its intrinsic qualities but in what it foreshadows. On the one hand it is undoubtedly written in the same key as the language of the sonnets, where metaphor, simile, conceit, are used at a high degree of lyric intensity; on the other hand, it shows evidences of a more dramatic use of language where what is said, the imagery used, and the speaking character, are closely integrated. The more highly wrought and lyrical language is to be found in Romeo and Juliet's first meeting, the more dramatic in Mercutio's language (excepting, of course, the set-piece about Queen Mab).

A superficial view might suggest that the play could be regarded as dramatized poem – a lyrical exploration of young love doomed by circumstance and the operations of malevolent stars. But this view runs us into the danger of neglecting the skilful dramatic force which deepens and widens our experience of the events. The play indeed is not one of emotional simplicities. Rather it holds within itself one large tension from which certain complexities radiate, a tension well described by T.J.B. Spencer: 'There are constant and deliberate collisions between romantic and unromantic views of love.'[32]

The play involves two worlds – that which Romeo and Juliet inhabit, and that of all the rest of the characters. The lovers' world, based on the pathetic fallacy that to love is enough, seeks to be self-sufficient, nourished solely by the power of love. It admits of actions which are precipitately undertaken, for its self-absorption makes its feelings hypersensitive and liable to loss of control:

> 'O, tell me, friar, tell me,
> In what vile part of this anatomy
> Doth my name lodge? Tell me that I may sack
> The hateful mansion.'   [III.3.105–8]

It is perhaps Romeo, more than Juliet, who convinces us that their's is a world which seeks to insulate itself from any intrusion, and, indeed, when we first meet him, he is already isolated, his solitary self-indulgence not only implicit in his speech but in the comments of others:

> 'But to himself so secret and so close.'   [1.1.147]

His attraction to Juliet, at first more real than his dreams of the shadowy Rosalind, makes him more capable for a time of consorting with the jests and quips of his fellows. But it is not long before his love for Juliet drives him further into a situation where the outside world seems an irrelevance, an irritant and a danger:

> 'Unless philosophy can make a Juliet,
> Displant a town, reverse a prince's doom,
> It helps not, it prevails not. Talk no more.'   [III.3.58–60]

The irritation that lurks beneath our experience of his character in the theatre derives from the simple fact that, except briefly, he seems incapable of making any real concession to the realities of the everyday world. Juliet has more of our sympathy for we have the impression that, despite her youthfulness, there is a greater practicality in her nature. She is more conscious of other duties which lie outside a total indulgence to love and knows her duties to her parents; she is agonizingly aware of the different but powerful love that she bears for her kinsman, Tybalt. It is only towards the end of the play that Romeo shows a deeper sensibility about the existence of others. Certainly his reaction to Mercutio's death has about it a reckless courage, but our admiration for his quick response is tempered by the curiously effete mentality which shows itself in the weak reply he makes to Mercutio who asks why he came between him and Tybalt: 'I thought all for the best.' (III.1.101)

In a sense we find it difficult to trust the emotional spirit of Romeo for at no point in the play can we be sure that he is not being governed by passions whose consequence has never been considered by him. Juliet, however, engages our sympathies, not only as a more complete and reliable person, despite her youth, but also because she is shown to be taking the greatest personal risk in deciding to accept the Friar's caution. It is Juliet's more outgoing sensibility and greater sensitivity to outside factors that make the insulation which the two lovers try to coil about themselves seem so poignant and vulnerable.

The outside world is certainly not neglected in the play. The lovers are shown to be besieged from several sides, each sharply designated. The first scene of the play, for example, shows the restless, niggling and potentially dangerous condition of the Capulet/Montague feud. This is exaggerated by the presence of Tybalt who is, in fact, the active element in a feud which, for the most part, rumbles distantly, always seeming about to break into bloodshed. Shakespeare personalizes, and therefore heightens, the effect of this feud by means of this character – a spoilt darling of a noble family. He represents one of the chief dangers beleaguering the lovers, and the representation is given sharper focus because of Tybalt's relationship to Juliet.

Within the general context of the feud yet another, more precise, enemy to the lovers is embedded and personalized. Children, particularly daughters, must abide by the wishes and edicts of their fathers, especially in the matter of marriage. Whatever sympathies the Elizabethan audience had for Juliet, these would have been tempered by the plain knowledge that she was disobeying a law which, to them, was natural. What is remarkable, however, about the depiction of the disobedience, is the dramatic quality of the personal clash between Juliet and her father. Capulet is a superb study of a small-minded, well-meaning man accustomed, because of his wealth and position, to get his own way. Shakespeare understood the psychology of such men, who are prepared to show bonhomie in situations where they feel relaxed, in control, and the centre of attention. Capulet is even prepared to accept Romeo at his banquet:

'I would not for the wealth of all this town
Here in my house do him disparagement.'   [1.5.67–8]

He can afford, as the only begetter of the feast, to show what is, under the circumstances, a very temporary magnanimity. Yet the narrowness of his sensibilities is exposed in his tirade to Juliet when she begs not to be forced to marry Paris:

'Hang thee, young baggage! disobedient wretch!
I tell thee what – get thee to church a Thursday,
Or never after look me in the face.'   [III.5.160–2]

Capulet's world is a fundamentally insensitive and cruel place. It has many adherents, and its strongest citizen (and the lovers' most insidious enemy) is the Nurse.

She is a woman for all seasons, hunting with the hounds and running with the hares. She is Shakespeare's most effective study in fickleness, all the more impressive as a dramatic creation because she plays a dual role. On one level she is lined up on the side of the outside world. her bawdiness, her basic crudity of sense and sensibility, seem like a sore against the unblemished flesh of Romeo and Juliet's love. To her, love means sex, marriage means bed, and the swelling female belly the only possible affirmation of the existence of love. Yet she is more than a mere repository of all that is in contrast with the delicate lyrical world of the two lovers. She is their enemy in a more subtle, and certainly more dramatically telling, sense. It is, after all, only by her lumbering and creaking help that the lovers are able to come together – she becomes a conspirator on their behalf. She is the only female that Juliet can turn to to share her excited joy in her new-found love – to this extent she becomes the child's confessor. Both Romeo and Juliet, particularly the latter, accept her as a natural ally. The blow to Juliet when the Nurse, falling ponderously in step with the Establishment she serves, denounces Romeo, is great and painful. Her philosophy of expediency – telling Juliet that one man is as good as another – strikes at the very heart of the consuming love Juliet bears for Romeo. She blows a chill wind into a world of warmth and youth:

'I think you are happy in this second match,
For it excels your first;'   [III.5.223–4]

The Nurse's treachery has a double effect – it increases our sense of the growing isolation of the lovers as well as isolating Juliet herself who, unlike Romeo, has striven to maintain some commerce with her family. Our sympathy for her is further increased and given added dimension by the cold anxiety which strikes us as she prepares to take the potion. But, more than this, the Nurse's words, and Juliet's reactions to them, brings a new maturity, giving her a brave resolve to proceed in her course, alone if necessary:

'Thou and my bosom henceforth shall be twain.' [III.5.241]

It is in fact largely because of the Nurse that Juliet is confirmed as having much the stronger character of the two lovers.

Yet this nurse exists also on another level – one more attractive and dramatically direct. Shakespeare has unerringly created a picture of an old family retainer. Limited in intelligence, proud in her status, the recipient of family confidences, emotionally unstable – so that tears fall as readily as laughter – this type, which has since become familiar to us in countless novels and plays, is a kind of chameleon changing its colouring for the safest atmosphere it can find. The Nurse is Mistress Quickly domesticated, and she endears herself to us less for her actual chracteristics than for the perceptible limitations of those chracteristics. Both the Nurse and Quickly lack taste in everything: their laughter is always overdone; their sentimentality always slightly misplaced; their judgment non-existent; their anger unblest with rational excuse; their fidelity is confined to the proposition that they serve best he who pays the piper.

The insidious intrusion of the outside world is thus clearly expressed. There is one, however, who stands between both worlds and attempts to reconcile them. The traditional way of playing Friar Laurence emphasises a kind of holy ineffectiveness and reduces him to an effete and wordy fool. Granville-Barker refers to him as 'poor Friar Laurence' and as 'deplorable' as a man of affairs, claiming that his reproof of the lovers is 'near to cant'.[33] Recently, T.J.B. Spencer, showing less dismissiveness, still inclines to disparage the man – 'well-meaning, kindly, good humoured'.[34] The majority of actors in twentieth-century productions concentrate their interpretations on overwhelming simplicity. Yet the Friar occupies a vitally important position in the play.

His first speech, when he is discovered collecting herbs, is often accepted by actors and directors as a testimony to the verbose ineffectuality of the man but, in fact, it is a reflection of some of the themes which are developed in the play's action. Romeo and Juliet's precipitate action is defined in the words:

'Virtue itself turns vice, being misapplied.' [II.3.21]

The situation in the city is mirrored in the lines:

> 'Two such opposed kings encamp them still
> In man as well as herbs – grace and rude will;'   [II.3.27–8]

And the speech prepares us for the Friar's offer of a potion for Juliet to take and for the poison which Romeo buys. The Friar is not a remote eremite. He is far more precise and direct about Romeo's state of mind than even Mercutio:

> '. . . Young men's love, then, lies
> Not truly in their hearts, but in their eyes.
> Jesu Maria, what a deal of brine
> Hath wash'd thy sallow cheeks for Rosaline!'   [II.3.67–71]

He is well aware, long before the crisis initiated by Tybalt's death, of the dangers that Romeo invites:

> 'Wisely and slow; they stumble that run fast.'   [II.3.94]

He is purposeful in committing himself to helping the two lovers, though the possible consequences are clear to him:

> 'So smile the heavens upon this holy act
> That after-hours with sorrow chide us not!'   [II.6.1–2]

His strictures on Romeo after the killing of Tybalt far from being 'cant' are a model of righteous anger, followed by practical advice. It is noticeable that his words to Romeo for the greater part of the scene are delivered in short clear sentences. He does not sermonize to this blubbering young man but is unequivocal in what he says; and when he does essay a long speech in this scene, it is not merely well-meaning, but a passionately rational series of points. It is altogether correct, psychologically, that he should make a long speech just after Romeo has attempted to stab himself, for what Romeo needs at this point are the home truths that the Friar hurls at him. He is no less direct and practical when Juliet visits him after being told that she must marry Paris.

In personality then he is far from ineffective and simple. He helps the lovers; his advice, under the circumstances, is rational and he cannot be blamed that events turn all his well-made plans awry. Standing between two worlds, the Friar represents what the ideal solution could have been – an acceptance of the love of the two young people and its legal sanction. His humanity enables him to accept their love, his profession urges him to legalize what he has, as a human being, already accepted. It is no fault of his that such a solution proves impossible – he cannot control the precipitancy of love, and he has no legislation over ill-crossed stars and intransigent parents.

Shakespeare is perhaps more precise in this play than in any other about giving time-checks on the duration of the dramatic action. The events take place in summer, beginning on a Sunday morning and ending early morning of the following Thursday. Romeo appears soon after nine on Sunday morning; the lovers meet in the evening, their conversation taking place about midnight; at nine on Monday morning Romeo is at Friar Laurence's cell; marries Juliet that afternoon; kills Tybalt about an hour later; the lovers part at dawn on Tuesday morning; later, the same day, Juliet gets the potion from the Friar; on Wednesday morning Juliet is discovered apparently dead; Romeo arrives at the tomb in the early hours of Thursday morning.

All these details are expressly given or unequivocally implied, often with such emphasis that it seems that Shakespeare was taking great pains to ensure that his audience knew where it was on the time-scale. The effect is one of precipitancy further boosted by the bringing forward of Juliet's proposed marriage from the Thursday to the Wednesday.

This sense of haste is also underlined in a naturalistic way, by the frequent references of the Friar to the dangers of haste and the skilful deployment of the temperaments of the leading characters. The first scene of the play with its sense of quick danger, the volatile Mercutio jumping from thought to thought, the itchy fingers and abrasive temper of Tybalt – all conspire with the play's clock-time to give a sense of impetuous haste.

The text also gives the stage-director a deal of opportunity to reinforce that sense of speed. The first scene, and that in which Mercutio taunts Tybalt, take place in the hot July Italian sunshine. There is a telling paradox in that such swift action should take place at a time which is traditionally siesta. In Franco Zeffirelli's production at the Old Vic in 1960 this paradox was emphasized so that there was an impression of danger and pointlessness in the feud, with the poignancy of Mercutio's death taking place in hot sunlight – a context for living not dying.

The naturalistic evocations of time moving quickly and actions and people keeping pace with it is paralleled by the imagery by which

Romeo in particular, and Juliet, to a less extent, express themselves about life and love:

> 'Too like the lightning, which doth cease to be'
> 'Ere one can say "It lightens" ...'   [II.2.119–20]
> 'A lightning before death.'   [V.3.90]
> '... too rash, too unadvis'd, too sudden.'   [II.2.118]

Both lovers show a consciousness of what their love is bound by; both see it as a swift incandescence. Indeed, one part of their minds and feelings, which sees their love thus, moves even faster than the relentless clock-time which dictates the action that surrounds them.

Yet perhaps Shakespeare's most conspicuous triumph is his ability to make the clock-face of the action transparent as it were. Other timescales, and consequently other values, can be perceived, and, in our perception of them, a poignant irony enters into our experience of the whole action. There is, for example, the ruminative timescale which the nurse reveals and, to an extent, Capulet. She is given to journeying, in a mumbling way, into the past: 'I remember it well', 'I never shall forget it'. Capulet, with the nostalgia of an elderly man, feeling the neural itch of youth, is also given to slow remembrance: 'I have seen the day', ''tis gone, 'tis gone, 'tis gone.' The effect of this timescale is to provide a pathetic contrast to the actual time the lovers have at their disposal. As Spencer says: 'The four days are framed, as it were, by many years', and this in itself suggests the impossibility of the two lovers ever growing into old age together.

There is also the implicit timescale which exists as a kind of wry aspiration in the two lovers. Their conscious minds tell them that their love is a thing of lightning, their desires force them to indulge in the pathetic fallacy that the lightning flash is, indeed, eternal in duration. They attempt to annihilate the temporary at several points as their imagery tries, from time to time, to identify their mutual love with something other than a lightning flash. For Romeo, Juliet's beauty is often identified with eternal verities:

> 'The brightness of her cheek would shame those stars.'   [II.2.19]

And she is 'as a winged messenger of heaven'. Even at the end, 'beauty's ensign yet is crimson in thy lips and in thy cheeks'; he knows she is dead but believes she has conquered death itself. Juliet is no less apt in this process:

> 'My bounty is as boundless as the sea,
> My love as deep: the more I give to thee,
> The more I have, for both are infinite.'   [II.2.133–5]

On their wedding night the fallacy of this attempt to defy the facts of time comes to the surface. They are both prepared to deny the natural evidence of clock-time, even to sacrifice themselves on behalf of the sweet counterfeiting they indulge in:

'I'll say yon grey is not the morning's eye.'   [III.5.19]

The language and imagery enable the audience to see through the clock face to the heart of Romeo and Juliet's experience of love. This is no more starkly experienced than in the scene of Capulet's banquet, where simultaneously two different timescales exist. There is the bustling present tense, with its reminders of normal chronology, in Capulet's references to the past, his conversation with his cousin about age, in Tybalt's fierce reactions to Romeo's presence, in Capulet's remark about the lateness of the hour. Within this undecoratedly expressed present tense there lies the exquisitely lyrical, timeless moment of Romeo and Juliet's first meeting. The audience is almost jolted from one timescale to another by the contrast in the language-patterns. Tybalt's words:

'I will withdraw; but this intrusion shall,
Now seeming sweet, convert to bitt'rest gall.'   [1.5.89–90]

are followed by:

'If I profane with my unworthiest hand
This holy shrine, the gentle fine is this.'   [1.5.91–2]

and the gentle and kissed farewell of the two lovers is followed by a raucous return to the present tense in the nurse's shout:

'Madam, your mother craves a word with you.'   [1.5.109]

The different time values of these scene are underlined by the contrasting language-patterns of the two worlds which are brought into existence in the banquet. No more striking confirmation of this contrast and its effects could be imagined than in Franco Zeffirelli's production of the scene. The restless present tense was depicted in bustling movement, gay dancing, laughter, and loud music at backstage. Out of this the two lovers emerged to meet frontstage. At the moment of recognition of love and beauty, both the visual and aural impression of the present tense began to fade and, as the love-dialogue between the two developed, the present-tense action in the background was deliberately slowed down, coming almost to a stop. The impression was as if a timeless moment had been created and had begun to dominate the present tense – almost to the point of annihilating it. Romeo and Juliet pathetically aspire for a perpetuation of this moment; their tragedy is that their aspiration is impossible.

The play's whole movement, however, is dominated by inevitability. It does not really allow of any change of direction so surrounded is it with a sense of malevolent fate. Destiny is an utterly dominant *dramatis persona* in the play, its presence announced by the chorus, by Romeo, Juliet, and the Friar. And perhaps the play's main weakness is that the insistence upon the malevolent stars, producing an inevitable result, is at variance with the busy mechanics of the plot line. One part of us will say that the outcome is inevitable, but another cannot help reflecting that a mere slight turn in the mechanics of the plot could change the conclusion. This weakness should perhaps be measured against Shakespeare's relative immaturity when attempting to write a tragedy which was more than the mechanical horrifics of Seneca. When the play is measured against the great tragedies in which fate, human will and choice are in exact tension, it may seem deficient. Yet in this play, a combination of theme – the indefinable attraction of young love – theatrical action, and the sheer power of the lyricism of the language may well override any minor quibbles.

The Merchant of Venice

This play, written between 1596 and 1598,[35] is one of the most popular in the whole canon. The first quarter records that it was 'divers times' performed by the Lord Chamberlain's company; in the eighteenth century Thomas Betterton played Bassanio and a well-known comic actor (John Downes) played Shylock; in 1741 Charles Macklin rejected the comic vein and created a villainous criminal from the part, playing it, to great acclaim, on twenty-two occasions; intermittently between 1784 and 1804 John Kemble played Shylock with Sarah Siddons as Portia; Edmund Kean followed, interpreting the Jew as a man as much sinned against as sinning, and Charles Macready continued the process of making Shylock into something sympathetic to the audience; the culmination of this process, taking Shylock from comic to villain to noble proud victim of a vindictive society, was seen in Sir Henry Irving's performance in the late nineteenth century. In the twentieth century it is the noble Jew that has dominated the innumerable versions of the part that have been presented.

Appraisal of the play is difficult, since the experience of it, either in the study or in the theatre, is likely, more than with most others, to be conditioned by strong personal predispositions. Is the reader, or member of the audience, Christian or Jew? How far does racialism (a pregnant consideration nowadays) affect one's estimate of the play? For the, perhaps rare, reader or viewer of the play who is able, by some process, to submerge such considerations, there still remains a factor which may colour his view of the play. This factor is literary rather than social, religious or racist. It is simply that some find the play inherently cynical because of the disparate elements in it. It is perhaps naive to state that the romantic resolutions of Belmont are hard to swallow after the stern judgments of the trial scene, or, indeed, to suggest that if this is so it may be an implied condemnation of Shakespeare's inability to reconcile what is seemingly dramatically irreconcilable. Looking at it from a different standpoint, one might ask if it is not possible that Skylock is built too large to be destroyed by mere legality, and this at the hands of characters who have not been created with the understanding and richness of human perception which has been expended on the Jew. Ten Brinck, writing in 1895, had no doubts about this:

> But it is not merely poetic justice that our feelings demand. Shylock
> has come too close to us, we have learned to know too intimately the

grounds of his hatred, of the intensity of his resentment, his figure has become too humanly significant, and the misfortune which overtakes him appeals too deeply to our sympathies, to permit us to be reconciled to the idea that his fate, which moves us tragically, should be conceived otherwise than as a tragedy.[36]

The play bristles with problems involving interpretation, and the nature of the response we are expected to make to it, both of which are reflected in the extraordinary diverse critical responses that it has induced over the years. In 1896 Georg Brandes, writing of the play as bringing us to the threshold of a period in Shakespeare's life 'instinct with high-pitched gaiety and gladness' adds that 'His poetry, his whole existence, now seems to be given over to music, to harmony'.[37] In 1927 E.E. Stoll uttered the warning that 'The time is passed for speaking of Shakespeare as utterly impartial or inscrutable'.[38] Yet, in 1962, Dover Wilson was certain that Shakespeare 'is neither for nor against Shylock. Shakespeare never takes sides'.[39] Frank Kermode, in 1961, writes that the play is 'about judgment, redemption and mercy',[40] although John Russell Brown had earlier assured as that 'Shakespeare does not enforce a moral in this play – his judgment is implicit only'.[41]

It is within the areas of two basic themes that these variations of response and judgment occur. The first is succinctly described by John Russell Brown: 'Shakespeare was so deeply concerned with the ideal of love's wealth in The Merchant of Venice that we may presume that it was fundamental to his thinking and feeling about human relationships.'[42] In this context, Portia is presented to us in such a way as to reconcile us to the otherwise unattractive means by which some characters achieve love's wealth. Bassanio has more than a touch of extravagant fecklessness about him. Although he chooses the right casket for the most estimably expressed reasons, the speech of acceptance does not square with the impression we have of his character; it seems a set speech ministering more perhaps to Shakespeare's own preoccupation with the ideal of love's wealth than to the reality of character. Jessica's ungenerous (to say the least) actions are hardly counterbalanced by what we know about her father's character. Lorenzo seems to fall 'for' rather than be in love 'with' Nerissa – it has the smack of delighted convenience. Portia alone gives a sense of the wealth of love. She, like Perdita and Rosalind, has a total generosity of spirit and, through this, she alone creates a sense of the wealth of love. Her beauty, her honesty, her fidelity and intelligence but, above all, her grave wisdom about the meaning of the depth of real love, radiates from her, sanctifying, as it were, what very much needs to be sanctified:

> 'I never did repent for doing good,
> Nor shall not now; for in companions
> That do converse and waste the time together,
> Whose souls do bear an equal yoke of love,
> There must be needs a like proportion
> Of lineaments, of manners and of spirit.'   [III.4.10–15]

It is important to stress that in the play itself this gravity of spirit rests in its quality rather than in its appearance. But curiously there has been a tradition for actresses to play Portia in their maturer years, and to create an impression of a woman of the world who has long awaited marriage and, in the interim, devoted herself to an assiduous study of the law. She is often dressed maturely, and delivers her speeches with a kind of judicial, grave and elderly sincerity. But the Portia whose task is to irradiate this play with the spirit of love's true wealth cannot be anything but young (a state well supported by the text, not least in the scene when she and Nerissa excitedly plan the donning of men's attire) and her qualities, like Rosalind's and Perdita's, cannot be anything but natural and inborn.

The other basic theme of the play is expressed by Moelwyn Merchant: 'We accept the seriousness and technical gravity of the trial scene, whatever doubts the juristic side of our minds may plead; we respond gravely to the nature of usury and to the contrasts of charity, compassion and equity.'[43] He goes on to show how the intertwinings of legal and theological niceties and the moral questionings which are engendered by the confrontation of legal quibbling and the idea of charity, mercy and compassion, are made. Such a confrontation, embedded within the stern framework of opposition between Christian and Jew, is not simple – the mercy expected from the Jew is not seen to be given to him by the Christians when their turn comes to show it. The differing attitudes of Christian and Jew towards usury are not shown as simple black-and-white contrast. In his abhorrence of usury, Antonio seems a plain dealer, but he also has a naive holier-than-thou self-satisfied streak in him. Shylock, in his promotion of usury, may seem something of a money-grabbing speculator, but he has also a persuasive fierce loyalty to his own religious principles and practices. Although, therefore, the play may be capable of communicating on several speculative levels, at the same time, its wide popularity with audiences of all ages (including children) make one doubt whether it is these themes to which the majority of audiences are responding . One can only say with certainty – respond they do, and enthusiastically, to something.

In the first place there are indications in the structure of the play of a careful design on Shakespeare's part to maintain a strong sense of that kind of narrative plot associated with the intriguing and the unknown. Quite simply, the play frequently puts its audience in the position of asking – what will happen next? Will Shylock demand the fulfilment of the bond? Will Antonio's argosies arrive in time? Will Portia's disguise be noticed in court? Who will choose the right casket? Will Shylock cut the flesh from Antonio and, if so, how? Will Shylock become a Christian? Will the business of the giving away of the rings mean a happy ending? Putting ourselves in the position of one seeing the play for the first time, we realize that these questions are very much in the forefront of our experience of the action. One question after another is posed and answered (except what happens to Shylock), mostly with a kind of convenient adherence to the demands of the plot at any given moment. It is meet, for example, that Antonio should not lose out on the general share out of happiness at the end so, conveniently, the news comes that his enterprises have not foundered. Possibly the popularity of the play rests firmly, though not of course exclusively, upon these questions and the answers that are given to them.

Then there is the question of credibility. We are given no reason for Antonio's melancholy; he just is so. (It could be suggested that Shakespeare has created him thus to produce a sense of isolation which in turn will increase the *frisson* of sympathy from us in the predicament he calls upon himself). Whatever the reason, there is something unreal about the character. This quality of unreality is increased by the fact that we are continually conscious that many incidents and episodes, in themselves, have a contrived, framed, unreal flavour. The casket episodes may be delightful but are scarcely credible; the bond may inject excitement into the plot, but its terms are in the realm of fantasy; Moelwyn Merchant says, 'The whole legal structure of the play is, of course, fallacious',[44] and certainly the trial may be exciting, but, is, in the last analysis, incredible; the appearance of Portia in a High Court, masquerading as a renowned lawyer, although an occasion for satisfying our romantic sensibilities, is palpably beyond the realms of possibility. And as if to emphasize this fantasy element in the play, the last act in Belmont, where any moral compunctions about what has happened before are wholly ignored, making the Belmont scene an idyllic haven, is immured from the harsh issues which have been enacted near the Rialto.

The creation of this unreal world through a set of incredible circumstances is reinforced by the disposition of certain scenes. The audience is lured into an aura of fantasy by the casket episode, and it is noticeable that Shakespeare extends this aura by separating the casket affair into four distinct parts. Morocco makes his debut in Act II.2 and his choice in Act II.7; Aragon chooses wrongly in Act II.9 and Bassanio, correctly, in Act III.2. On each occasion the fantasy quality is reinforced. Morocco's first speech to Portia, after he had asked her to lead him to the caskets, has all the inconsequential bravado of a pantomime potentate:

> '... By this scimitar
> That slew the Sophy and a Persian prince,
> That won three fields of Sultan Solyman,
> I would o'er-stare the sternest eyes that look,
> Out-brave the heart most daring on the earth,
> Pluck the young sucking cubs from the she-bear,
> Yea, mock the lion when 'a roars for prey,
> To win thee, lady ...'   [II.1.24–31]

His reactions to the contents of the casket are in the best traditions of rhodomontade melodrama:

> 'Cold indeed, and labour lost.
> Then farewell, heat, and welcome, frost.'   [II.7.74–5]

Aragon, in his turn, no less reinforces the mode of delightful fable:

> 'I am enjoin'd by oath to observe three things:
> First, never to unfold to anyone
> Which casket 'twas I chose; next, if I fail
> Of the right casket, never in my life
> To woo a maid in way of marriage;
> Lastly,
> If I do fail in fortune of my choice,
> Immediately to leave you and be gone.'   [II.9.9–16]

These three promises take us unequivocally into the realm of fairy story and give us a standpoint from which to take stock of the world which Portia inhabits. A young and beautiful princess attended only by minions waits for the outcome of an edict made by her head father. She is visited by two exotic potentates but her heart is a'quiver lest one of them should open the right casket and claim her. She need not fear – only Prince Charming will open the right one, for he is true in heart. All might well end very happily, except that this particular Prince Charming has involved himself in an enterprise which endangers a near and dear friend. The happy ending must be postponed until the danger is removed and its wicked progenitor cast away.

Yet how wicked is Shylock? It is remarkable how easy it is to assume that Shylock's intentions, from the very beginning, are utterly vicious, but this is not so. In order to believe that, we have both to deny completely the emphasis on fable in the play and to overstress the implications of one particular speech of Shylock. When he first encounters Antonio he rails to himself about Antonio as a publican. He hates him for being a Christian, he despises him for his attitude to usury. He says he will not forgive him and hopes that 'if I can catch him upon the hip' he will be happy. To 'catch upon the hip' does not suggest killing. It has the flavour of those threats which melodramatic villains whisper to themselves about the hero. It is a wrestling term, suggesting Shylock will be happy to give Antonio a fall which will be painful and humiliating.

Indeed the whole of the preliminaries to the signing of the bond are conducted by Shylock with the excited expectation of humiliating his adversary but no more. At first he and Antonio spar with each other, then, the sparring over, Shylock begins the process of real humiliation. Antonio is the challenger, Shylock speaks from his position of advantage. He taunts Antonio whose former jibes at Jewry have now turned to requests for Jewish help:

> 'Fair sir, you spit on me on Wednesday last,
> You spurn'd me such a day; another time
> You call'd me dog; and for these courtesies
> I'll lend you thus much moneys?'   [1.3.121–4]

Throughout this scene the atmosphere is compounded of Shylock's fierce joy in humiliating Antonio and Antonio's grim determination to swallow the jibes for the sake of Bassanio. Up to Act III.1 the motivations of Shylock are presented, albeit strongly, within the terms of the fabulous world which the casket scenes in particular have created, but suddenly, in this scene, the rules of fairy tale are broken. Jessica's departure from her father's house with his money is, in itself, of a piece with the fairy tale atmosphere. The beleaguered young maiden, tied to a mean and cruel father, escapes romantically by night from his clutches into the waiting arms of her dashing young lover. If Shylock had been allowed by Shakespeare to remain in the mode of the surrounding actions of the play – that of fairy story – the morality of Jessica's taking of her father's money would not arise in our minds; the villain would merely be getting his deserts. In Act III.1, however, Shylock moves from one mode into another. He associates the departure of his daughter with Christian perfidy. It is, very significantly, as if a piece of his own flesh had been torn from him:

> 'I say my daughter is my flesh and my blood'   [III.1.32]

It is at this point that the bond as an element in the plot acquires a more realistic significance and when, immediately following upon his cry about his daughter, he shouts that Antonio must 'look to his bond', Shylock himself moves from his position as agent in a fantasy into human dimensions. He is no longer confined within the conditioned reflexes of the fairy tale mode and is beginning to generate his own reactions to situations. Yet what surrounds him is still largely cast in that fairy tale mode. Immediately after Shylock's declaration about fulfilling the bond we have a casket scene (when Bassanio makes the right choice) and we are jolted back to a world of fable. This itself is interrupted by the news about Antonio's ships. Yet, even now, the element of happy-ever-after is strong, for Portia's almost merry speech, offering money to pay Shylock, has all the flavour of that confidential optimism by which the pantomime princess assures her audience that, in the end, all will be well:

> 'When it is paid, bring your true friend along.
> My maid Nerissa and myself meantime
> Will live as maids and widows. Come, away;
> For you shall hence upon your wedding day.'   [III.2.310–13]

Portia maintains her relatively merry mood in the delight she displays with Nerissa at the prospect of disguising themselves, a scene which induces that feeling of excitement we feel in a fairy story or pantomime when the fragile heroine leaves to take arms against the cruel monster:

> 'But come, I'll tell thee all my whole device
> When I am in my coach, which stays for us
> At the park gate; and therefore haste away,
> For we must measure twenty miles today.'   [III.4.81–4]

But the villain himself has stepped out of the cage of fairy tale and, by Act III, he is a wounded, dangerous, and strangely pitiable creature.

he has gone far beyond the simple function of being a mere melodramatic impediment to the romantic course of true love.

Perhaps the most common attitude towards Jews in Elizabethan England dictated Shakespeare's outline of the character. There was no generally expressed fierce hatred of the Jews in London in the 1590s; on one occasion only did a basic and inherent attitude show itself in positive demonstration. This was during the trial of Roderigo Lopez for high treason.

Lopez, a Portuguese Jew, professed Christianity like the majority of the relatively small number of his race who were in the capital. He had been physician to the Earl of Leicester and subsequently to the Queen, when a claimant to the Portuguese throne arrived in London (1592) and Lopez was alleged to have engaged in political intrigue with him. The Earl of Essex denounced him, adding to the allegation of treason that he had attempted to poison the Queen. His execution on 7 January 1594 occasioned great and angry public excitement. However, the Jew of Elizabethan imagination was a dark figure, half real, half out of fable, and his characteristics – cupidity, obsessive, self-indulgent thrift, meanness of spirit and a set of religious beliefs at variance with Christianity – are all put before us by Shakespeare in his character, Shylock. But there is much more. Shakespeare allows Shylock free play on our emotions. Antonio's sparse reponse to Shylock's taunts:

> 'I am as like to call thee so again,
> To spit on thee again, to spurn thee too.'   [1.3.125–6]

only serves to make us wonder whether he does not have some justice in his attitude to Antonio. The defection of Jessica in complicity with a Christian although by itself merely a part of the fable, becomes, when set against Shylock's tortured grief, something to make us pause. His plea to be granted the benefit of the letter of the law may seem, in isolation, irrationally spiteful, but against Portia's legal petit-point, it becomes no more than a demand for the equity of an eye for an eye and a tooth for a tooth. These factors, in themselves, cause us to wonder whether, in fact, Shakespeare, having accepted the semi-mythological conception of the Jew as the basis of his character (after all, he knew his box office), bent a little backwards, not so much to avoid taking sides as to allow his own sense of fair play to manoeuvre. Certainly, to put Shylock legalistically, as he does, on a dramatic par with Christian legality, argues for a disposition on his part to favour Shylock.

There are, however, two other factors which push the figure of Shylock away both from the conventional idea of the Jew and, most certainly, from the fable mode of his context. The first is the man's pride. He has the virtue of total fidelity (expressed without mealy-mouthed compromise) to his heritage as a Jew. He clings to usury, not only because it is profitable but because it is a built-in tenet of his religion. The small details of his pride swell into largeness when he bases that pride upon strictly human grounds, 'Hath not a Jew eyes?' In the speech from which this line comes, Shakespeare opened the doors for an audience response which, in depth and variety, take one's experience of the play far beyond the realms of fable.

The second is in the implied reconciliation between the Christian and the Jewish attitude. The 'punishment' of Shylock is conceived, particularly by Antonio, less as a punishment than an opportunity for Shylock to allow himself the possibility of eternal grace by entering the Christian religion. But is this, for the audience, a fair and acceptable bargain? Having already been taught to admire Shylock's fidelity to his race and religion – we are now asked to welcome his defection from it. We are asked to applaud a man being brought to the true religion when we have been convinced that, for this man, Jewry is the only religion.

Shylock in fact becomes too human to be accommodated within the fable. However much scholarship may point to the processes of reconciliation in this play, it is only if we can continue to regard Shylock as a monster/comic, that we can join in the dance. Portia, and Portia alone, is raised to a level which can be regarded as on a par with what Shakespeare makes of Shylock from the time of the news of his daughter's elopement to his own final shuffling departure. It is not without significance that the truly successful productions of this play have always depicted Shylock and Portia, in the trial scene, as equal adversaries, and, mutually recognizing the other as equal, they both demand, and should receive, an equal amount of sympathy and understanding from the audience. Portia represents Christian law and a spirit of reconciliation, Shylock no less, represents a Jewish law, and a fidelity to his own religious principles. If the tension, strung between two poles of equal strength, is maintained in the theatre, speeches like Portia's on mercy and Shylock's 'What judgment . . .' ennoble the whole action. If the poles are of unequal strength, the sense of the agencies of a fable overcoming, by trickery and sententious moralising, a powerful human figure is, not to exaggerate, sickeningly obvious.

The play can only be made, as a whole, compatible to itself in production by allowing the strength of the fable element *and* the strength of the Shylock element full play. The result is inevitably a powerful demonstration of the singular *theatrical* effectiveness of what is, dramatically, irreconcilable.

NOTES

1 Lord Chamberlain's Men, 1594–1603 (later The King's Men, 1603–1642). Company of actors including Shakespeare, Richard Burbage and Will Kempe, acting first at the Theatre, later at the Swan, then at the Curtain, and finally (1598/9) building their own theatre, the Globe.

2 On the great religious festivals, eg Christmas, Easter, Whitsun, plays were performed in many towns. See E.K. Chambers, *The Medieval Stage* (1913).

3 Roderigo Lopez, Jewish-Portuguese doctor, hanged 7 June, 1594 for attempting to poison the Queen.

4 Robert Devereux, 2nd Earl of Essex (1566–1601) was the favourite of Queen Elizabeth. But he was convicted of treason for his attempt to dethrone the Queen in 1601, and executed.

5 *Holinshed's Chronicle as used in Shakespeare's Plays*, eds. Allardyce Nicoll and J. Calina (1927).

6 Ibid.

7 A.C. Sprague, op. cit., p. 29.

8 'Foul Papers' – a MS. in Shakespeare's own hand.

9 See J. Dover Wilson's Introduction to the New Cambridge edition of *King John* (1939); P. Ure, Arden Series (1956); and E.A.F. Honigman (ed) on the problems of *King John* in the Arden Series (1954).

10 The two parts of *Henry IV* are regarded as having been written successively in late 1596 and early 1597.

11 J. Dover Wilson. Introduction to the New Cambridge edition of *Henry IV* (1946).

12 J.B. Priestley, *The Engish Comic Characters* (1925), p. 90.

13 William Empson, 'Falstaff and Mr Dover Wilson', in *Kenyon Review*, 15 (1953).

14 A.C. Bradley, 'The Rejection of Falstaff', in his *Oxford Lectures on Poetry* (1909).

15 John Wain, *The Living World of Shakespeare; A Playgoer's Guide* (1964), p. 66.

16 *Henry V* is usually ascribed to the period March–September, 1599.

17 J. Dover Wilson. Introduction to the New Cambridge edition of *Henry V* (1947).

18 Winston Churchill in a broadcast, 14 July 1940; printed in *Into Battle*, 1941.

19 Barrett Wendell, *William Shakespeare, a Study in English Literature* (1894).

20 Arthur Humphreys, Introduction to the New Penguin edition of *Henry V* (1968).

21 Derek Traversi, *Shakespeare from Richard II to Henry V* (1957).

22 See Georg Brandes, *William Shakespeare*, 2 vols. (1898).

23 Peter Alexander, *Introduction to Shakespeare* (1964), p. 58.

24 See Leslie Hotson, *Shakespeare versus Shallow* (1931).

25 John Dennis, *Epistle Dedicatory to The Comic Gallant* (1702).

26 Jan Kott, *Shakespeare Our Contemporary* (1965), p. 72

27 Ovid, 43 BC–AD 18 Roman poet. Metamorphoses published after his exile (AD 8) from Rome. Lucius Apuleius. c. 125? Orator. His *The Golden Ass* was translated into English by William Adlington, 1566.

28 Children of the Chapel, 1501–1616. A group of children, known by various names, renowned for their music and acting ability. The group became a serious rival to the adult acting companies c. 1600.

29 From Dylan Thomas, 'And Death Shall Have No Dominion'.

30 See T.J.B. Spencer, *Elizabethan Love Stories*, in Penguin Shakespeare Library (1976).

31 Brooke's poem was based on a version in Belleforest's *Histoires Tragiques* (1559).

32 T.J.B. Spencer, Introduction to New Penguin edition of *Romeo and Juliet* (1967).

33 Harley Granville Barker, *Prefaces to Shakespeare* (1927–30).

34 T.J.B. Spencer, op. cit.

35 Moelwyn Merchant in the Introduction to the New Penguin edition of *The Merchant of Venice* (1967).

36 B. Ten Brinck, *Five Lectures on Shakespeare* (1895).

37 Brandes, op. cit.

38 E.E. Stoll, *Shakespeare Studies* (1927).

39 J. Dover Wilson, *Shakespeare's Happy Comedies* (1962).

40 Frank Kermode, 'The Mature Comedies', in *Stratford-upon-Avon Studies* 3 (1961).

41 J. Russell Brown, Introduction to the New Arden edition of *The Merchant of Venice* (1954).

42 J. Russell Brown, *Shakespeare and his Comedies* (1957), p. 75.

43 W. Moelwyn Merchant, op. cit.

44 Ibid.

4 The Romantic Comedies

The so-called Romantic plays – *Twelfth Night, As You Like It*, and *Much Ado About Nothing* – provide clear evidence of how much Shakespeare's conception of comedy had matured since the writing of *A Midsummer Night's Dream*. Indeed, even that exquisite play at times shows some signs of the immaturity of the earlier *The Comedy of Errors, The Two Gentlemen of Verona* and *Love's Labour's Lost*. They display a sharp, sometimes mechanistic differentiation between their various ingredients: farce, knockabout humour, aerated language mix, not altogether successfully, with pathos, melodrama and a pleasing lyricism. The occasional lurches between extremes of theme, characterization, mode and expression, sweet and sour, dark and light, largely disappear or become accommodated in a more graceful unifying elegance by the time Shakespeare picked up his pen to evoke Arden and Illyria. It is almost as if he had discovered that autumnal twilight, with its blending of sunlight and shadow, was a more satisfying emblem and expression of the human condition than the garishly uncertain meteorology of the earlier comedies. Now, opposites are reconciled as the plays seem intent on embodying a vision of life as a blend of joy and disappointment, expectation and regret.

There is perhaps no more positive indication that in the sixteenth century the seasons of human life were differently disposed from ours than these romantic plays written between late 1598 and 1601. Shakespeare's confident matching of expression and content gives the impression of having been achieved early – they seem to be plays written by someone in their late twenties – but in 1599 Shakespeare was thirty-five. By this time, in every aspect of the art and craft of dramaturgy, Shakespeare was on a steeply ascending graph of creative activity. Language, character, the handling of plot and theme all give evidence of a huge energy. In particular, his manipulation of a mature lyrical language is authoritative while still having reserves of rhythmic and melodic beauty, and his plotting has a cunning efficiency – character and action are harmonized whereas before they often seemed yoked together with some discordancy.

In the first of the plays – *Much Ado About Nothing* – and, to a degree, in the other two, Shakespeare was writing very much under the influence of the plays of an older contemporary, John Lyly. Lyly specialized in romance, involving highly mannered courtly characters and, in their way, equally sophisticated country rustics. In his earlier comedies Shakespeare took from Lyly the characteristic artificial language of punning wit, allegorical reference, relentless alliteration, antithesis of phrase and flowered imagery. He learned, too, how to write bantering love-dialogue which he used in the verbal contests between Berowne and Rosaline in *Love's Labour's Lost* and Beatrice and Benedick in *Much Ado*. Indeed the whole convention of love-games, verbal and otherwise, derives from Lyly, though, in his mature romantic comedies, Shakespeare subtilizes their significance.

But perhaps Shakespeare's greatest achievement is his transformation of the so-called 'pastoral' mode, changing, enriching, and, in an important sense, dignifying this ubiquitous type of dramatic writing. In its common form, in the works of George Peele, Greene and Lyly, the pastoral mode was crammed with innumerable conventions, manipulated by each dramatist with varying degrees of success, so that even as they give us unexpected felicities, gaucherie often awaits us around the play's next corner. Indeed one of Shakespeare's achievements was to train these heterogeneous elements to take their proper place in a designed and controlled order.

Pastoral drama is replete with reluctant or frustrated wooers, of high and low estate; rejected swains and pouting shepherdesses; endangered or dispossessed noble ladies and disinherited noble Lotharios; banished Dukes and unaccountably malevolent male relatives; mistaken identities; females in disguise; wise and witty Fools; village wooings and arboreal assignations. Unknown dangers abound as cynical, soured men of no fixed abode haunt the woods and forests. All these elements are herded into a bosky venue, where sad knots are untied and happy ones new made. In Shakespeare's hands this tinsel became gold and he achieved the metamorphosis by deploying five elements which in their quality and usage give these plays an unarguable individuality.

The first is the pre-eminent status given to Love, for in Shakespeare's romantic comedies Love is the generator of theme, plot and character, not merely an important activity in human affairs, but as the source of all that makes for virtuous action, thought, feeling, and so – for happy fulfilment.

The second concerns the effects of Love. This element is an almost obsessive assertion of the power of Love to overcome the destructive forces of disorder and hatred. These comedies celebrate unity, reconciliation, order and concord, and their heroines, by word and example, either heal or organize, with thought and feeling, those they encounter who are deficient, bereft or ignorant of Love and are, therefore, unable to find either true concord or fulfilment.

The third is the extent to which Shakespeare puts the sophisticated society of the upper-crust in intriguing tandem with below-stairs riff-raff. Although Shakespeare found his courtiers in his source stories, he carved his lower orders from his own experience. Already, in the characters of Launce, Bottom and his artisan companions, he had shown how much he owed to his own Cotswold hinterland. Now, in his depiction of William, Audrey, Martext and Belch he added to that debt. Certainly none of his contemporaries saw and heard the rougher sort of mankind as accurately, warmly or, indeed, with as much respect, as he did.

The fourth element is one of his most original contributions to English drama – his use of the professional Fool. Feste, Touchstone and, later, Lavache and Lear's unnamed shadow, have a far deeper role in the plays they inhabit than any of the comic knockabout clowns or country bumpkins who abound in his earlier plays and continue to appear throughout his later ones. The professional Fools are different in status and function from the Dogberrys, Dulls, Launces and Gobbos, because their source of origin is different. In 1599 Will Kempe, the chief comedian, left the Lord Chamberlain's Company, of which Shakespeare was a member, and his place was taken by the playwright and actor, Robert Armin. Little is known of him except that he acted Shakespeare's Fools, was a minor dramatist and a pamphleteer. Among his published works are: *Foole upon Foole* (publ. 1600); *Two Maids of More-clack* (publ. 1609); *Phantasma, The Italian Taylor and his Boy* (1609); *Quips upon Questions: A Nest of Ninnies*.

One suspects that from these books and even more from the influence of Armin himself, Shakespeare derived his professional Fools. Armin describes some of the real Fools of history who belonged to royal and noble households, and who, like Touchstone, Feste, Lavache and Lear's Fool, had well-defined characteristics of both personality and function. From these Shakespeare created an unusual but important kind of character – an individual who used his function as professional funny-man to couch his expression of a wry, even sad, wisdom.

From Armin, and elsewhere, Shakespeare would for example have heard of Thomas More's Fool – Henry Paterson, Henry VIII's Fool – Will Somers, and Wolsey's Fool – Will Patch.[1] These men were accounted to be men of notable intellectual distinction and political shrewdness, often acting as advisers to their masters or as carriers of messages between them. In *Twelfth Night* we recall Feste who 'wears not motley in his brain' and 'he is holden wise that reputeth himself a Fool': in *As You Like It* Jaques expresses a desire to be a Fool so that he may the more easily exercise a licence to speak his mind and 'cleanse the foul body of the infected world': and, above all, we realize that if King Lear had accepted the shrewd strictures of his Fool, he may well have been wise earlier.

The importance of the emergence of this type of character in the romantic comedies cannot be overestimated. Shakespeare had discovered that he could insert into his plays an agent which, though acceptable as a natural part of the play's milieu, could also stand aside from total committal to the fictional world of the play and speak, as it were, from a neutral corner. We can, in fact, see Lear both as he is and as he ought to be, because the Fool is there to tell us; we can see the exaggerations of Olivia's mourning because Feste tells us, and her, about them; sometimes the Fools, in their wisdom, operate on our behalf – expressing for us, within the world of the play, our own unspoken comments on what we see or hear.

Perhaps one may also be allowed to see in the Fool-figure the presence of Shakespeare himself. Both helped, by their professions, to sustain a world of illusion; both, from behind the mask of folly, the disguise of comedy, tried to express the truth behind the illusion.

The fifth element which contributes to Shakespeare's supremacy over his contemporaries is his use of language. By the time he wrote *Twelfth Night* and *As You Like It* he had effected a remarkable liaison between a dramatic version of Elizabethan vernacular speech and a richly-conceived imaginative lyricism. He had moved away from the thumping iambic regularity of his early comedies, the sudden swoops of lyricism of *A Midsummer Night's Dream*, and the tortured sophisticated prose with which his apprentice plays are festooned, to a kind of language where it is difficult to detect the seams which join verse and prose. He had learned much from writing the highly-charged language of *Richard II* and *Romeo and Juliet* and the controlled prose of *Henry IV*, and had come within striking distance of a mode of expression in which the customary divisions between prose and verse were being annihilated.

There is no more telling evidence of Shakespeare's growing command of language than the fact that *Much Ado About Nothing* is almost entirely written in a prose medium, yet possesses to a high degree the effectiveness, associativeness and lyrical force of poetry.

The writing of these romantic comedies, then, enabled him to benefit from the dramaturgical problems they set. The need to tame the pastoral convention taught him much about the organization of plot and theme; the liaison with Armin, which produced the professional Fool as a character, enriched his awareness of the subtle interplay of illusion and reality – what 'is' and what 'seems' – a basic preoccupation in his later plays; and his ability to find an easy commerce between prose and poetry, gave his language an ordered, unified power, and a fluency, both of which served him well in the task he set himself in the tragedies. There he sought to explore mankind's darker heart and head, and needed to command all the skills of both dramatist and poet.

Much Ado About Nothing

The least satisfying and least gracious part of *Much Ado About Nothing* is the plot involving Claudio and Hero – which Shakespeare took from an earlier story. What affords us most delight are the Beatrice/Benedick episodes – Shakespeare's own invention. The first plot was most probably found in his reading of an Italian novella by Bandello,[2] though a version of it occurs in Ariosto's *Orlando Furioso*. The rest, including Dogberry and Verges, comes from the chambers of his own imagination. The differences between the two in terms of emotional atmosphere, characterization and spirit can create serious problems for our acceptance of the play as an entity. Claudio seems priggish, mentally under-developed, self-indulgent and, in the end, reaps a reward which seems flattering to his desserts. Hero, though wronged and victimized, never completely conquers our affections. She is a somewhat faint and fainting maiden suitable for inclusion among the wilting heroines of nineteenth-century melodrama, lacking any brave spirit that would make her presence poignant rather than, as it is, irritating. She becomes a mere mechanism in a plot which, by itself, is curiously tasteless in its absurdity.

By contrast, the Beatrice/Benedick story has a fresh, acidic quality, sweetened by its conclusion, and made especially palatable by the tartly clever wit which characterizes their relationship. These two are no less under the spell of illusion than Claudio or, for that matter, the other characters, but they seem to be half aware of it and, sustaining it to the end, seems part of a game they are prepared to enjoy. Regarded separately and superficially, the two plots appear incompatible, both in their quality and in their effects upon the audience, the one tending to drive us away from the play, the other inviting us in.

It is all the more remarkable, therefore, that the play is among the popular favourites of audiences and that, in good performance, it seems to have a firm unity and balanced construction. The reasons for its success on stage are many but the decisive variety of its moods would seem to be one of the most important. The first two scenes have an almost festive atmosphere reminiscent of the early comedies: warriors are returned from wars, ladies and celebrations await them. The scenes between Don John and his confidants – Borachio and Conrade – have the half absurd quality of bare-faced melodramatic villainy. the Dogberry/Verges scenes are superbly farcical. The

164

garden scenes, in which Beatrice and Benedick are duped, have the artful shape, movement, and verbal dexterity of Restoration comedy. If the church scene takes us beyond unreal melodrama towards the edge of dark realism, the conclusion, even if in our hearts we know it to be forced by the plot-mechanics, still satisfies that yearning, which never abates in audiences, to see, if not justice, at least theatrical logic.

This variety is given a cohesion by strong dramatic and theatrical bonds. All the sub-episodes – like Don John/Borachio/Conrad scenes and the Dogberry scenes – serve to guide the main direction of the play. The Claudio/Hero plot would be impossible without them and the Beatrice/Benedick story would lack meaning without the results of the intrigue which is initiated by Don John and which Dogberry, like a lucky Bassett hound with no sense of smell, eventually uncovers.

The fact that the play is largely written in prose both aids the credibility of the whole and provides an element of contrast. As Foakes has pointed out: '. . . the characters whose speech is almost wholly in prose . . . have more life and depth than those who speak verse most of the time . . . Benedick and Beatrice deliberately reject:

"Taffeta phrases, silken terms precise
Three-piled hyperboles, spruce affectation,"

in favour of witty prose. . .'[3] It is in fact correct wit which is held in tension with over-pretty sophistication in this play, and, in the end, the innate honesty and candour of the former overcomes the self-deception of the latter.

In the three mature comedies (*Much Ado, As You Like It*, and *Twelfth Night*) a young woman dominates our experience of each play and by her presence makes acceptable a series of events and characters which are, to say the least, unpalatable. Claudio's priggishness, Hero's ineffectiveness, Don John's perfidy, the hedonism of the court – are all irritants to our sensibilities as are Orsino's self-indulgence, Orlando's relative effeteness, the Duke's sudden excess of anger. It is the romantic heroines, Beatrice, Viola, Rosalind, who sweeten the unpleasant pill and edge the play into the status of happy contented comedy.

Something of the nature and dominance of Beatrice's character is given at her very first appearance. In the first place he would be a brave person who was prepared to take her on in a battle of wits. Her taunting reference to Benedick bespeaks a tough spirit – one for attack not defence.

'Oh Lord he will hang upon him like a disease, he is sooner caught
than the pestilence, . . . God help the noble Claudio, if he hath caught
the Benedick.'   [1.1.70–4]

Secondly, Beatrice seems at ease in the presence of men. She
displays no wilting femininity, no suggestion of subservience either
to men's whims and foibles or to any convention of society. She
speaks as an equal and has to be accepted as an equal. For, although
all three romantic heroines – Beatrice, Rosalind and Viola – may have
strong personalities, it is Beatrice who more than holds her own in
men's company without her will having to be shored up by disguise.
When Viola and Rosalind revert to female dress they become
beautiful spouses; disguise aids their determination to find love but,
when it is dropped, they become their man's willing mate. Beatrice,
having no such aid, seems to be in a position of greater loneliness.
Once having established herself as the equal of men, she has to
preserve that equality without the hope of any concession on their
part to her femininity. The price she has to pay for being accepted as
man's intellectual equal is, for a long time, to be misunderstood; the
price Viola has to pay for her solitary harbouring of love for Orsino,
is to watch with anguish the possibility of him marrying another. The
difference is between a willed and a fated isolation. The attitude
Beatrice takes up towards Benedick drives her into a position where
her constant engagement in verbal banter gives her the reputation of
being a man-hater, a 'professed tyrant to their sex' who cannot abide
to hear tell of a husband. What at times her attitude reveals is a
curious strain of comic pathos:

'Thus goes everyone to the world but I, and I am sunburnt. I may sit
in a corner and cry "Heigh ho for a husband".'   [II.1.286–8]

It is all part of a kind of game, and the attractiveness of her character
lies in the fact that within the game there is a serious, often heart-
catching truth. Her nature forces her to banter, to appear recklessly
gay in her strictures on men and in the idea of a husband, yet deep
inside her a silent battle is going on.

She makes one very touching and precipitate exit from the action.
She is bantering with Don Pedro about how she would marry his
brother if he had one and he reminds her of what everybody expects
from her:

'To be merry best becomes you, for out of question, you were born
in a merry hour.'

She answers, as if to confirm the general view:

> 'No sure my lord, my mother cried, but then there was a star danced, and under that was I born.'

But when Leonato asks:

> 'Niece, will you look to those things I told you of.'

She turns quickly upon him:

> 'I cry you mercy, uncle, by your grace's pardon.'   [II.1.299–307]

and one suspects leaves his company crying. For a moment the battle between her given 'disposition' and her own desires have become too much for her. Moments like this suggest there is more to Beatrice than dancing star, and these moments prepare us to accept the mood she displays in the church scene, where her curt directness is so different from the playfulness of the earlier cut and thrust:

> BEATRICE: I love you with so much of my heart, that none is left to protest.
> BENEDICK: Come bid me do anything for thee.
> BEATRICE: Kill Claudio.
> BENEDICK: Ha! not for the wide world.
> BEATRICE: You kill me to deny it. Farewell.   [IV.1.284–9]

Benedick is indeed foil to Beatrice; we never feel he will better her in any of their verbal battles. His sallies often seem less a result of willed determination than hers, and, indeed, Don Pedro speaks truly of him – 'He doth indeed show some sparks that are like wit'. [2.3.171] In Beatrice's presence his witty weapons are never so effectively cutting as when he is with others. There is something comparable here to the relationship between Rosalind and Orlando, and Viola and Orsino. Orsino's aristocratic and autocratic leadership of his court pales to nothing in the shadow of his curious ineffectiveness in the company of Viola; Orlando's physical courage is, in the Forest of Arden, overshadowed by his emotional subservience to Rosalind. The difference in fact between these three heroines and their male wooers is that the females are intellectually, morally, and emotionally more mature than the males. The church scene in *Much Ado* confirms this. Here the true spirit of Beatrice is revealed – a woman of great fidelity to those she loves, of great moral determintion, and entirely truthful. For the sake of truth, she is prepared to stake all that her love for Benedick means, for she can only love a man

167

who can come near to matching her own intellectual resource, her fidelity, and her sense of what is true and what is false. By teaching him the true meaning of love she releases in him a new maturity, as Rosalind does in Orlando, Viola in Orsino, and even Kate in Petruchio. As John Russell Brown comments – when Benedict 'truly loves, he must ... believe his lady's soul against all outward testimony...' and 'if he has truly looked upon her with a lover's imagination he will have seen the beauty of that (inward) spirit and will now trust and obey'.[4]

The Claudio/Hero plot, though tasteless by comparison, is a variation on the same theme. Claudio is Benedick without the capacity for intellectual maturity or emotional resilience. He is a spoilt whippersnapper, a boy thrown into the army with only the trappings of manhood and little, if any, inward maturity. To some extent he is perhaps more sinned against than sinning, a victim of his own youthfulness, his own profession and his own class – which have taught him little but that (like a child) he should have whatever he desires. He has been provided with no inner resources by which he can test the veracity of Don John's outrageous accusations. Like every young hero of courtly romance (from whence he comes) he responds to every situation self-indulgently.

Equally, Hero is the conventional heroine of courtly romance, a literary code which was the staple diet of the very class to which both she and Claudio belong. She is designed to be a victim, blown by every conventional whim. Foakes underlines the 'artificiality' of the Claudio/Hero story: 'He is a romantic lover for whom ardour is unnecessary, since he loves an image other than a person, and is never seen making love to Hero. Her name signified devotion in love, as the legendary Hero, a priestess of Venus, loved Leander...'[5] The outcome of their story is 'happy', as is Beatrice and Benedick's, and supposedly Claudio eventually learns, as does Benedick, a maturer conception of the nature of true love. But there is an essential difference in the effects of the two plots upon the audience's imaginations. The Claudio/Hero story remains within convention – its resolution the inevitable and mechanical result of the working out of the ploys of a convention. The Beatrice/Benedick resolution, however, is based upon the logistics of the human heart and mind, and as a result, their love is more 'real' to us. They have discovered one another, whereas Claudio and Hero have been 'put together'.

All the other characters in the play, of whatever kind – the well-meaning Leonato and Don Pedro, the villainous Don John and his crew, the farcically pompous Dogberry – minister to the working out of the two main plots. They are all under-developed as characters, although two of them, Dohn John and Dogberry, deserve more than a cursory mention. Don John, like the Duke in *As You Like It*, is a man of ungovernable anger, malice, and envy. In both cases the force of their villainy lies in their relationship to their own brother. Don John says of his brother, 'I had rather be a canker in a hedge than a rose in his garden'. He is also rancorously envious of Claudio's youth, 'That young start-up'. In Bandello's novella he is a rejected suitor, and a bastard, and Francis Bacon, the contemporary essayist, states that those most subject to envy were 'deformed persons, old men and bastards'. Shakespeare does not mention rejected suitorship; he makes little of bastardy; he concentrates on the fact of envy. There would have been no need for him to be explicit. Such characters were well-known figures of the literature of the time.

It is strange how possible it is to write of so many of the ingredients of this play without feeling forced to comment on their comic 'qualities'. There is much that is not comic; towards the end the play does, indeed, seem to lurch in the direction of blood and tragedy. The opening scene, Beatrice and Benedick's witty games, the garden scenes, sprinkle rather than suffuse the whole with drops of comic spirit. The uninhibited laughter Shakespeare gave decidedly and only to Dogberry, and here we move from Sicily to Warwickshire. For English audiences this is not only reassuring in itself but it is the means by which we are reassured that the events in Sicily will have a happy conclusion. Dogberry has all the comforting presence of the now virtually defunct village policeman. The very fact that he was there, largely present in the village, was sufficient. On some dark night in the Cotswolds, when evil was abroad, the great, slow-moving bulk of officialdom, galumphing against the moonlight like a large family-dog, banished all fears that evil would triumph. The creation of Dogberry's character, however, is far more subtle than often appears on first acquaintance. He is inefficient, conceited, pompous, a sycophant to higher officialdom, all those things we dislike when we imagine their presence in the lower reaches of the Civil Service. Yet Dogberry is entirely lovable and for many reasons. In the first place, largely because he gives us a sense of comfortable permanence. He stands, in his comic way, for a tested status quo and he is even more lovable because he is also an implied mockery of that status quo – mispronouncing and malapropping his way through every situation. He is undoubtedly the mould out of which have come countless self-mocking policemen in countless comic-thriller plays. He is lovable because he is essentially warm-hearted – he has more of a care for possible broken pates in his Watch than he has for the exact execution of duty. He wants all manner of things to be well, and if he seems to want to be recognized as being the creator of a happy commonwealth, we can forgive him, for it is a laudable aim. And finally, he is lovable because, out of his own mouth, he is given words to mock his own pomposity. Like a fat copper relentlessly pursuing the wrong clue he is determined that he shall not be set down an ass. In passing judgment on himself he has set his place in our affections. His is the triumph of naïve candour.

The language of the play, for the most part, is prose. It is partly for this reason that the play lacks a full romantic glow and calls for a more intellectual response. In *Love's Labour's Lost* and *The Comedy of Errors*, the earlier plays of his younger days, Shakespeare is more explicit about what he means by full and real love, and the warmly lyrical passages of verse in those plays convey the meaning with passion. In this play the basic theme has to be worked out in the rational parts of the audience's experience. In the writing of *Henry IV* he began more and more to exploit prose as a dominant medium of communication and the prose language of *Much Ado* represents a complete mastery of that medium. Shakespeare shows himself capable, at different points in the play, of rendering glittering wit, malaprop farce, true tenderness, and controlled pathos – all in the medium of prose. Perhaps, indeed, at this point of fame, recognition, and relative affluence in his career, he 'relaxed' his imagination (if only for a very short time) from the pressures and demands of writing dramatic poetry. Perhaps even after the tremendous poetic achievement of *Romeo and Juliet, A Midsummer Night's Dream, Henry IV*, his imagination required, in a way, to be refreshed. The prose of *Much Ado*, in all its manifestations, seems easy-running. It may not, indeed, have come easy, but Shakespeare as an artist found refreshment not by absenting himself from creative activity, but by changing the direction and mood of his creative imagination. Yet the period of relaxation was short, and the subsequent plays – *As You Like It* and *Twelfth Night* – suggest that, poetically, he benefited much from this exquisite excursion into prose.

As You Like It

In his introduction to *Elizabethan Love Stories*, T. J. B. Spencer writes:

> [Shakespeare] had the ability to go and find out the best that was known and thought in his day; to get it quickly (as a busy writer must, for Shakespeare wrote a million words in twenty years); to get it without much trouble and without constant access to good collections of books . . . ; to deal with his material and sources of information his intelligence and discrimination . . . Perhaps he was a good listener, not self-assertive in the company of his supposed betters, and was therefore able, with that incomparable serenity of mind of his, to profit from any well-informed acquaintance.[6]

As You Like It is an excellent demonstration of Spencer's remarks. The play was written in 1599, at a time when the vogue for pastoral romance was at its height and when the taste for it was satisfied by plays like Anthony Munday's *The Downfall of Robert, Earl of Huntingdon* (1598), *The Death of Robert, Earl of Huntingdon* (1598), by Munday and Henry Chettle, and by popular translations from Matteo Bandello's *Novelle*. Shakespeare's source for this play (used quickly enough to catch the height of fashion) was Thomas Lodge's *Rosalynde, Euphues' golden legacie* (publ. 1590). His intelligence and dramatic skill are triumphantly shown in the extent to which the original source is deepened in meaning, enlivened in incident, sharpened in characterization. His own penetrating imagination transformed Rosalynd from a typical pastoral-romantic heroine into one of the most pleasingly devious and full-blooded young women in dramatic history. That same imagination gave the romantic material of the play a piquant sauce by its invention of Touchstone, Audrey, William and Oliver Martext, and that disturber of speculations – Jaques. As to what unconsidered trifles he picked up – transforming them into gold – this play, again, gives ample testimony. In the characters of Touchstone and Jaques there may be seen the outcome of the impact made by the entry of Robert Armin to the company of players and with his arrival that new kind of character – the Fool – appears in Shakespeare's plays, built from basically comic material but with indications of something beyond single comic communication and response.

All this resulted in the making of a more complex meaning behind the fable and in raising the play above the rut of typical pastoral comedy. The stark contrast between sunshine and shadow, the conventional behaviour, the typed characters, the mechanical resolution of the plot – all typical of pastoral romance – are present in *As You Like It*. Yet, despite the quality of the fable and the action, despite the fact that this Forest of Arden has about it something of the never-never aspect of contrived romance, the exploration of the theme is sharply realistic. As a result, the audience is able to enjoy the play on two levels. It may gambol its imaginations in the delights of the fable, but it would be an insensitive theatregoer who did not realize that the theme reaches deeply into the meaning of love and the irony of life.

In general terms Shakespeare develops the theme already announced in the early comedies – the necessity for order, fidelity, truth, and honour for a successful outcome in love. We have seen the working-out of the theme of order (and its opposite) in the history plays; in this play, for the first time, the theme is seen in the geography of the human mind, heart and imagination.

Rosalind is at the centre of the action and the theme – she is both the 'creator' of right order and its most positive and acceptable symbol. Her 'teaching' to Orlando of the ways of love is a demonstration of the theme in depth, her conducting and disposing of the love affairs of others is a demonstration of the theme latitudinally. Her education of Orlando is never sententious; the need for love to be certain and faithful is never preached at him. She teaches by the example of her own feelings, and her seriousness of purpose is expressed in flashes, quicksilver proofs that, for her, all the gamesomeness and the antics in the forest are more than words and appearances:

'Good my complexion! dost thou think, though I am caparison'd like
a man, I have a doublet and hose in my disposition?' [III.2.181–3]

The absence of sententiousness allows Rosalind to stand as an example of the best kind of woman – gay, tender, loyal, witty, faithful, and sprightly in body and mind, and the love she teaches she also embodies. The keynote of her character is a delicacy of spirit, and there is no other character in the play whom we can trust, respect, and delight in with the same confidence she inspires in us.

Shakespeare exploits this delicacy of spirit in a number of ways – her recoil from physical injury, for example:

'But is there any else longs to see this broken music in his sides? Is
there yet another dotes upon rib-breaking?'   [I.2.125–7]

Her generosity:

'The little strength that I have, I would it were with you.' [I.2.174–5]

Her courageous sincerity:

'Unless you could teach me to forget a banished father, you must not learn me how to remember any extraordinary pleasure.' [I.2.2–5]

Her vulnerability to love:

'What did he when thou saw'st him? What said he? How look'd he? Wherein went he? What makes he here? Did he ask for me?'
[III.2.205–8]

She emerges as the leader of the trio which, self-banished from court, ventures into the Forest of Arden, but in taking up the leadership, loses nothing of her femininity. The audience is thus prepared to accept, without embarrassment, her obvious mental superiority to Orlando and her determination to take the reins into her own hands. All the lineaments of her character are enchanting to our eyes and ears but there is another quality in her which is likely to be obscured by her more dominant characteristics, and which amounts to more than enchantment. She has within her a secret sadness, often taking the form of a reflective wryness, which never becomes bitter and gradually comes to be seen as the real source of her honesty and of her insistent quest for plain-dealing in love.

The first appearance of this element in her character comes in the exchange with Celia (I.2) which is interrupted by Touchstone. Although his interevention side-tracks the conversation into witty badinage, we have heard enough before his entrance to make us reflect upon Rosalind's words:

'Fortune reigns in the gifts of the world, not in the lineaments of Nature.' [I.2.38–9]

Fortune has dealt hard with her and it is to deal her another, harder blow by the Duke's decree of banishment. She has been prevented by Fortune from enjoying the full happiness which her own personality, her social status and the companionship of close relatives would have given her. She knows from her own experience the truth of her own remarks about Fortune, and alludes to it again, after Orlando has defeated the wrestler, when she hopefully declares:

'He calls us back. My pride fell with my fortunes;' [I.2.231]

She has been the victim of bad fortune; she has learned that it is realistic not to expect too much of 'nature'. Man is a creature dominated by the unknown workings of favourable or unfavourable fortune. Rosalind can scarcely credit the possibility that love has entered her heart – can it really be that at last good fortune has come her way? And certainly the assiduous way in which she tries to discover whether a true and good 'nature' lies behind that fortune, suggests the question is never far from her mind.

The Forest of Arden is where better selves are found. The rancour and fury of Duke Frederick is there converted into happy piety: the jealousy and disgust of Orlando's brother is transmuted into warm affection; the banished Duke and his men discover a relaxed companionable ease there, learning mutual respect and interdependence – thus creating an ordered society.

In Shakespeare's plays there is copious evidence that his imagination was deeply attracted to a conventional renaissance concept of woodlands as potential agents which, after first disorientating individuals, brought about changes in their behaviour – usually for the better. *As You Like It* is but one example in a group which includes *Love's Labour's Lost*, *A Midsummer Night's Dream* and *The Merry Wives of Windsor* where the magic of woodlands or forests plays a large part in human disposition. And even in other plays where the effect is less compulsive there is frequently a quickening of the play's pulse, a sudden awareness of magical influence when a wood, a forest, a glade, or a grove are mentioned.

In marked contrast to the natural life is the court. There, sharp anger erupts suddenly; violence is near the surface in the confrontation between Orlando and Charles, and in the motive behind it: inhuman cruelty is implicit in the burning of Orlando's house. There is a touching symbolism in the fact that the most 'naturally' good man in the court – Old Adam – feels that he must leave and when he is received graciously and proudly by the banished Duke's society, it is as if he has come home to die happily in his right and proper soil.

Only two people remain untouched by the translation from the sophisticated artificial court where capricious fortune operates, to the Forest where beneficent nature works: they are Touchstone and Jaques. Touchstone is a professional court fool, not a natural idiot. He is a man of sophistication who has become part of the organization of the court. His confrontation with Corin confirms this and, at the same time, illustrates clearly the contrast, basic to the whole play, between the simple efficacy of what is beneficently natural and the deviousness of what is sophisticated. Touchstone is worsted by Corin, whose natural common-sense overcomes Touchstone's self-conscious verbal dexterity:

'Not a whit, Touchstone. Those that are good manners at the court are as ridiculous in the country as the behaviour of the country is most mockable at the court. You told me you salute not at the court, but you kiss your hands; that courtesy would be uncleanly if courtiers were shepherds.'   [III.2.41–5]

His wooing of Audrey is little more than a kind of charade. His tone to her is always mocking: 'Doth my simple feature content you?' he asks her, and this leads him to a display of word-mongering in the middle of which something of his sardonic philosophy of life is revealed:

'for here we have no temple but the wood, no assembly but horn-beasts. But what though? Courage! As horns are odious, they are necessary.'   [III.3.42–7]

Touchstone performs a triple role in the play. The first is his professional one as court Fool – a witty and licensed obbligato to the action of the play. The second involves his thematic function (with Jaques) as a resistant to the beneficial effects of the natural order of the Forest of Arden. The Duke's words:

'. . . Are not these woods
More free from peril than the envious court?
Here feel we not the penalty of Adam,
The seasons' difference, . . .'   [II.1.3–4]

is given its thematically important answer in Touchstone's words to William:

'Truly, shepherd, in respect of itself, it is a good life; but in respect that it is a shepherd's life, it is nought.'   [III.2.14–15]

Touchstone's third function is as a sharp sauce to contrast with the romantic diet of the play. Shakespeare, by this time, had learnt that the art of dramatic writing is, to a large extent, that of representing contrasts in mood, style, and character. Without the presence of Touchstone's cynical sharpness, the romantic food would cloy and grow tiresome.

Jaques shares this function with him; certainly we begin to yearn for the romantic diet after the taste of Jaques' sour melancholy. Yet

175

there is more to him than this. We learn much about him before he actually appears, and it is well to take heed for Shakespeare is always conspicuously careful about preliminary information he gives his audience. Often what is given is intended to implant in our minds a dominant characteristic (courage and martial prowess in Macbeth, melancholy in Hamlet, pride, status and bravery in Othello) upon which the subsequent situations and scenes of the play will work.

Jaques, we learn, has been observed 'weeping and commenting' upon a deer wounded by a hunter and abandoned by the rest of the herd. Jaques compares their horrid indifference to the ways of the human world:

> 'Sweep on, you fat and greasy citizens;
> 'Tis just the fashion. Wherefore do you look
> Upon that poor and broken bankrupt there?'   [II.1.56–7]

We have learnt of a man who could be described as sensitive and philosophical, but might well also occasion the cynical view that he is sententious and emotionally self-indulgent. We incline to the second view, when we hear the Duke say:

> 'I love to cope him in these sullen fits,
> For then he's full of matter.'   [II.1.67–8]

This inclination is given some justification when we first meet Jaques. He protests too much about his state of melancholy: he is an inward-looking man:

> 'I can suck melancholy out of a song, as a weasel sucks eggs.'
>   [II.5.12–3]

There follows the superb speeches to the Duke and his followers, in which Jaques anatomizes the condition of being a Fool.[7] In Touchstone he has come across one he believes to be a fellow-traveller – one who finds the world an odd place but who, unlike himself, has, because he is a Fool, a liberty, a charter to blow on whom he pleases. Jaques in these speeches communicates an aspiration for a status of Fool which will allow him to reflect upon, and judge the world, without commitment to it, to be one who can use his folly as 'a stalking horse' and 'under the presentation of that' can 'shoot his wit'.

Yet the 'wit' he yearns to be able to expend is of a kind which must, for him, have a practical purpose. Tired of the world,

possessed of a 'melancholy of mine own' (the result of his experience
of the world) he wishes to speak his mind to some purpose and so:

> '. . . through and through
> Cleanse the foul body of th'infected world.'   [II.7.59–60]

We have enough evidence of Jaques by now to know that he could
not wear the coat of wise motley properly, for he lacks the
ingredients of the true professional Fool – like Touchstone. And yet
Jaques seems sincere in his protestations to achieve a status from
which he can cleanse the infected world. Why, however, should such
a man be found in Arden?

Many interpretations have been offered of the source and nature
of this character. The frequently expressed theory is that he is a
delineation of the Italianate Englishman, who has travelled widely,
become bored with experience and affected a melancholy. Beginning
as an affectation, this has now become an amalgam of conceit and real
action-sapping sadness. Some have seen him as a lampoon on Sir John
Harington, the courtier and translator of Ariosto's *Orlando Furioso*;
others as Shakespeare's comment on Ben Jonson or an embodiment
of the melancholy dramatist, John Marston; but the speeches given
him seem conspicuously free from references which could unequivocally associate him with actual people.

Jaques is a self-centred man who has not the equipment to be a
full professional Fool. He becomes therefore a wild card in the pack;
a shadow in the sunlight of Arden. He is governed by a self-conceit
which he cannot control. Very soon Shakespeare was to create
another such – Malvolio – whose shadow casts, if only fleetingly, a
darkness across Illyria; and later still he was to create Thersites, a
monstrous sore of a man – one on whom self-conceit has turned into
the sourest rancour. Such characters need to be distinguished quite
clearly from the professional Fools like Touchstone, Feste and Lear's
nameless Fool. They do not have the blessing which the true Fools
have of 'allowed' witty effrontery, of licensed opportunity to speak
what, behind their wit, they know to be the truth. Above all, because
they do not have professional skills of entertaining, and, behind the
mask of amusing others, of remaining insulated from and uncommitted to that which they comment on, they lack objectivity.

Why then do Jaques, Malvolio and their like, exist in the play?
Their presence can be superficially explained by regarding them as
contrast-agents in a romantic world. To this extent they are a simple
but effective means of subtilizing the comic mode. A more searching

yet more contentious explanation is that they are the palpable indications of a shift in balance in Shakespeare's view of the world. It cannot be too often emphasized that his view was all of a piece but that, from time to time, one facet is explored more searchingly than others. In the midst of the joyous and affirming romantic comedies, the darker hues of tragedy can be glimpsed. The comedies demonstrate the construction of an ordered world; the tragedies witness the destruction of order. Jaques and Malvolio are warning signs of Shakespeare's recognition that there is a kind of human belief, attitude and action which sits ill with order and the acceptance of it. The better part of the self-indulgent Jaques sees a foul infection in the world and seeks to cleanse it – but he is defeated by his own conceit. The worst part of him nags at our enjoyment of the order which, by the ministrations of Rosalind, the play is making for. It is Jaques's presence which makes the ordered world ceated in Arden the more poignant and, in a sense, the more to be wondered about. The effective theatrical result is that the world of *As You Like It* seems fragile; its affirmation of the efficacy of good nature trapped in a present tense. Its declaration of future intent seems a sad illusion.

Yet, while we are given leave by the play itself to speculate upon these graver issues, and while the affirming joy of the resolution seems fragile, we cannot forget how superbly happy we are made by the world Shakespeare orders for us. The comedy of the play is not only rich in quality, but of great variety. Rosalind's wit is not only sharp but warm – our laughter has, as it were, a contented smile upon its face simply because the wit has a happy purpose:

> 'I'll have no father, if you be not he:
> I'll have no husband, if you be not he:
> Nor ne'er wed woman, if you be not she.'   [V.4.116.1–8]

Touchstone's sharper sallies arouse the kind of appreciative laughter reserved for the professional who is good at his job. At times we respect him, with a little reserve, because he has the unnerving and disquieting ability to seem more clever than any one else about him. At other times this kind of laughter loses its reserve; the wheel turns and we find ourselves laughing at Touchstone because the natural wisdom of the countryman confounds him: the comedy of Martext and of Audrey induces in us laughter of the most primitive kind, coming from a delighted feeling of total superiority to the characters who create it. Audrey's enormous ignorance and innocent bawdy, Martext's crazy assumption of clerical status, are the victims of our laughter, but we do not despise them – firstly because the characters are themselves happy people, and secondly because they are natural people: both of them have an innocence which excuses their palpable defects.

All these forms of comic presentation and response are, however, contained within an essence whose effects suffuses them all. It is expressed neatly by Helen Gardner:

'*As You Like It* is the most refined and exquisite of the comedies, the one which is most consistently played over by a delighted intelligence ... The essence is one in which intelligence and emotional sensitivity combine. In their combination we are neither over-provoked by too assiduous an exploration of intellectual meaning nor too lavish a presentation of emotional experience. It is as if Shakespeare had himself achieved a kind of civilised contentment – fleeting but true – and shared it without exaggerating or cheapening it.'[8]

Twelfth Night

The occasion of the first performance of *Twelfth Night* may well have dictated its colouring and temperature. It was written for a festive occasion. John Manningham, a barrister, reports in his diary, having seen the play acted in the Middle Temple on the 2 Feb. 1602:

> At our feast we had a play called 'Twelve Night' or 'What You Will', much like The Comedy of Errors, or Menechmi in Plautus, but most like and near to that in Italian called Inganni. A good practise in it to make the steward believe his Lady Widow was in love with him, by counterfeiting a letter as from his Lady in general terms, telling him what she liked best in him, and prescribing his gesture in smiling, his apparel, and etc, and then when he came to practise making him believe they took him to be mad.

Leslie Hotson believes that its first performance was at Court on the Feast of the Epiphany in January 1601, at celebrations to honour the visit of a Tuscan ambassador – Duke Orsino.[9] Either of these occasions suggests a special commissioning. The alternative title 'or What You Will' indicates a happy flippancy – the nomenclature does not matter, the occasion is the thing. However, it could not, from internal evidence, have been written before 1599 and, with Manningham's diary in mind, it could not have been written after 1602.

Its plot is similar to the translation of *Gl'Ingannati* which was performed at Cambridge on the occasion of a visit from the Earl of Essex.[10] The more direct source, however, is Barnabe Riche's story of *Apollonius and Silla*, itself deriving ultimately from *Gl'Ingannati* by way of prose versions in Bandello's *Novelle*, and Belleforest's *Histoires Tragiques* (1559–82).[11]

Barnabe Riche's version contains two questions which Shakespeare's play, in some measure, answers. First, 'what is the ground, indeed of reasonable love whereby the knot is knit of true and perfect friendship?'; second, in T. J. B. Spencer's words,

> To love them that hate us, to follow them that fly from us, to fawn on them that frown on us, to curry favour with them that disabuse us, to be glad to please them that care not how they offend us, who will not confess this to be an erroneus love, neither grounded upon wit nor reason?[12]

Shakespeare's answer is, in effect, to demonstrate different kinds of love – fawning love, misplaced love, witless love, unexpected love, and true love. Malvolio, Orsino and Olivia, Andrew, Sebastian, and Viola are agents for each particular demonstration and it might be said that Toby and Maria also play their part in this dance, their love being based on admiration, affection, and expediency. Although each kind of love is presented to us, and we are left to decide which, in Riche's word is the least 'erroneous', the important point is that whatever decision we make, we are left in no doubt that all kinds of love play a part in the everlasting human dance.

Two kinds are announced at the very beginning of the play. Orsino's first speech has all the languid self-indulgence of a man of wealth and comfort for whom love is a bitter-sweet adaggio accompaniment to his existence. His personality is firmly established from the first. He is a curiously inert man, prepared only to give commands for actions to be taken by others on his behalf, the sort of man who is likely to live in an illuson of love, since he never can take steps to discover for himself the truth or otherwise of his indeterminate affections.

Viola's personality is immediately established in sharp contrast. Her very manner of speaking – quick, urgent, directly questioning – seems like a fresh breeze by comparison with Orsino's hothouse phraseology. Moreover, what she says about Orsino to the sea-captain suggests an active, purposeful creature prepared to seek the truth of emotions which stir her. It may well be that she already harbours some romantic feelings for Orsino before she actually meets him:

'I have heard my father name him.
He was a bachelor then.' [I.2.28–9]

'. . . I'll do my best
To woo your lady. (*Aside*) Yet, a barful strife!
Whoe'er I woo, myself would be his wife.' [I.4.39–41]

Although these are strong hints, they are admittedly less definite than in the source story where Viola (Silla) had previously met Orsino (Apollonius) in her father's house where 'she fed him with such amorous baits as the modesty of a maid could reasonably afford', but they are piquant enough.

Viola's personality also sharply contrasts with Olivia's. When she first visits the 'marble-breasted' and mourning creature, we note the difference between a self-indulgent and, for a moment, inert person, and one for whom word and deed are as one. Yet Olivia responds to Viola's urgent sincerity and directness, her request to Viola to return again being perhaps the most positive decision she has made in her life. Shakespeare points the difference [I.1] between the Orsino/Olivia type and Viola through the language. When Viola is reporting or quoting Orsino, her language is cast in the conventional romantic mode:

'Most radiant, exquisite, and unmatcheable beauty...'   [I.5.160]

and, replying to Olivia's question, 'How does he love me?', says:

'With adorations, fertile tears,
With groans that thunder love, with sighs of fire.'   [I.5.239–40]

On the other hand, when Viola is speaking from her own heart and mind the language is more direct, unadorned with wild filigree:

'Make me a willow cabin at your gate,
And call upon my soul within the house;
Write loyal cantons of contemned love
And sing them loud even in the dead of night;'   [I.5.252–5]

Although in this speech she is talking about the outward appearances of love – the visual and aural proof of it – she, unlike Orsino, gives a sense of conviction; the appearance is an earnest or a deeper validity, not an empty substitute for it.

Viola, like Rosalind, is at the centre of the play's positive meaning. She shares Rosalind's courage, determination, fidelity and wit, but the total effect of her personality on us is quite different. There are two reasons for this. The first is that whereas Rosalind shares her disguise with both Celia and Touchstone, both talkative characters, Viola shares hers only with a sea-captain, who promises to stay mute and, indeed, disappears for much of the action. Viola, then, is virtually alone in her disguise.

The second reason is that Rosalind dispenses her exquisite advice on love with an extrovert largesse. Viola does not. Rosalind's position is therefore far more public, Viola's is private and, at times, secretive. Celia knows Rosalind loves Orlando; no one knows that Viola loves anyone. Rosalind may be vulnerable in a general sense, simply because she is a woman; Viola is vulnerable in a particular sense because she is a woman with a secret.

This gives Viola a poignant solitariness making her a more sweetly sad heroine than Rosalind. The latter, we feel, would be capable of enduring even more in order to achieve her love for Orlando but Viola, we suspect, has gone as far as she can go – alone. 'My father had a daughter loved a man', she says but cannot, in her secret solitariness, convey the pith of the meaning to anyone; Rosalind however is free, with Celia, to question and debate upon her love for Orlando. Orsino's remark about men:

'Our fancies are more giddy and unfirm,
More longing, wavering, sooner lost and won,
Than women's are.'   [II.4.32–3]

is a shrewd comment upon himself and, by implication, upon the other males in the play. Malvolio's 'love' for Olivia is entirely self-seeking; Toby's for Maria smacks of insurance against old age; Sebastian's for Olivia is thrust upon him without his having to stir; Sir Andrew's, seeking a contract which is impossible, is hopeless – perhaps what he really needs is some show of kindness.

These various kinds of love are shown with insistent clarity by Shakespeare. He does not specifically designate the relative value of each as they are displayed; rather he seems to be saying – humankind is like this. He stops short of explicit judgement, except to imply a distinction between love that is the product of fortune – ill or good – and love which is a natural growth. Malvolio's words, ''Tis but Fortune, all is fortune', may be taken as the motto of all the lovers except Viola. It underlines the contrast between the active pursuit of true love by her and the inert or time-serving predispositions of the others.

It is, however, important to emphasize the joyous and comic direction which the play takes. To dismiss the Belch/Aguecheek/Maria scenes as mere sub-plot is to minimize and falsify their importance in giving impetus to the play's direction, for if we imagine the play without them we are left with a sense of loss and irritation. The comic scenes activate movement in the play and, importantly, create a society, a world, around what would otherwise be a claustrophobic privacy. Illyria would not be wholly credible without Belch, Aguecheek and Maria.

Perhaps the most significant feature of the comic scenes is the clarity with which Shakespeare distinguishes the personalities. In one sense Belch and Aguecheek are in similar positions, relying on their 'connections' – in Belch's case, his family relationship with Olivia, in Aguecheek's, the tenuous associations which his (no doubt meagre) legacy might assure him. Yet they are immensely different in temperament.

Toby Belch is a scaled-down Falstaff – one who has so far avoided

being banished from the bosom of an outraged family to trick and
finagle through the darker reaches of the commonwealth. He is the
black sheep of a noble family who has battened upon his niece and is
suffered with limited patience and, perhaps, with a slight grudging
acceptance of some military prowess he displayed in battles now
forgotten. It is only impecuniosity, and the necessity to ensure that
sack will continue to flow, that keeps him in Illyria, relentlessly
picking at Aguecheek's legacy. Sir Toby has, however, reached a
crisis in his life. Unable much longer to rely on the continuance of
Olivia's thin patience, his adventurous reckless spirit is prepared to
enter upon stratagems of whose outcome he is never sure. His
participation in the gulling of Malvolio is hedged about with a queasy
fear:

> 'I would we were well rid of this knavery. If he may be conveniently
> deliver'd, I would he were; for I am now so far in offence with my
> niece that I cannot pursue with any safety this sport to the upshot.'
> [IV.2.65–8]

He jests, he is one of the boys, he has 'connections', but he really
does not know what to do with himself. Sack, quips, cunning, are
almost all he has left of identity, yet he is never a bore. He is shifty
and can be inhuman, sentimental and admiring when he finds a spirit
as recklessly expedient as his own:

> 'She's a beagle true-bred, and one that adores me.'   [II.3.168–9]

We like him because he still enjoys life and because he has the courage
of his own immediate reactions to a situation. He does not attempt to
fool either himself or us about his feelings. When he has eaten
unwisely he is windily honest about the 'pickled herrings'; he loves
his niece in his own way:

> 'I'll drink to her as long as there is a passage in my throat and drink in
> Illyria.'   [I.3.36–8]

He makes no bones about what he is doing to Sir Andrew:

> 'I have been dear to him, lad – some two thousand strong, or so.'
> [III.2.51–2]

He is, in fact, an honest rogue. But more than this he is a rogue who
can accommodate his words to the reality of a situation. He is
sensitive to events and the verbal means by which those events can be
embodied. In the drunken way, his words have the slithering largesse
of bonhomie induced by alcohol:

'To hear by the nose, it is dulcet in contagion. But shall we make the welkin dance indeed? Shall we rouse the night-owl in a catch that will draw three souls out of one weaver? Shall we do that?'   [II.3.55–9]

In the cunning way of strategy his words smack of 'fashion' calculated to persuade Sir Andrew that he is at the centre of modishness, and in the gamesome way he effects the grandeur and solemnity of vital military deeds, pregnant with sombre implications:

'That defence thou hast, betake thee to't. Of what nature the wrongs
are thou hast done him, I know not; but thy intercepter, full of
despite, bloody as the hunter, attends thee at the orchard end.'
[III.4.210–14]

A man for all seasons, he is a stylist, and no man of real style can ever be boring.

Sir Andrew is a natural victim for such a man. He was, one feels, born into the world with the extreme liability of being the mentally underdeveloped son in a family of some means. He has been sent off to find what fortune he can, with limited resources that will soon, with the depradations of Sir Toby, be frittered away. One cylinder is not firing at all in the clattering engine of his mind. He is always out of phase with the circumstances of the moment, coming around the corner hopefully just when faster creatures have left. He utters modish precepts like an automaton, but we know that nothing of account is moving in his brain:

AND: Good Mistress Accost, I desire better acquaintance.
MAR: My name is Mary, sir.
AND: Good Mistress Mary Accost, –
TOBY: You mistake, knight. Accost is front her, board her, woo her,
   assail her.   [I.3.49–53]

He is essentially a creature to be laughed *at* not *with*, but by the same token he arouses sympathy simply because he is comically defenceless.

Not so Malvolio. He is here to be scorned, though the trend of modern stage productions reveals that modern sensibilities cannot be content with a figure who is laughed out of court. Malvolio and Shylock have crept under the shawl of modern sentimentality and conscience, and ironically we are more ready to condemn the black Othello than either of these two – one of whom is a stupid, arrogant sycophant, the other wants flesh and revenge.

Explanations of Malvolio's character have ranged from the notion that he is a caricature of the Puritan to an under-documented assumption that he is a picture of a real individual – Sir William

185

Knollys, comptroller of the royal household from 1596 to 1602. Perhaps he might, if we had the proof, turn out to be something of an amalgam of both. Yet his dramatic presence is not explained entirely by both or either of these suggestions. Malvolio is mean-spirited, ludicrously ambitious, and humourless – as perhaps some Puritans and Sir William were. He is, however, more. Shakespeare's plays which are stamped with the label 'romantic' achieve their potency and maintain their interest because they are superb exercises in the art of contrast. They reach, in their resolution, an ideal condition, but the journey towards that resolution always involves the concept of an un-ideal world. Every word and every activity of Malvolio's is, in effect, un-Illyrian. Everything, except him, moves in a direction which will finally release happiness, correct partnership and generosity of spirit. Malvolio's meanness is completely out of place – all that is left for this man whose ambitions and pretensions are absurd, and who is discovered to be absurd himself is to cry out for revenge. It is this final cry which has occasioned much heart-searching in modern commentators and audiences. But to be sorry for Malvolio is to forget both that the word he uses is 'revenge' and that he has played a large part in bringing himself to this condition. He has been 'ill-used', condemned to darkness, has made himself, and has been made, to look and sound like a presumptuous idiot. Yet he has asked for much of this simply by breaking the rules of Illyria, by trying to be what he is not – in love with Olivia and bigger than his station. Of course she herself, as Feste sharply reminds us, is overaffected in her mourning. Viola, in disguise, is also to a degree what she is not. Orsino's misdirected passion is a measure of his self-delusion. Yet all of these are purged of their illusions – by love. Only Malvolio seems completely incapable of being purged (Aguecheek could be, we feel, but is not given the chance) and is unequipped to adjust to Illyria. Some attempts are made to enable him to make an adjustment and to modern sensitivities these attempts may seem hard and disproportionate to his faults. Yet we must disabuse ourselves of such sentimentality in the light of what is revealed by the existence of Feste, and, in particular, by his relationship to Malvolio.

Most of the Fools of whose historical existence in medieval Europe we know, with something of their activities, present a common set of characteristics which bear a remarkable similarity to those of Feste and Lear's fool in particular and, to a lesser extent, to Touchstone. First, they seem to have occupied an indeterminate status in noble or royal households. Very often the Fool had finally arrived at a noble or royal domicile by a series of steps from humble and lowly surroundings – from village-green entertainment to court entertainment. They do not thereby seem to have changed their social status in any precise sense, for such was their dependence on pleasing their lord and master they could, at any time, have been thrust out of doors. Yet, having physically removed themselves from an originally low social status, they could no longer be said to belong there either. In fact, they seem to have existed in an odd limbo. They were classless; they slipped in and out of social stratifications very easily, but were committed to none of them. Feste, in particular, exemplifies this. He has easy commerce with high, middle and low, and yet he seems not to belong to any particular group or home. He wanders from Orsino's court to Olivia's. He is everyone's acquaintance but no one's friend.

Second, the Fools of history were possessed of a licence to utter things which, if they came from another's mouth, might have been deemed discourteous, libellous, treacherous or disloyal. An 'allowed' Fool's licence was bestowed upon him because he was regarded as entertainer and because his actual social status was so indeterminate – he had the privilege of comment only because he was uncommitted, in both social and human terms. Feste exercises this licence to the full for, surely, he is the only one who would have been allowed to say to Olivia what he does about mourning:

CLO: 'Good madonna, why mourn'st thou?
OL: Good fool, for my brother's death.
CLO: I think his soul is in hell, madonna.
OL: I know his soul is in heaven, fool.
CLO: The more fool, madonna, to mourn for your brother's soul
being in heaven. Take away the fool, gentlemen.'   [I.5.61–8]

Yet there was an irony involved here. The licence was tenuous and revokable, the Fool's freedom an illusion. Both Feste and Lear's Fool are threatened with the whip for what they say. The mankind of both plays cannot stand too much of the reality, the truth, which these men utter. 'He is holden wise that reputeth himself a fool' is the hallmark of both some of the notable Fools of history and of Shakespeare's Fools.

Feste's virtual uncommittedness to the action is quite obvious. As R. H. Goldsmith says: 'It ought to be remembered that Feste, although he confesses to a part in the intrigue, actually is not present at the baiting of the yellow-stockinged, cross-gartered gull. Instead, his role as ironic commentator is taken over by the less subtle

Fabian.'[13] This posture of near isolation – as if the fool were holding himself back in order to preserve the freedom to exercise his licence – is confirmed when we examine the famous drunken scene with Aguecheek and Belch, where, as soon as Maria reveals the plot against Malvolio, Feste plays no further part.

The sense that the relationship between the Fool and others is on a commercial basis, rather than an intellectual or emotional one, is emphasized in Act V.1. Here Feste has indulged in some witty badinage with the Duke Orsino. He seems, for a moment, to be part of the company, then:

> DU: Thou shalt not be the worse for me. There's gold.
> CLO: But that it would be double-dealing, sir, I would you could make it another.
> DU: O, you give me ill counsel.
> CLO: Put your grace in your pocket, sir, for this once, and let your flesh and blood obey it.   [V.1.24–8]

Immediately the truth of the Fool's position is revealed. It is allowed, tolerated and the function it performs is paid for.

Why then does Feste seem to commit himself so much to the attempt to purge Malvolio of his 'madness'? If withdrawal, a desire to hide behind the mask of folly in order to shoot forth his wit and truth, is the real motivation of Shakespeare's fools, then why should Feste thus expose himself? In the Sir Topas scene, he mercilessly taunts Malvolio:

> 'Madman, thou errest. I say there is no darkness but ignorance; in which thou art more puzzled than the Egyptians in their fog.'
>   [IV.2.41–3]

It is this scene which renders the modern conscience uneasy about what is being done to Malvolio.

The occasion of Twelfth Night is the feast of the Epiphany when, during the Middle Ages, the Feast of Fools was performed widely in Western Europe, including England. Churches and Cathedrals were taken over by the irreverent – fools, clowns, tumblers, riff-raff of society – and a ceremony guying the rites and customs of religion was indulged in, involving obscenity and profanity. At these events, the chief figure – the Lord of Misrule – presided over the noisy and chaotic activities. He did so in the guise of a priest or bishop, shouting dog-Latin, ridiculing the litany, substituting low comic business for church ritual. The tradition of a connection, however bizarre, between cleric and Fool (who, the records show, was often cast as the Lord of Misrule) is both long and tenuous. It may, for example, be implied by the extraordinary number of depictions of Fools found carved under misericord seats in English churches (notably at Beverley in Yorkshire, and at Worcester Cathedral). The tradition of the clerical Fool is persistent in both near-Eastern and Western history.

> During the first centuries of the Christian era . . . the old pagan rites not only survived . . . they actually penetrated into the interior of the churches and at length gave rise to that famous clerical saturnalia, in which mighty persons were humbled, sacred things profaned, laws relaxed, and ethical ideals reversed, under the leadership of a Patriarch, Pope or Bishop of Fools.[14]

The ceremony of the Feast of Fools is known to have been performed in England (the last recorded occasion was at Beverley in the fifteenth century), and modified versions of it were performed on Twelfth Night at the Inns of Court. The appearance of Feste in *Twelfth Night* to purge a madman would, one suspects, have been no surprise to the students of the Middle Temple, or indeed to a public or private audience to whom the Twelfth Night ceremonies were an accepted part of the actual experience of their folk memory.

Feste, in this scene, is therefore not stepping out of his posture as a relatively uncommitted observer of the human scene. Rather as Sir Topas he is fulfilling the function of the clerical Fool – mocking and purging, or at least going through the motion of purging. Putting on the gown of Sir Topas, he says, 'I would I were the first that ever dissembled in such a gown'. This is a double-edged comment – on both the iniquities of some priests and the long tradition of the Fool as cleric. The irritant of Malvolio is therefore subject to comic purging – and it is on this level that an Elizabethan audience would have accepted it. Malvolio is 'mad' only in the sense that his disposition is at variance with the play's disposition. He is driven 'mad' by fooling and his medicine is properly administered by the Fool. The fact that it does him no good, does not cure him so as to accept the prevailing climate of Illyria, is neither here nor there. Lords of Misrule have to have their victims, and if the victim is a pompous ass with an aversion to 'cakes and ale' – so much the more is the comic experience.

Feste, in comic context, fulfils that function of the Fool most seriously described by Jaques in *As You Like It* [II.7.44–61]. He is to be free to comment and to blow wisdom through his folly, and, given the opportunity, he will purge the infected world if it will patiently receive his message.

By the time he came to write *Twelfth Night*, Shakespeare was himself approaching middle years, and that part of his spirit which had always incited him never to take or create matters merely at face value began to haunt him, to demand some expression. In *Twelfth Night* he found a way both to cater for the romantic appetites of his audience and to give his own awareness some palpable expression. The means lay in the character of the Fool. The Fool was an entertainer – so was Shakespeare. The Fool, as part of his professional function, created, through his wit, a world of illusion – so did Shakespeare. The Fool, as Armin had taught, used illusion and wit, but as a mere frontage to his lonely apprehension of the truth behind illusion. Shakespeare, the dramatist, was only too aware of this approach. We see the beginnings in Feste, more certainly than we do in Touchstone, of what amounts to a new order of characterization in Shakespeare's plays, one which fulfils more than one function. The Fool, and of course Lear's Fool is the ultimate embodiment of this, is, on the one hand, professional entertainer, a natural inhabitant of the world of the play. Yet he is also non-naturalistic agent - a means by which Shakespeare is able to express, and we are enabled to receive, a dimension of imaginative truth which the play's action does not, of itself, demonstrate. The fool is as lonely as the artist; he, like the artist, creates matter to beguile, to please, to incite, to entertain. Yet, like the artist, he holds some things very close to his chest – a knowledge, a truth, an ironic vision, a wry reflection, which in the end becomes a poignant and sharp comment on the beguiling illusions the imagination has created. Feste's song at the end of the play is to be celebrated, not only because the traditional tune by which (despite new versions) we remember it is so plangent and bitter-sweet, but also because its sentiments embody, albeit naively, the nature of the Fool's status – an awareness of the eternal hard irony of reality amidst the illusion with which mankind surrounds itself. A production which gets nearest to the heart of this play is one which, at the end, leaves Feste alone on stage, while the citizens of Illyria fade into a receiving darkness. They have, one might say, existed only in the mind and imagination of the Fool and now he dismisses them. The realist has charmed himself and us by satisfying our yearnings to be told of happy places and happy times – now it is time to turn once again away from the sunlight. Feste does so, and in his eyes we can catch an expression of sadness and grief which surely he shares with his own creator.

NOTES

1 See Enid Welsford, *The Fool, his social and literary history* (1935).
2 Matteo Bandello, c.1480–1562. Italian author of *Novelle*, 1554–1573; translated into French by Belleforest as *Histoires Tragiques*, 1559–1582.
3 R. A. Foakes, Introduction to the New Penguin edition of *Much Ado About Nothing* (1968).
4 J. Russell Brown, *Shakespeare and his Comedies* (1957), p. 118.
5 R. A. Foakes, op. cit.
6 T. J. B. Spencer (ed.), *Elizabethan Love Stories* (1968), pp. 11–12.
7 cf. Welsford, op. cit.
8 See Helen Gardner's essay in John Garrett (ed.) *More Talking of Shakespeare* (1960).
9 Leslie Hotson, *The First Night of Twelfth Night* (1954).
10 Comedy, first acted in Sienna in 1531, first published in 1537.
11 Barnabe Rich(e) 1540?–1617. Writer and soldier (*Riche his Farewell to Militarie profession*, 1581).
12 T. J. B. Spencer, op. cit., p. 97.
13 R. H. Goldsmith, *Wise Fools in Shakespeare* (1957), p. 103.
14 Welsford, op. cit., p. 199.

5 The 'Problem' Plays

Troilus and Cressida, *All's Well That ends Well*, and *Measure for Measure* are commonly designated 'problem' plays, though scholarly definitions of this term show a great variety of emphasis. The most frequent gloss concerns the so-called 'tone' of the plays, because they fit in neither with the happy atmosphere of the romantic comedies nor the awesome darkness of the great tragedies; they are 'in-between' – at one moment they seem to be taking us in the direction of comedy, at another towards a tragic destination. This indeterminacy is increased by the emotional and intellectual stance which the playwright seems to have taken up in relation to the incidents and characters, sometimes looking upon them with eyes sharply satirical or cynical, sometimes gravely moralizing. He seems to want to show humanity in its most unpleasant guise yet, at the same time, to remind us that it also has a thoughtful, pleasing, and caring aspect. Parolles, Thersites, and Angelo leave bitter tastes in our mouths. Helena, the Duke, the Countess of Rossillion, despite the fact that some of their actions are not entirely unquestionble, allow us to taste of the better part of mankind.

These plays therefore may be deemed 'problems' in that their ultimate meaning is difficult to grasp. The impression of a drive towards the demonstration and proof of the existence of order in the universe is far less certain, and although there is, admittedly, a theatrically-contrived resolution of the 'disorder' in *All's Well* there is some doubt as to whether, for example, the positive virtues of Helena and the fickle temperament of Bertram will ever make good bedfellows. Certainly, in *Measure for Measure*, lives are saved, unpleasant situations are corrected, but the means by which this is brought about do not really allay a certain moral uneasiness which we feel. Indeed, the coming together of man and woman at the end of the play seems the result less of an inevitable ordering than of a theatrical theorem. *Troilus and Cressida*, designated by some critics as a comedy, placed in the First Folio between the histories and the tragedies, leaves us equally puzzled, for the play talks much of the need for 'order' but demonstrates, with fierce cynicism, the opposite.

More pertinently, these plays do not seem to have Shakespeare's usual sense of balance – by which the motivation of character and the actuality of situation move together harmoniously. Our critical sensibilities are split; we find ourselves involved in making moral judgements on characters on the basis of what they say, or what is said about them, yet their actions apparently contradict the judgements we have been led to make. The case of Helena is a sharp example. Her 'goodness' is unquestionable, but the ease with which she allows herself to be impregnated by Bertram (for this is what it amounts to) when he believes he is taking another woman bewilders our opinion of her. It is not morally satisfying to say that, after all, Bertram is her husband and that, therefore, she is not committing a sin or a covert trick. She has, in a sort, tried to buy love when, all the time, we have been led to believe that of them all she is the one whose moral and emotional correctness and tact we can trust.

Neither is it satisfying to explain this contradiction between our conception of a character and his or her actions by falling back on the argument that we must accept these plays as examples of conventional plots and character-types. If we compare our experience of these plays with that of the romantic comedies, we are aware of a disturbing hiatus. The incidents of *As You Like It* are, equally, based on conventional plot-lines and, in their familiar sinews, there is duplicity, equivocation, and false-dealing. Yet, in the long run, a total reconciliation between structure and meaning takes place. In the problem plays Shakespeare forces us to come to certain intellectual conclusions while, at the same time, contradicting their validity. As William Empson says of *Measure for Measure*: 'In a way, indeed, I think this is a complete and successful work of the master, but the way is a very odd one, because it amounts to pretending to write a romantic comedy and in fact keeping the audience's teeth slightly but increasingly on edge.'[1]

Yet, can it be that we are uneasy with these plays because we are suffering the shock of finding Shakespeare writing in a new form – one totally unexpected after what we have known from him before? From 1599 onwards Shakespeare had to contend with the shrewdly keen genius of Ben Jonson, whose *Every Man Out of his Humour*, probably first produced at the new Globe Theatre in 1598, introduced a new type of play which Jonson himself called 'comic satire', which caught the interest of the audience. He ransacked classical comedy and Commedia dell'Arte seeking material to satisfy his talent for ridicule, satire, and cutting comment, and his characteristic method was to set up a figure, notable for folly or knavery, to draw out these qualities in an exaggerated form, and then either to show him reformed or, as in *Volpone* (first published in 1607), pushed into outer darkness beyond redemption.

Cases have been made for Malvolio and Parolles as Jonsonian character-types. Certainly the pretences of both are mercilessly exposed. Thersites has many of the characteristics of Jonson's misanthropes – men who stand back, castigating folly with verbal destructiveness. Mosca is typical:

'Are not you he, that filthy covetous wretch,
With the three legges, that, here, in hope of prey,
Have, any time this three yeare, snuft about,
With your most grov'ling nose; and would have hir'd
Mee, to the pois'ning of my Patron?'   [*Volpone*, V.3.67–71]

Jonson's view of the world was shrewd in observation, merciless in judgement, and cynical in hue. His knowledge of the contemporary conditions and activities of his society was, on the evidence of his plays, not only starker than Shakespeare's but excited a bigger portion of his imagination. That gentleness of spirit which is so characteristic of Shakespeare's vision of humankind was absent in him. Nevertheless, Shakespeare was an artist whose nature rarely failed to respond to the challenge of new modes in the theatre – it was, anyway, expedient for his livelihood. He not only knew Jonson but probably played in *Every Man in his Humour* and was, undoubtedly, very aware that Jonson's drama was new, powerful, and a certain rival to his own. An explanation, then, for the sharp dissonances, the seeking out and destruction of order, the puzzling inconsistencies between character and action, the access of cynicism, in the problem plays, may be found in an attempt by Shakespeare to combat Ben Jonson by taking up for himself this new mode of comic satire. As O. J. Campbell comments: 'The strong infusion of satire in the "problem" plays accounts to a considerable degree for their dark and pessimistic tone. If these plays give the impression that their disparate elements are imperfectly fused, it may be that Shakespeare was forcing his art into channels uncongenial to his mind and art.'[2]

This persuasive explanation, which could account for much in the plays, does not, however, completely satisfy. Shakespeare, in his earlier days, had not found satire uncongenial, as *Love's Labour's Lost* testifies. Neither had he found the mocking of self-indulgence, duplicity and folly, inimical – Armado, Holofernes and others in the gallery of his satire are ample evidence of this. There seems, therefore, to be some factor missing in this explanation of the plays as 'problems', and it may be suggested that there is a further group of possibilities, none of which deny that Shakespeare was, to some extent, striving to emulate Jonson, but which perhaps modify the degree and the nature of his addiction to the Jonsonian mode.

They are based on an assumption that the undoubted strains of pessimism and cynicism, which so considerably mutate his essentially optimistic view of the universe, are the result of a personal catastrophe which overwhelmed him at the time of writing these plays. But here we enter into the dangerous quicksands of biography. What is certain, however, is that these plays are linked by several common themes – themes which also, intriguingly, dominate Shakespeare's sonnets. The hero or heroine, for example, loves another who is obviously unworthy of love; lies and cruelty originating in a third party injure the prospects of love; what 'seems' and what 'is' are at extreme variance and sex consistently shows its uglier side.

All three plays, it seems, were written near the turn of the century[3] – a time much given to the inducing of *mal-de-siècle* – and all show marked, even severe, differences in tone and theatrical treatment from anything he had ever written before – with the possible exception of *Julius Caesar* (1599). But perhaps even more to the point, Shakespeare, after this 'problem' period, never relinquished entirely the darker vision of existence found in these plays. With varying degrees of intensity and emphasis, in his subsequent plays he evinces a firm realization that the mixture of good and evil, light and shade, order and disorder, is of a far more complex nature than he had hitherto comprehended. To put it crudely, a sense of the tragedy of human existence, and the disparity between motivation and action came to occupy an equal place with the characteristic optimism which, one suspects, he was born with. Why or how this change of focus came about we do not know – we can merely note it and marvel that what happened to his imagination as a result, far from eroding his dramatic genius, shaped it to a new, even greater architecture.

The position, then, might be that *Hamlet* was written as the first outright manifestation of his sense of complexity; that the problem plays attempted to express it with a due regard to the modes and methods of Ben Jonson. The problem of interpretation they present to us can be regarded as a direct reflection of the enormous challenge Shakespeare gave himself in trying to wrestle with an unfamiliar inner force and to represent it objectively in a relatively new mode of expression. The triumph of the problem plays is that they are such forceful images of some turmoil within Shakespeare's mind; that, theatrically, they are so effective; and that they encompass a number of characters worthy to stand with the best Shakespeare ever created.

Their failure amounts to a lack of correlation between their thematic content and its embodiment in character and action, and if we do try to concentrate wholly on the plays' thematic aspects, we may well find ourselves, not only uneasy and discontented, but very liable to judge the plays themselves as dramatically unsound.

All's Well That Ends Well

One significant difference between Shakespeare's source (Boccaccio's *Decameron*) and his play is that in the former Helena is rich and besieged by suitors; in the latter her material possessions are few. At one stroke Shakespeare has introduced an irritant into the Bertram/Helena confrontation – it seems hardly apposite to call it a love-story. It is her lowly status which first induces Bertram to cavil, then to rebel, at the prospect of marrying her:

> 'I know her well:
> Shee had her breeding at my father's charge.
> A poor physician's daughter my wife! Disdain
> Rather corrupt me ever!'   [II.3.112–14]

Shakespeare seems at pains to emphasize the difference – Helena is as sensitive to it as Bertram:

> 'The Count Rousillion cannot be my brother:
> I am from humble, he from honoured name:
> No note upon my parents, his all noble.
> My master, my dear lord he is; and I
> His servant live, and will his vassall die.'   [I.3.146–50]

This irritant lies at the heart of the play's meaning, and is one of the major reasons why both the progress of the action, and its resolution, are so curiously unsatisfying to our sense of fitness.

When we first meet Helena there is no equivocation whatsoever about the nature of her character, and her standing. She is secretly in love with Bertram, and has something of the winsome grace of Viola – certain about love, yet baulked by circumstance. Under the scathing and searching examination of Parolles, whose catechism on virginity is a barely disguised paean on lust and fornication, she shows a similar mettle to Viola – a witty presence of mind. Yet this heroine has also qualities which marks her off from all her romantic colleagues. Her first soliloquy:

> ''Twere all one
> That I should love a bright particular star
> And think to wed it, he is so above me.'   [I.1.79–80]

though it superficially reminds us of Viola's situation, has an element

of desperation never found in Viola. The second soliloquy is certainly
in a different key:

> 'Our remedies oft in themselves do lie,
> Which we ascribe to heaven. The fated sky
> Gives up free scope; only doth backward pull
> Our slow designs when we ourselves are dull.
> . . . Who ever strove
> To show her merit that did miss her love?
>
> . . . . .
> But my intents are fix'd, and will not leave me.'   [I.1.202–15]

It may remind us of Viola's determination to stay close and be of
service, but there is more to it than this. Between the two soliloquies
Parolles has spoken shrewdly to Helena about virginity and in reply
to Helena's question:

> 'How might one do, sir, to lose it to her own liking?'

declares:

> '. . . ill to like him that ne'er it likes.'   [I.1.141–2]

This, sharpening her determination, makes her restless, impatient to
carry out her 'intents' and, instead of the steadfast patient Viola, we
are left with a somewhat volatile, unpredictable woman.

When next we meet her, in the company of the Countess, she is
cautious, almost mulishly taciturn, very aware of her own social
position. Despite the fact that she has inherited her father's virtues, is
accepted as daughter by the Countess, and has Lafeu's confidence,
neither she nor Bertram can dismiss the problem of her social
inferiority. She is just 'a poor physician's daughter' who is out to win
her man by trickery – the only way she can see to get him. Never
before has Shakespeare placed such emphasis on the effects of social
status on the course of true love. Viola, for example, 'appears' to be
of lower status than Orsino, but her problem merely consists of
biding her time until her true status is revealed.

Certainly when Helena comes as supplicant to the King, to buy
status, in order to buy love, she speaks with a very different voice –
with unsycophantic humility, grave wisdom and the courage of
determination:

> 'If I break time, or flinch in property
> Of what I spoke, unpitied let me die;
> And well deserv'd. Not helping, death's my fee;
> But, if I help, what do you promise me?'   [II.1.198–9]

The King says of her:

> 'Methinks in thee some blessed spirit doth speak
> His powerful sound within an organ weak.'   [II.1.174–5]

When, after curing the King, she is called before the court to make choice of her husband, it is as if a goddess were being presented.[3] The reactions of the various people present are deferential to the point of awe:

> HEL: Heaven hath through me restor'd the King to health.
> ALL: We understand it, and thank heaven for you.   [II.3.63–5]

The transformed Helena, it seems, has, indeed, overcome by her wisdom, honesty, and healing power, the petty considerations of inferior status, and at this point the play, as a short, simple but powerful demonstration of the power of goodness, virtue, and love, might have ended – with the glamorous noble youth, Bertram, willingly accepting the hand of one in whom social status had become an irrelevancy. Parolles, with his rampant sexuality, would have vanished from the play, vanquished by Helena's purity as spirit, her virtue irradiating the scene. Certainly at this point she seems, in Wilson Knight's words, like 'a divine or poetic principle' acting 'as a bridge between religion and the court, between humility and honour. In a world of divided, sin-struck humanity she is a redeeming power, a perfect unit; that is her function.'[4]

As a description of the symbolic reality of Helena, this seems fair, if a shade over-enthusiastic. Moreover, such a view of Helena may be corroborated in the encomium spoken of her upon her presumed death, when even Lavache, the cynic, refers to her as 'the sweet marjoram of the sallet, or rather herb of grace'.

Yet, although we may agree with this view in part, it hardly squares up with Helena's presence elsewhere in the play. One man alone, Bertram, is the catalyst which stirs us to see deeper, and, in a sense, so move Helena into a different dimension of dramatic reality.

Although by healing the King she achieves a status far transcending her actual social position, this new status is sought for one reason alone – to get Bertram. All the transfiguration in heaven or earth could not equal for her the kind of acceptance she really desires. The ironic truth is that as Helena climbs the pinnacle of admiration, one voice pushes her – and the play – back on its original course:

> 'I cannot love her, nor will strive to do't.'   [II.3.145]

Bertram cannot love, and will not marry a physician's daughter, earthly angel though she may be, and that is the end of it. G. K. Hunter confronts the difficulty which the audience has to face in judging Helena's actions after Bertram's rejection by suggesting that: 'She expiates her "ambitious love" by abandoning worldly position and her journey to Great St Jaques (via Florence)'. This is to be a journey of contrition and abrogation which Hunter suggests: '. . . is accepted as such by the Countess and the two gentlemen, whose comments seem to reflect a norm Shakespeare intends us to accept'.[5] But can we accept this? Hunter pauses on this point. 'Of course there are difficulties in the way of this view. In her conversations with the Widow Helena appears as a schemer, and the reader may well feel that no single view of her conduct is possible.'[6]

Helena appears to the Widow as a 'holy pilgrim'. She tells her her secret. The widow says she does not want to become involved in any 'staining act'. Helena persuades her to help – saying that she will not be guilty of any crime, since Bertram is her husband. Helena explains her scheme:

> 'The Count he woos your daughter,
> Lays down his wanton siege before her beauty,
> Resolv'd to carry her. Let her in fine consent,
> As we'll direct her how 'tis best to bear it.
> Now his important blood will nought deny
> That she'll demand. A ring the County wears,
> That downward hath succeeded in his house
> From son to son, some four or five descents
> Since the first father wore it . . .'   [III.7.17–25]

The Widow replies:

> 'Now I see
> The bottom of your purpose.'

In her argument that her plan is lawful, Helena is reduced to logic-chopping:

> 'Why then to night
> Let us assay our plot; which, if it speed,
> Is wicked meaning in a lawful deed,
> And lawful meaning in a lawful act;
> Where both not sin, and yet a sinful fact.'   [III.7.43–7]

The words themselves may bespeak lawfulness, but the glib devious-ness of their expression does nothing but convince the audience that this is verbiage disguising conscience.

The bed-trick is the result of the 'negotiations' with the Widow. Doubtless, as Hunter points out, 'There was little sense among Shakespeare's contemporaries that this was a degrading and unsatisfactory way of getting a husband, either in real life or on the stage', yet, equally, 'The psychological reality of Helena and the realism of the background make the facile substitution of one body for another seem irrelevant and tasteless'.[7]

Indeed – what has happened to our angel? The truth is that Helena, having been raised in the centre of the play to a symbolic level where 'grace', 'love', and 'virtue' co-mingle, has now become a woman of physical appetite; fierce, active desire has taken the place of inert virtue. She has, in fact, reverted to what she was at the beginning – slightly desperate, expedient, willing to buy love. The effect on us is as if Portia had covertly directed Bassanio to the right casket, or as if Viola had persuaded Olivia to feign love for Orsino, and substituted herself in his bed. A sense of fitness is destroyed. The result of Helena's enforced actions is to cast doubt on the validity of the play's very title – will love so bought be well? Moreover, her character is diminished in the sense that we are now convinced more of the appetites of her love than of its truth. The angelic Helena, the redemptive force, is, after all, a woman who wants her man.

The dichotomy thus presented in Helena is present (in an extreme form) in Bertram. Quite simply, we are asked to find him both acceptable and unacceptable. He 'stands for' the admirable young courtier-type; he is 'virtuous' in the sense of military virtue; he is 'honourable' in seeking martial glory; he is patently aristocratic. He is a younger Coriolanus, brought up to fixed conventional standards of attitude and behaviour. To this extent he is the embodiment of an idea – the accepted Elizabethan courtier. Yet, he is also a 'Proud, scornful boy', a 'rash and unbridled boy', susceptible to bad influence, who can be 'foolish and idle'.

All these descriptions could be contained, in a way, within the elastic notion of the young courtier – the apprentice nobleman – without destroying the ideal. Yet Bertram's conventional nobility, honour, and virtue are completely overshadowed by his priggishness, insensitivity, and deceit. We find it no excuse that he has been brought up to a certain sense of class, and that marriage to Helena would constitute a slight to his high birth. We find it difficult to believe that his behaviour, his cast of mind, is dictated entirely by the malevolent influence of Parolles. Such an influence exists, but does not fully account for the inner qualities of this young man. The explanation is that Bertram, though essential to the plot-line, is, as a personality, almost irrelevant. As Hunter says, '... he is not the central character; he illustrates ideas and tendencies that the play develops elsewhere and in other (sometimes more striking) ways.'[8]

These are best developed in the character of Parolles. For all the wayward eccentricities of the production, Sir Tyrone Guthrie's interpretation of the play at the then Shakespeare Memorial Theatre in 1959 was notable for the way in which it 'fixed' the nature of Parolles. He was a cross between mercenary soldier and dirty-mouthed braggart. He haunted the rear of any battlefield picking up largesse and repaying it with reckless gossip and lewd bonhomie. He was, as played by Paul Hardwick, a most instinctive coward. He is, in fact, the most carefully and consistently drawn character in the play, but it is important to realize that all his characteristics do not add up to a credible creature who can positively incite either our pity or our admiration. In a sense we have no point of view on Parolles; we know what he is from the outset – a collection of follies and vices – but we are not required to do more than note how predictable his actions and words are; this, however, is not to say that we are not caught up with them as they appear. He is, indeed, in Lafeu's words, 'muddied withal'.

Yet he plays an important role in the play. It is through Parolles that we learn to regard, with some cynicism, the brave announcements about honour, chivalry, bravery, which are an integral, if standardized, part of Bertram's make-up. The emptiness of these concepts is more vividly embodied by Parolles than by Bertram, who lives in his shadow. Like Falstaff, Parolles sees through (in part himself helps to corrupt) the images of honour, bravery, and virtue. Unlike Hal, Bertram does not learn anything of human value from what he sees and hears. Both he and Parolles are oddly empty figures – they wear all that there is of them upon their sleeves. In Parolles's case we have no compulsion to explore what is underneath; in Bertram's case not only do we know that we will find nothing there, but that this knowledge, in itself, turns awry all our feelings about the play and its meaning.

Because Bertram and Parolles are thus, the case of Helena becomes more equivocal. The dialogue about virginity, at the outset, is, for Parolles, a playful, cynical, witty demonstration of lewd appetite. And Bertram's dialogue with Diana, for all its fine phrases, is no less appetite-ridden:

'Stand no more off,
But give thyself unto my sick desires,
Who then recovers. Say thou art mine, and ever
My love as it begins shall so persever.'   [IV.2.34–7]

Helena, then, is partly surrounded (and her eventual actions are governed) by attitudes which render entirely cynical the near-angelic status to which she was raised, and from which she has such a fall. She is more sinned against than sinning, but the pitch of Parolles and Bertram has defiled her nature and made sourly ironic her quest for the fulfilment of a particular love.

The play also has, deep in its centre, one character whose presence not only casts a sour look upon love but also upon life itself. This is Lavache, described as Clown but who is, in fact, the least clownish of all Shakespeare's Fools. He is called 'A shrewd knave and an unhappy'. This is meticulously accurate. He is very much the observing and commentating wearer of motley, but his cynical view of the world is seldom mitigated by the traditional leavening of the fool's zany wit which usually characterizes the Fool figures. Even Lear's Fool has more in him of 'court entertainer' than Lavache. Hardly anything he says is uncomplicated. His verbal responses to particular cirumstances always bear with them a double-meaning, or imply a half-mocking, half-cynical conception of life which is dominated by a kind of dismissive despair. He is a very obvious example of the cynic who knows the price of everything and accepts the value of practically nothing. The only really warm sentiment he expresses is his remark about Helena's 'grace':

Lavache's presence and personality, then, confirm an impression of the uneasy cynicism which lurks about the play. Yet, more than this, he establishes a connection between the mood and spirit of this play and of *Troilus and Cressida*. In that play one of the most insistent features is the contrapuntal effect of opposites – true love and false love, true honour and false honour, high political theory and mean practice. It is remarkable that so many of Lavache's remarks and speeches display a similar play of opposites or, at times, a cancelling out of positive assertion by negative assertion, so that the final communication becomes a nothing.

There is, however, one aspect which, in itself, might be regarded as a mitigation of the implicit and explicit cynicism of the rest. The Countess (a woman of Volumnia's strength of character but with greater sensitivity), the King, and Lafeu have a grace of spirit, a gentility of demeanour, a kindness of disposition, and a grave and pleasing wisdom. They seem, very much, to belong to an older and different world from the others – one whose values are more certain, both in conception and execution. Indeed, part of the initial 'charm' of Helena is derived from her association with these people, and from their glowing report of her. There is no doubt that much of the wisdom she displays, the grace she has, seems the result of her own quite unequivocal recognition of the values of this other world. For, as Hunter says, 'Helena, no less than Bertram, has to forget her father and abandon her foster-mother the Countess, as he has to abandon his mother and his foster-father the King.' This abandonment of the old world coincides with her entry into the new, younger world, whose values are directed less by principle than by expediency; it also coincides with her loss of the audience's total sympathy. The old world of the play is not represented as defeated; rather it seems tired, almost reaching the point of immobility. For this reason its values seem passive and, though their presence cannot be overlooked, nor their potential influence rejected, they exist largely as a kind of nostalgia. In dramatic terms, they do not strikingly affect the movement of the play's theme and action.

This play, then, is puzzling to the sensibilities. It is compact of cynicism, satire, wisdom, sadness, fleeting gaiety. It is not, by any means, desperately pessimistic, nor does it entirely lose sight of optimism. It does, however, deny its title – all's well that ends well. The words of the King come nearer to its mood. He says, at the end, 'All yet seems well.' It is in all the implications of 'seems' that our problem, as an audience, lies.

Measure for Measure

The mood in which Shakespeare wrote *Troilus and Cressida* and *All's Well* was still present when, some time in 1604, he committed *Measure for Measure* to paper. Matters of import concerning the world, man and his usages, had turned sour on him, as this play, no less than the other two, shows. What is most remarkable is that during the period 1600 to 1606 he was also writing, or in process of conceiving, other plays (the great tragedies) which, dark as is their picture of humanity's ways and means, still powerfully convey a sense of man's innate nobility.

There is nothing worthy or noble in *Measure for Measure* – the 'good' characters, including Isabella and the Duke, leave us with a taste of dissatisfaction at the contradictions which exist between their principles and their practice. The tying up of knots at the end is done with fingers that are theatrically dextrous but clumsy as far as dramatic logic is concerned. In short, there is a credibility gap in the play between the moral issues that are raised and their resolution in acceptable human terms.

The Duke is a case in point. He is, in the end, the one who pardons from his magisterial height and dispenses judgement 'like power divine'. Yet his actions are full of inconsistencies which suit ill with such a station. He gives up his place to Angelo, leaving us with a conspicuous feeling that he has decided to leave a mess for someone else to clear up; his action in forcing Angelo to make Mariana his wife, and then threatening to execute him, smacks of sadism; in the theatre his request to Isabella for her hand in marriage is too sudden, scarcely heart-felt.

Isabella's conduct is no less puzzling and irritating. She is a woman of great courage, intellectual subtlety and apparent moral strength; yet it is precisely the 'apparent' which is worrying. The Elizabethan audience may very well have been far less squeamish than we are about, for example, Isabella's easy agreement to the Duke's plan to substitute Mariana for herself in Angelo's bed. As W. W. Lawrence writes: 'The point of importance to keep in mind is the relation between Angelo and Mariana. The fact that they had earlier been affianced is of the utmost significance in drawing conclusions as to the morality of the story.' And in considering Isabella's actions in the light of her novitiate as a nun, Lawrence continues: 'An Elizabethan audience was not likely to be scandalised by the heroine's leaving a convent. ... Small niceties of ecclesiastical infringement were not shocking to Protestant England in Shakespeare's day.'[9]

The generalization about 'Protestant England' itself begs many questions, but, in any case, one wonders why Shakespeare bothered to stress Isabella's addiction to the sisterhood, if he did not want to make some dramatic capital out of the 'niceties of ecclesiastical infringement'. Whether Lawrence is right or not about the Elizabethan reception of Isabella, audiences today cannot swallow completely the several inconsistencies in her character – why, for example, should Shakespeare have emphasized Isabella's desire to have even stronger restraints in the sisterhood if he did not, at some point, want her to appear as most severely moral and pure? Surely one who looks for more restraints is not going to regard the substitution of herself by another in a man's bed as an irrelevant nicety?

Some critics have tried to reconcile the irreconcilable elements in the characters by claiming that the play is a comedy. R. W. Chambers suggests: 'Shakespeare's audience expected a marriage at the end: and, though it may be an accident, the marriage of Isabel and the Duke makes a good ending to a Christmas play.'[10] One wonders whether even an Elizabethan audience, in the mood Chambers suggests, would have found that the whole play satisfied a festive lightheartedness and laughter. The 'low-life' scenes and characters may well have done; the implied satire on the law and those who practice it may well have appealed to its sense of humour; the bed-trick may have aroused some wry smiling. Yet what kind of comedy is it that has such scenes as the confrontations between Isabella and Angelo, such weighty moral arguments upon whose resolution lives depends, such terrifying verbal realizations of the horror of death, and such an underswell of cynicism? There is as T. M. Parrott notes an '... incongruity between the tragic theme, the tragi-comedy technique and the realistic background.'[11]

Like *The Merchant of Venice*, *All's Well*, and *Troilus and Cressida*, the play perplexes, even irritates, our sense of fitness, even though it is at the same time satisfying as a piece of theatre. It is its theatrical power which commands attention despite its unpleasing inconsistencies of motivation, action, principle and practice. The heart of the play's theatrical and dramatic potency is in the two scenes of confrontation between Isabella and Angelo [Act II.2 and Act II.4]. In no other play does Shakespeare demonstrate, at such length and concentration, his skill in writing dramatic, dialectic language. The scenes between Isabella and Angelo with their brilliant display of argument in dramatic form demonstrate how Shakespeare has solved the problem of presenting thesis and antithesis without losing a grip on the need to provide dramatic interest and a sense of action. Psychological tension, the ebb and flow of emotional and intellectual responses, are both implicit and explicit in these two scenes. Even reading the text one cannot help but feel and visualize the human drama that is taking place. At the beginning [Act II.1], Angelo hardly notices Isabella; her carefully worded statements, models of logic, are punctuated by his sharp, offhand, peremptory phrases:

'Well; what's your suit?'

'Well: the matter?'

'Maiden, no remedy.'

'He's sentenc'd; 'tis too late.'

'Pray you be gone.'   [II.2.29–62]

and as Angelo becomes more dismissive, so Isabella's speeches become more emotionally charged. She moves from the plain urgency of:

'No ceremony that to great ones longs,
Not the King's crown nor the deputed sword,
The marshal's truncheon nor the judge's robe,
Become them with one half so good a grace
As mercy does.'   [II.2.59–63]

to the penetrating passion of:

'Why, all the souls that were were forfeit once;
And He that might the vantage best have took
Found out the remedy. How would you be
If He, which is the top of judgement, should
But judge you as you are? Oh, think on that;
And mercy then will breathe within your lips,
Like man new made.'   [II.2.73–9]

Shakespeare is unerring in his psychological exactitude. At the point where Isabella's words involve Angelo personally and she turns from abstract argument into the particularity of the judgement, he looks at her, one feels, for the first time. His early address – 'Maiden, no remedy' – changes to – 'Be you content, fair maid'. That word 'fair' signifies the depth of his looking – a fuse which, later, will explode

his passion. From this point onwards he argues with her with a
respectful recognition of her intellectual equality. Yet the word 'fair'
sticks in his mind and as he cannot argue with her so closely without
looking upon her closely, he begins to find that he cannot separate
her intellectual from her sexual power:

> 'She speaks, and 'tis
> Such sense that my sense breeds with it.' [II.2.141–2]

The scene is a masterpiece of dramatic subtlety and dramatic truth. It
is also remarkable in its careful avoidance of a merely simple kind of
seduction. Isabella does not exert an explicit sexual pressure, but her
pressure brings about a vast change in Angelo. The tone on which the
scene ends is one of subtle irony. Angelo, who cannot be corrupted
by evil, is tempted by goodness.

> 'Most dangerous
> Is that temptation that doth goad us on
> To sin in loving virtue.' [II.2.181–2]

The arguments that each puts to the other concerning justice, mercy,
and the law, take second place, in the theatre, to the intensity of the
human situation which develops and to the irony which is involved.
Shakespeare, in fact, passes through dialectic and achieves dramatic
truth.

The second main confrontation between the two [Act II.4] is no
less dramatic. In terms of response from one to the other their roles,
at first, are reversed from the earlier meeting. Here it is Angelo who
is making propositions and statements, and Isabella who interrupts
with short peremptory phrases:

> ''Tis set down so in heaven, but not in earth.'
> 'How say you?'
> 'So.'
> 'True.' [II.4.49–87]

Again the shift from theoretically presented case to personal issue
appears. Just as, previously, Isabella slowly involved Angelo in her
arguments about law and mercy so, now, she finds herself enmeshed
in Angelo's question – 'what would you do?' He has pressed her to
make a personal decision about her reactions if the only way to save
her brother is by laying down the treasures of her body. By the end
of this second meeting the two are inextricably and personally
involved in issues which began as abstractions.

However, although it is the spectacle of human tensions which grips us in the theatre – the issues remaining secondary – nevertheless, these issues have some effect on the drama that is presented to us. If we take them on their face value a simple equation can be made. The Duke represents wisdom and mercy; Isabella represents chastity unwilling to compromise even to save a brother's life; Angelo represents law untouched by mercy. If we remain within abstractions, what happens in the play is the triumph of mercy and forgiveness over human weakness and corruption. As has frequently been pointed out, the play, with its title taken from the gospels, concerns itself with the idea – 'Judge not that ye be not judged'. This is the main issue, and we are aware, as the play proceeds, of the intricate variations that are being made upon it. But over and above this awareness is a much stronger and prevailing sense that Shakespeare is less interested in thesis drama than in revealing the unreliability of human response when faced with matters which ask for a direct moral decision. The Duke, for example, is in fact more memorable as a somewhat lazy, bumbling, self-indulgent autocrat than as a symbol of mercy and wisdom. Angelo engages us less as an example of legal severity untempered by mercy than as a weak man whose latent lasciviousness catches up with him. Isabella's innocence is a pliable thing and she is not far from being a priggish, holier-than-thou virgin, given to sermonizing:

> 'Take my defiance;
> Die; perish. Might but my bending down
> Reprieve thee from thy fate, it should proceed.
> I'll pray a thousand prayers for thy death,
> No word to save thee.'   [III.1.144–8]

Our sympathies do not go out to those three with their triangle of moral tensions; we are more drawn to those who are affected by that triangle. Claudio, Lucio, and the crew of bawds have at least the virtue of directness even if they are guilty of one crime or another. Because they do not wrap up their beliefs or motivations in precepts which are denied by their actions they seem more 'honest' than the holy three. Claudio merely wants to love and to live; Lucio, no less direct in his aspirations, is honest about his time-serving occupation, pretending to nothing else than to be a quick-witted bawd. What Nosworthy says of Lucio may serve to stand for the rest of the low-life characters: 'He speaks scarcely one word true throughout the play, and yet his lies and distortions shape themselves into a kind of truth.'[12] The 'truth' of Lucio and his fellows is a kind of transparent honesty to their own iniquities for their lies and distortions are not hidden from us. For this reason Lucio and the others bring a refreshing air of realism and non-equivocation into the play.

Lucio is more than a simple carrier of news and a tricksy leader of the low-life community. He has a little of Mercutio's braggadocio attractiveness, and although his dexterity with words does not extend to lyrical fantasy, he has a similar witty incisiveness of speech, which is characterized by punning and an exquisite sense of the humour of sound:

> 'Some report a sea-maid spawn'd him; some, that he was begot
> between two stock-fishes. But it is certain that when he makes water
> his urine is congeal'd ice; that I know to be true. And he is a motion
> generative; that's infallible.'   [III.2.100–4]

Lucio's relationship to his social group parallels that of the Duke to his, and he is as assiduous in his championship of the unlawful as the Duke eventually is of the lawful. He has a very clear idea of the situation – as is shown in his comments on the Duke's actions:

> 'It was a mad fantastical trick of him to steal from the state and usurp
> the beggary he was never born to.'   [III.2.86–8]

His asides in the first meeting between Isabella and Angelo form a chorus which increases our sense of the critical urgency of the argument that is taking place. His deep knowledge of commodity and opportunity in human affairs gives him a sensitive ability to know how far to press a claim, so when Angelo says to Isabella, 'Well: come to me tomorrow', Lucio immediately says to her, 'Goe to: 'tis well; away'. In the scene with the Duke [Act III.2] he is completely reckless, since he is unaware of the Duke's identity, in his insinuations about the Duke's character. Yet inside the free-ranging devilry of his tongue, we find matter to which we can only nod in acceptance:

> 'I would the Duke we talk of were return'd againe. This ungenitur'd
> agent will unpeople the province with continency;'   [III.2.162–4]

Lucio, indeed, is a realist. He well knows that Angelo's inflexible legality is at variance with the reality of human behaviour and when he speaks of 'mercy' it is not as an abstraction but as a practical matter. The Duke, he says, whom he loves because of his imperfections, showed mercy to transgressors because 'he had some feeling of the sport, he knew the service, and that instructed him to mercy'.

This is a different version of mercy from that exerted by the Duke, which has the quality of an indulgence ministered from on high. Even though the Duke, in the end, shows mercy and forgiveness, he seems at the same time to be making up for his past laxness by attaching severe penalties to his act. In the long run Lucio's conception of mercy is seen as not only more practical but more compassionate.

One reason why Lucio's compassionate realism overrides his viler qualities of time-serving, lying, and supporting of the forces of unlawfulness, is that it is more in keeping with the actualities of the society of Vienna. It is important to emphasize that Shakespeare gives us a brilliantly clear, detailed and naturalistic series of pictures of the low-life society of Vienna, whose flouting of the law has occasioned the Duke's decision to put affairs in the hands of Angelo. Nothing in the low-life scenes of any play of Shakespeare approaches the stark naturalism of the Pompey/Overdone/Froth scenes in this play. We might perhaps accept them as the closest evocations of contemporary London low-life that Shakespeare created. When we read:

> If these houses have a box-brush, or an old post, it is enough to show
> their profession. But if they be graced with a sign complete, it's a sign
> of good custom. In these houses you shall see the history of Judith,
> Susanna, Daniel in the lions' den, or Dives and Lazarus painted upon
> the wall. [13]

it is the low life of *Measure for Measure* that we recall.

> POM: Yonder man is carried to prison.
> MRS. OV: Well, what has he done?
> POM: A woman.
> MRS. OV: But what's his offence?
> POM: Groping for trouts in a peculiar river.
> MRS. OV: What! is there a maid with child by him?
> POM: No; but there's a woman with maid by him. [I.2.82–8]

The sharp reality of these scenes, coupled with the function of Lucio, deeply affects our conception of what the play is saying. By comparison with the low-life characters, the upper-class society, despite its references to justice, mercy and law, never seems to get to grips with the reality of the situations it has to face and any resolutions of these situations are achieved by mechanistic means. 'Justice' and 'mercy' are bandied about, but, in the event, it is the imposed 'accidents' of events which resolve the issues. What they may mean or ought to mean in practice is more clearly shown through Lucio and the realistic low-life scenes. What the play seems to be saying is that justice and mercy as abstractions run the risk of being confounded by action; that the law as a mere concept is an ass, and that the dispensing of justice and of mercy must always be temporized by a recognition of the true, albeit frail, nature of humankind. It is necessary to accept that this is an imperfect world, for

> 'There is scarce truth enough alive to make societies secure; but
> security enough to make fellowships accurst. Much upon this riddle
> runs the wisdom of the world.' [III.2.212–14]

It is a realistic view, mordantly expressed. It shows both human weakness in stark clear detail and even human virtues as tainted. If this be comedy, it has some sickness upon it.

Troilus and Cressida

The problems about the dating and textual condition of *Troilus and Cressida* have to take second place to the perplexities which the play arouses as a piece for theatrical realization. A play, probably Shakespeare's, was noted in the Stationers' Register on 7 February 1603, 'as yt is acted by my Lord Chamberlens Men'.[14] On 28 January 1609, 'A booke called the history of Troylus and Cressida' (certainly Shakespeare's play) was licensed, and the quarto to which the licence applied was issued in the same year. The original title page was changed before publication and the lines 'As it was acted by the Kings Majesties servants at the Globe' omitted. There was an addition to the effect that this was 'a new play, never stal'd with the Stage', and describing it as the wittiest of Shakespeare's comedies.

In 1623 the play was included in the Folio, and its position there formerly raised speculations as to whether it was a comedy, tragedy, or even history. Twentieth-century scholarship has established that it was intended to be placed after *Romeo and Juliet* amongst the tragedies, but that after three pages had been printed, for some reason the work on the play stopped and was not continued until the whole collected work was almost completed and then it was placed between the histories and the tragedies.

The first recorded performance was during the Restoration. John Dryden's 1679 version, *Troilus and Cressida, or Truth Found too late*, displaced the original in the late seventeenth century and held sway until 1734. After this date there is no record of Shakespeare's original being performed until 1907. Today it is no longer neglected, though the immense variety of contemporary stage interpretations is telling proof that no final solution to the play's basic problem – is it comic, satiric or cynical? – has been found. Modern productions have attempted, from time to time, to reconcile comic and tragic, satirical and cynical. Some contemporary directors have seen in it themes akin to those of modern absurdist drama - God is dead, life meaningless, traditional values supernumerary, indeed a little eccentric – and then tragic and comic become almost the same thing and to cry or to laugh, to fear or to rejoice, are mere responses which a dramatist may evoke. *Troilus and Cressida*, has also been particularly susceptible to a post-war Western attitude of mind which assumes that it can solve or reconcile matters which have remained asunder over centuries of civilization. Thus, the play, in production, has been used (notably by

214

John Barton in 1968[15]) to show how possible it is to make Shakespeare speak to the twentieth century. Certainly the play seems to reflect much that seems typical of today – political theory and practice, cynically, at odds with one another; romantic love at the mercy of sexual permissiveness; honour in personal and public action riddled with expediency; a world which has lost its belief in a moral order. There is little sense in the play that God or Gods exist in the heavens – time, rather than embodied fate and destiny, is the *deus ex machina* of the play.

The last few words spoken by the Prologue sum up the mood of 'take it or leave it' which seems to have dominated Shakespeare while he was writing the play.

> 'Like or find fault; do as your pleasures are;
> Now good, or bad, 'tis but the chance of war.'   [Prologue.30–1]

Yet, there is a paradox here. The dominant mood is inescapable, but it is equally obvious that it has had no enervating effect upon Shakespeare's imaginative power and dramatic skill. There are scenes of great emotional, dramatic and intellectual power, and characters who have been created with energetic subtlety. In fact we seem to be in the presence, not of a tired dramatist, but of one whose unabated skill is being used to communicate a sour and cynical vision of existence. Dover Wilson encourages us to keep 'a satiric purpose in mind' when we assess the play. He says that it amounts to an anatomizing of the folly of both the Greeks and the Trojans. This advice cannot be ignored for, at every turn of the play, we find examples of a pointed satiric purpose – there is unconscious irony in Pandarus's warning to Troilus of the dangers of 'mad idolatry' and again a little later in the condescension of Hector's rebuke to Troilus and Paris.

> After arguing in favour of the law of nature and of nations, which require the return of Helen, what he finally proposes is to keep her, 'For it is a cause that hath no mean dependence/Upon our joint and several dignities.' Here again, Shakespeare gives an ironic twist to his source by inventing a *volte-face* which makes Hector as vulnerable to satire as the thoughtless Troilus.[16]

To accept the satiric purpose in the play, it is necessary to be clear about what is being satirized. There is nothing original in Shakespeare's depiction of the Troilus and Cressida story. He is not satirizing it for its own sake; there would have been little need for him to do so, since Troilus, Cressida and Pandarus had been already firmly fixed in their symbolic roles by earlier writers. Cressida was already synonymous with faithlessness, Pandarus with bawdry, and Troilus with romantic gullibility – the employer of a bawd to ensure his liaison with Cressida.

Neither is Shakespeare's portrait of the other inhabitants of Greece and Troy uniquely pejorative. The status of those great heroes with reverberating names had declined during the fifteenth century. Shakespeare had read William Caxton's *Recuyell of the Historyes of Troy* (1475), itself based on an earlier medieval work – Guido delle Colonne's *Historia Troiana* (1287). What is common to most medieval writers on the legendary stories is the low opinion they held of the majority of the heroes. The Trojans are depicted as loose in behaviour, undisciplined in war, unamenable to reason and the Greeks (not least among them, Achilles) as a mob of brutes, bullies and fools.

Neither, therefore, in his treatment of the love plot nor of the legendary background, is Shakespeare original in the attitude he takes up, and the Elizabethan audience would not have been surprised by it. Yet, to regard the play simply as Shakespeare's satirical comment upon material which had already had its fair share of harsh and denigrating appraisal, is to deny the existence of a special potency. What Shakespeare seems to be satirizing ruthlessly are many of the themes and forms and attitudes which had created the life-blood of his earlier plays. The noble conception of history, the sense of its awful sweep and depth are here reduced from a grand to a domestic architecture. It is with a sense of acute irony that we recall the Choruses of *Henry V* when we hear the play's Prologue:

> 'To Tenedos they come,
> And the deep-drawing barks do there disgorge
> Their war-like fraughtage. Now on Dardan plains
> The fresh and yet unbruised Greeks do pitch
> Their brave pavillions:'   [Prologue. 11–14]

The sense of diminution of history is all the more telling since the *dramatis personae* of the play have names which, though despoiled of reputation during the medieval period, still have power to reverberate – Hector, Priam, Ulysses, Ajax. But God, and the rhythms of fate and destiny, have been removed, to be replaced by the notion of mere Time – an ill-serving, mean-spirited, voracious consumer of men and their deeds:

'Injurious time now with a robber's haste
Crams his rich thievery up, he knows not how.
As many farewells as be stars in heaven,
With distinct breath and consign'd kisses to them,
He fumbles up into a loose adieu, . . .'   [IV.4.41–5]

The reduction of history is accompanied by a demonstration of the
collapse of the natural order which Shakespeare's erstwhile conception of history implicitly involved. Ulysses's speech on Degree has
often been used by commentators as a set-piece definition of the
conception of order, and of the dangers attending disorder, which lie
at the basis of Shakespeare's history plays. The speech made in an
atmosphere of empty pomp and circumstance takes on a particular
and ironic tone. The great Greek leaders meet in council; they pay
high-sounding compliments to each other – 'Great Agamemnon' is in
his 'godly seat'; he is the 'Nerve and Bone of Greece'; Nestor is
'venerable' and 'most resolved'; Ulysses speaks 'Most wisely'. Yet
there is something verging on the ridiculous behind all this. The
studied formal gait of their language limps with rhetorical phrases:

'With due observance of thy godlike seat,
Great Agamemnon, Nestor shall apply
Thy latest words. In the reproof of chance
Lies the true proof of men.'   [I.3.31–4]

It is within an atmosphere of intellectual inertia and choked will that
Ulysses makes the speech on Degree. The rest acknowledge its truth
to their own situation, and ask what remedy his diagnosis suggests.
Ulysses has spoken political philosophy, germane to the war, and
yet, what follows? – references to Achilles's 'Lazy bed', 'Scurril
jests', undignified impersonations of the Greek leaders. We learn that
Ajax is grown 'self-willed'; that there is a scabrous man called
Thersites wandering about the Grecian tents: that Hector is casting
aspersions on Grecian womanhood and that, on this score, Nestor
and Agamemnon himself are prepared to meet him in combat. In
such a context, Ulysses's great speech becomes an ironic irrelevancy.
Ulysses speaks of both the earth and the wide universe in his analysis
of the nature of degree and order, but when his terms of reference are
applied to the Greeks, his universality is reduced to a lascivious, lazy
warrior, his probably homosexual friend, a mockery of leadership, a
self-conceit in a man of war, and a quarrel about whether Trojan
women are superior to Greek. Shakespeare's English history plays
may have their ridiculous and petty incidents and characters, their

217

peevishness of motives, yet at no point is the great theme of order and disorder cheapened and by implication ridiculed. Shakespeare, in fact, seems to have deliberately struck at the very heart of one of his most closely held and positive theses and satirized his own faith in a universal order.

This, however, is not all. The manner in which he deals with the story of Troilus and Cressida reveals him attacking another, most cherished conception which had informed many of his earlier plays. It has been noted how a concern for order and disorder is manifest not only in the history plays, but in all the comedies – both the early ones and the mature ones that he wrote at a time very near to the writing of *Troilus and Cressida*. Love is enhanced, made valid and true by order, and is destroyed by disorder, which induces faithlessness and fickleness. All of Shakespeare's comedies up to this point have affirmed the validity of true love, governed by a correct ordering of the mind, the feelings, the spirit. In this play, however, Shakespeare seems deliberately to concentrate on false love.

This has several aspects which revolve about the characters of Cressida, Troilus and Pandarus. Cressida is a flawless beauty with the instincts of a whore. There is little point in seeking subtlety in her character, since Shakespeare has not endowed her with much emotional sensitivity or moral scruple. She has a bright and brittle intelligence, with Viola and Rosalind's skill in witty badinage but without their delicacy of spirit:

CRES: Why Paris hath colour enough.
PAN: So, he has.
CRES: Then Troilus should have too much. If she prais'd him above, his complexion is higher than his; he having colour enough, and the other higher, is too flaming a praise for a good complexion. I had as lief Helen's golden tongue had commended Troilus for a copper nose. [I.2.95–101]

Her priorities of occupation are quite clear. When Pandarus says 'A man knows not at what ward you lie', she replies:

'Upon my back, to defend my belly; upon my wit, to defend my wiles; upon my secrecy, to defend mine honesty; my mask, to defend my beauty; and you, to defend all these...' [I.2.252–6]

Her sexuality is implicit from the very first, both in her unblushing responses to Pandarus's bawdry, and in her own language: 'joy's soul lies in the doing'; 'Men prize the thing ungain'd, more than it is';

'That she was never yet, that ever knew/Love got so sweet, as when desire did sue'. Her sexuality is the more emphasized by her impersonation of coyness at the first meeting with Troilus. She has already told us, 'That though my heart's Contents firm love doth bear,/Nothing of that shall from mine eyes appeare'. So we may expect deception. When it comes it is precisely of that kind practised by the sexually devious female – a pretended reluctance:

TROY: O Cressida, how often have I wish'd me thus!
CRES: Wish'd, my lord! – the gods grant – O my lord!   [III.2.60–61]

Her very nature, however, prevents her from keeping up the act for long and she is soon tantalizing Troilus with a curiously professional sounding assessment of sexual possibility:

'They say all lovers swear more performance than they are able, and
yet reserve an ability that they never perform; vowing more than the
perfection of ten, and discharging less than the tenth part of one.'
[III.2.81–4]

and follows this by a demonstration of her ability at sexual titillation!

TROY: What offends you, lady?
CRES: Sir, mine own company.
TROY: You cannot shun yourself.
CRES: Let me go and try.
    I have a kind of self resides with you;
    But an unkind self, that it self will leave
    To be another's fool. I would be gone.
    Where is my wit? I know not what I speak.   [III.2.140–7]

Her reiterated appeals to Troilus to 'Be true' in the parting scene before she is taken to the Greek camp, and her avowals of love seem, in themselves, genuine enough, but Shakespeare does not allow us to harbour for very long any idea that we may have earlier misjudged her. The scene in which she is greeted with kisses by the Greek commanders assures us that her previous protestations to Troilus to 'Be true' are very much like the cry of the natural libertine who, having given herself to a man, claims an exclusive possession of his affections which, ironically, she herself is often the first to betray. Ulysses has her measure exactly; the Cressida he describes is the Cressida who gradually unfolds herself in the play – a beautiful harlot who will 'Sing any man at first sight'.

'There's language in her eye, her cheek, her lip,
Nay, her foot speaks; her wanton spirits look out

At every joint and motive of her body.
O these encounterers so glib of tongue
That give a coasting welcome ere it comes,
And wide unclasp the tables of their thoughts
To every ticklish reader! Set them down
For sluttish spoils of opportunity,
And daughters of the game.'   [IV.5.55–63]

Cressida herself confirms Ulysses's judgement, having no illusion about herself, attributing her failings rather to the infirmities of the female sex:

'The error of our eye directs our mind.
What error leads must err; O, then conclude,
Minds sway'd by eyes are full of turpitude.'   [V.2.107–9]

By comparison with Cressida, Troilus seems a paragon of the romantic lover. He expresses himself with a fiery passion; his descriptions of Cressida take exaggerated flight. He is urgent in his pursuit of her love; her perfidy strikes him to the heart and his expression of grief is as profound as his protestations of love. Yet he is not altogether unattractive, perhaps because he seems over-anxious, and therefore ludicrously emotional in praising Cressida (as Romeo lays himself open to mockery in his exaggerated claims for Rosaline). This unattractiveness, however, is not entirely the result of his own personality. It also comes from the context in which his love is placed. His kind of young, urgent romanticism seems entirely out of key in a society which harbours expedient people like Diomed, sophisticated deceivers like Helen and Paris, devious men like Pandarus and, above all, time-servers like Cressida. Love is largely presented as a pawn in a political chess game and as a means of sexual satisfaction. Troilus's rarefied notions of love are entirely out of place – he looks foolish because he is an outsider; his rightful place is the Forest of Arden, not these Trojan wars. Even his emergence as a powerful young commander towards the end of the play does little to alter the image that we retain of him.

The irony with which Shakespeare has treated the love story of Troilus and Cressida is increased by the presence of Pandarus. In the long run, the kind of love that Cressida is capable of giving and the kind that Troilus requires are incompatible – the expedient and the romantic do not make for permanent bed-fellowship. Moreover these two are brought together by one who cannot have any conception of Troilus's notion of love. As Tillyard comments: 'Pandarus does not stand for good sense and he does not inhabit the same world as Troilus. He is good natured but he is coarse; and the kind of love that possesses Troilus is quite outside his experience or power of imagination.'[17] In these words Tillyard indicates how absolute is the separation of Troilus and Pandarus, pointing out that it is reflected even in the opening scenes where Troilus speaks verse and Pandarus prose. The effect is striking:

> TROY: Still have I tarried.
> PAN: Ay, to the leavening; but here's yet in the word 'hereafter' the
>   kneading, the making of the cake, the heating of the oven, and the
>   baking; nay, you must stay the cooling too, or you may chance to
>   burn your lips.
> TROY: Patience her-self, what goddess e'er she be,
>   Doth lesser blench at suff'rance than I do.
>   At Priam's royal table do I sit;
>   And when fair Cressid comes into my thoughts –
>   So, traitor, then she comes when she is thence.   [I.1.22–31]

and because Pandarus is far more interesting than Troilus, Troilus is pushed even further out of our sympathies, and his kind of love seems even more incompatible with Pandarus's and Cressida's. We cannot help wanting to hear the innuendoes cackling of this cunning old gossip; he has a far greater sense of humour, his intelligence is sharper, his attitude, if oiled with lechery, is more down to earth than Troilus's. The reduction of the romantic conception of love by irony and satire is further intensified by the fact that there is such a consanguinity of spirit between Pandarus and Cressida, who are, basically, of the same breed, and are creatures of appetite. Cressida can match his innuendoes word for word, responding to the lascivious excitement of his verbal sexuality without demur. Troilus – and romantic love – become mere encounters in the game which these two are playing.

There is no mitigation by Shakespeare of the judgement of Cressida which she forces upon us. The scene in which Troilus observes her with Diomed serves only to emphasize the kind of woman she is, harshly making his own romantic postures seem even more pathetically ludicrous. In this scene Cressida proves in action her own assessment that the weakness of woman is that 'The error of our eye directs our mind'. Her feelings for Troilus take on a kind of nostalgia which mixes with her disposition to flirt and to yield to anyone:

> DIO: I do not like this fooling.
> THER: Nor I, by Pluto: but that that likes not you pleases me best.

DIO: What, shall I come? The hour –
CRES: Ay, come – O Jove! Do come. I shall be plagu'd.
DIO: Farewell till then.
CRES: Good night: I prithee come.
    Troilus, farewell! One eye yet looks on thee;   [V.2.100–5]

Order and true love – the twin focuses of Shakespeare's vision of human existence – are thus smashed in this play, and the extent of the destruction which he indulges in should be emphasized. Order, which involves honour, fidelity, chivalry, reason, grandeur of spirit, is comprehensively annihilated. In Achilles martial courage is seen as laziness, honour as treachery, nobility of spirit as lascivious hedonism; in Ajax soldierly strength is shown as brute, ignorant, conceited, physical strength – even in Hector chivalry is self-indulgent. Where love is portrayed it is shown as false, blind, ministering to appetite, and its consummation served by lechery.

There are two particular characters whose presence and function suggests the depths of speculation and feeling out of which the play was born. The first is Thersites. One of the most significant things about this scurrilous, physically disgusting rag of a man is that he is well-known and, furthermore, the close acquaintance of so many of the characters. That he should be the confidant and acquaintance of men in high position is in itself a terrible reflection of the disease which Ulysses so eloquently diagnoses. His position among the Greeks is one of allowed Vice. His presence adds a fog of disgust to our sense of disorder and chaos, darkening the dismal and pessimistic view of the world which the play reflects. Yet he is, in fact, used to specify and to confirm in detail all that we learn from the play's actions and characters. He is a Fool in the sense that he sees behind appearances, but he is less than Fool in that he is disgusting in himself, totally committed to his own opinions and so lacks that curious objectivity which, in different degrees, makes Feste, Touchstone and Lear's Fool both mysterious and sympathetic. His indictment is comprehensive. He satirizes Agamemnon, abuses Achilles and Patroclus, rails unmercifully at Ajax, he tells us of Ulysses's and Nestor's mouldy wit, wishes the 'bone-ache' on the whole camp – 'For that me thinks is the curse dependant on those that war for a placket.' He 'sums up' – 'Still wars and lechery, nothing else holds fashion. A burning devil take them.'

If Thersites symbolizes Shakespeare's pessimistic, dismissive, disgusted conclusions about the world, yet he is confronted by an opposing symbolism – that of Ulysses. It is Ulysses who comes nearest to occupying the status of the true Fool in his role as a repository of wisdom. Ulysses, of course, does not wear motley, and there is certainly none in his brain; he is not a professional entertainer, though he has the power to command listeners; he is not disconnected or incompletely connected to a particular class in society, and yet the nature of his wisdom marks him off from the others. He is Fool in the sense of Jaques's words:

> '... give me leave
> To speak my mind, and I will through and through
> Cleanse the foul body of th'infected world,
> If they will patiently receive my medicine.'
>
> [*As You Like It.* II.7.58–61]

The Greeks do patiently listen to his medicine – he calls it himself 'Derision medicinable' – and it is acted upon, though not with the expected results. He affirms order, though he knows it to be gone; he knows the difference between true and false love; he speaks about man's works and the operations of time with a grave and wry wisdom. He is, in fact, as much of a realist as Thersites, but with important differences. His realism is derived from a positive view of the universe. He regrets the world's condition but has not lost faith in what its true state should be. His assessment of people is accurate (as in the case of Cressida) without being harsh; his wisdom is kindly. He is marked off from Thersites as clearly as white is from black and he is the only character in the play who upholds human dignity, both by being dignified in himself, and through his words and deeds.

The question rises as to why such a positive and creative agent is found in a play which so conspicuously paints a negative picture of the world. Perhaps he is a powerful residue of that optimism which had previously governed Shakespeare's plays. Nothing can prevent us from taking away with our experience of this play a sense of disillusion, cynicism, irony and satire. Ulysses remains as a reminder of the brighter times of Shakespeare's spirit and imagination, and perhaps as a notice that there will be a return to them. Ulysses's wisdom, grave kindliness, insight and mysterious intuitiveness are not far removed from the qualities of certain characters in Shakespeare's last plays which re-affirm an optimistic faith in human kind: in considering Ulysses we are perhaps dimly aware of the eventual approach of Prospero.

NOTES

1 William Empson, *The Structure of Complex Words* (1951), p. 284.
2 O. J. Campbell and E. G. Quinn, *A Shakespeare Encyclopaedia* (1966), p. 136.
3 See G. Wilson Knight, in Kenneth Muir's *Shakespeare, the Comedies* (1965), pp. 135–51.
4 Ibid.
5 Hunter, Introduction to the Arden edition of *All's Well that Ends Well* (1959).
6 Ibid.
7 Ibid.
8 Ibid.
9 W. W. Lawrence, *Shakespeare's Problem Comedies* (1969), p. 94.
10 R. W. Chambers, *Shakespeare's Unconquerable Mind* (1939), pp. 307–8.
11 T. M. Parrott, *Shakespearian Comedy* (1949), pp. 347–55.
12 J. M. Nosworthy, Introduction to New Penguin edition of *Measure for Measure* (1969).
13 Donald Lupton, *London and the country carbonadoed* (1632).
14 Stationers' Register. Records of the Stationers' Company giving titles of works they intended to publish. The Company consisted of printers and publishers who held the monopoly for publishing, from 1557.
15 Production at the Royal Shakespeare Theatre, 1968; subsequently at the Aldwych, 1969.
16 J. Dover Wilson, (ed.) Introduction to New Cambridge edition of *Troilus and Cressida* (1969).
17 E. M. Tillyard, *Shakespeare's Problem Plays* (1957), p. 63.

6 The Tragedies

Unlike so many of his commentators and critics, Shakespeare was no theorist. He responded to experience with a natural urgency and transformed it into imaginative truth without striving to conform to convention or rule, in form or expression. If he had been a conformist his tragic plays would doubtless have embodied an acceptance of Aristotelian rules. They do not. The spirit of a Shakespearean tragedy is essentially different from that of Greek tragedy. Moreover, he did not find it necessary to demonstrate the authority of Aristotle by resorting, for example, to the unities or to the ubiquitous tragic chorus.

And whereas Thomas Rymer writes, 'In tragedy he appears quite out of his element; his Brains are turn'd, he raves and rambles, without any coherence, any spark of reason, or any rule to controul him, or set bounds to his phrenzy,'[1] Alexander Pope reminds us that there is another way of looking at it:

'To judge therefore of Shakespear by Aristotle's rules, is like trying
a man by the laws of one country, who acted under those of
another.'[2]

Only in his apprentice days did Shakespeare show any conscious subservience to classical tragic models. The debt of *Titus Andronicus* to Seneca has been noted, yet one of the most notable features of that play is the indication it gives of Shakespeare's imagination – a pulling-away from fixed conventions. He enters the territory of Seneca, but very quickly emerges on the other side, tentatively flexing his own muscles.

The scholarly investigations of the sources of Shakespeare's tragic patterns are prodigious, both in number and in theory. His debt to medieval drama, to classical drama, to renaissance 'humanism', have been copiously audited. The net result of these investigations has been a valuable indication of possibilities and a revelation of certain specific debts. Yet none of them, either alone, or in consort, really deliver the true coinage of the tragic plays. For all the profit that has accrued from asking the question, 'Who and what influenced Shakespeare's tragedies?', it remains token payment compared with what is gained by asking the question, 'What is our experience of the tragedies?'

For Shakespeare life is more important than death, and although

225

his tragedies accept the irony that the fact of life implies the inevitability of death, it is the first part of the proposition on which he most concentrates. Hamlet, King Lear, Othello, and Macbeth suffer, in the end, the common fate of all human kind, yet this is nothing compared with the force of life which each one of them generates on his journey towards doom. Shakespeare's interest in what happens after death is merely implied; almost offhandedly, we are made to feel that there is a reward for the good and damnation for the wicked. He does not tie his tragedies to the Christian myth. Because of this we, as members of an audience (although we may in the study), do not become involved in questions about Christian dogma – the nature of sin, for example, and its possible redemption in the after-life.

What captures our hearts and imaginations is the spectacle of lonely men, capable of conscious thought, deep feeling and willed action, trying to assert their grip on the fact of being alive. In Shakespeare's tragedies lies a most affirmative statement about the sheer importance of man. This is the first and most compelling magnetism of these plays. We leave the theatre bereft and shrived of that pessimism which tells us that life is not worth living. We are, on the contrary, restored to accept the proposition that it is the very irony, cruelty, hardness, of being alive which confirm the necessity to live life to the full.

This proposition is not presented in a straight, didactic fashion; it is not bright-eyed optimism. Its force derives, to a large extent, from the fact that it is presented dramatically and with verbal splendour. Indeed, it might be said that life is worth living if only because we can experience these plays.

Drama exists only by contrasts – by the pull and push of opposites. In order that we may feel exhilarated, and not a little ennobled, by the fact of being alive, we have, also, in the tragedies to be chastened, frightened and conscience-stricken by examples of life's other colouring. We cannot accept the lonely and gracious sacrifice of Hamlet without experiencing his stubborn, self-indulgent indeterminacy. We cannot admire Lear's acquisition of wisdom, without journeying with him through his disordering blindness. We cannot feel Othello's proud sense of self and of love without learning to condemn his folly. And (the greatest testimony of all to the exciting effects of dramatic contrast) we cannot, at the last moment, when the head of tyranny is displayed before us, condemn Macbeth peremptorily, because we remember the reckless courage that prompted him to try to survive against augury and circumstance.

These characters affect us because of the powerful disposition of opposites both within and without them. It is not so much the question of whether they are good men *or* evil men, which engages us, but the fact that they have elements of both qualities in them, and moreover these mixed qualities are large in appearance. The natural courage, the conscience, the moral compunctions of Macbeth loom as large as his evil ambitions, his cunning and his cruelty. Hamlet's princeliness, intellectual strength and emotional sensitivity are as great as his self-indulgence and emotional instability. Lear's physical and spiritual courage, his intermittent tenderness, are not less apparent than his unthinking anger, his intellectual caprice. Othello's nobility of bearing and spirit, his martial bravery, his honesty, are as affecting as his pitiable gullibility, mental instability and cruelty.

It is because both opposed sets of qualities are present in these men, in such large proportions, that they are able to envelop our imaginations so completely. Our tragic experience is, indeed, less closely associated with the dramatic action of the whole play, than with the singular action within the tragic hero. We naturally think of them as tragic heroes rather than as tragic villains – this is important. They are heroic in the accepted sense because what they embody in mind, imagination and action is on such a vast scale, and because the catastrophes involved are so widespread in their effects. Yet, although they are the agents of death and catastrophe, they cannot be classified as villains. Foolish, misled, self-indulgent, intermittently unbalanced they may be, to an inordinate extent, but we baulk at final and complete condemnation. Even Macbeth, the most relentlessly cruel of them all, leaves us, at the end, with an ineradicable, if grudging access of admiration – because of his immense, stark, and fruitless courage. If it were simply the courage of a trapped and vicious brute, we would have no hesitation in condemning him out of hand. Yet, at the last, we remember that Macbeth has suffered the agony of having not only to fight a better self, but of being tortured by his own terrifying imagination. It is this human self-knowledge that rescues him for us.

Also they are placed in situations which test them beyond the breaking-point and over which they eventually lose control. We encounter them at a crisis point in the most severe sense. The drama which excites us as we witness the clash within them is heightened by our realization that the events of the plays are of a uniquely critical kind. It is as if we meet these men at the one and only point in their lives when all the lines of temperament, fate and circumstance, join, at the moment of birth of a totally unique catastrophe.

This quality of special circumstance – allowing the heroes something of the posture of victims – also serves to give them with a very particular status of loneliness. It is they, and they alone, who have to meet the ultimate and fatal implications of the crisis. Others, of course, are meshed into the dark pattern and their lives are changed or, indeed, ended, and yet none of them in a Shakespeare tragedy ever seem to be facing the full consequences of the crisis – where, as well as actual catastrophe, the whole personality is tested, tortured and, above all, is ruthlessly exposed.

Some of them may come near to it – Gloucester, Macduff, Claudius, Michael Cassio. Yet we feel that they are spun about on the edges of a whirlpool whose dark centre reaches down to depths that only one man – the tragic hero – really enters. In a very certain sense these other characters, much as they suffer, exist to minister to our experience of the tragic hero; they are second-class citizens of the tragic world.

The solitariness of the tragic hero at the centre of the whirlpool increases the tragic experience for us. There is a terrible poignancy in contemplating such total loneliness of the spirit and the imagination. Hamlet's reaching out for the comfort of Horatio only serves to convince us that there is little that Horatio can do for him; Lear's fumbling to find the hands of the Fool and of Mad Tom and, eventually, of Cordelia, is a gesture which only too piercingly confirms that he is in an agony of mind and spirit no touch of hands can divine or comprehend; Macbeth's removal from any real human association (including, eventually, that with his wife) gives us ample proof that he is journeying upon seas of the imagination no one else can encompass; Othello is ironically and irretrievably solitary at those very times when he seems closest to human relationship – when he is with Iago.

The victims of the events do not give this experience of total isolation. Perhaps Gloucester and Lady Macbeth come closest to it, but there is an important qualification. Out of Lady Macbeth's lonely and shattered state there come few of those profound intimations and revelations, unique to the tragic heroes, about the battle that is being fought inside the personality. 'The Thane of Fife had a wife, where is she now?', she asks. 'All the perfumes of Arabia will not sweeten this little hand', she cries, and we are aware of conscience and fear. Her husband, however, in his loneliness, takes us fathoms further into the deeps of what his conscience is, what his fear is. She describes, he creates them for us.

Gloucester's loneliness, given a pathetic emphasis by his blindness, is intensely affecting, but it is little more than that. His deprivations, his victimization by filial ingratitude, is a close *obbligato* to Lear's case. Yet it is Lear, not Gloucester, who is the epitome of the reality of suffering.

These tragic heroes are larger than anything around them, and this is not only because of the scale of their personalities, but because they arouse in us a belief that they embody universal qualities – both good and bad. As we watch them we are not only in the presence of Hamlet the Dane, the Thane of Cawdor, the dispossessed King, the proud blackamoor General, but of archetypes, who are also part of ourselves. It is a simple, perhaps hackneyed, but certain fact, that they have all come to stand for certain human verities, have become interchangeable with the abstractions they have come to embody – Hamlet and melancholy have become synonymous, Macbeth and wicked ambition, Lear and aged folly, Othello and tragic jealousy. We do not make the same automatic and categorical associations with the other characters in the tragedies. These tragic heroes are not only larger than life – they are massive emblems of certain unchanging and, indeed, familiar qualities in the human animal.

Yet unique as they are in the power of their dramatic presence, monopolistic as they certainly are of our attentions, they do, within the plays, inhabit a world. They stalk it, set traps for it, and shake its ground. When they leave it, it is with the force of super-beings. The different worlds of each tragedy are literally disordered because these men have inhabited them. Shakespeare's great theme – the demonstration of the effects of order and disorder – which, in one way or another, informs all his plays, persists in these tragedies. Yet, since completing the cycle of histories he had widened and reorientated his comprehension of the meanings of disorder. His obsession with individual character – most explicitly announced in Richard III – had, one suspects, grown in phase with a realization that disorder within the state is personified by disorder within the single human being. Ulysses's famous speech in *Troilus and Cressida*, long utilized by scholars to confirm their view of Shakespeare's conception of order and disorder within the political matrix, can equally be taken as a perfect general description of what happens within the commonwealth of individual personality, of what, in fact, happens to Hamlet,

Othello, Lear, and Macbeth. A balance of forces is upset and 'hark what discord follows'. But although the world of the tragedies is one of total disorder, both within and without, in the plays Shakespeare's greatest interest is in the protagonist's inner catastrophe.

Julius Caesar

The problems of the chronology of the plays between 1599 and 1608 are great and, in some cases, insoluble. *Julius Caesar*, one of Shakespeare's most popular plays, is not immune from these problems. It has variously been assigned to 1599, 1600 and, less credibly, to 1607. What is crucial is whether it precedes or follows *Hamlet*. Is it a link between the incipient tragedy of the 'problem' plays and its full, awesome appearance in *Hamlet*? Many scholars and critics have either noted or expatiated upon apparently close affiliations of these two plays. Mary McCarthy's comment, for example, might equally well refer to *Hamlet*: '*Julius Caesar* is about the tragic consequences that befall idealism when it attempts to enter the sphere of action.'[3]

Since the dating of *Hamlet* is at present uncertain, it is of little consolation to record that many recent scholars regard 1599 as the most likely date for the composition of *Julius Caesar*. This conclusion has, at its base, an account by a Swiss doctor, Thomas Platter, who visited London in 1599, saw two plays, and described one: 'After dinner on the 21 September, at about 2 o'clock, I went over the river with my companions, and in the thatched house saw the Tragedy of the first Emperor Julius Caesar, with at least 15 characters, acted very well.'[4] It is assumed that this refers to Shakespeare's play. It should also be recalled that Ben Jonson's *Every Man Out of his Humour*, entered in the Stationers' Register on 8 April 1600, contains a possible reference. In Act III there seems to be an echo of the line from *Julius Caesar* – 'O judgement, thou art fled to brutish beasts' – in 'reason long since is fled to animals', though this may be mere coincidence. Whatever the truth of the chronological relationship of *Julius Caesar* to *Hamlet* or any other play written in the period 1599 to 1605, there can be little doubt that there is a consanguinity between it and the tragedies, particularly *Hamlet*. Brutus's nature – whose inner complex is tested by outer circumstance to breaking point – recalls to the mind that of the great tragic protagonists. Secondly, there is the impression that a weakness, a corruption, having its source within men of power, can spread to destroy the society around them; this theme of proliferating disorder is as strong in *Julius Caesar* as in the tragedies. Thirdly, as in the tragedies to one degree or another, portents and supernatural occurrences function as symbolic comments upon the action. Finally, and most obviously, Brutus has in large measure that introspection, with its torturing self-knowledge, which in varying degrees is characteristic of the tragic protagonists, particularly Hamlet. These words from Brutus are closely akin to Hamlet's self-analysing soliloquies:

'Between the acting of a dreadful thing
And the first motion, all the interim is
Like a phantasma or a hideous dream.
The Genius and the mortal instruments
Are then in council; and the state of a man,
Like to a little kingdom, suffers then
The nature of an insurrection.'   [II.1.62–9]

Indeed, it is not difficult to make out a strong case for this play as a companion piece to the great tragedies. Yet there is much to set against it. Firstly, though one may see in *Julius Caesar* the tension created between the inner man and outward circumstances, this tension has a good deal of slack in it. Brutus in his self-deliberations never 'follows-through' to such terrible and self-wounding conclusions as does Hamlet or Macbeth. The tension is too 'commonplace'; of a kind that we normally believe to be present in all men who, having some goodness and conscience, are involved in the equivocations of political action. Brutus's personality in fact lacks uniqueness in what it reveals of its response to external events. Secondly, although the theme of disorder, of spreading corruption, is vividly, almost naturalistically, presented to us, particularly in the scenes where the mob is on the rampage, in a sense this also seems too ordinary, too expected. We know from experience that social strife often follows political assassination, that men will be killed and property destroyed, and although we may marvel at Shakespeare's depiction of this in *Julius Caesar* we do not, as in *Hamlet* and *Macbeth*, shudder at the 'unnaturalness' of it. In the great tragedies nature itself seems disarrayed; in *Julius Caesar* it is 'merely' a particular society that is shaken. Indeed the supernatural elements are more of personal superstition than mysterious portent – the other world never surrounds Rome as it pervades Elsinore.

In the theatre *Julius Caesar* does not engage us as a tragedy in the highest sense, though it has its own magnetism which has its source and power in the play's ability to seem (and, indeed, often to be) 'contemporary'. The play has, in successive decades, not only provided its readers with points of reference for contemporary political events, but has seemed particularly amenable to being presented in contemporary dress. From the 1940s, for example, the possibility of dressing and setting the play to align it to the Fascist world of the 1930s proved too strong a temptation for a number of theatre directors.[5] However, politics and political men are always of high news-value, exerting a fascination which is compelling and unfailing, and it is precisely this compulsion that the play exploits with such skill. More than this it gives the kind of insight into the political world demanded by our curiosity and imagination. We are shown the inside workings as well as the outside configurations of that world; our view is double-focused. We are, for example, given glimpses of the reasons why Caesar held such sway, but these singularities are shown in parallel with other elements in him which are common to lesser and weaker men. Some qualities he shares with modern dictators, his courage, his bravura, his ability to command, his expectation of immediate obedience, his peremptory assumption of absolute authority, yet we are also shown the pettiness of mind, the fears, the almost absurdly ordinary emotional response of the man. The contrast between public and private, between great singularity and petty plurality – titillations of our curiosity about political men – is vividly encapsuled in a play of remarkable political and human insight.

If *Julius Caesar* counterpoints our own experience of the twentieth-century world of politics, it is surely not beyond possibility that for the Elizabethans (especially those who strode very near to the corridors of power) it came near to the quick of actual events in their own time. How much, for example, of the Earl of Essex is in Brutus and what taffeta'd courtier is partly hidden behind Casius's thin smile? The questions are unanswerable, yet worth posing since the kind of political and human insight revealed in the play could surely have been gained only by a man who had himself sat very near the seats of power. Shakespeare's literary sources gave him much, but only keen and close observation could give him the ability to convey a sense of actuality and fidelity to political and human affairs. The tense and quarrelsome meeting of Cassius and Brutus before Philippi is told in North's translation of Plutarch's life of Marcus Brutus – Shakespeare's source:

> 'Therefore before they fell in hand with any other matter, they went unto a little chamber together, and bade every man avoid, and did shut the doors to them. Then they began to pour out their complaints one to the other, and grew hot and loud, earnestly accusing one another, and at length both fell a-weeping.'[6]

In Shakespeare's play it is transmuted into this:

> CASS: Most noble brother, you have done me wrong.
> BRUT: Judge me, you gods! wrong I mine enemies?
>
> . . . . .
>   Cassius, be content;
> Speak your griefs softly; I do know you well.
> Before the eyes of both our armies here,
> Which should perceive nothing but love from us,
> Let us not wrangle.   [IV.2.36–45]

Such scenes induce in the reader and the theatregoer the feeling,

> 'Tut, I am in their bosoms, and I know
> Wherefore they do it.'   [V.1.7–8]

Julius Caesar demonstrates that Shakespeare's prevailing detestation of disorder, his celebration of order, his loathing of irrationality in thought and action, had not abated. The Boar's Head, the Courts of Richard of Gloucester, of Harry of Monmouth, of Bolingbroke, Richard II, Henry VI and, indeed, the Forest of Arden, are now joined by Rome as emblems of Shakespeare's view of what makes for good and bad societies. But what gives *Julius Caesar* such a sharpness of outline is the number of different ways in which the perils of disorder are displayed and manipulated. Each one of the characters – Caesar, Brutus, Cassius, Antony and Octavius Caesar as well as the mob – is a distinct example of the incompatibility of political and private moralities, particularly where the element of power dominates. The play shows the corrosive effect of power on these men, ranging from Octavius Caesar's cold embrace of it to Brutus's self-torturing attempts to allay its destructive force.

Julius Caesar we see after power has completed its work of raising the public man high at the expense of ruining the private man. It is on Caesar that Shakespeare exerts the fullest rigour of his bifocal view, showing us relentlessly his effortless, conceited, assumed public domination and, at the same time, his pettiness. For most onlookers the public man is respected, not for his humanity, but for his power:

> 'Who else would soar above the view of men,
> And keep us all in servile fearfulness.'   [I.1.75–6]

When we first meet him it is as a public spectacle, surrounded by his courtiers and a great crowd. He is like some Eastern potentate, addressed with fulsome repetitiveness as Caesar, and addressing himself in the third person. Shakespeare does not make the mistake of presenting too violent a contrast between the image of public authority and the private man, for Cassius's account of Caesar's physical weakness and feat when swimming the Tiber is prevented from destroyed the first image by the envy in Cassius's tone:

> 'And this man,
> Is now become a god; and Cassius is
> A wretched creature, and must bend his body
> If Caesar carelessly but nod on him.'   [I.2.115–18]

In virtually the same breath Cassius refers both to Caesar's 'feeble temper' and to his bestriding the world 'like a Colossus'. As a result the Caesar presented in this play is both strong and weak – he has both a good and a bad profile, is shown from different angles so that we receive a constantly changing impression of the reality of the man.

Caesar's ability to assess those around him is peremptory but superbly accurate:

> 'Yond Cassius has a lean and hungry look;
> He thinks too much. Such men are dangerous.'   [I.2.194–5]

His stoicism seems natural, not assumed, yet there is a self-pride in it:

> 'It seems to be most strange that men should fear,
> Seeing that death, a necessary end
> Will come when it will come.'   [II.2.35–7]

His authoritarianism has a petulance about it:

> 'The cause is in my will; I will not come.
> That is enough to satisfy the Senate.'   [II.2.71–2]

Even egocentric authority – a most obviously typical characteristic – is made to appear a form of self-indulgence - his vulnerability to believing what he wants to believe. He is taken in by Decius's speciously flattering interpretation of a dream which his own wife regards as ominous and his self-conscious assumption of the mantle of Caesardom is both dignified and slightly absurd:

> 'But I am constant as the northern star,
> Of whose true-fix'd and resting quality,
> There is no fellow in the firmament.'   [III.1.60–2]

Shakespeare gives Caesar one characteristic which indicates the shrewdness of his perceptiveness about the political animal. Shakespear was aware that the art of politics involves histrionics – the most successful politician usually turning out to be a consummate actor and none has a greater sense of histrionics than the authoritarian/ dictator type. In the following report there is a clear indication of Caesar's use of histrionics to gain sympathy, utilizing a disability for dramatic effect:

> 'Marry, before he fell down, when he perceiv'd the common
> herd was glad he refus'd the crown, he pluckt me ope
> his doublet, and offer'd them his throat to cut. . . . Three
> or four wenches, where I stood, cried, "Alas, good soul!"
> and forgave him with all their hearts. But there's no heed to
> be taken of them; if Caesar had stabb'd their mothers, they
> would have done no less.'   [I.2.262–74]

We may recall, too, that Richard of Gloucester opened his doublet and offered his bare chest. The occasion was different, but the method and the intention were exactly the same. There is evidence that Shakespeare consciously emphasized the histrionic quality of Caesar's activities in this scene. By a slight departure from his source in North's Plutarch[7] he immensely increases the sense of the theatrical in Caesar's behaviour. Plutarch has Caesar departing 'home to his house, and tearing open his doublet collar, making his neck bare, he cried aloud to his friends that his throat was ready to offer any man that would come and cut it'. This is dramatic enough but is presented to a limited audience – in a private theatre, as it were. Its effect is as nothing compared with the sensational theatricality of his doing it before a vast audience. Casca, who knows political men and their ways, has the pith of it - 'if the tag-rag people did not clap him and hiss him, according as he pleas'd and displeas'd them, as they use to do the players in the theatre, I am no true man'.

When this Caesar dies our emotions are mixed. On the evidence presented by the play his death seems unnecessary, and while we are not over-sorry for him – his death may seem a relief – neither are we completely glad. The likes of him fascinate our curiosities, turning awry our judgements and our power to be sure of what we feel and think, which is why they are so dangerous yet so attractive.

Brutus could never become a Caesar because he is too honest a man and incapable of play-acting. Yet we as listeners and observers lack confidence in him. His courage, his fidelity to a cause, his intellectual and emotional honesty – none of these are in doubt; yet we constantly wonder if his heart is indeed capable of being, committed to the pursuance of those actions which will be necessary once he has thrown in his lot with the conspirators. He is unequipped for the harsh political word; the private, the human and the personal are at odds with the public, the political, the expedient, and his purpose is blunted. We observe him at various stages of the journey that starts with Caesar's death and which ends at Philippi. It might have ended back in Rome with laurel wreaths about his head, but in our hearts we know all along that Philippi will be the end. The fight between political necessity and personal sensibility atrophies his well-meant intentions. He is a man to whom introspection is natural, who is happiest when least in company, when:

> 'I turn the trouble of my countenance
> Merely upon myself.'   [I.2.38–9]

He gives the impression that he is not a natural leader of active opposition, least of all of the kind which will lead to assassination. His observation of Caesar causes him to reflect pessimistically to fear the direction which Caesar's rule is taking, but he has to be cajoled into taking action. Although he says to Cassius, 'What you would work me to, I have some aim', we cannot really believe that he would have contemplated assassination except as an abstract solution. It has gone unremarked by most commentators that Brutus is finally pushed to commit himself to the conspiracy by a cheap trick. The letters that Cassius throws through his window are forged:

> 'I will this night,
> In several hands, in at his windows throw,
> As if they came from several citizens,
> Writings, all tending to the great opinion
> That Rome holds of his name;'   [I.2.314–18]

Brutus's decision is founded upon a deception:

> 'Am I entreated
> To speak and strike? O Rome, I make thee promise,
> If the redress will follow, thou receivest
> Thy full petition at the hand of Brutus.'   [II.1.55–8]

The effect of our knowing that the letters are forgeries is, or should be, twofold. First, that Brutus should be thus so easily deceived increases our sense of his vulnerability in the harsh political world; second, that he should so quickly respond to them initiates a conviction that he is politically naive. From the moment of the delivery of the letters Brutus's vulnerability and political insufficiency are frequently emphasized by Shakespeare. Cassius's calculating practicality is in stark contrast to Brutus's impracticality. Cassius says, 'Let Antony and Caesar fall together' and Brutus replies, 'Let's be Sacrificers, but not Butchers Caius.' Cassius is right but Brutus is the more human. Later, after the assassination, Brutus says of Antony, 'I know that we shall have him well to Friend', and Cassius, right again, replies:

> 'my misgiving still
> Falls shrewdly to the purpose.'   [III.1.146–7]

Brutus commits simple, fundamental errors of political tactics. The first is to invite Antony to speak at all at Caesar's funeral, then, having done so, to allow him to have last voice. The emergence of Antony as a leading character in the play serves, among other things, to underline Brutus's *naïveté*. Antony is a natural politician. The difference between his and Brutus's handling of the funeral speeches is immense. Brutus, idealist and theorist, indulges in rhetoric – we feel that speech-making (certainly to a mob) is not his forte – idealism is:

> 'Romans, Country-men, and lovers! hear me for my
> cause, and be silent, that you may hear. Believe me for
> mine honour, and have respect to mine honour, that you may
> believe.'   [III.2.13–17]

Antony manipulates his audience as if they were puppets, making most of his points succinctly but never failing to labour the one theme he knows will appeal to the acquisitive appetites of his listeners – the contents of Caesar's will. He is completely aware of what he does:

> 'Mischief thou art afoot,
> Take thou what course thou wilt.'   [III.2.261–2]

and, like Octavius Caesar, is ruthless and Machiavellian.

The relationship between Octavius and Antony is based entirely on expediency. They are both amoral. Their relationship is in marked contrast to that which develops between Brutus and Cassius reaching fulfilment in Act V, where Cassius, who in the early scenes gave evidence of knowing the price of everything and the value of nothing, is 'tamed' into more human responses through his friendship with Brutus. There is an acute dramatic irony in the fact that Cassius, who rightly describes himself as 'older in practice', should accede to Brutus's decision about the battle-plan. Cassius is practical:

' 'Tis better that the enemy seek us;
So shall he waste his means, weary his soldiers,
Doing himself offence, whilst we, lying still,
Are full of rest, defence, and nimblenesse.'   [IV.3.198–200]

but Brutus bases even his battle-plan upon abstraction:

'The enemy increaseth every day:
We, at the height, are ready to decline.
There is a tide in the affairs of men
Which, taken at the flood, leads on to fortune:'   [IV.3.214–17]

These are worthy sentiments, but battles are won by shrewd plans
not noble words. Yet Brutus persuades Cassius. In the emotionally
charged scenes between Cassius and Brutus before Philippi we see the
conversion of a political man by a man of intellectual and emotional
sensitivity. Cassius discovers what humanity means, what love is
through his introspective, vulnerable, sensitive friend. He begs
Brutus:

'Have not you love enough to bear with me,
When that rash humour which my Mother gave me
Makes me forgetful.'   [IV.3.117–17]

No other play of Shakespeare's has such a valedictory atmosphere
as has *Julius Caesar* in its final act. Foreboding, resignation and death
are in the air. The discovered love between the once entirely political
man and Brutus makes the very enterprise on which they are
embarked seem irrelevant. Victory or defeat seems less important
than that Brutus and Cassius have found love and respect for each
other. Portia's death is of greater moment to Cassius than discussions
about tactics and strategy and it seems more to the point that Cassius
and Brutus should part well and lovingly than that Brutus 'gave the
word too early' and ensured defeat for his army. Cassius, in fact,
makes no response to this revelation – his thoughts and feelings seem
already to have left this world.

The relationship between these two men comes to dominate the
last act of the play, leaving us a feeling of having seen a personal
rather than a social tragedy – finally, we are less concerned about
Rome and its future than with the sad fate of the two noble Romans.

Yet, up to this last act, *Julius Caesar* is less concerned with
individual tragedy than with a vividly naturalistic evocation of
historical events. Shakespeare's ability to give a present-tense actuality

to those events is proven in several scenes – in Act I.1, where Flavius and Marullus berate the common citizenry, in Act II.1, where Brutus greets and talks to the conspirators, and the following scene, where we see Caesar in his domestic habitat before departing for the Capitol. One scene is remarkable also for other reasons. In Act III.3, the poet Cinna is massacred by the Roman mob. It is not difficult, with Cinna's opening words in our minds, to imagine the fiery glow of burning property with, perhaps, a context of sultry thunder and vivid lighting:

> 'I dreamt to-night that I did feast with Caesar,
> And things unluckily charge my fantasy:' [III.3.1–2]

The brutality of the scene, achieved with such economy, attaches itself inexorably to the imagination. It is, in a sense, just one painful minor event in a day full of important and unimportant happenings, and is often cut by theatre directors who claim that we already know that this Roman mob is dangerous and brutal and that the death of an obscure, frightened poet is of little dramatic consequence. Such argument ignores the fact that the scene is a clear example of Shakespeare's superb sense of thematic and theatrical values. Shakespeare realized what, so often, his modern directors fail to grasp – that the brutal reality of mindless killing is best conveyed to an audience not when groups confront other groups with physical violence but when a single individual is menaced by a group. The death of Hector in *Troilus and Cressida*, of York in *Henry VI* and of Cinna in this play, are ample testimony. The doomed individual takes on a terrible vulnerability becoming representative of all threatened men, and his loneliness in the face of calculated death makes cruelty all the more vicious.

In the particular instance of Cinna the poet, another sensitivity of Shakespeare's is revealed. One of the first victims of social anarchy is a society's culture – modern history bears ample testimony to this – for what unreason fears most is the reason, order, and imaginative and intellectual freedom represented by art and culture. This Roman mob which, in any case, probably cannot read, is prepared to 'tear' Cinna for 'his bad verses'. Ironically, it is even more poignant evidence of the rule of anarchy when even minor poets are killed.

Finally, as one further testimony to the foolhardiness of those who, in the game of trying to make Shakespeare speak to the twentieth century, cut this scene, one may turn to William Shirer's 1960 book, *The Rise and Fall of the Third Reich*. There he recounts the story of Willi Schmidt, a minor musician, whose flat was invaded one evening in the 1930s by a group of Hitler's thugs while Schmidt and his family were having a musical evening among themselves; they inquired his name, demanded his presence, and the last his wife ever saw or heard of her husband was that as he was brutally pushed downstairs he cried that he was not Willi Schmidt the politician, but Schmidt the musician. Across the centuries poor blubbering Cinna's cries are echoed in the words of another victim – 'I am *Cinna* the poet – I am Cinna the poet'.

We are reminded of the most obvious quality, then, of *Julius Caesar* – its innate ability to be always 'contemporary'. Shakespeare's sense of politics, of man in society, of the tension between personal sensibility and public necessity, is so accurate that this play remains an eternal reflection of the ironies, cruelties, and pains which the individual suffers in a politically organized society in trying to reconcile the (probably) irreconcilable – private and public morality, wisdom, and sensibility.

Hamlet

A young man, in black doublet and hose, a white and collared shirt, opened wide to reveal his breast; around his neck hangs a pendant with a miniature; the hair is awry, the eyes deep, searching, and passionate; the movements are graceful, the voice melodious, but never far away from the tones of grief and bewilderment. This, perhaps, is the most prevalent image of the character of Hamlet the Dane which has lodged in the imaginations of countless readers and theatregoers through the decades. Any departure from this, by an actor, seems always to occasion surprise – as if a fact of nature had been interfered with. A scrap of evidence about the appearance of an early Hamlet – perhaps Richard Burbage - suggests that the image is not perhaps after all a romantic fantasy. Antony Scoloker refers to the actor who:

> 'Put off his clothes; his shirt he only wears,
> Much like mad-Hamlet; this as Passion Tears.'[8]

The illustrations which exist of Thomas Betterton's way and David Garrick's way of presenting the part visually also suggest that they did not entirely abandon what some would call this romantic image. Yet it is the illustrations of Henry Irving's Hamlet of 1874 which, more than anything else, in comparatively modern times, give credence to the image. The gaunt pale face, the slim body, the black suit and open shirt. His hair was described as 'black' and 'disordered', it was 'carelessly tossed about the forehead, but the fixed and rapt attention of the whole house is directed to the eyes of Hamlet: the eyes which denote the trouble – which tell of the distracted mind. Here are the "windy suspiration of forced breath", "the fruitful river in the eye", the "dejected haviour of the visage".' This is the Ur-Hamlet of our imaginations, and countless actors over the centuries have, apparently willingly, succumbed to it.

It is worth considering the reasons why this embodiment of Hamlet should be, so to say, the received one. What, in fact, is involved? The black suggests mourning and melancholy; the open white shirt suggests not only distraction but, paradoxically, a kind of romantic insouciance. The tousled hair suggests active engagement with mental problems. The beautiful voice we expect to hear conjures up the idea of a poet; the grace of movement we anticipate from the limbs within the suit, ministers to our expectation of princeliness, of

242

an awareness of a being cutting a figure of grace and beauty across the air. In short, we are in the presence of a sensitive artist – one who wrestles with chaos, yet who, in his speech, his tones, his actions, tries to give that chaos not only a local habitation and a name, but one that is calculatedly formal and excitingly elegant.

There is a unique and very particular relationship between any actor who performs Hamlet, and the part itself. With the other great tragic heroes we always have a sense that the actor's fundamental problem is to enter into the character; with Hamlet, we have a sense that the actor's problem is to control the extent and the nature of the way in which the character enters into him. The character of Hamlet is a direct challenge to the very core of what we call the actor's art – fluency of expression in face and eyes, grace and correctitude in the movements of the limbs, an infinitely variable melodiousness of voice, an overall necessity to seem at one and the same time pleasingly vulnerable to and dominant over the moods and predilections of spectators. All these qualities are those of the character and they are, of course, all the qualities which are required of any actor who is more than an impersonator or exploiter of personality. What Hamlet expects from the actor is, curiously, what we expect, all the time, of Hamlet:

> '... whose end, both at the first and
> now, was and is to hold, as 'twere, the
> mirror up to nature.'   [III.2.23–5]

The greatest actors have always exemplified the truth of Hamlet's words not only in their awareness of their own art, but in the way in which they have conceived and embodied Hamlet the Dane. The potent grace of presence, the willed artistry which we expect from Hamlet were, it seems, present in Garrick's performance:

> When Horatio says, 'Look, my lord, it comes!' Garrick turns
> sharply, and at the same moment staggers back two or three paces
> with his knees giving way under him; his hat falls to the ground and
> both his arms, especially the left are stretched out nearly to their full
> length, with the hands nearly as high as the head, the right arm more
> bent, the hand lower, and the fingers apart; his mouth is open; thus
> he stands, rooted to the spot, with legs apart, but no loss of
> dignity...[9]

Academic and insoluble speculations as to whether the hero is mad, is in love with Ophelia, has an 'Oedipus complex', is dilatory, is really 'fat and scant of breath', have to give place to the one undeniable

243

effect of Hamlet upon an audience – that he is a man of civilized mind, emotional sensibility, grace of speech and movement; in fact combining many of the attributes of what is conventionally known as 'the artistic temperament'. This emblematic figure of the artist spans the centuries, signally lonely, singularly articulate, and the most lasting impression left by the play, after we may have ceased to care about the immediate fate of Hamlet or anyone else in Denmark, is the feeling of having been in the presence of that fragile grace.

In a very precise sense Hamlet's dilemma is that of the artist who is required to come to close terms with reality, a man of imagination, who places more validity on the unreal than on the real, is trapped. A merely cursory glance at the play's events supports this contention. Hamlet is, in a way, most himself when by himself – when he can isolate himself from the snarls of reality, and exercise his particular artistic gifts in order to distil and comprehend, in an imaginative way, the meaning of what is happening to him and others. At several points he recoils from engagement, not because he is simply a dilatory man, but because his temperament is such that actual engagement is of less consequence to him than the imaginative conclusions that he can draw from the contemplation of action. His 'explanation' for not killing Claudius at prayers has a kind of logic about it, but this impresses us less than the manner in which he communicates himself. His 'baiting' of Polonius confirms, certainly, his decision to put on an antic disposition, but what is most remarkable is the consummate skill with which the baiting is executed.

As the play proceeds we witness a number of manifestations of Hamlet: sober-suited, grief-racked Prince; sardonic respondent to mother and uncle; urgently intimate semi-confidant of Horatio; distracted man of passion with Ophelia; wryly witty ex-student with Rosencrantz and Guildenstern; masterful, almost gay *aficionado* of the theatrical arts with the players – and so on. This is, in fact, what happens in *Hamlet* – a dazzling variety of images are presented to us, the common denominator of which is that each is a conscious creating of a particular image at a particular time.

The 'reality' of the situation is that Hamlet knows his mother has married with his uncle hastily, that the visitation of the Ghost confirms the prompting of his 'prophetic soul' that some foul deed has been committed. His immediate reaction is to warn Horatio –

'As I perchance hereafter shall think meet
To put an antic disposition on . . .'   [I.5.169–70]

– not to seem surprised if he finds Hamlet acting in a manner 'unreal' in relation to situation and event. The conscious artist who wishes to exercise his will over his own appearance, his attitude to events, has taken over, and if we inquire what kind of artistic imagination this most brings to mind, we are surely forced to the conclusion that it is the actor's. Granville Barker writes:

> A large part of the technical achievement of Hamlet lies in the
> bringing home his intimate griefs so directly to us. In whatever
> actor's guise we see him he is Hamlet, yet the appeal is as genuine as if
> the man before us were making it in his own person.[10]

this is as much to say that the actor's temperament and the character of Hamlet are consanguineous.

It has been noted how, in both Prince Hal and in Richard III, there is a large element of that kind of dissimulation which we associate with the art of the actor. Both Hal and Richard (see Chapters 1 and 2), in their very different ways, 'put on' an antic disposition in order to achieve their purposes. They attempt to create the reality they desire by exercising the art of illusion. Hal 'puts on', deliberately, a 'loose behaviour', Richard self-consciously congratulates himself on his ability to change shape with the chameleon. It is, indeed, remarkable how baulked we can be, when we ask ourselves what is the true nature of characters like Hal, Richard and the Fools (all of whom have this quality of dissimulation). We can, of course, say that Hal is ambitious, Richard evil, the Fools wittily wise, but their talent for a kind of disguise is so developed that any final revelation of their personalities is really denied to us. We can give chapter and verse about Othello and Macbeth and Lear's personalities – why they believe in such and such a way and for what reason. Our minds, however, are made to slide off these other men, just as so often, when we meet an actor, we are unable to declare – yes, this man is like this or like that. Now, he is here, now he is gone; now he is this, now that. So it is with Hamlet. All the baffling questions we ask about motivation, about the true condition of his mind, his attitude to Ophelia, to his mother, are utterly unanswerable, because all the apparent contradictions we experience when we see Hamlet are, in fact, not contradictions at all – they are elements of the acting temperament.

The evidence of Hamlet's cleaving to the histrionic is both varied and abundant. His immediate decision to put on an antic disposition is followed, very soon, by two pieces of evidence that he is very capable of such a putting on. He baits Polonius as a great Fool would bait an oaf. Indeed he becomes the witty Fool, whose jokes and taunts bear along with them the strain of truth. That his putting on, in this scene, is a conscious act of will, consciously controlled, is sharply underlined by his comment after Polonius's departure: 'These tedious old fools!' This has all the sardonic effect of the great actor who, having bent his audience to his magic fingers, bows with mock humility, then behind the fallen front curtain lifts up two insulting fingers to his hidden victims. He appears before Ophelia

> '... with his doublet all unbrac'd,
> No hat upon his head; his stockings fouled,
> Ungart'red and down-gyved to his ankle;
> Pale as his shirt, his knees knocking each other...'   [II.1.78–80]

What occurs, she describes in detail:

> 'He took me by the wrist, and held me hard;
> Then goes he to the length of all his arm,
> And, with his other hand thus o'er his brow,
> He falls to such perusal of my face,
> As 'a would draw it...'   [II.1.87–91]

The announcement of the arrival of the players to Elsinore provides another opportunity to show us, in a now more objective, less involved way, Hamlet's intimacy with the world of the actor. He inquires if they hold the same reputation as they once did; he has strong views on the child actors who are rivalling the adults for public acclamation; he welcomes them all as friends, but one, in particular, as an old friend; even Polonius is constrained to forget his bafflement, and to exclaim, when Hamlet speaks a speech, ''Fore God, my lord, well spoken, with good accent and discretion.' His warm respect for the profession is definite:

> '... they are the abstracts and brief chronicles of the time; after your
> death you were better have a bad epitaph than their ill report while
> you live.'   [II.2.517–19]

His speech to the players (so much scanned by scholars seeking to find the heart of Elizabethan acting-practice) is of that kind which bespeaks a close relationship with the actuality of performance. He knows the commodity involved:

> 'I heard thee speak me a speech once, but it was never acted; or, if it
> was, not above once; for the play, I remember, pleas'd not the

million; 'twas caviare to the general...'   [II.2.428–431]

It is the enactment of a play that, he believes, will 'catch the conscience of the king', for he observes:

'That guilty creatures, sitting at a play,
Have by the very cunning of the scene
Been struck so to the soul that presently
They have proclaim'd their malefactions...'   [II.2.585–8]

This far, there can be little doubt about the fact that Hamlet is a willing suitor to the world of the theatre. The extent of his committal to it involves us, however, in deeper reaches. Hamlet tells the Queen:

'That I essentially am not in madness,
But mad in craft.'   [III.4.187–8]

The bewildered Polonius himself cogitates on the seeming fact that 'though this be madness, yet there's method in't'. Hamlet's actions puzzle Elsinore; it is as if the various claims that he is mad have a reserve clause to them. Discussing the question, 'Was Hamlet, at any time and in any sense, really mad?' R. W. Chambers writes,

> It has been held, sometimes with much learning of the alienist, that in course of time, under the strain of the situation, the pretence adapted as a mask passed into a reality. I do not think that the text, fairly read, supports this theory, and in the abstract it is surely untenable.
> ... only of one thing we may be sure. Shakespeare did not mean Hamlet to be mad in any sense which would put his actions in a quite different category from those of other men. How could it be so, since the responsibility of the free agent is of the essence of psychological tragedy, and to have eliminated Hamlet's responsibility would have been to divest his story of humanity and leave it meaningless.[11]

Within the context of Chambers's words, it is apposite to reflect on the fact that both Othello and Lear show more evidence of what, in modern psychiatric parlance, would be called 'abnormal conditions', yet we would never consider making with any certainty the judgement upon them that they are 'mad'. We recognize a temporary distraction of their mental faculties, a condition these men have been driven to rather than a 'disease' of the mind, and certainly the text, fairly read, does not support the theory of a diseased mind. On the contrary it supports the idea of a particular kind of mind and imagination given to histrionics.

At the same time it would be folly to attempt to explain Hamlet's behaviour merely on the basis described up to now. Once an actor has played a part he moves on to the next one. But with Hamlet there is a continuing set of themes in every 'role' he adopts during the course of the play. He is, as it were, trying to mutate reality by taking up histrionic postures, yet, at the same time, there is that within him which refuses to be translated, however hard he tries, into mere image, shadowplay.

The dominant tones in Hamlet's speeches are wryness and irony; these are sometimes harmonized with melancholy, with gaiety, with wit, sometimes with emotional fury, sometimes with bleak despair. They are present in his first asides:

'A little more than kin, and less than kind.'   [I.2.65]

They appear, too, in the baiting of Polonius, in the exchanges with Rosencrantz and Guildenstern, in the nunnery scene with Ophelia. It should be remarked that they also manifest themselves on those occasions, in the soliloquies, when we overhear him communing with himself:

'What's Hecuba to him or he to Hecuba,
That he should weep for her?...'   [II.2.552–3]

'To sleep, perchance to dream. Ay, there's the rub...'   [III.1.65]

The cast of his mind is completely permeated by irony and wryness. What, in fact, is the source of this?

A man is often given to wryness and to the use of irony when he realizes that the posture he is forced to take up relative to an event and to other people is not one that he would choose himself. There is a touching and disturbing example of this, as it applies to Hamlet, at the outset of the play, when after reflecting upon the words and the injunctions of the Ghost, he cries:

'The time is out of joint. Oh cursed spite,
That ever I was born to set it right!...'   [I.5.189–90]

These words are all the more telling coming as they do at the end of the scene, after the hot words that he has used in swearing that he will avenge his father's death. He sees that the times are disordered, and equally regrets that it is he who has been enjoined to restore them to order. We get a strong impression that this regret is because he feels he is the wrong man to set them right, an impression underlined by his decision to 'put on' an antic disposition. All his attempts to put things right are out of phase with what is required. He should 'sweep to his revenge', but he cannot; he should confront his uncle, but he does not; he should make his intentions clear to Ophelia, but he does not; he reflects so keenly that even Horatio, at the graveside, impatiently says that his inquiries are 'too close'. One of the traditional answers to this way of going about things – that is, to suggest that since he is not sure of the Ghost's validity he must be cautious – is not entirely satisfactory because we know from Claudius's own testimony that the Ghost tells the truth:

> 'O, my offence is rank, it smells to heaven;
> It hath the primal eldest curse upon't –
> A brother's murder.'   [III.3.36–8]

And indeed, if Hamlet suspects the Ghost on one score – the murder – why then does he believe it so easily on the other - the 'crime' committed by Gertrude in marrying Claudius? It is quite remarkable that Hamlet reacts much more credulously to what the Ghost confirms about Hamlet's mother (that she has lustfully conjoined with a murderer) than to what the Ghost relates about the fact of the murder. It is equally remarkable that whereas his attitude towards the murderer is sardonic, never seeming to threaten more than verbal taunt, his attitude towards his mother, especially in the closet scene, is full of a dangerous passion.

It is at this point that the posture which the Ghost has tried to force Hamlet into begins to look at odds with the posture that Hamlet, since he has to take some kind of action, wishes to assume – what is wished upon him, and what is desired by him, are at variance. Even before we are witnesses of Hamlet's first meeting with his father's Ghost we have a clear indication of the manner in which he has responded to his father's death. He is in a state of acute melancholy – to the extent of reflecting upon suicide – about what has happened. Yet what has darkened his mind seems less the fact of the loss of a dear father than the precipitancy of his mother's marriage, and all that it implies about the fragility of her fidelity:

> '... Frailty, thy name is woman! –
> A little month, or ere those shoes were old
> With which she followed my poor father's body,
> Like Niobe, all tears – why she, even she –

> O God! a beast that wants discourse of reason
> Would have mourn'd longer – married with my uncle,
> My father's brother...'   [I.2.146–52]

Hamlet is in fact called upon to avenge the wrong deed. The Ghost wishes him to leave his mother to heaven, and reminds him in the closet scene that his 'true purpose' (the avenging of his father's death upon Claudius) is almost blunted. The Ghost has cast Hamlet in the role of avenging angel, when all his faculties cry out for him to be a moral scourge. The Ghost has asked him to be active, but his disposition is to be reflective, intellectually questioning, and, in moral terms, admonitory. All Hamlet's soliloquies point to this, but one in particular, the most searing in the directness of its meaning and the effect of its language, describes the torturing irony which inhabits the soul of this man called up to be one thing but, by disposition, capable only of being another. In the 'rogue and peasant slave' soliloquy, two Hamlets confront each other. The actor-prince most certainly now has a dual role. The reflective man and the reluctant man of action face each other in stark contrast:

> 'Yet I,
> A dull and muddy-mett'd rascal, peak
> Like John-a-dreams, unpregnant of my cause,
> And can say nothing;...'   [II.2.560–3]

And, what, in the end, is the result of this drama in which Hamlet faces himself upon the stage of his own sensibilities? It is a decision of superb, and at the same time, pathetic compromise. He will not be merely reflective, nor merely active. He will concoct yet another drama wherein 'the conscience of the King' will be caught. He retreats, yet again, into his disposition not to come to full terms with the reality of the situation, but to push it into the realms of histrionic illusion. His reason, as always, seems subtle and logical enough. He has heard 'that guilty creatures sitting at a play' will be so conscience-stricken by what they witness that they will reveal their guilt. Yet we are not convinced of two unspoken things. First, that it is a half-hearted, half-cocked motivation and, second, that the plan suits his disposition more than it seems likely to achieve its avowed intention of revealing Claudius's guilt. Hamlet's delight that the mouse-trap play does, in fact, prise out from Claudius a guilty reaction is the delight of a man who unexpectedly finds that his plan has worked, rather than of one whose suspicions have now been proved.

It has already been noted that Hamlet's arguments for not killing

Claudius at prayer are both subtle and logical – too subtle, in fact, considering the enormity of Claudius's deed and the virtual certainty that Hamlet now possesses of his guilt. Yet he holds back his sword – his heart does not seem to lie in its blade. He is almost cool in his reflectiveness as he speaks behind the back of the unsuspecting Claudius:

> 'Now might I do it pat, now 'a is a-praying,
> And now I'll do't – and so 'a goes to heaven,
> And so am I reveng'd. That would be scann'd:
> A villain kills my father; and for that,
> I, his sole son, do this same villain send
> To heaven ...'   [III.3.73–7]

Yet, if we compare this with the temperature of his language when he speaks to his mother, the proposition that he has been called upon to avenge the wrong deed, begins to acquire confirmation. He is so fiercely outraged by his mother because her deeds offend his intense moral susceptibilities – and in a very particular way. He feels himself to be a tainted wether of the flock. The kind of self-indulgence which feeds Hamlet's histrionic temperament is also present in his reflections on his mother's crime, that she has not merely stained herself, but has also stained Hamlet.

One of the most prevalent explanations of Hamlet's wildness of behaviour and words to Ophelia is that they show the extent to which his mind has become unbalanced. If, however, we accept the explanation that he himself feels tainted by his mother's deed, his words and actions to Ophelia have a poignant logic about them and, moreover, his rejection of her makes sense – a strained, nervous sense assuredly, but nevertheless one not dissociated from a clear theme. The truth of the paradox he speaks to her (which he himself recognizes as a paradox) is now proven:

> '... the power of beauty will sooner transforme honesty from what it
> is to a bawd than the force of honesty can translate beauty into his
> likeness. This was sometime a paradox, but now the time gives it
> proof.'   [III.1.111–15]

These words call to mind the 'dishonesty' in which his mother has involved herself, and his next words refer directly to the concept that he feels tainted by his mother's action:

> '... for virtue cannot so inoculate our old stock but we
> shall relish of it...'   [III.1.118–19]

The implication of this remark, in the context of Hamlet's feeling of having been tainted by his mother's deed, is amplified considerably when put against the accusations that he later hurls at his mother in the closet scene. He will show her, he says, her 'inmost heart', he will 'wring her heart', and when he asks if it is the King who has slumped dead behind the arras he cries:

> 'A bloody deed! – almost as bad, good mother,
> As kill a king and marry with his brother.'   [III.4.28–9]

When he compares the portrait of his father with that of Claudius he does not dwell upon the horror of murder, but on the superiority of the one to the other, and the conclusions he draws from the contrast between the two pictures amounts to a passionate, morally outraged, condemnation of Gertrude's crime in marrying Claudius. Her act 'blurs the grace of blush and modesty', it takes away the rose from 'the fair forehead of an innocent love'; it has made 'marriage-vows as false as dicers' oaths', it is for him an act of 'rank corruption' which 'infects unseen'.

Melodramatically as all this is expressed, with Hamlet's typical acting-out in his words of the nature of deeds and thoughts, the moral indignation seems to come from some deep source in Hamlet himself, and the meaning of his previous words to Ophelia begins to take on an importance in terms of the nature of his moral indignation. No virtue, he says, is capable of cancelling out the taint with which his mother's deed has infected his 'stock' – that is, his blood and lineage. As a result his cruel assault on Ophelia's emotions, therefore, has the aspect both of a kind of protection of her, and a condemnation of himself. She is to get to a nunnery lest she be 'a breeder of sinners' (got by Hamlet himself upon her). He could, he says, accuse himself of such things 'that it were better my mother had not borne me'. He rationalizes what his faults are – pride, revengefulness, ambition; he pictures himself an arrant knave 'crawling between earth and heaven', but these rationalizations hardly explain the anguish with which he tries to dismiss Ophelia from his heart. His manner of protecting her against herself as a breeder of sinners, shows the extent to which his mother's crime has infected his moral and emotional susceptibilities. In the nunnery scene, one of the most pitiful elements is the way in which his fierce and implied protectiveness of the single female shades into outright condemnation of the whole female sex. Gertrude has outraged womanhood; she has tarnished and corrupted its image and its reality. To this extent all womanhood has become as one foul and objectionable thing.

All this, Ophelia does not know and if she did would not, we are assured, understand. She responds, one may say, conventionally, remembering the Hamlet that was – renowned as courtier, soldier, scholar, man of fashion – and grieves, like any affronted and jilted girl, at the loss of her dear lover.

One of the most poignant elements in the tragedy of Hamlet is that his moral susceptibilities, kindled into fierce hate by the deeds of one woman, cancel his desire to love another woman. He can only express his love for Ophelia when she is dead (she is then beyond the need for his curiously self-abnegating kind of protection) and is shrived by death of her connection with the tainted image of womanhood that his mother has created for him.

The offence of his mother is against the order of love and all its tenets. It is this which Hamlet wants to avenge by 'cleansing' like Jaques the 'foul body of the infected world'. But Hamlet is pacific by nature, governed by a high conception of the order and validity of love. For him to kill would be to be guilty of an offence against his nature and against the spirit of love as he so deviously expressed it. The fact that love, in terms of order, fidelity, honesty, truth and indeed beauty (witness his description of his father) is a governing element in his personality, is evidenced by the fact that the offence Gertrude has committed against it has (even before the Ghost's revelations) taken away from him any zest for life itself. It is as if the heart has been taken out of his universe. A sense of the corruption of life stains his thoughts and his words, and what we may take to be a former apprehension of life's purpose, beauty and order, exists now as a kind of nostalgia. B. Ifor Evans makes this point in another way, but one which underlines, very forcibly, the cast of Hamlet's mind:

> We have in Hamlet a mind that strikes out to undiscovered beauties,
> and then, by some complex anatomising of experience, destroys the
> beauty he has created. 'Why', he asked Horatio, 'may not
> imagination trace the noble dust of Alexander, till he find it stopping
> a bung-hole?' Horatio answered with a comment that might apply to
> a number of Hamlet's speculations: ''Twere to consider too
> curiously, to consider so.'[12]

The 'case' of Hamlet, then, is that of a perfectionist in thought and feeling, subjected to the most severe undermining of the very thing which is the object of his sense of perfection – the spirit and truth of ordered love. The wryness and irony of so much of his tone of address is a kind of emblem of the 'fractured and corroborate' state of his mind and feelings now that they have been bereft of that which made life meaningful for him – the belief in the efficacy of love. Beneath his wryness and irony, his cynicism and despair, can be glimpsed, in so many of his dealings with people, vestiges of what he has lost. He is asked to excise when what he wants to do is to heal.

Hamlet's religion is that of love, and his involvement in it is complete. Love as friendship he worships in Horatio but he finds its negative in Rosencrantz and Guildenstern; love as true marriage he has witnessed in the union of his father and mother, but he has found its negative in that of Gertrude and Claudius; love, catching him in the nearest way, as that which binds men and women together, he has found in Ophelia, but once his faith is shattered, he cannot share himself with her or with anybody else.

Hamlet is often regarded, mistakenly, as the first of a group of 'tragedies' marked off in theme and tone from what has gone before. It is, in fact, the first most profound exploration of a theme present by 1599 in all his plays. *Twelfth Night, As You Like It, Measure for Measure*, and *Troilus and Cressida*, in particular, are concerned with the theme of love encompassing both romantic affirmation and cynical doubt, and although the 'tragedies' take the exploration much further, it still remains a unifying spirit. In *Hamlet* love as the ultimate exemplar of fidelity, honesty and human kindness is the obsession of the protagonist; in *Othello*, love as the victim of stupidity, rancour and jealousy is the burden of the play; in *King Lear*, love betrayed by cupidity, filial ingratitude and mulish pride is the dominating theme; in *Macbeth*, love in the shape of duty, honour, is the victim of ambition.

Shakespeare thus moves not into a new terrain, but through varied aspects of the concept of love – from its more obvious and pleasing manifestations in the romantic coupling of man and woman to profound examinations of the disorder, grief and tragedy that ensue when love is despoiled.

It is a mistake to let any discussion of *Hamlet* become a total obsession with the protagonist at the expense of the other characters, although there is perhaps some justification for this. In no other play of Shakespeare's do the minor characters so definitely subserve the presence of the protagonist. We find ourselves obliged to consider Polonius, Gertrude, Claudius, Ophelia, only to find, time and time again, that they hardly exist except in terms of Hamlet himself. They are 'partial' characters in a sense which is far from true of, for example, Gloucester, Regan, Goneril, and Iago. It is only because

Polonius is accidentally killed by Hamlet that we have cause to consider his position in the play; it is only because Gertrude is Hamlet's mother that we regard her; it is only because Claudius is Hamlet's uncle and also his intended victim that he is important; it is only because of Hamlet's communication of the nature of his relationship with her that Ophelia enters into our sensibilities. In fact, so comparatively under-developed are they as characters, they occasion a kind of puzzled questioning – is Polonius a mere old fool, or has he more shrewdness than folly?; was Gertrude a willing and active partner to actual murder or is she a simple, over-sexed, unintelligent woman?; how 'innocent' is Ophelia?; how 'evil' is Claudius? Such questions arise at every reading of the text and, significantly, at performances of the play. Polonius has been played both as grave elderly statesman, stumping along the final corridors of power, and with equal success as a senile comic. Gertrude has been played as a gorgeous, sexually alive, dark beauty and, with equal success, as a bewildered pawn in power politics. Ophelia has been played as a sexy miss (revealing in her 'mad' scenes the bawdy configurations of her sub-conscious), and as fragile innocent hammered into madness by grief for her father and for the loss of Hamlet's love. Claudius has been played as rodomontade villain, vicious, dangerous, but, with equal success, he has been depicted as a man of intellectual and moral sensitivity, suffering pangs of conscience for the deed which was an inexplicable aberration in an otherwise noble man.

Although the text does give some scope for such variations, simply because these characters are not fully developed in their own right, nevertheless each one of them is given one scene in the play in which each is, if only for a short time, 'rounded out', as it were. Polonius's precepts to Laertes; Gertrude's reactions in the closet scene; Ophelia's 'mad' scene; Claudius's 'prayer' scene – these scenes give body to characters who, on the whole, lack substance. The significant feature of the scenes is that, in their different ways, they allow the characters to come closer to our sympathies and to our understanding.

If Polonius is made to look foolish in his scenes with Hamlet and in his tautological encounters with Claudius, the speeches to Laertes – full of saws as they are, long-windedly as they are expressed – bespeak a caring man, and a man who, though the practice of virtue has ossified into theorizing, has principles and has known the world shrewdly. If we tend, overall, to be impatient of Polonius, this scene tempers our impatience. He is a well-meaning old man in whom tautological speculation has replaced shrewd practice, but he has retained feeling and a sense of duty and has much love in him. Again, to see Gertrude merely as an unthinking loose woman, driven by expediency and sexual appetite, is an over-simplification when we witness her pitiful demonstration of half-realized conscience, fear and bewildered affection in the closet scene; if we are disposed, at first, to see Ophelia as a mere pathetic victim of circumstances, we are forced to reach deeper into our sympathies when we contemplate, in the 'mad' scenes, the extent to which her mind and heart have been broken. Up to this point she is a victim of circumstance but, upon her madness, we realize what the word 'victim' means – she ceases to be a mere cog in the plot machine, and becomes a deeply suffering, deeply affecting human being.

Claudius shows few signs of being more than a nervous autocrat until we witness him at prayer. It is in this scene that we learn that any simple decision about the nature of this man is misplaced. He is pulled out of the status of secondary victim in a revenge play and placed in a more credible light.

These four episodes, while they have the effect of subtilizing the characters and drawing them nearer to our sympathies, have another important role in our experience of the play. They help us to realize, despite the concentration by Shakespeare on Hamlet's viewpoint of the world of Elsinore, that this world exists independently and has its own tensions and realities. At certain points, well distributed throughout the play, it is as if we suddenly leave the immense chambers of Hamlet's own mind and find ourselves standing, with the rest, in an uneasy society, all of whose inhabitants are in a state of apprehension.

Apprehension is indeed the keynote of the society of Elsinore, a society which is essentially political in the manner in which it responds to circumstances. One of the most skilful features of Shakespeare's handling of his plot is the manner in which the events, and particularly Hamlet's responses to them, are 'naturalized'. Without the shrewd pointing of its political nature, the play might well be in danger of seeming to be a profoundly poetic demonstration of an unusual man's over-exaggerated point of view. We have, for example, a sense of the existence in this court of a faction, to which Horatio seems to belong, which disapproves of Claudius's accession. We have a glimpse of the reasons why Polonius is so privy to the King's ear – he has, it seems, been instrumental in ensuring

Claudius's election to the throne. We are given a powerful demonstration of the force of autocratic intrigue and the way in which the political minion will cleave to the seat of power, in the episodes involving Rosencrantz and Guildenstern; we watch, with unsurprised amusement, the political dilettante and sycophant Osric – on the first rungs of the ladder of service on which, perhaps, years before, Polonius had stepped on his way to the most private rooms of state secret and intrigue. But, above all, the 'naturalizing' of the play by its political elements is achieved by the presence of Fortinbras, who comes, shining, from a world elsewhere than Elsinore, to broaden out the context of the play's action. Like the rest of them he is a political man come to establish his politically conceived rights.

It is such elements which make Elsinore 'real' and, at the same time, increase, the tragic loneliness of Hamlet himself. Although he mentions his succession and election, Shakespeare never puts so much emphasis upon this as to make us think that Hamlet is, like the rest, a political man. He remains an outcast, an outraged artist, finding, as Shaw says, 'the duties dictated by conventional revenge as disagreeable a burden as commerce is to a poet.' Shaw, in reviewing Forbes Robertson's Hamlet at the Lyceum in 1897, said:

> Mr. Forbes Robertson is essentially a classical actor. ... What I
> mean by classical is that he can present a dramatic hero as a man
> whose passions are those which have produced the philosophy, the
> poetry, the art, and the statecraft of the world, and not merely those
> which have produced its weddings, coroners' inquests and
> executions. And that is just the sort of actor that Hamlet requires.[13]

Shaw had perceived what a few great actors have perceived – that the tragedy of Hamlet the Dane is that of an artist called upon to execute the work of an artisan.

Othello

It is partly because Othello is built on a much more ordinary human scale than any of the other tragedies that the play has always held a particular popularity for theatre audiences. Its attraction can also be attributed to the insistent 'domesticity' of its plot and theme. It concerns itself with love, hate, deceit, treachery, brutality, affection, duty (as do the other tragedies), but here they are scaled down to familiar proportions. The kind of marital jealousy shown by Othello we recognize immediately – sometimes with a shock – as a very close reflection of what we may have encountered in actual experience. The kind of 'accidents' by which Othello is duped are almost ludicrously obvious in the manner in which they dictate the actual plot-line; yet the very disproportion between their petty nature and the terrible tragedy which they trigger off, makes the play seem agonizingly 'true' to what we call real life. Iago, alone, seems not to fit exactly in with the recognizable and the familiar. It is true that we catch sharp glimpses in him of a kind of reasonless envy, malice and duplicity, and we realize, with a start, that we have known men like this; at the same time so enormous is the build-up of hate, so puzzling is the question of motivation, that he seems to stand apart from the mode of the rest of the characters.

Why Shakespeare should have turned to write a play in which a Moor is the protagonist is not known. He continually surprises with the manner in which he grasps firmly at stories and source plots, which are in themselves unremarkable but, for him, proved most valuable ore. In this case he found the story in Cinthio's *Hecatommithi*, a book divided into ten decades, each one dealing with a different subject.[14] The seventh novel in the book begins: 'There once lived in Venice a Moor, who was very valiant and of a handsome person; and having given proofs in war of great skill and prudence, he was highly esteemed by the Signoria of the Republic, who in rewarding deeds of valour advanced the interests of the state.' Perhaps, indeed, Shakespeare was intrigued by the possibilities of what could be done with such a character and two other sharply distinguished characters described by Cinthio:

'A virtuous lady of marvellous beauty named Disdemona fell in love with the Moor.'

'Amongst the soldiery there was an ensign, a man of handsome figure, but of the most depraved nature in the world.'

Shakespeare's play moves very strictly within the boundaries of this triangle. There is no highly developed sub-plot; the destinies of everyone are held closely within the triangle. Yet, although the play is architecturally neat, and the most insistently domestic of the great tragedies, it poses a number of questions, many of which do involve subjective decisions. 'What motivates Iago?' 'How innocent is Desdemona?' 'Are the "accidents" of the plot too obtrusive, and do they, in fact, rob the play of that relentless inevitability which characterizes the other tragedies?' 'What part is Othello's colour meant to play in the development of the plot and theme?'

This last question is, for the contemporary audience, the most intriguing of all. It involves all the susceptiblities and prejudices about colour which have forced their way into humanity's consciousness in the last few decades of this century. It is a truism to state that the depth and variety of both our emotional and intellectual preoccupation with the 'problem' of colour were unknown in Shakespeare's time, yet it is worth emphasizing now that modern directors are so obsessed with the principle of making Shakespeare's plays vital for the twentieth century that there is a danger that specifically twentieth-century notions about colour are likely to be grafted on to Othello. This is not to say that the play has nothing, of itself, to say to us about 'colour', yet we must be clear what it does, in fact, declare, and what it does not. O. J. Campbell has a timely warning on this matter: 'In present-day North America a Negro Othello is likely to pervert the meaning that Shakespeare gave the situation, to twist it into a problem of miscegenation ... this is disastrous to a correct interpretation of the action, for Othello is no struggler up from slavery for status, but an aristocrat who fetches his "life and being" from "men of royal siege".'[15] Campbell's words are the more to be regarded in the light of the contradictory and emotionally expressed conceptions of Othello that have appeared in critical works throughout the nineteenth and the twentieth centuries. The complications of the problem may be indicated by two nineteenth-century comments. First by Mary Preston, an American critic: 'Shakespeare was too correct a delineator of human nature to have coloured Othello *black*, if he had personally acquainted himself with the idiosyncracies of the African race ... *Othello* was a *white man*'.[16] Second, by G. H. Lewes: 'Othello is black – the very tragedy lies there.'[17] It is unlikely that Shakespeare would have had close contact with the Moorish race from which, he is careful to emphasize, Othello came. On the other hand it is more than possible that he had seen and met with Moorish ambassadors or seamen. What he is very aware of is the close relationship between Venice and the Moors. They traded with Venice, and their mercenary warriors had fought both with and against the Venetians. They were a proud, martial and civilized race; the rich blood of their stock is well described by Henry Reed:

> (Othello) was one of that adventurous race of men who, striking out
> from the heart of Arabia, had made conquest of Persia and Syria;
> and, overturning the ancient sovereignty of Egypt, swept in victory
> along the whole Northern coast of Africa; and, passing thence across
> the narrow Frith of the Mediterranean, scattered the dynasty of the
> Goths...[18]

This, then, is the basis of Othello's character, pride of race, martial courage, with centuries of civilized achievement as well as fierce barbarism behind him. Yet, he is also black, and it is well to examine, in general terms, what kind of 'placement' his colour and race has in the play. Certainly it plays some part in Brabantio's outraged condemnation of Othello's marriage with Desdemona. The word 'black' is mentioned several times and is used later by Othello himself when he speculates as to why Desdemona has been unfaithful to him. There can be little doubt that an association is made, by Othello's enemies, between his colour and what they take to be his vices. Iago makes the most violent association when he goads Brabantio with what has happened to his daughter:

> 'Even now, now, very now, an old black ram
> Is tupping your white ewe...'   [I.1.89–90]

Yet, Othello occupies high status; he is well regarded by many people; he is trusted by the state to important office. Othello does not live in a racialist society which would deny him the opportunity for advancement. He is not a pariah; he is debarred from nothing that any white man would accept as a natural right. On the contrary, in the context of the society of Venice, Othello takes precedence over many eminent white people. 'Colour' then is most definitely not an issue, in this play, in the sense in which it has become an issue in modern society and in many examples of modern literature. The three most specific attitudes towards Othello in this play are those of Iago, Brabantio and Desdemona, and in each, although 'colour' plays some part, it is peripheral compared to the part it plays in the consciousness of the twentieth century.

Iago uses 'colour' only as an additive to a hatred whose real source lies elsewhere. He does not despise Othello because he is black, but the fact of his blackness may be said to be an additional reason for disliking him. Brabantio's affronted fury leaps to its height when he thinks of the black ram tupping his ewe, but it is very significant that the accusation that he hurls at Othello is that he has used 'magic' to ensnare Desdemona. For Brabantio, Othello is a dangerous stranger he does not understand; he has come, with pride and status, from some dim exotic land where mesmeric arts are practised. Desdemona's expression of love for Othello and, importantly, her explanation of how she grew to love him, is based (in a somewhat childlike way) upon the appeal of mystery – the fairy prince, from places unimaginable, has come to life for her. It is curiously ironic that Desdemona loves Othello for the very reason that Brabantio rejects him. They both see him as the mysterious stranger but with completely opposed results.

Othello is therefore no more reviled simply because he is black than he is respected because he is black. He is an exotic stranger, an outsider in the world of Venice. For those who love him or can appreciate his qualities and his value to them he is a welcome outsider – a saviour to the hierarchy of Venice, a fairy prince to Desdemona. For those who hate him he is an outsider, but in the sense of one that is to be reviled, either for some real or imagined vice (to suit Iago's purposes) or for his utter difference from an accepted and familiar social norm (to Brabantio). To the former he is a 'lascivious Moor', a 'Barbary horse'; to the latter he is one who has 'enchanted' Desdemona, bound her 'in chains of magic' and used 'foul charms', 'a practiser of arts inhibited'.

The first speech of consequence that Othello makes seems to emphasize the strangeness of the man. We catch glimpses of a life led in far places, in stern circumstances. When the Duke gives him permission to tell of his wooing of Desdemona, the outlines of that life are filled in with exotic and romantic colourings. He has had 'hair-breadth scapes', wandered in 'deserts idle', and has met

'The Anthropophagi, and men whose heads
Doe grow beneath their shoulders.'   [I.3.144–5]

Moreover, he has, from the age of seven, led the hard life of a soldier – from childhood he has wandered with rough, harsh assembly. Desdemona has grown to love him for he is an unusual man, and because she pities the sufferings of his youth. What Othello tells us in his speech is the story of a romantic girl who has found her dreams and imagination realized, and of a man who has unexpectedly found beauty, worship and pity. The basis of their love is that both the romantic, innocent child and the experienced man have a dream realized.

The passionate extent, the blind fury of Othello's jealousy, is explicable entirely within the context of these two factors – his own 'outsider' position and his unexpected realization of a dream. The tragedy is the result of the wilful and clever increasing of Othello's sense of being an outsider and a deliberate destruction of his belief that his dream of love, fidelity and beauty has been realized in Desdemona. It cannot be over-emphasized that behind all that Othello says of Desdemona, up to the point where Iago's jealousy begins to work its poison, there is a note of joyous surprise that he has won her. It expresses itself in his pride in her as his wife; it lurks in his description of how she reacted to his stories; it comes to the surface in his greeting to her at Cyprus:

> 'It gives me wonder great as my content
> To see you here before me. Oh my soul's joy.'   [II.1.181–2]

And, as if joy is bursting his heart, he cries,

> 'I cannot speak enough of this content;
> It stops me here; it is too much of joy.'   [II.1.194–5]

Criticism of the kind which sees Othello as a blind dupe from whom a thin veneer of civilized behaviour is easily removed, does not take sufficient note of what Desdemona means to him. He has discovered something in her he never before possessed; a beautiful woman who has overlooked men of her own clime and come to love him, to become 'the joy' of his 'soul'. When he says that it is 'too much of joy' it is almost literally true – he never imagined that reality could fulfil desire, hope, imagination, in this way.

This man whose dreams have come to life is opposed by one who is a conscious artist in villainy. Like Richard III, Iago has been designated, by critics, as a form of medieval Vice; yet, as with Richard III, this description does not seem, in the closest analysis, to give more than a general framework to something that is more subtle and complex. Iago is, like Richard and the Vice, an emblem of evil, but, like Richard, there is a quality in him which goes beyond the mere allegorical. The Vice in medieval drama manifested evil in as definite a manner as an angel manifested good.[19] When drama was a fixed ritual, ministering to stated and accepted beliefs, its constituent parts – plot, theme, language and character – had, to a large extent, a symbolic value. The plot stood for a known series of events, the theme bespoke and underlined the meaning of those events, the language memorialized conditioned reflexes of response, the characters pictorialized in action a natural equation – on one side stood the plus of good, on the other the minus of evil. There was no cross-over. On the minus side the Vice worked.

The heirs of this stock theatrical representation of evil are abundant in Elizabethan drama. There can be little doubt that Iago himself is made up of the basic ingredients of the Vice figure. He is completely amoral; he patently enjoys being and doing evil; his 'reasons' for committing wrong are unconvincing; he seems to acquire motive from some dark evil force of which he is an earthly agent; he is mentally agile in his pursuit of wrongdoing; he is a master of deception. Such characteristics exist also in different degrees of intensity within Richard III. To an extent such characters, for an Elizabethan audience, would have been accepted as stock 'props' in any play where evil was pitted against good in an intent fashion. Yet neither Richard nor Iago are simply this. Shakespeare building upon traditional and conventional material gives his 'Vice' characters the additional dimension of seeming actual. There is always much in them that is only too human while, at the same time, we are kept aware of dark affiliations they have with the supernatural. Kenneth Muir comments: '... Iago is both a stage devil, deriving ultimately from the Vice of the Morality plays, and a character in a more sophisticated Elizabethan tragedy. He hates goodness, at the same time as he has psychological motives for hating Othello.'[20]

These 'psychological motives' are difficult to credit yet, paradoxically, they give this particular tragedy an awful patina of reality, for none of the reasons given by Iago are ever proven, yet they might always be true. Even more important we readily recognize their mode and manner of expression as only too typical of the processes by which envious, rancorous and dangerous men serve their own ends.

One aspect of this play is, however, unique. In no other of his plays does Shakespeare concentrate so much upon the minutiae of a relationship between two men. Yet it is a relationship of an unusual and terrible kind for it is based entirely upon duplicity. It is a most terrible demonstration of the difference between what is and what seems. Iago, with the most slender resources of evidence, and dangerously near being unmasked at every stage, mounts an offensive of terrible ferocity and audacity, the various stages of which are shown with remarkable dramatic skill.

The reasons given by Iago, at different points in the play, for his hatred of Othello are firstly, that Cassio has been appointed lieutenant instead of himself; secondly, that it is 'thought abroad' that Othello has had sexual relations with Emilia; thirdly, that Cassio has also had relations with Emilia; fourthly, that he wants Desdemona himself, and fifthly because Michael Cassio:

> '... Hath a daily beauty in his life
> That makes me ugly.' [V.1.19–20]

There are three themes running through these 'reasons' – envy, sexual jealousy and self-regard. Of these, the last is the most persistently expressed; indeed the other two become subservient to Iago's immense self-regard as the play proceeds. At the very beginning he tells Roderigo, 'I know my price, I am worth no worse a place.' His every soliloquy implies a fear that he is not being regarded as he should be. The extent to which even sexual jealousy is subservient to his self-regard is clearly shown in his references to his own wife's alleged infidelity with Othello. In Act I.3, he says:

> 'I hate the Moor;
> And it is thought abroad that 'twixt my sheets
> 'Has done my Office...' [I.3.380–2]

Later on in Act II.1, he says,

> 'For that I do suspect the lustful Moor
> Hath leap'd into my seat...' [II.1.289–90]

As Kenneth Muir says: 'Iago, however, is not so much concerned with Emilia's unfaithfulness, as with the fact that he is despised or pitied, or an object of ridicule as a cuckold; and this is intolerable to his self-esteem.'[21]

It is noticeable how the word 'I' runs with repetitive frequency through Iago's soliloquies and noticeable, too, how, like Richard III, part of his self-regard has a kind of chuckling celebration of his own cleverness and duplicity:

> 'How am I, then, a villain
> To counsel Cassio to this parallel course,
> Directly to his good? Divinity of hell!

When devils will their blackest sins put on,
They do suggest at first with heavenly shows,
As I do now.'   [II.3.337–42]

Even at the very end when all his villainy is revealed he preserves a
kind of mocking self-assurance, a determination to assert the
immense self-conceit of 'I am what I am'. Even his last words are a
refusal to explain, and so debase himself:

'Demand me nothing. What you know, you know.
From this time forth I will never speak word.'   [V.2.306–7]

We have to see all his alleged 'reasons', and indeed his machina-
tions against Othello within the matrix of this self-regard. If no
'reasons' were ever given or implied, we would find it quite
acceptable that a man of such extraordinary self-conceit would be
highly likely to find opportunity to display it by wicked deeds.

The process by which he destroys Othello has much in it which
displays the skill of an actor. It is often forgotten, especially by those
who see Othello as a stupid, blind dupe, that Iago succeeds in duping
everyone. He is, like Richard III, a consummate actor who can exert
his power over the most intelligent, as well as the most gullible.
Michael Cassio trusts him, Desdemona seems almost to admire his
forthrightness, the stupid Roderigo is mesmerized by him. The basis
of the deception he practises is his studied 'putting on' of the face of
honesty. Othello trusts him completely – to him he is simply 'honest
Iago'. It is often held that Iago is a complete liar, but, in point of fact,
his duplicity is subtle for he uses honesty itself in the service of
deception. This is shown with superb effect in the scene where the
tipsy Cassio has wounded Montano and Othello is seeking the truth.
He gets it – from honest Iago.

His account is absolutely correct. It is so true, so mild in its
expression, so 'fair' to Cassio, that Othello immediately suspects that
the honest teller of the circumstances is deliberately playing down
Cassio's part in the brawl:

'... I know, Iago
Thy honesty and love doth mince this matter,
Making it light to Cassio.'   [II.3.237–9]

Iago has achieved his purpose – by honesty.

He does, in fact, make his attack on Othello not only with the
simple device of lying, but with a subtle usage of calculated candour.
We can believe him when he says:

'Good name in man and woman, dear my lord,
Is the immediate jewel of their souls . . .'   [III.3.159–60]

He does no more than echo Brabantio when he says:

'She did deceive her father, marrying you;'   [III.3.210]

He confirms what Othello knows when he claims:

'And when she seemed to shake, and fear your looks,
She lov'd them most . . .'   [III.3.211]

He is ironically right in his advice:

'My lord, I would I might entreat your honour
To scan this thing no further; leave it to time.'   [III.3.248–9]

He is probably telling the truth when he says that he saw Cassio wiping his beard with the handkerchief that Othello gave to Desdemona. Even if he did not actually witness the occurrence, he knows perfectly well that the handkerchief is in Cassio's keeping. It is wrong to assume that Othello's belief in Iago's honesty (or indeed Cassio's belief) is entirely misplaced. Iago, indeed, is no simple deceiver – he can wreak havoc and create corruption by a shrewd exercise of plain speaking.

Even his use of the direct lie is a mixture of cool calculation and breath-taking opportunism. A good deal of the play's dramatic impact on us is, indeed, the result of watching and listening to a man walking a knife-edge between what is, for him, success and disaster. Some of his lies are as blandly calculated as his truth-telling. He prides himself upon his patient calculation of his intentions:

'Thou know'st we work by wit, and not by witchcraft;
And wit depends on dilatory time.'   [II.3.360–1]

He gives several examples of his careful assembly of false evidence. He tells Othello that he does not think it could have been Cassio sneaking 'away so guilty-like' from Desdemona's presence. 'My lord, you know I love you,' spoken right at the moment of the birth of Othello's suspicions, is outright and calculated hypocrisy. Yet, what is most striking about Iago is his audaciously correct reading of the reaction that his evidence, false or honest, will receive. When he says 'Ha! I like not that', in order to incite a reaction from Othello to Cassio's meeting with Desemona, Othello asks 'What dost thou say?'

He replies, 'nothing, my lord; or if – I know not what'. The onus is thrown upon Othello to consider whether what Iago has said means 'nothing' or 'something'. When he reports Cassio's lascivious behaviour when dreaming, we have no proof that this is a lie, although we are prepared to believe that it is; more to the point is Iago's reply to Othello's 'O monstrous! monstrous!' Iago says, 'Nay, this was but his dream.' There is a terrible and frank reasonableness about it – it could, quite, simply, be a truth. This awesomely accurate 'placing' of traps, rather than, in most cases, the nature of the traps themselves, constitutes the real evil genius of Iago. He is able to snap up the slightest chance of setting traps, and to foretell the certain result. Although he has obviously thought of a use for the handkerchief previously, he has no idea that it will fall into his hands at a particular time, yet when it does, there is a certainty in his knowledge that it will serve his purposes well:

> 'Trifles light as air
> Are to the jealous confirmations strong,
> As proofs of holy writ.' [III.3.326–8]

There is one further aspect of Iago's superb evil craftsmanship which not only indicates how well he can calculate his victim's reactions, but reminds us of the joy that he takes in his histrionic art. He is able to 'pace' the sequence of events which leads to Othello's final breakdown. The first 'act' of his baiting of Othello he sets at a slow pace; it is composed of offhand remarks, insinuations, affronted dignity. He is in the first stage of playing his line, jerking it slightly, pulling the hook away from his victim, then with a slow swoop advancing it again towards him. This 'act' ends with a sudden jerk of direct assault:

> 'She did deceive her father, marrying you;
> And when she seem'd to shake, and fear your looks,
> She lov'd them most.' [III.3.210–12]

He begins now to increase the pace of his attack, by making more direct statements, and interweaving them with an urgent confidentiality:

> IAGO: I see this hath a little dash'd your spirits:
> OTH: Not a jot, not a jot.
> IAGO: I'faith, I fear it has.
>   I hope you will consider what is spoke
>   Comes from my love; [III.3.219–21]

The next 'attack' follows an interval in which he has obtained the handkerchief from Emilia. Now, he is prepared to let Othello have free reign with the passion that has built up in him. Over thirty-seven lines all Iago says is,

'Why, how now, General? No more of that.'
'How, now, my lord!'
'I am sorry to hear this.'
'Is't possible, my lord?'
'Is't come to this?'
'My noble lord.'   [III.3.339–71]

For the rest, Othello holds the stage and swamps it with his rage, grief and despoiled pride. As the rage begins to abate, Iago comes more into the spotlight, eases the pace a little, then increases it to a terrifying speed with his images of goats and monkeys, his account of Cassio's alleged dream, and then he achieves his supreme climax by kneeling to pledge his service to Othello. Up to this point, Iago has invented, so to say, a play in which passion has risen, abated, then risen again. The final episode of this superbly well-organized drama of passion which Iago is realizing, takes on a different tone, pitch and pace. Hitherto Iago has used innuendo, truth, half-truth, has played on emotion and passion, but now he becomes explicit; he bursts through Othello's flimsy guard with short staccato thrusts and makes the final cut exactly on the right spot:

IAGO: What,
    To kiss in private?
OTH: an unauthoris'd kiss.
IAGO: Or to be naked with her friend abed
    an hour or more, not meaning any harm?   [IV.1.2–5]

His trick, by which Othello overhears Cassio seeming to confess to Desdemona's love for him, leads to the final stage of his play, when everything he has said to Othello seems to have been proved, and he can afford to give direct and vicious advice:

'Do it not with poison; strangle her in her bed, even
the bed she hath contaminated.'   [IV.1.203–4]

When we contemplate the singular craftsmanship and art of Iago's assult on Othello, and remember the extent to which others have succumbed to it, we have to pause before condemning Othello as a simple gull. The Moor, whose whole life has been dedicated to the raw simplicities of battle, and whose status has come entirely from his prowess and bearing, is subjected to an entirely new experience both in Desdemona's love and in the intellectual subtlety of the way in which that love is destroyed. The Othello whom we see at the beginning of the play is, in Granville Barker's words, 'Confident, dignified, candid, calm'.[22] He is far from simple-minded. His life has given him the ablity to think quickly if not deeply. He is capable of gaining respect by his qualities of leadership and his palpable honesty. His downfall is the result of the very pride which he has surrounded himself with through his marriage to Desdemona. He is as vulnerable as a child who has had snatched from him the one gift that he has dreamed about. In a sense the question that is sometimes asked 'Is Desdemona completely guiltless?' – is an irrelevancy. We can never answer it, and in any case it is enough for a man of Othello's quick mind and huge joyous pride to be suspicious. He asks for proof but even when it is (apparently) given to him, it seems of less importance than the agony and pain of his personal loss. Time and time again, after the poison has begun to work, what was surprised and joyous pride is replaced by the bewildered suffering of shattered pride:

'For she had eyes and chose me.'	[III.3.193]
'She's gone; I am abus'd.'	[III.3.271]
'Ha! ha! false to me, to me?'	[III.3.338]
'I had been happy if the general camp, Pioneers and all, had tasted her sweet body, So I had nothing known.'	[III.3.349–51]
'. . . he had my handkerchief.'	[IV.1.22]

It is, indeed, the admixture of consuming pride, and apparently crass gullibility in the man which has occasioned a fairly common judgement that Othello is of less 'status' than the other tragic heroes. As he plunges into the traps laid by Iago, and as he reveals more and more of what seems to be self-centred pride, we almost forget the better qualities he revealed at the beginning of the action. In a sense we learn as an audience certain positive things from the other tragic heroes. Hamlet 'teaches' us the quality of a noble, if misguided spirit; Lear's agonies 'inform' us of the realities of great suffering; even Macbeth presents the evidence of the tragedy of fine qualities corrupted, and, with this specific education, there is also involved a general realization of the potential greatness of the human animal.

Othello lacks the potentialities of Shakespeare's other tragic heroes and what we learn from him does not seem to have a largeness of import. To learn not to listen to lies, not to believe calumny and place credence upon ridiculously false evidence seems of less consequence than what we apprehend from Hamlet, Lear and Macbeth.

It may be added, too, that Othello is less intelligent, and of narrower sensibilities, than the others. He does not acquire, with cumulative force, their self-knowledge; although, at the end, he is aware of the crime he has committed, he is more pathetic in his apprehension of it, than profoundly tragic in total realization. He does not 'enlarge' himself in our experience as he falls towards his doom. It is because we can say, of his fall – 'There, but for the grace of God, go I', that the protagonist seems smaller than the other three, who take us beyond mere identification.

There is another aspect of the 'smallness' of this play when set against the context of the other tragedies. Apart from Iago, no other character or element in the drama intensifies the attendant atmosphere, or implies meanings beyond what is specifically given. Nothing supernatural exists to give the play a dark and brooding hinterland; the sub-plot, dominated by the goofy pretensions of Roderigo, seems minuscule, lacking the pressure on the main plot which, in *Lear* particularly, increases the emotional and psychological weight of the whole; Michael Cassio, Desdemona, Bianca, minister to the plot without imprinting themselves as deeply on our imaginations as do for instance Edgar, Ophelia or Lady Macbeth.

The language of the play too, so indebted to prose, lacks the profound associativeness of the other tragedies. Kenneth Muir says that 'Othello's speech cannot be used to undermine his nobility. To most sensitive critics his lines ring true'.[23] Indeed, they are only too true. When they reverberate, it is the reverberation of rhetoric which we hear. When they do not, the reader's and the theatregoer's imagination does not take flight – we taxi earth-bound, only too aware of the immediate landscape, but ignorant of what is beyond the horizon.

Yet, even if its tragic hero is not great, and its own contours are within a limited area, this is still a great play. Its poetry is at the service of a present-tense immediacy of effect; its characters are held within a matrix of action and experience which, on the whole, is likely to be familiar to an audience. It tells a terrible story with an intensity of concentration upon immediate response by the *dramatis personae*. There is little implied or direct philosophical reflectiveness in them, nor are we incited to reflectiveness by what we witness. Its greatness lies in its stark exposure of the pitiful and pathetically thin line which divides pride from pettiness, truth from falsehood and love from hate, – a line which, daily, we tread ourselves or see others treading. *Othello* memorializes man's constant and daily vulnerability to his own frailties.

King Lear

The four great tragedies share two general features. The first is the close domesticity of the initial setting and exposition of the events which will eventually broaden out, both directly and indirectly, to encompass wider horizons and universal human implications. The second is the careful insistence upon the locations of the plays' actions and events. We never allow 'A Wood Near Athens' to disabuse us of our certain intuition that it is really a sixteenth-century English wood, people by English lovers; we do not allow ourselves to pretend that Kate and Petruchio and Sly have anything but sixteenth-century English blood coursing through their hearts – this Padua is no more than a few leagues from London Bridge. Yet Elsinore, Venice and Cyprus, Dunsinane and Lear's Court remain, either in time or place, far removed from contemporary Elizabethan England. In the tragedies, though, their protagonists, their language, the implications of their themes, are forged out of English Renaissance modes of thought, feeling and attitude, are distanced, apparently deliberately, from specific connections with Shakespeare's contemporary world. It is partly because of this that they achieve a free universality of meaning uncramped by those holding lines which attach, even in the great histories, to certain particular and fixed Elizabethan concepts.

King Lear begins as the most 'domestic' of the tragedies but it is also the one which, although its location is Britain, is furthest removed in time from Shakespeare's own age. The place is 'Britain' not 'England', the time is neither contiguously medieval nor virtually contemporary to Shakespeare. The word 'Britain' itself, if only emotively, conjures up a remote Celtic time where fable is prinked only a little by fact, its morality pre-Christian, its emotions primitive, – stark with the possibility of violence and unnatural deeds. Hazlitt, writing in 1826, comments:

> There are no data in history to go upon, no advantage is taken of
> costume, no acquaintance with geography, or architecture, or dialect
> is necessary; but there is an old tradition, human nature – an old
> temple, the human mind – and Shakespeare walks into it and looks
> about him with a lordly eye, and seizes on the sacred spoils as his
> own.[24]

Remote in time and place though it is, *King Lear*, in its exploration of human nature, is blazingly familiar. Its 'domesticity' climbs out of the time where it is placed, and out, therefore, of myth, and stalks along into the present tense of any reader or theatregoer who happens upon it. No one who has lived within the ebbs and flows of family life can read or see *King Lear* without being aware of its piercing relevance, and in that sense the events it depicts are so terribly ordinary and familiar. Age, with its slackening of reason, and its atrophying of sensibility; youth, with its covetousness and bland, self-indulgent assurance – these are the two poles between which the play voyages, and between which so many families have foundered.

Not least familiar in the play's thematic movement is the demonstration of how little parents know about their own children. This strand in the story of Lear and his daughters brings out an irony made the more intense by the fact that what Lear cannot see is so plain to others around him and to us in the audience. We know Lear's daughters at first better than he knows them just as, perhaps, our neighbour knows our daughter better than we do. This familiar domesticity is very intense, very affecting and the marvel is that the play both expresses the tragedy of the domestic issues *and* transcends them – in the end it is the family of man which has suffered the tragedy.

There is an implied question which precipitates the tragedy. It is put by an old man to his three daughters, and it is probably the most spoken (or unspoken?) query in the history of families. Indeed there are few fathers who have not begged, silently or vociferously, for an answer from his progeny – 'How much do you love me?'

The play begins with no hint that so much humanity is to be given pain, even destroyed by the implications of the separate answers to this question. It is asked not by an enfeebled old man merely seeking reassurance in the shadow time of his life, but by a king who has the power to command and to give. When we first meet Lear he is not a shuffling relic of greatness but at the height of his power. The court which he commands shines and reverberates with pomp and cere-mony. True, he talks of conferring his responsibilities on 'Younger strength, while we unburthened crawl to death'. But his intention is expressed with regal determination and complete clarity of mind and strength of purpose. His intent is 'fast', his will is 'constant'. He has not reached that state of mental decay when anyone could distract him from a purpose which is palpably going to lead to problems. When Kent attempts to do so, his fate is peremptorily settled; each daughter, as she comes forward to present her love, does so with a formal regard not only for parenthood but for the state of kingship. The situation is domestic, certainly, but it is girt about with the trappings of high royalty.

Lear, then, is not senile but he is tainted with a weakness, in which two elements dominate. The first is that he transfers into blood relationships the kind of peremptory autocracy he employs, as king, in political relationships. He is really demanding from his daughters the answers he wants; ones that will completely satisfy his expectations. It is the prerogative of kingship, as it is often manifested in Shakespeare's plays, for the monarch not to be crossed in his purposes. Lear makes no allowances for the ties of blood or for the rights of others to interpret what amounts to a rhetorical question in their own way. Lear has, in fact, committed the crime of 'unnatural' parenthood before Cordelia speaks words which seem to him to be unnatural, for he has put his three children in exactly the same position as a king might put the courtiers surrounding him. Goneril and Regan give the 'correct' and expected answers. Cordelia gives the 'incorrect', but the truly human and the unexpected reply, and the response she gets is one which Lear might have directed to any courtier:

> 'Mend your speech a little,
> Lest you may mar your fortunes.' [I.1.93–4]

It may be recalled that the answer which Cordelia gives is very similar indeed to that of Desdemona to her father. Brabantio asks,

> 'Do you perceive in all this noble company
> Where most you owe obedience?' [*Othello*.I.3.179–80]

Desdemona replies:

> 'I do perceive here a divided duty:
> To you I am bound for life and education;
> My life and education both do learn me,
> How to respect you; you are the lord of duty –
> I am hitherto your daughter; but here's my husband, . . .'
> [*Othello*.I.3.181–9]

Lear asks:

> 'Which of you shall we say doth love us most?' [I.1.50–2]

Cordelia replies:

'Good my lord,
You have begot me, bred me, lov'd me; I
Return those duties back as are right fit,
Obey you, love you, and most honour you.
Why have my sisters husbands, if they say
They love you all?'   [I.1.95–8]

Yet, whereas Brabantio's question is the simple request of a simple
man, used to being obeyed and expecting obedience, Lear's is that
of a man whose sense of human values is dangerously warped.
This is the second and more potentially tragic element in his
weakness. His question invites three human beings, tied by blood,
to vie with each other for his favour and bounty, making the
communication of the amount of love they feel for him into a kind
of tournament. Moreover, his question really invites them to
distort their true natures. 'Where nature doth with merit challenge'
suggests that the award will be in due proportion to the amount of
affection they are able to display. If he has made a tournament out
of love, he is at the same time making 'nature' into a kind of
commodity. He has, in addition to his own unnatural procedure in
treating his daughters as servile subjects, the moral weakness which
cannot assess true value. He is, in effect, asking for the impossible
– he wants, at one and the same time, the most naturally true and
the most expectedly satisfactory answer from his daughters.
Goneril and Regan find no difficulty in providing the answer,
giving in a sense the answer that his question deserves, and so to
this extent, responding to the examination in the spirit in which it
is being conducted. No one whose nature is true and is unable to
measure either love or merit by Lear's standards can possibly
answer the question to his satisfaction. Cordelia's 'nothing' is the
truest answer to his particular question. For him to accuse her of
being 'untender', to refer to her as a wretch of 'whom nature is
ashamed', is terrible proof of Lear's basic flaw. He is less guilty of
senile stupidity than of a blindness of the spirit. Kent's outburst
shows his awareness of Lear's weakness. He recognizes that
'power' has 'bowed' to 'flattery'; that the answers Lear has been
given by Goneril and Regan are 'empty-hearted'; that Lear's sense
of human values is completely false. A phrase of France's, too,
shrewdly pinpoints this falseness of the values:

'Love's not love
When it is mingled with regards that stands
Aloof from th'entire point.'   [I.1.238–40]

275

Lear, in his words about Cordelia to Burgundy, still speaks in terms which, by implication, equate 'nature' and 'commodity':

'When she was dear to us, we did hold her so;
But now her price has fallen. Sir, there she stands;
If aught within that little seeming substance,
Or all of it, with our displeasure piec'd,
And nothing more, may fitly like your Grace,
She's there, and she is yours.'   [I.1.196–201]

'Price' and 'substance' are the coinage of Lear's estimate of human values.

The first scene of Act I is remarkable among the tragedies for the comprehensiveness of its information about the nature of the tragic protagonist. Unlike Macbeth, Othello and Hamlet, where the fatal evidence of weakness is built up slowly and methodically, in this play the facts flare out with a primitive freedom, and the inevitability of tragic consequence is assured by what we are taught of the nature of this king. The possible extent of the consequences is suggested by Cordelia's banishment, Kent's banishment, but, above all, by Cordelia's words about her sisters. What she says is no mere confirmation of the unctuous flattery which they have used upon Lear, but a strong suggestion that this usage is not an isolated example of ill behaviour. Cordelia's speech seems to look back to a time before the play began, as if she did not find their flattery in the least surprising.

'The jewels of our father, with wash'd eyes
Cordelia leaves you, I know you what you are;
And, like a sister, am most loth to call
Your faults as they are named. Love well our father,
To your professed bosoms I commit him;'   [I.1.268–72]

The parting speeches of Goneril and Regan are superbly modulated by Shakespeare so that any judgements we may be prepared to make on the sisters, first by their flattery and, second, by Cordelia's speech, are subject to some doubt. They have not yet been starkly categorized as evil. Indeed, what they have to say, given what we have learned of Lear, seems reasonable, for in the face of Lear's caprice the precautions the two sisters desire seem neither illogical nor particularly sinister:

GON: I think our father will hence to night.
REG: That's most certain, and with you; next month with us.
GON: You see how full of changes his age is; the observation we have

made of it hath not been little. He always lov'd our sister most; and
with what poor judgement he hath now cast her off appears too
grossly. [I.1.285–94]

Moreover, Goneril and Regan, like Cordelia, seem to look back to a
time before the play begins, giving a context for Lear's actions. Age
may have exaggerated his nature, but it is not the cause. In fact
Shakespeare seems at pains not to attribute Lear's state of mind and
spirit to the accident of age, possibly because he realized that the
highest tragedy is not a bedfellow of unavoidable accident but is the
issue of fate and human weakness. The accident of Lear's age does not
explain his actions – he is blind and insensitive and has always been
so.

> 'The best and soundest of his time hath been but rash; then must we
> look from his age to receive not alone the imperfections of long –
> engraffed condition, but therewithal the unruly waywardness that
> infirm and choleric years bring with them.' [I.1.294–9]

The stage, then, is set for events whose course will be unpredictable
but whose form is likely to be dark and disquieting. The whole of Act
I.2 is concerned with the Edmund/Gloucester plot which serves,
immediately, to widen the context of the main story, providing a
mournful and ironic *obbligato* to the main theme. The closeness
between the two is established from the beginning. The deception of
parent by child, the animosity between children, the dislocation of
the meaning of 'nature' (in this case given an additional twist by the
fact that Edmund is a bastard), the precipitate haste with which the
parent is prepared to think the worst of the child, on the basis of
flimsy evidence that is never investigated. Lear and Gloucester even
employ similar rhetorical language. Lear's:

> 'For, by the sacred radiance of the sun,
> The mysteries of Hecat and the night;
> By all the operation of the orbs
> From whom we do exist and cease to be;
> Here I disclaim all my paternal care...' [I.1.108–12]

is paralleled by Gloucester's:

> 'These late eclipses in the sun and moone portend no good to us.
> Though the wisdom of nature can reason it thus...

love cools, friendship falls off, brothers divide; in cities, mutinies; in
countries, discord; in palaces, treason; and the bond crack'd, 'twixt
son and father.'   [I.2.100–8]

What really binds them together, however, are the limitations of their
parental affections; Gloucester's crime may be less than Lear's for he
could at least declare that the hand of villainy helped to push him into
false judgement, yet the threshold of his love for his children is
terribly low. Like Lear's, his crime is a failure of the spirit of love. He
is truly, as Edmund says, 'a credulous father'.

One of the most affecting features of the play is the speed which
attends the decay in Lear's status. By Act I.3, the trap he has placed
himself in is on the point, already, of closing on him. Various
attempts to calculate exactly the time taken up by the action are
inconclusive, largely because the play (unlike *Romeo and Juliet* for
example) is niggardly in the provision of time signposts. In any case,
what is important is the impression of a relentless precipitancy in
Lear's fall, and, accompanying it, an access of increasing isolation for
Lear. In Act I.3, Goneril can no longer endure Lear's 'riotous'
knights, nor the fact that he

> '. . . himself upbraids us
> On every trifle.'   [I.2.7–8]

We recall Goneril's conversation with her sister about Lear's fickle
temperament at the end of Act I.1, and certainly what we have seen of
Lear thus far seems only to confirm the truth of their words. A
critical point is now reached where the extent of the sisters' infamy
may be clarified. Are they merely guilty of expedient flattery or are
they prepared to disturb muddier waters? When Goneril rails about
his knights and Lear's pernicketiness is there any justification for her
words? or is she preparing herself for an unwarranted assault on the
foolish fond old king? Lear's first words in Act I.4, on his return to
Goneril's home, would seem to give some justification. They have
the tone and colour of a bad-tempered autocrat:

> 'Let me not stay a jot for dinner; go get it ready.'   [I.4.8–9]

The treatment Lear gets from Oswald, in which his dignity and status
are affronted, is no more nor less than a demonstration in action of
Goneril's earlier orders to Oswald:

> 'Put on what weary negligence you please,
> You and your fellows; I'd have it come to question.'   [I.3.13–14]

Oswald has been instructed in his behaviour so that the matter should come out into the open. Goneril speaks reasonably:

> 'Not only, sir, this, your all-licens'd fool,
> But other of your insolent retinue
> Do hourly carp and quarrel, breaking forth
> In rank, and not-to-be-endur'd riots.'   [I.4.199–202]

Indeed the keynote of Goneril's passionate attempts to persuade Lear to 'disquantity' his knights is exasperation. He is incapable of rational reply to anything she says, and in the end he utters his terrible curse upon her. There are few who could, if pushed to decide, condemn Goneril completely while absolving Lear. His words, his curse, are a tremendous demonstration of the temperament which at 'the best and soundest of his time hath been but rash', and the reaction of Albany to the departure of Lear from his home, however strong the rational grounds for what Goneril has said, rouse lingering doubts about their rightness:

> 'Well, you may fear too far.'   [I.4.328]

> 'How far your eyes may pierce I cannot tell.
> Striving to better, oft we mar what's well.'   [I.4.346–7]

Moreover, the 'love' which Goneril is demonstrating now towards her father is certainly not the love she expressed with such unctuous fluency upon command. If we examine the rationality of her attempts to 'disquantity' Lear, what strikes us is, precisely, the reasonableness of it. It is what Hazlitt calls – 'cool didactic reasoning'.[25] There is no love involved. Goneril, for her own satisfaction and convenience, is demanding of Lear as impossible a self-sacrifice, as utterly servile a response, as he demanded of her and her two sisters. He asked them, in effect, to disabuse themselves of that element in personality which says – 'this is mine to give, and I will give it on my own terms and in my own words'. Lear, when he divested himself of the property of kingship wished to maintain the status and appearance of kingship:

> 'Only we shall retain
> The name, and all th'addition to a king:'   [I.1.134–5]

and Goneril's requests are a terrible *quid pro quo* for the request made of her.

So, by scene 4 we are less conscious of 'guilt' on the part of Goneril, than of the extent to which she is, ironically, her father's daughter. Together, Lear and Goneril and, so far, to a lesser extent, Regan, have given us a grim introduction to what lack of true 'nature', lack of love that gives more than it takes, means. Thus a terrible irony is created – Lear is beginning to receive no more than he deserves. By the end of scene 4 the characters are moving out of the domestic relationships towards a symbolic state where they stand for aspects of dis-nature, dis-love (to employ a repeated prefix of the play).

Act II.1 and 2 are concerned with externalizing, and therefore widening the implications of, the unnatural relationships that have been revealed in the first Act. The use of a forged letter, a pretended wound, and false report (devices very reminiscent of those Shakespeare had recently used in *Othello*) by the 'unnatural' Edmund, serve to put this melancholy condition into the category of a crime. Edmund's actions are, in a way, a proof that 'dis-nature' is not a merely static quality, but is capable of active and sinister movement. The putting to flight of his brother widens and activates what has been like a grumbling of a half-sleeping volcano, and the later blinding of Gloucester, in which Regan plays a positive and leading part, serves not only to deepen the sinister and cruel context of dis-nature, but to point, most horribly, through her, the parallel situations of Gloucester and of Lear.

In the first four scenes of Act II a clear distinction is drawn between the characters of Goneril and Regan, and between their domestic environments. Goneril, at first, is cruel by default rather than apparent will. Her default is a lack of true love and a lack of intelligence. Her letter to Regan is her chief actual crime. It prepares the more subtle and dangerous woman for positive action. Regan, ironically, has all her father's peremptory autocracy:

'I have this present evening from my sister
Been well inform'd of them; and with such cautions,
That, if they come to soujourn at my house,
I'll not be there.' [II.1.101–4]

The court in which she is a dominant figure seems, by comparison with Goneril's, rife with potential cruelty, faction and intrigue. In marrying Albany a weak woman has met a weak man. In marrying Cornwall a dangerous and very intelligent sadist has joined with one who has a great stomach for cruelty. For Shakespeare seems to go out of his way to make Regan sadistic. It is she who increases, with a curious relish, Kent's sentence in the stocks.

'Till noon! till night, my lord; and all night too.' [II.2.130]

If we had any doubts about her sadism, the blinding of Gloucester would remove them. She instructs the ropes to be bound 'hard, hard'. It is more than likely that it is she who commits the indignity on Gloucester of pulling his beard. She cries out for Gloucester's other eye to be put out; she kills the remonstrating servant from behind; she, it is, who says of Gloucester:

'Go thrust him out at gates and let him smell
His way to Dover.'   [III.7.92–3]

The difference between these sisters is often ignored and they are played as if the evil they each harbour is entirely similar, but at first Regan's evil is far more active than Goneril's, the atmosphere she engenders around her initially, more dangerous. It is through Regan rather than Goneril that we learn that 'dis-nature' is not only inhuman but capable of being evil. Yet, finally, Goneril out-paces Regan, climbing slowly but inexorably into criminality, while the other, having swiftly revealed her vicious side, falls a victim to some unknown disease (conscience?) then to poison administered by Goneril.

For the first two scenes of Act II Lear is absent from the action. It is noticeable that in all four of the great tragedies Shakespeare removes the protagonist from the stage for some time. No doubt practical considerations are involved; any actor playing these parts needs breathing space from the physical and intellectual demands of the role. Shakespeare usually makes capital out of such necessity. In the case of *Hamlet*, *Othello* and *Macbeth* and, it may be added, most conspicuously in *Richard III*, the opportunity is taken either to give additional information from others about the protagonist or to condition us for some change in the protagonist which is manifest when he next appears. In the case of Lear himself there is no change in character. When he reappears, he is still the ranting self-pitying man we have seen previously:

'The King would speak with Cornwall; the dear father
Would with his daughter speak; commands their service.
Are they inform'd of this?'   [II.4.99–101]

It is not until immediately before his exit into the storm that he speaks words which begin to change our feelings about and towards him. He, albeit faintly, shows signs of reaching inside himself and his wayward, narrow spirit discovers a nobility and a certain courage. His self-indulgence for the first time begins to transform into a quality which begets our sympathy. He does not ask the gods to take vengeance on his behalf, but to teach him 'patience' and 'noble anger'. It is true that the wilder part of him still bursts forth, as when he cries:

> '. . . No, you unnatural hags,
> I will have such revenges on you both . . .'   [II.4.277–8]

but even in his wildness, the seeds of that kind of noble fortitude which he is going to need and reveal later on begin to generate:

> 'You think I'll weep.
> No, I'll not weep.
> I have full cause of weeping; but this heart
> Shall break into a hundred thousand flaws
> Or ere I'll weep.'   [II.4.281–5]

Just before he goes out into the storm where his reason will be beleaguered and finally capitulate, Lear is thus presented to us in a new light and we become prepared for pity as surely as he is being prepared to go through the darkness.

Subtle peparations for our change of attitude have in fact begun before. First by the concentration on the story of Gloucester during Lear's absence which almost ousts, for a time, the Lear story from the action. Our imaginations are conditioned, before we meet Lear again, to react against the treachery of Edmund and the mental blindness of Gloucester – that is we are already conditioned to the idea of filial treachery. This pushes our sensibilities, albeit unconsciously, in the direction of sympathy for all victims of such treachery, and when these victims (however much we find blame in them) are seen to be gradually isolated, the possibility of sympathy is further increased. Paradoxically, in Lear's case, this isolation is furthered by the very two people who, physically and intellectually, never forsake him – Kent and the Fool. These are two other agencies by which our attitude to Lear is caused to change. Kent knew the dangers of Lear's actions as they were being performed in the first scene of the play. His blunt, honest sense of duty, and his caring humanity shine like gold in the multiplying dross of the society that surrounds Lear. In Kent, Lear, in simple terms, has a doughty champion and friend whose resolution to succour the king will never fail. Yet, curiously, Kent's very directness of word and deed serves to increase the fractious relationships between Lear and his daughters. In his determination to speak truth, Kent exacerbates the situation. His handling of Oswald, justified though it may be by Oswald's studied insolence, is incautious. His words to Cornwall before he is put in the stocks are hardly calculated (considering he is known as Lear's servant) to lessen Cornwall and Regan's determination to rid Lear of his unruly attendants, and when he is discovered in the stocks, the nature of his replies to the King raises the temperature of Lear's mind and heart:

LEAR: What's he that hath so much thy place mistook
    To set thee here?
KENT: It is both he and she,
    Your son, and daughter.
LEAR: No.
KENT: Yes.
LEAR: No, I say.
KENT: I say, yea.

        . . . . .

LEAR: By Jupiter I swear no.
KENT: By Juno, I swear, ay.   [II.4.11–21]

Equally, the Fool, no less than Kent, but with a pungency of illustration, wit and truth, goads Lear's temper:

FOOL: If I gave them all my living, I'd keep my coxcombs myself.
    There's mine; beg another of thy daughters.
LEAR: Take heed, sirrah – the whip.
FOOL: Truth's a dog must to kennel; he must be whipp'd out, when
    Lady the brach may stand by th' fire and stink.   [I.4.106–12]

Indeed the Fool is no mere purveyor of innuendoes, half-hidden hints. He goes directly to the mark. He is fulfilling absolutely the aspirations of Jaques in *As You Like It* – attempting to 'cleanse the foul body' of Lear's infected mind. He is also fulfilling exactly the function of the true Fool in that his shafts are given irony by wry humour. What is so conspicuously lacking in Lear and in all his progeny is a sense of humour, of wit. As Wilson Knight says, 'If Lear could laugh – if the Lears of the world could laugh at themselves – there would be no such tragedy.'[26] What the Fool says in fact is – see what an absurd situation you have placed yourself in. But Lear cannot hear the message because a self-indulgent sense of status and dignity has atrophied his sense of the difference between what is absurdly wrong and what is absolutely right, proper and human.

The Fool, then, in the first two Acts, joins the Edmund/Gloucester plot and Kent as agents which, at one and the same time, ironically exacerbate the conditions for tragedy *and* increase the possibilities of our eventually achieving the right grounds for pity.

There is a distinct and, in its implications, immense break in the atmosphere and the form of this play at the beginning of Act III. Up to this point the 'domestic' nature of the events has predominated; dark tragedy which will engulf both the inner and outer lives of men has barely been hinted at. Indeed, like *Romeo and Juliet* and *Othello* there is something curiously 'absurd' about the events. They are cavilling; they are the result of somewhat petty inflexibilities of mind and self-indulgence. The crises created could, we believe, easily be reversed by the exercise of simple reason. The events and crises are familiar, never involving the interventions of the supernatural. We know of such domestic stupidities in everyday life and one has marvelled that people should be so crass as to refuse to see the relatively simple way to redress such absurdity.

The very first words of Act III take us into darker, stranger countries of experience. The language used by Kent and the Gentlemen on the heath has a startling effect:

KENT: Who's there, besides foul weather?
GON: One minded like the weather, most unquietly.   [III.1.1–2]

For the first time the elements and man's mind are equated. Certainly, we have had in the previous two Acts Lear's raging in which the heavens, the gods and nature have been involved. Yet all this was the grand rhetoric of mood. Even before we see him he seems to have become a victim, a confidant of nature itself, and his great speech in which he addresses the elements is no mere invocation. It is as if he is in the process of total identification with natural catastrophe. The problem for the actor in this great speech, as phrase after phrase piles up, has been taken to be one of producing enough volume to do justice to the extraordinary 'impersonation' of a storm which the words and images are creating.

With modern electronic and mechanical aids, the actor can be helped, but, in the final analysis, the onus is upon him. Indeed too much mechanical aid can be as much of a liability as none at all. The reason is that it is not simply that the actor, in purely technical terms, is asked to 'impersonate' a storm, but that, in a sense, Lear and the storm have become identified. This speech is the proof positive of the immense change in form and atmosphere that the play has taken. Lear is no longer a foolish old man; the dramatist has plucked him out of domestic familiarity and made of him a great symbol. Now we no longer think of Lear in terms of his original guilt, or his mental blindness; neither do we regard him simply as a realized character in a play. He seems to have been made to transcend both himself and the confines of what we call dramatic form. The storm scene not only makes us forget the particularities of the play's dramatic action but engulfs us in an experience of human suffering utterly naked in its presentation. Even the phrase 'human suffering' seems a poor cypher to stand for the complexity of what happens on the heath. Lear's self-identification with the storm purges him of his passion as it begins to drop away, leaving him with a grieving quietude against whose sadness the jingling words of the Fool play ironically. The Fool recalls the particularities of his case as Lear is slowly entering into a condition where his whole inner being is to be changed – like a tin whistle playing at a great man's obsequies:

> LEAR: Come on, my boy. How dost, my boy? Art cold?
> I am cold my self. Where is this straw, my fellow?
> The art of our necessities is strange
> That can make vile things precious . . .
>
> . . . . . .
>
> FOOL: He that has and a little-tiny wit
> With heigh-ho, the wind and the rain –
> Must make content with his fortunes fit,
> Though the raine it raineth every day.   [III.2.68–78]

Kent's arrival, and his mention of the storm, bring Lear again to passion, but it is a poor thing now compared to its former appearance. The purging is terrible; its final spasm is agonizing to contemplate:

> 'I am a man
> More sinn'd against than sinning.'   [III.2.59]

We accept Lear's self-pity now, when before we did not, because the play has moved from a depiction of mere plot into an embodiment of human suffering.

The Fool continues to jingle his ironic *obbligato* to events that are now happening inside Lear's very soul. Passion which was formerly the very pith of Lear's personality is vanquished in him and as yet he can find nothing to take its place, so:

> 'My wits begin to turn.'   [III.2.67]

Yet they do not yet completely fall away from him. When Kent reappears and asks Lear to enter the hovel, we have the first positive indication of the changes happening inside him. His cries of 'filial ingratitude', his threats that he will 'punish home' are a mere vagrant flotsam and jetsam of the old wild Lear, and as soon as he has cried them, he remembers:

'O, that way madness lies; let me shun that;
No more of that.'   [III.4.21–2]

Kent repeats his request that he should enter the hovel. The answer he gets – utterly simple in its expression – is profound in its implications:

'Prithee go in thyself; seek thine own ease.'   [III.4.23]

The peremptory man, accustomed to first place and to obedience, puts another before himself. This line is a direct and moving proof, expressed in simple personal terms, of what it is that is beginning to replace the old passion. Lear, alone, while the others clamber into the hovel, tells us and himself what it is:

'Take physic, pomp;
Expose thyself to feel what wretches feel,
That thou mayst shake the superflux to them,
And show the heavens more just.'   [III.4.33–5]

Yet the shock to his system compounded of what both Goneril and Regan have done, and the spiritual metamorphosis that is occurring in him, is too much for him to bear. His wits now do begin to turn and the manner of their turning and the advent of Edgar and Poor Tom signal even further departures of this play from conventional dramatic modes. At the height of the storm Lear identified himself with it and, as it died away, so did his passion. Now, he comes to identify himself with the 'madness' of Tom, and as its whirligig presence increases, so Lear's wits increase their distance from reason – he now begins to identify himself with madness. The Fool and Kent stand helplessly by while Lear, with a kind of muted, almost half-contented frenzy, begins to walk with madness. The theatrical impact of this is uniquely strange and compelling. Certainly there is nothing in European drama which gives us anything approaching it. The movement of the scene has a mesmeric effect. We seem not to be in the presence of stage characters, but in the midst of an enveloping pattern of rhythm and sound. Edgar's speeches sway in a kind of demented liturgy; Lear's responses are, for the most part, staccato and intellectually numbed; the Fool's little pipe of reason whistles with ever-growing ineffectiveness. Kent speaks only one

286

sentence – this blunt man from the world of humans is, in this supernatural place and time, almost an irrelevancy. Gloucester's arrival comes between us and the spell that has been woven about us, but we can still hear it – and by the end of scene 4, Edgar and Lear are joined in a pitiful consanguinity. A kind of agonized wit comes into Lear's distempered mind; he has all the confiding, urgent, almost chuckling content which we see in the deranged, who begin to create their own worlds with their own rules, and to people them with their own creations:

> LEAR: O, cry you mercy, sir.
>   Noble philosopher, your company.
> EDG: Tom's a-cold.
>
>   . . . . .
>
> LEAR: Come, let's in all.
> KENT: This way, my Lord.
> LEAR: With him;
>   I will keep still with my philosopher.'   [III.4.167–72]

In scene 6, this process of creation proceeds one stage further. Lear puts himself at the head of his new world, and proceeds to arraign its recalcitrant citizens.

If we marvel at Shakespeare's achievement in scene 4 where Lear seems, as has been said, to step out of the territories of mere drama, what word can be used to describe the skill by which, in scene 6, he maintains the strange, unique atmosphere and, at the same time, begins to remind us that what we have seen and experienced does have its source somewhere in familiar event and motivation. We have been pulled away from the particularities of Goneril, Regan and Edmund and have seen the human spirit naked in agony. Now the particularities begin to swirl and their coming serves to give the agony a moving point of reference, as Lear, in his arraignment of the citizens of his new dark world, drifts in and out of reason and reality. It is as if we see his mind opening and closing, with intermittent light attempting desperately to vanquish the darkness. Sometimes he is a child:

> FOOL: Prithee, nuncle, tell me whether a madman be a gentleman, or
>   a yeoman?
> LEAR: A king, a king!   [III.6.9–11]

Sometimes he has the quick but wild authority of the deranged:

> 'It shall be done; I will arraign them straight.
> Come, sit thou here, most learned justicer.'   [III.6.20]

287

˙Sometimes, in his dark mind, Goneril appears, but it is another Lear she has wronged:

> 'Arraign her first; 'tis Goneril. I here take my oath before this
> honorable assembly she kick'd the poor King her father.' [III.6.46–8]

And once, his mind wanders into the past and it is he himself who is the victim:

> 'Then let them anatomise Regan; see what breeds about her heart. Is
> there any cause in nature that make these hard hearts?'   [III.6.75–7]

There is created a terrifying contrapuntal effect between delusion and reality, which is an indictment not only of the idea of human cruelty, but of the particular facts of the cruelty that has been practised on Lear. The dramatic balance is perfect and the play, in these two scenes, treads superbly and unerringly between poetic symbolism and theatrical reality.

In Act III.7, the play returns, for a time, to the domestic familiarities of the first two Acts. The scathing revenge on Glouces-ter, the news of the landing of the King of France's army, the implications of a sexual relationship between Edmund and Goneril, the wounding of Cornwall – all these matters are concentrated into a short sharp time, and the effect is, first, to re-establish the realistic cause-and-effect plot line and, second, to imply, as Shakespeare so inevitably does in his tragedies, how evil and cruelty are never contained, but always spread out affecting those about them.

The blinding of Gloucester, on stage, has been condemned as unnecessary. It is indeed not often that Shakespeare, in his plays, so explicitly and starkly depicts such bestial cruelty. Yet, to accuse him of specious sensationalism is to ignore a particular effect of the scene. As in the Cinna the Poet scene in *Julius Caesar*, Shakespeare is here using direct cruelty for a purpose beyond itself, so the servant who, when Gloucester cries for help, says:

> 'Hold your hand, my lord.
> I have serv'd you ever since I was a child;
> But better service have I never done you,
> Than now to bid you hold'   [III.7.72–4]

is the embodiment of the scene's purpose. It is the reality of human pity as much as the fact of human cruelty that the scene is intended to display; just as in *Julius Caesar* when Cinna cries: 'I am Cinna the

Poet', it is the irony of human misjudgement as much as the fact of
mob violence that makes its effect. After the blinding of Gloucester,
the emotions and practices of revenge and cruelty which inhabit
Goneril and Regan's world begin to turn inward and over a series of
scenes we witness the piece by piece disintegration of their world –
through outward pressures, sexual jealousies, hatred and distrust.
Indeed, after the Gloucester scene, the play presents clear divisions of
interest, effect and mode. The Goneril/Regan scenes present domestic broil; the scenes in which Cordelia and her husband are
presented have a spirit of amity, of succour and love; the scenes
between Edgar and his father introduce the element of healing, of
kindness, filial love and the expunging of Gloucester's mental
blindness. Lear, alone, until he is rescued and recognizes Cordelia,
belongs to none of these categories. Shakespeare very deliberately
keeps him isolated – he wanders, fitfully, through the air, having
consort with people, but in essence, utterly by himself. It is as if
while the action itself is moving towards a state where evil and cruelty
may be overcome, Lear is disconnected. The world is moving, but it
seems to move past him – as if he were a creature moving without
purpose in a stream whose different currents and eddies have no
effect on him. He is himself, alone.

Although his mind still flickers fitfully with light, there are certain
things about this mad Lear which are above and beyond mere
madness. In his meandering words we discover that the purging
which destroyed most of his sanity has given him, paradoxically, a
clarity of truth, not only about the events which led to his state, but
about the whole world and its ways. If he had said in Act I.1 what he
says in Act IV.6:

> 'Ha! Goneril, with a white beard! They flatter'd me like a dog, and
> told me I had the white hairs in my beard ere the black ones were
> there. To say "ay", and "no" to everything that I said! "Ay", and
> "no" too was no good divinity.'   [IV.6.96–9]

he would not have suffered, and there would have been no tragedy. If
he had had the 'wit' in Act I.1 to see his kingship in the way he sees it
in Act IV.6 he would not have been fond, foolish, autocratic and
narrow-minded. If he had had the sensitivity of mind and feeling to
know the difference between natural love and commodity-love in Act
I.1 he would have known which of his daughters spoke the truth. In
Act IV.6 he knows the difference clearly, for he has been taught to
observe the ways of the world:

'What, art mad? A man may see how this world goes with no
eyes. Look with thine ears. See how yond justice rails
upon yond simple thief. Hark, in thine ear: change
places and, handy – dandy, which is the justice, which is the
thief?'   [IV.6.150–4]

Lear has, indeed, learned wisdom. Yet no amount of sifting through
his mad later scenes to discover the abstract 'developments' in the
character can equal the effect of experiencing him as a theatrical
presence. It is almost unbearable to support the variety of emotions
which his presence arouses in us. He is the communicator of that
wry, clipped poetry in which Shakespeare seems to be able to harness
images and concepts, in themselves incompatible, but when miraculously joined, speak harsh truths:

'The wren goes to't, the small gilded fly
Does lecher in my sight.
Let copulation thrive; for Gloucester's bastard son
Was kinder to his father, than my daughters
Got 'tween the lawfull sheets.
To't, luxury, pell-mell . . .'   [IV.6.112–116]

He is, at times, like some embittered sage, mocking the world with
ironic truth:

GLOU: O, let me kiss that hand!
LEAR: Let me wipe it first; it smells of mortality.   [IV.6.132–133]

He is, fleetingly, like a child again, but one grown old in cynicism:

GENT: You shall have any thing.
LEAR: No seconds? All myself?   [IV.6.195]

Towards the end, he wrings our hearts by his gentle vulnerability, his
fearful gratitude, his frail dignity:

'Pray do not mock me:
I am a very foolish fond old man,
Fourscore and upward, not an hour more nor less;
And, to deal plainly,
I fear I am not in my perfect mind.'   [IV.7.59–63]

It is because the character of Lear is made to arouse in us such a
maelstrom of emotion that it is difficult to come to a conclusion
about the 'philosophical' implications of the play. One's mind veers
from concluding that the experience we have had is in itself too

various and huge to allow of intellectual formalization, to a conviction that the play is so powerful that Shakespeare must intend us to find in it some particular intellectual truth. Critics, over the centuries, have ranged themselves fairly equally on opposite sides. For some, the play, piling on evidences of cruelty upon cruelty, subjecting, as it does, one man to the uttermost purging of his soul and then depriving him of the benefits of the purge, is a vision of a desperately meaningless universe. To others, the filial love of Edgar, the radiant truth of Cordelia, the very purging of Lear so that he achieves wisdom, dignity and an awareness of true love, cancels out the spectacle of mankind's darker side. For some the play is the nearest Shakespeare ever came to presenting an 'absurd' view of the universe; for others it is an affirmation of Christian faith – man pays a price for guilt, inhumanity, and the penance is hard, but the outcome is a reconciliation and peace.[27]

Yet, so often what we experience in the theatre is at variance with what intellectual probing discovers. The end of the play cannot, as we watch it, either be said to be happy or sad, dismissive or affirmative. We experience a rare and touching joy when Cordelia is re-united with her father; we suffer a corresponding grief when that re-uniting is smashed by a death which, if Edmund had spoken moments earlier, might have been avoided. We share the quiet frail satisfaction of Lear in recognizing his daughter, yet we are forced almost to avert our eyes and stop our ears.

The self-sacrifice of Kent who determines to follow his master into the grave seems, to us, both a joyful affirmation of love and duty and, at the same time, an additional unnecessary grief. Edgar's assumption of authority is a logically correct representation of the restoration of order and humanity, yet, like the coming of Fortinbras in *Hamlet*, fails to wipe out from our minds and imaginations what we have just experienced. Edgar's final words in fact sum up the truth of our experience:

> 'The weight of this sad time we must obey;
> Speak what we feel, not what we ought to say.
> The oldest hath borne most; we that are young,
> Shall never see so much nor live so long.'   [V.3.322–6]

Much of the play's reality is encased within these lines. Of all Shakespeare's tragedies this is the one we apprehend most through our feelings. The very pith of our emotional experience is created from the spectacle of old age suffering so much and so long, and we leave the play convinced that no man has ever lived so long or suffered so much as King Lear. His tragedy is, in essence, therefore, that of mankind itself, the extent of whose tenancy of this planet is incommensurate with the amount of love, wisdom and humanity it has acquired. Neither optimistic nor pessimistic, it is an immense evocation of the reality of human existence. We would not be human if we were not irrational, faithless and treacherous, but we would be more human if we more closely harboured reason, fidelity and love.

Macbeth

Macbeth is Shakespeare's most haunting play. It not only stirs but frightens the imagination. It is also a 'favourite' play of many readers and theatregoers. There is a connection between what it does to the imagination and its attraction for it. There are certain places, certain books, certain pieces of music, certain pictures, certain people, which, when we meet or recall them, energize our emotions in a particular way, causing them to rise to a point almost beyond tolerance, and while we are caught within their power almost anything seems possible. *Macbeth*, perhaps especially when read, offers many moments when the play seems likely to leap from the page, embodying itself into some monstrous shape which will engulf the reader. Perhaps, indeed, the power of the play rests in its curious ability to make us believe, even in reading, that it will come alive.

Any inclination to dismiss this as idle fancy can be given pause by reflecting upon the play's strange status in the history of theatre. Not only does it seem to escape from the printed page and haunt our waking senses, but it has, in a sense, escaped from the confines of the workaday theatre itself. All actors treat *Macbeth* with awesome respect, not only because it is a great play but because so many performances of it throughout history have been accompanied by tragic, sinister, and disquieting events. In fact the stage history of *Macbeth*[28] is full of 'coincidences' – a word used conveniently to encompass the inexplicable – in which death, accident, and strange occurrences figure large.

The play is about evil and it seems to generate its own evil atmosphere. Clairvoyance may provide one explanation of this; criticism however is obliged to inquire what makes this play different from others in Shakespeare's canon.

There is one certain quality which distinguishes it and that is the language. It is memorable language – the imagery being more consistently 'pictorial' and much more redolent and evocative of action than in any other play of Shakespeare's. There are few lines in which any character speaks reflectively, without his thoughts implying tremendous action, either of the mind or of the body. Thought, and consequent human movement, have become one in this play. Hearing Hamlet speculate upon life and death, we speculate too. He gives us an intellectual and emotional exposition of a point of view:

'To be, or not to be – that is the question;' [*Hamlet*.III.1.56] but when Macbeth weighs up the pros and cons of killing Duncan, the deed itself and the immense voyaging of his hot imagination catches us, and we are forced to follow him not speculatively, but with every nerve and sinew full of the expectation of what may happen:

'If it were done when 'tis done, then 'twere well
If were done quickly. If th' assassination
Could trammel up the consequence, and catch,
With his surcease, success; that but this blow
Might be the be-all and the end-all here –
But here upon this bank and school of time–
We'd jump the life to come.'   [I.7.1–7]

The language of the play does indeed 'Blow the horrid deed in every eye'. Every soliloquy Macbeth speaks is not only, of itself, pictorial and active, but implies action – evil action. In no other play of Shakespeare for example is the supernatural so malevolent and so starkly presented. The presence of three witches seems totally apt as a dank background to the evil generated by Macbeth's own thoughts and deeds. We tolerate the benevolent supernaturals of *A Midsummer Night's Dream*, the symbolic appearances in *The Tempest*, because their presence leads to satisfactory and pleasing conclusions – our innate scepticism is allayed by joy. In *Hamlet*, *Richard III* and *Julius Caesar*, however, the supernatural elements seem, in the final analysis, no more than additives which we ourselves could, easily, dismiss from our experience of the play; even the Ghost of Hamlet's father cannot quite escape our tendency to be sceptical, irritated, or even faintly amused. Not so the witches. The fact that they are 'weird sisters', and not described as 'ghosts', in itself gives them a status disquietingly near to 'the natural'. Like Hamlet's father their appearance is given in detail, but unlike him, they seem to have an intercourse with human affairs which is constant, close, and malevolent. They do not come intermittently out of hell's regions to descant upon what has happened in life, and to grieve loudly about the sufferings of the unanealed; they live within man's society, seizing the thumbs of a shipwrecked sailor, killing swine, taking revenge upon a sailor's wife with chestnuts in her lap, and meeting with victorious soldiers upon a blasted heath in Scotland.

Their presence makes the supernatural curiously domestic. They are around the next bend in the dark lane and not amorphously appearing out of graves at midnight. Their power is ambivalently expressed in the play. George Hunter claims that 'The mode of evil they can create is potential only, not actual, till the human agent takes it inside his mind and makes it his own by a motion of the will.'[29] This is true, but only to an extent. Their ability to influence the fate of the master of the Tiger would seem to have little to do with *his* 'will'. It is the First Witch who will 'Drain him dry as hay', who will withhold sleep from him, who will cause him to 'dwindle, peak and pine'. It may be argued that only when Macbeth wills it can the evil they exemplify become active. Yet they are 'active' in that they present themselves to him on the first occasion. He does not call them up, any more than Banquo does. It seems that they activate, by the fore-knowledge they have, the seeds of evil ambition which exist, unfertilized, in Macbeth's mind, and it is clear that these seeds *are* present. After Ross and Angus confirm the witches' prophecies about his elevation to the Thanedom of Cawdor, Macbeth, in his asides, allows his secret expectations to surface:

> 'Glamis, and Thane of Cawdor!
> The greatest is behind.' [I.3.116–17]

> 'Two truths are told
> As happy prologues to the swelling act
> Of the imperial theme.' [I.3.127–8]

One of the most teasing critical questions in the play concerns how much Macbeth is 'influenced' towards evil by his own will, how much by the witches, and how much by his wife. What is rarely taken into account is the nature of Macbeth's immediate reaction to the prophecies – before he has met his wife and after receiving honours. He is in a state of turmoil. Apart from the asides which reveal the secret ambitions, he displays a bewildered reaction. He wants the witches to tell him more, he wishes they had stayed; he turns to Banquo as if for confirmation and asks 'And Thane of Cawdor too, went it not so?' He is like a child who is unable to believe that his secret dreams seems to be on the point of becoming realities. In his disturbed state he rationalizes – the prophecies cannot be either ill or good. He balances 'ill' against 'good' and they cancel each other out:

> 'This supernatural soliciting
> Cannot be ill; cannot be good. If ill,
> Why hath it given me earnest of success . . .
>
> . . . . .
>
> If good, why do I yield to that suggestion
> Whose horrid image doth unfix my hair . . . ? [I.3.130–5]

Before he meets Duncan and, importantly, before he meets his wife, he is in a state of almost totally inactive acceptance. He has pushed to the surface his secret thoughts: has had one of them confirmed; has concluded that the prophecies have no moral value, being neither ill nor good – they merely 'are'; that it is chance that has come to roost; time and the hour will run through the roughest day. Only one caveat to inactive waiting remains. He wants to talk over what has happened, at some time, with Banquo when:

> 'The interim having weigh'd it, let us speak
> Our free hearts each to other.'   [I.3.154–5]

The Macbeth we meet before he rejoins his wife is, basically, a morally weak man. His military prowess is certain, his status in the hierarchy of Scotland is lofty, his reputation assured. Yet it appears that he has little will-power over his baser instincts. What we witness is a present-tense revelation of the vulnerable interior of a man of high place. The tentative tone of his letter to his wife giving the impression that he requires some strong catalyst to make him come to a decision one way or the other for 'ill' or 'good' echoes his weakness. He writes that when he heard the witches' prophecies he 'stood rapt in the wonder of it', adding, 'This have I thought good to deliver thee, my dearest partner of greatness' – as if to say 'now, you can make the decision for me'. This weakness is underlined by the first words Lady Macbeth speaks after reading the letter. She 'fears' his 'nature', recognizing the softer virtues in him of wanting status without being prepared to accept that it cannot be gained without 'illness'. When he appears his first words only serve to emphasize his tentative state of mind:

> 'My dearest love,
> Duncan comes here to-night.'   [I.5.55]

Behind this statement lies one of the most potent hidden questions in the whole of Shakespeare's plays, – 'What shall we do?' It is significant that when she comes out with a plain statement of intention – 'He that's coming must be provided for' – he falls back into the same mood that possessed him after he had decided to leave all to chance, yet at the same time telling Banquo that they should speak about the prophecies on another occasion. He says to his wife, 'We will speak further', echoing his earlier words:

> 'The interim having weigh'd it, let us speak
> Our free hearts each to other.'   [I.3.154–5]

At his first meeting with his wife, then, Macbeth is at his most indecisive. The better part of him is not strong enough to dismiss its opposite, and Lady Macbeth has not yet summoned up all her power to push his 'compunctious visitings' away. In fact, after Duncan has arrived, he comes nearest to grasping 'good' rather than 'ill'. The soliloquy 'If it were done when 'tis done' reveals, for the first time that Macbeth, even if he is weak in will, is strong in both intelligence and, particularly, imagination. The soliloquy shows he is capable of knowing what 'good' is, just as his soliloquy before the murder of Duncan shows his imaginative awareness of the reality of evil. His arguments against doing the deed are comprehensive and subtle. First, they are self-indulgent; he would do the deed *if* the *act* of doing had no consequences, if it were insulated from both past and future, so that no judgement on it were possible. Second, they are conventionally honourable – you do not kill either as a 'subject' or 'kinsman', and as host, your duty is to protect not destroy your guest. Third, Duncan is a good man, and so such a deed would be an offence to heaven. Finally, he turns back to himself, recognizing that the sole justification for such a deed is 'vaulting ambition' which will end only in his own downfall.

The witches have done no more than objectify secret ambitions; they have not prompted him to act. His wife, as yet, has not played her ace card and that card alone – starkly simple in its potency – is responsible for forcing him to declare his own hand, so changing the whole direction of Macbeth's relationship, both to himself and to the whole society in which he lives. She attacks his love and his manhood:

> 'what beast was't then
> That made you break this enterprize to me?
> When you durst do it, then you were a man;
> And to be more than what you were, you would
> Be so much more the man.'   [I.7.47–51]

This softens him up for the final attack, and it is at this point that Macbeth changes irrevocably from the wavering, tentative being we have seen so far into, first a potential, then an actual, strong, murderous man. The change is indeed achieved by Lady Macbeth showing how easy the deed will be. In the plethora of critical exposition of Macbeth's state of mind up to the murder of Duncan, it is often forgotten that this man is a soldier – a very successful one – and that, given a logistic situation, he is eminently capable of solving it. He knows the art and craft of professional killing in massed battle and to kill one man is, in itself, a simplicity for him. Lady Macbeth plays her card – it is an order of battle:

> '... When Duncan is asleep,
> ... his two chamberlains
> Will I with wine and wassail so convince
> That memory, the warder of the brain,
> Shall be a fume, and the receipt of reason
> A limbec only. When in swinish sleep
> Their drenched natures lie as in a death,
> What cannot you and I perform upon
> Th'unguarded Duncan?' [I.7.61–70]

Lady Macbeth quells his thoughts of 'good' and 'ill' by giving him a problem he is only too capable of solving. He accepts the problem and with it pushes away, without speculation, its moral implications:

> 'Away, and mock the time with fairest show;
> False face must hide what the false heart doth know.' [I.7.81–2]

After this practical decision, he is a different man, becoming a soldier again, exercising his ability to execute that which is presented to him as a problem to be solved. Moral compunctions which had always been faint are overcome by a realization that the task in hand is, as Lady Macbeth suggests, simple to execute. Macbeth is essentially a man of action. Like Othello he is most himself when *doing*, not thinking or feeling. The combined 'influence' of the witches and Lady Macbeth upon him is to confirm him in this correct element. When he says earlier that 'Chance will have him king', he has to an extent given up. When Lady Macbeth points out that 'chance' can be expedited by action, he is determined.

Yet, like Othello, this soldier is cursed by something that inhabits him, making his status in the play far more profoundly subtle and powerful than that of mere brute, physical man. Macbeth is cursed by imagination. He can perform no deed without testing its uttermost consequences. His wish that 'this blow might be the be all and the end all here' is, considering his mental make-up, terribly ironic. The mere brute man commits murder with immediate access of physical violence, having no imagination to project motive or consequence either backwards or forwards in time. But Macbeth is saddled with the frightening ability both to remember and to foresee in images of engulfing power – in a man of action set upon a course of treacherous murder, this is a curse. In his soliloquy spoken before Duncan's chamber, his imagination can be seen working in phase with the present-tense action of the deed – the real dagger he is about to use being also a dagger suspended in the chambers of his own mind. The real steps he is taking must be unheard, otherwise they might 'prate' of his intentions. Yet as soon as he returns from the chamber his imagination begins to work in the past tense, he remembers a noise he heard; he recalls that one laughed in his sleep, the other cried 'murder', then 'God bless us', then 'Amen'. His memory pushes inwards upon him, like mounting waves, knocking his words into a growing rhythm of imagined guilt:

> 'Still it cried "Sleep no more" to all the house;
> Glamis hath murder'd sleep; and therefore Cawdor
> Shall sleep no more – Macbeth shall sleep no more.'   [II.2.41–3]

However, the fact that this man of action has omitted an elementary precaution – to bring back the daggers from the murder chamber – is surely a measure of the extent to which his ranging imagination has accompanied and fractured the simple performance of the deed. At this point, two considerations enter into the critical estimation of Macbeth's state.

The first concerns his realization of his guilt. To what extent, indeed, at this stage, has Macbeth a conscience? To the extent that conscience implies regret at a deed committed which is subsequently wished uncommitted, he has a large one. In the murder scene his huge imagination frightens his conscience into activity, and the implications of the images it conjures up – the voice saying that he shall sleep no more, his bloody hands – eventually come to mean one thing:

> 'Wake Duncan with thy knocking! I would thou couldst.'   [II.2.73]

Yet, at this point, Macbeth does not have the kind of conscience which shows any pity for the victim of a deed committed. Indeed, far from regret over killing Duncan, the implication is that the real regret he feels is for himself and what the deed's implications have in store for him – moral conpunctions have been replaced by self-indulgent imagination.

The second important matter of interpretation concerns the nature of the relationship between Macbeth and his wife. It is customary to imagine them and, indeed, to depict them, as a closely-knit 'fiend-like' duo. Indeed, they have sometimes been used to illustrate the idea that every great man, good or evil, should have, behind him a woman of will and determination, urging him on. The extent of Lady Macbeth's urging has been noted; their mutual involvement in the crime is signified by Lady Macbeth's return to the chamber with the daggers and her reappearance with blood on her hands. Later, we see them together, and in the banquet scene she performs an act of tremendous will in holding together (if only just) her shattered husband. Yet it is at the point of the murder when they are 'but young in deed' that, paradoxically, these two begin to draw away from one another, or rather, Macbeth draws himself away from his wife. George Hunter writes: 'The deed itself is a denial of all social obligations, all sharing, all community of feeling even with his wife.'[30] But the separation has another element in it as well for where drawing away from Lady Macbeth is concerned, the simple fact is that she cannot follow him into the regions to which his imagination is taking him. As his imagination weaves around the words 'Amen', 'God bless us' and 'sleep', pushing him into the final horror of:

> 'Will all great Neptune's ocean wash this blood
> Clean from my hand?'   [II.2.60]

her responses are remarkably banal. 'Consider it not so deeply'. 'What do you mean?' and she reveals her profound imaginative insensitivity when she says:

> '. . . The sleeping and the dead
> Are but as pictures; 'tis the eye of childhood
> That fears a painted devil. If he do bleed,
> I'll guild the faces of the grooms withal,
> For it must seem their guilt.'   [II.2.53–57]

And there can be no doubt about her inability to follow Macbeth in his journey through hells of his own making, after her remark that:

> '. . . retire we to our chamber:
> A little water clears us of this deed.'   [II.2.66–7]

– in itself an ironic reversal of Macbeth's belief that his hand will turn all the ocean to red.

Macbeth, then, becomes isolated from society because of the murder, and isolated from individuals, even the closest to him, because of the far greater imaginative power he has. He is the loneliest of the four tragic heroes – utterly isolated on a sea of horrible imaginings whose shore harbours on the one side haunting images of the past, and, on the other, a limitless dark future; his eyes are sharp enough to see both simultaneously.

The loneliness, however, which cloaks him at the death of Duncan gives him also, paradoxically, a new kind of strength. The Macbeth we see after Macduff has arrived to wake Duncan is not the tortured man of the previous scene. There is an icy kind of calm about him. In reply to questions and remarks, he is terse, as if screwing his courage for a posture of strength. 'Good morrow both'. 'Not yet'. 'I'll bring you to him'. ''Twas a rough night'. He keeps his head while the discovery of the murder creates its own chaos and, in the end, takes charge of the situation:

> 'Let's briefly put on manly readiness
> And meet i' th'hall together.'   [II.3.133–4]

His calm is the more remarkable in the face of the atmosphere of suspicion which the murder of the grooms has created, for in this and the following scene, Shakespeare, by hints and innuendoes, gives us a faint but ineradicable sense that Macbeth's action has not passed without whispers of suspicion. 'Wherefore did you so?', inquires Macduff, and a little later phrases his answer to Ross's inquiry about who has done the deed most curiously 'Those that Macbeth hath slain'. Even more pointed is Macduff's reply to Ross's disbelief that the two grooms could gain anything from murdering Duncan. He says:

> 'They were suborned.
> Malcolm and Donalbain, the King's two sons
> Are stol' away and fled; which puts upon them
> Suspicion of the deed.'   [II.4.24–26]

Suspicion has been 'put upon them' – Macduff says no more on this score – but again phrases his answer to Ross's question most curiously:

> 'Then 'tis most like
> The sovreignty will fall upon Macbeth'   [II.4.29–30]

He emphasizes the haste with which the sovereignty has fallen upon Macbeth:

> 'He is already nam'd, and gone to Scone ...'   [II.4.31]

He says he will not go there himself, though Macbeth's succession, in the face of the apparent treachery and defection of Malcolm, is legal.

Naturally, not to go would be inviting danger, but more than this, his decision not to go, together with the implications of his remarks, emphasizes the state Scotland is in after Duncan's murder. Shakespeare seems at pains to demonstrate the chaos, suspicion, and disorder that has fallen upon the society of which Macbeth is now head. The scene between Ross and the old man underlines this, as if the deed has unlocked unnatural and dark forces and the fair times of Duncan have become foul almost within the hour. All has become unnatural 'even like the deed that's done'.

The range of Shakespeare's imaginative grasp of the meaning of evil is demonstrated superbly in both this scene and in Macduff's conversation with Ross. Up to now we have seen evil as it is embodied in and corrodes one single man. This scene broadens the implications. The evil of one man, like that of Richard III, corrupts a whole society, selective evil leading to evil on a total rampage. But whereas the history plays cover large canvasses of time and space to show the spread of the forces of destruction and evil, *Macbeth* achieves it with an amazing brevity. The murder, its discovery, the comments upon it, the chaos it engenders, the unnatural portents which have accompanied it, are all gathered up into fearful immediacy of both time and place. Macbeth's earlier desire to have the deed and its consequences insulated within the present tense is here ironically counterpointed by a swift presentation of those consequences.

The seeds of suspicion in Macduff's mind are germinated when he leaves for Fife, and Banquo's reaction, III.1 is:

'Thou hast it now – King, Cawdor, Glamis, all
As the weird women promis'd; and I fear
Thou play'd most foully for't;'   [III.1.1–3]

Suspicion, disorder, have come to the surface. Where now does Macbeth stand?

First, his isolation is virtually complete; second, his acquisition of the throne has, from the very beginning, been attended by disorder, suspicion and a perplexed mind for himself and his queen. However, as long as Macbeth can remain active, can at least give himself the illusion that he has some control over his destiny, he seems decisive, authoritative, and unswamped by imagination. He is courteously authoritative in the scene with Banquo before Banquo rides out for his last journey; he is scornfully in charge when he gives directions and probably lies to the two hired assassins. The possibility of action balances him. He has pulled himself together after the air-drawn dagger speech with the couplet:

'Hear it not, Duncan, for it is a knell
That summons thee to heaven or to hell.'   [II.1.63–4]

echoed in the couplet following the scene with the assassins:

'It is concluded: Banquo, thy soul's flight
If it find heaven must find it out to-night.'   [III.1.140–1]

The couplet, in itself, seems to lock the acting of the deed into an unassailable, insulated present tense.

The extent to which the acquisition of kingship gives Macbeth a quality of decision is seldom noted by critics, nor is it always communicated by actors. It makes itself quite manifest in Act III.2 when Lady Macbeth enters and asks him why he keeps himself so much to himself. The answer she receives is clear-headed, rational. He knows exactly the position he is in, and knows, equally exactly, what his next step will be: 'Let your remembrance apply to Banquo.' Just as significant as this access of authority and rationality is a pronounced shift in the way in which his imagination works as he moves from a state when it controls him, to a state when he seems able to call upon it, exults in its power, making it do what he asks. It is as if the fulfilment of his ambition (though it has cost him much) has strengthened the man, and there is irony in the fact that his rationality, control, and authority suggest that, were all the circumstances different, he would have been an efficient and respected monarch. This possibility is the more distinct when we see him at the beginning of the banquet scene, when he is completely in command – gracious and regal:

'Our self will mingle with society
And play the humble host.'   [III.4.3–4]

Even when the first murderer enters covertly to tell him that though Banquo is dead, Fleance still lives, Macbeth has only a moment of the old weakness, losing control but for an instant.

'But now I am cabin'd, cribb'd confin'd, bound in
To saucy doubts and fears.'   [III.4.24–5]

He quickly recovers himself, making plans to talk further with the murderers, and returning to his guests, even allowing himself a wry remark about the absence of Banquo:

'Who may I rather challenge for unkindness
Than pity for mischance.'   [III.4.42–3]

The 'fit' which comes upon him with the appearance of Banquo's ghost is, in effect, a struggle between the 'new' rational Macbeth, and the former weak, indecisive man, cursed by imagination. The rhythmic movement of the scene is superbly controlled by Shakespeare. The first wave knocks Macbeth out of sense:

> 'Thou canst not say I did it; never shake
> Thy gory locks at me.'   [III.4.50–1]

The second wave plunges his mind into a cauldron of uncontrollable images:

> 'If charnel-houses and our graves must send
> Those that we bury back, our monuments
> Shall be the maw of kites.'   [III.4.71–3]

The third wave sucks all away, leaving him shattered but momentarily restored to equilibrium:

>   'I do forget:
> Do not muse at me, my most worthy friends;'   [III.4.84–5]

With the return of the ghost comes the fourth wave, which causes his anguished mind to try and will this horrible image into a shape and a situation which he can control:

> 'Approach thou like the rugged Russian bear,
> The arm'd rhinoceros, or th'Hyrcan tiger;
> Take any shape but that, and my firm nerves
> Shall never tremble.'   [III.4.100–3]

The fifth wave is a return of the third – imagination overpowers him; exhausted as he is, neither authority, will nor reason can hold back the monstrous images:

>   'You make me strange
> Even to the disposition that I owe,'   [III.4.112–3]

Finally, when all have left, this battered man returns to some semblance of order within himself. He grasps again at the one thing which is indigenous to him, which gives him equilibrium and rationality – the possibility of action:

> 'Strange things I have in head that will to hand,
> Which must be acted ere they may be scann'd'   [III.4.139–40]

These two lines sum up Macbeth's personality. He is of that kind whose disposition is to act and then to speculate. His tragedy is that his weak moral fibre, in combination with his powerful imagination, confounds his will to control himself in acting 'rightly' or 'wrongly'.

His resolution to act takes him again to the witches. Here he is presented with images which equal in intensity and implication anything that he himself can conjure out of the resources of his own imagination. He is shown the future and it appals him. Yet, from the deep recesses of his mind, the impulse to contain the future within the present tense – 'If it were done when 'tis done' – still works. After the witches disappear he says:

'Let this pernicious hour
Stand aye accursed in the calendar.'   [IV.1.133–4]

When Lennox informs him that Macduff is fled to England he remonstrates with Time for having anticipated what he plans to do – he wants the deed and its consequences to proceed together. He chastises Time for its treachery:

'Time, thou anticipat'st my dread exploits.
The flighty purpose never is o'ertook
Unless the deed go with it.'   [IV.1.144–6]

Again, it is the thought of action that restores his equilibrium:

'To crown my thoughts with acts, be it thought and done:'[IV.1.149]

Speculation, act and consequence must in fact become one.

Shakespeare's skill in counterpointing individual disorder with social disorder is brilliantly demonstrated in the scenes that follow this second visit to the witches. Any actor playing Macbeth must welcome the break; what it achieves for the audience is twofold. The results of spreading evil are seen, first, in a domestic and harrowing sense – the murder of Macduff's family – and, secondly, in a political sense – the conversation between Malcolm and Macduff in the court of England.

The scene between Malcolm and Macduff, often condemned as dull by commentators and directors who frequently cut it down, is of immense importance in re-establishing the context of large disorder which had, for a time, become dramatically subservient to the active analysis of the disorder within Macbeth himself. Moreover its opening atmosphere of suspicion and dissension in the State's high places is in direct and ironic contrast to the earlier scenes of Duncan's court where all is amity, fidelity and order. With the Malcolm/Macduff conversation, faint optimism and a glimmer of order to come, again enter into the play. The rhythm of history once more asserts itself and in this scene and the ones that follow, Scot and Englishman join to destroy evil. Rightful degree and order is restored, confirming that Shakespeare's access to pessimism, revealed so darkly in *Troilus and Cressida*, had not defeated his inherent faith in an ordered universe. Within the terms of this play, the Lady Macduff scene, the Malcolm/Macduff confrontation, followed as they are by the whispered words between the Doctor and the Gentlewoman and Lady Macbeth's sleep-walking, play an essential part in emphasizing Macbeth's loneliness. During these scenes he is 'lost' from the action; when we next see him he is utterly alone, an inhabitant of an empty castle, with empty dark space around him:

'Those he commands move only in command,
Nothing in love.'   [V.2.19–20]

No other tragic hero reveals quite such a separation from humanity, ordered society and love. The theatrical effect of this is heightened by giving him only two visible companions – the 'lily-livered' Seyton and the Doctor who, were he 'from Dunsinane away and clear,/ Profit again should hardly draw' him there. Where, we may ask, are Macbeth's forces? His 'false Thanes' have fled. We are given an almost ridiculously frightening impression of a man determined to fight a whole army alone. Yet it is only 'almost' ridiculous. At this point in the play, perhaps for the first time, we begin to feel twinges of pity for the man. He has passed through moral compunctions, through indecision, through fear even and the irony is that, at last, he is in complete command of his imagination:

'I have almost forgot the taste of fears.
The time has been my senses would have cool'd
To hear a night-shriek, and my fell of hair
Would at a dismall treatise rouse and stir
As life were in't. I have supp'd full with horrors;
Direness, familiar to my slaughterous thoughts,
Cannot once start me.'   [V.5.9–15]

The death of his wife enables him to put his imagination to its final task – to assess the meaning of existence. Having done this, imagination itself dies – there is nothing more it can do since even its prophetic powers add up to nothing:

'Life's but a walking shadow, a poor player,
That struts and frets his hour upon the stage,
And then is heard no more; it is a tale
Told by an idiot, full of sound and fury,
Signifying nothing.'   [V.5.24–8]

So, with fear gone, imagination dispossessed, Macbeth is left with that one quality which, without ambition, without imagination, without moral weakness, might well have made him a man of greatness – the will to act. One by one the witches' equivocating prophecies are revealed for what they are, but at each withdrawal of illusory safety, Macbeth makes renewed decisions to act:

'At least we'll die with harness on our back.'   [V.5.52]

'But bear-like I must fight the course.'   [V.7.2]

'Yet I will try the last. Before my body
I throw my warlike shield. Lay on, Macduff;
And damm'd be him, that first cries, "Hold, enough!"'   [V.8.32–4]

Macbeth is often relegated to the status of 'unsympathetic' tragic villain. His stark and violent butchery contrasts with Hamlet's wavering, Othello's misguided pride, Lear's foolishness, as having no excuse with which to command any kind of admiration or pity from reader or audience. Yet, if we place him alongside Iago, who *seems* equally blandly and totally evil, can we in the final analysis relegate him to a role of total infamy? Throughout the whole play of *Macbeth*, but most notably in the early acts, there is a sense created that here is a man who could, most positively, be good and great and what we witness is a tragedy of the most painful, and yet pure kind – that of a man in whose personality there is a dissociation between certain characteristics which, in themselves, are potentially admirable. He has a will for action, a powerful imagination, self-knowledge, an ability to distinguish between good and evil, a strong awareness of love, fidelity and honour. As they are mixed in this play, what emerges is evil; but in the inevitability with which he surrounds himself with evil, and in the searing self-knowledge which accompanies it, Macbeth becomes a suffering man. Iago suffers nothing; his self-knowledge is a wry self-indulgence; his imagination is practical rather than transcendental.

It may be, too, that there is another quality which absolves him from total condemnation. George Hunter comments that though there is 'nothing morally admirable about the capacity to speak well, we are in fact held sympathetically by a sense of surviving significance in his rhythms, even in those final speeches whose content is devoted to the meaninglessness of existence.'[31] Macbeth's enormous desire to survive, his unabated capacity to take action in order so to do, may in themselves elicit from us a feeling of respect. But more than this, the language through which he expresses this desire and this capacity is of a soul-searching eloquence. Such language in the service of good would order kingdoms and inspirit commonwealths. In the service of evil it astounds our minds and feelings by its power and apparently limitless possibilities of invention. The 'butcher' Macbeth confirms, paradoxically, the dignity of human communication.

The play is, to all intents and purposes, a one-man play. The theme of disorder painfully transmuted into order is present, but only in the shadow of the spotlight which plays upon Macbeth. The characters surrounding him play their roles but only under the sway of Macbeth's presence. There is no greater measure or demonstration of this than the character of Lady Macbeth herself. Brave and great actresses have tried to find a 'personality' within her which has a coherence and a validity in its own right – few seem to have succeeded. Even one of the most famous of Lady Macbeths (Sarah Siddons) failed, it seems, to find the interior of the character.

> Mrs. Siddons was at first much agitated; in the scenes with Macbeth immediately brought before and after the murder of Duncan she was admirably expressive of the genuine sense and spirit of the author; but in the banquet scene in the third act, her abilities did not shine to so much lustre. In several passages of the dialogue she adopted too much the familiar manner, approaching to the comic; this may be called her epilogue style in which she has already experienced an entire failure. In this scene an exception must be made to her rebuke of Macbeth (though even that had not the powerful effect we might have expected from Mrs. Siddons) and the congé to her guests, which last was delivered with inimitable grace.
>
> In the taper scene she was defective; her enunciation was too confined . . . the faces she made were horrid and even ugly, without being strictly just or expressive. She appeared in three several dresses. The first was handsome and neatly elegant, the second rich and splendid, but somewhat pantomimical, and the last one of the least becoming, to speak no worse of it, of any she ever wore upon the stage. Lady Macbeth is supposed to be asleep and not mad, so that

custom itself cannot be alleged as a justification for her appearing in white satin.[32]

Lady Macbeth, like the rest, ministers to the presence of Macbeth. She is so small a creature by comparison with her husband, especially when we compare her 'imagination' with his. Only once, in the soliloquy in which she calls upon the spirits to unsex her, does she display anything like the creative force of his imagination, rising beyond her normal and customary station. Ordinarily she is a creature devoid of the sensitivity or complexity of that kind of mental power which suggests either strong will or subtle imagination. It is easy for her (before Duncan's murder) to exhibit some willpower over her wavering husband. No deed has been committed up to this point. In fact, her mood at this time is nearer to bravado than anything else. But when the deed has been committed her lack of sensitivity shows; she believes a little water will clear away the deed, adding with appalling off-handedness that she would have done the deed herself had not Duncan resembled her father. This statement gives perhaps the key to her mental make-up. Whereas Macbeth haunts himself by the creative scope of his imagination, Lady Macbeth is destroyed by mere memory. Her mind can pre-figure nothing, is only astonishingly retentive. What destroys her reason is her memory; she discovers the untruth of her own remark 'what's done is done'. In the banquet scene a courageous bravado again sees her through. She remembers the air-drawn dagger and dismisses it. We next hear of her through the Doctor's reports, which imply that she has now become a prey to memories she cannot dismiss:

'I have seen her rise from her bed, throw her nightgown upon her,
unlock her closet, take forth paper, fold it, write upon't, read it,
afterwards seal it, and again return to bed . . .'   [V.1.5–7]

Is this a memory of a letter she wrote to her husband before the murder of Duncan? We do not know, but what she says during her sleep-walk suggests that images of palpable and concrete happenings from the past are dominant in her mind. She remembers the blood on her hands – 'Out damned spot'. She remembers Lady Macduff – 'Where is she now?' She remembers Macbeth's susceptibilities – 'You mar all with this starting'. She remembers the smell of blood – 'All the perfumes of Arabia will not sweeten this little hand'. She remembers the night of the murder – 'Wash your hands, put on your nightgown, look not so pale.'

This accumulation of memories destroys Lady Macbeth, and as her imagination only moves backwards, she is doomed to be isolated from the man whose imagination moves in many directions. She is the smaller of the two because of her limitations, and, perhaps, the more pitiful. She is, certainly, not fiend-like. Rather she is a female with little sense of reason, no sense of morality, and the ability – the bravado – to put on a false face to hide what the false heart knows.

Banquo is, theatrically speaking, a dull character. Occasionally he comes near to developing into an interesting man, but Shakespeare, seemingly deliberately, stops him short. The first occasion is after the first appearance of the witches when he agrees 'very gladly' to discuss at some future time what has happened; the second occasion is immediately before Duncan's murder when he is alone with his thoughts:

> '... Merciful powers
> Restrain in me the cursed thoughts that nature
> Gives way to in repose!'   [II.1.7–8]

How near are these cursed thoughts to Macbeth's? How near is Banquo to uttering them and, indeed, acting upon them? We are never allowed to know. He slips back into his mechanistic role in the plot line, emerging only once more to give up hope that there is subtle mettle in him:

> 'Yet it was said
> It should not stand in thy posterity;
> But that myself should be the root and father
> Of many kings. If there come truth from them –
> As upon thee, Macbeth, their speeches shine –
> Why, by the verities on thee made good,
> May they not be my oracles as well
> And set me up in hope?'   [III.1.3–10]

Banquo is, in fact, a conventionally good and honourable man, given just enough temptation to arouse in him unworthy thoughts and feelings. These are very intermittent but sufficient to give the action a touch of piquancy when they occur.

Macduff, also, is little more than a pawn. Arguments which have been conducted about the moral rightness or wrongness of his leaving his home and family at the mercy of Macbeth seem irrelevant. We know too little of him to judge whether he is acting rightly or wrongly. The moments when an actor may find sufficient to help him present a cogent characterization are few and far between. The

England scene between him and Malcolm gives some opportunity for a dispay of emotional variety, but even here there is a curious negativeness about the man. He seems to respond automatically, to say exactly the right things as Malcolm tests his integrity and purpose. This feeling of 'automatic' response is strong even in the scene where he learns of the murder of his wife and family, a scene infinitely touching yet without arousing our pity for Macduff himself. It is as if he were a mere symbol, not the direct human recipient of grief. In fact, by comparison with the man he eventually destroys, he seems wooden in intellect, lacking in imagination, uncertain in motivation.

Duncan is constantly presented to us as an image of goodness. Many of the qualities Malcolm lists –

'As justice, verity, temp'rance, stableness,
Bounty, perseverance, mercy, lowliness,
Devotion, patience, courage, fortitude . . .'   [IV.3.92–4]

– Duncan is either expressly or implicitly shown to have. Shakespeare goes out of his way to keep this golden image before us even after the murder. In the scene immediately ensuing the murder the words 'Duncan', 'The king', 'His Majesty', 'royal master', 'royal father', toll continuously like a mourning bell through the action, and whenever Duncan is referred to, the image presented is always in stark contrast to the present-tense actuality of Macbeth's reign. His body goes to 'the sacred storehouse of his predecessors'. Macbeth calls him 'gracious Duncan'; 'after life's fitful fever he sleeps well'. We are never allowed to forget this man, and certainly in no other tragedy of Shakespeare's is there such a consistent implied and direct opposition made between good and evil, as in this opposition between the image of Duncan and the actuality of Macbeth.

His son, Malcolm, whose elevation as Prince of Cumberland gives Macbeth his first speculations about the barriers to be overcome for the fulfilment of the prophecies, could be a glowing dramatic figure in the play, but is not. All there is of him may be summed up in the word 'representative'. He is representative of the forces of order which will restore peace to Scotland; he is representative of the orderly progression of dynasty, rudely interrupted by Macbeth; even the doubts which he plants in Macduff's mind about his fitness to be king strike us more as representative of an argument than as an embodiment of his own speculative nature. An actor has, virtually, to 'make' a character out of Malcolm because there is so little positive to interpret.

311

In the end, however, all the characters pale into insignificance in comparison with Macbeth himself and the curious fact is that whatever moral judgements one makes on him, whatever allowance of sympathy one is prepared to grant or to withhold, he cannot be forced out of one's imagination. As Kemble noted: 'In the performance on the stage, the valour of the tyrant, hateful as he is, invariably commands the admiration of every spectator of the play.'[33] Shakespeare's theatrical power in fact can exert such a fascination on us that it can weaken any disposition we have to question intellectually the moral pattern of the play. Chaos is expunged in the end, order reasserts itself, the commonwealth, tested sorely by evil, is brought back to health. Yet it is not this that we remember when we leave the book or the performance. We remember only that we have experienced (in John Wain's words): '. . . not so much with our visual imagination as with our hands, teeth, throats, our very skin, hair and nails, a terrifying reality.'[34]

NOTES

1 Thomas Rymer, 1641–1713. Historian and critic. *A Short View of Tragedy* (1693).
2 Alexander Pope, 1688–1744. His edition of Shakespeare appeared in 1725.
3 Mary McMarthy, *Theatre Chronicles, 1937–1962* (1962).
4 Thomas Platter. Swiss physician who visited London in 1599 and wrote descriptions of theatre-going in London. Translated from German, in Chambers and Williams, *A Short Life of Shakespeare* (1933).
5 Cf. Frank Dunlop's production at the Nottingham Playhouse, 1962.
6 T.J.B. Spencer, (ed.) *Shakespeare's Plutarch* (1968).
7 Ibid.
8 Anthony Scoloker, in his poem, *Daiphantus, or the Passions of Love* (1604).
9 M.L. Mare and W.H. Quarrell (trans.), *Lichtenberg's Visits to England as Described in His Letters and Diaries* (1938), pp. 45–6. See also Gareth Lloyd Evans, *Shakespeare in the Limelight* (1968), p. 38 *passim*.
10 Granville Barker, op. cit., p. 29.
11 R.W. Chambers, op. cit., p. 46.
12 B.Ifor Evans, *The Language of Shakespeare's Plays* (1952), p. 105
13 See E. Wilson, (ed.) *Shaw on Shakespeare* (1969), pp. 102–3.
14 Cinthio (Giovanni Baptista Geraldi) 1504–1573. Italian playwright and novelist. His *Hecatommithi*, c.1565, was a collection of stories linked by narration.

15 In O.J. Campbell and E.G. Quinn, op. cit., p. 599.
16 In H.H. Furness, (ed.) *Othello*, Variorum Shakespeare edition (1886), p. 395.
17 Ibid.
18 Ibid, p. 393.
19 See Chapters 1, pp. 34–35 and 3, p. 107.
20 Kenneth Muir, (ed.). Introduction to New Penguin edition of *Othello* (1968), p. 17.
21 Ibid, p. 12.
22 Granville Barker, op. cit., p. 266.
23 Muir, op. cit., p. 44.
24 In Furness, (ed.) *King Lear*, Variorum Shakespeare (1880), p. 423.
25 William Hazlitt, 'On Kean's King Lear', in *The London Magazine* (June, 1820).
26 G. Wilson Knight, *The Wheel of Fire* (1930), p. 57.
27 Ibid.
28 Dennis Bartholomeusz, *Macbeth and the Players* (1969), *passim*.
29 G.K. Hunter, (ed.). Introduction to New Penguin edition of *Macbeth* (1967).
30 Ibid.
31 Ibid.
32 John Taylor, in *The Morning Post* (3 February 1785).
33 John Kemble, *Macbeth Reconsidered*, 1786 (in Bartholomeusz, op. cit.).
34 John Wain, op. cit., p. 212.

7 The Classical World

When one compares the evidence of the nature and extent of classical learning in Shakespeare's plays with that of some of his contemporaries – Ben Jonson, for example, or Christopher Marlow – it is easy to conclude that he had not the deep grounding they had in classical literature and culture.

For the Elizabethans 'classical' meant mostly 'Latin', for though they had knowledge of the Greeks, it was often at second hand through the Roman tongue and Roman sources. Shakespeare does not exhibit the kind of easy commerce with the classical world nor the habitual meticulousness of references that one finds in many of his literary contemporaries and which he would have learnt from a university education. Indeed, it is the customary, random insouciance of his use of the classics and of the Latin language which gives the greatest confirmation to the probability that his education ended at grammar school level. By comparison with Ben Jonson's Shakespeare's Latin was not only 'small' and his Greek 'less', but it had a strange mixture of restriction and waywardness about it which suggests he ceased formal acquaintaince with it in his 'teens.

But no serious Elizabethan writer could escape the influence of classical culture and, in Shakespeare's case, there is abundant evidence that, though his formal education in the classics was bound by a grammar school curriculum, his imagination was irresistibly drawn to classical history, politics, society, myth and legend. One of the simplest but forgotten facts about Shakespeare's career is that he never lost what amounted to a very deep curiosity about the classical world, which began early in *Titus Andronicus*, appeared in many ways in his subsequent plays and intensified in focus in his later years.

During the period following the writing of the tragedies (about 1606) Shakespeare's mind turned very decisively in the direction of the classical past. In the next few years he wrote two of his greatest plays, both of them having a classical source – *Antony and Cleopatra* (c. 1607/8) and *Coriolanus* (c. 1608) – and the first of them is of such potency that some critics assign it a place amongst the tragedies. Yet whatever it is – romantic tragedy or historical romance – *Antony and Cleopatra* owes its existence to Shakespeare's ability to immerse himself into an evocation of classical history. His sources were the then accepted historians and chroniclers – Plutarch, whose *Parallel*

Lives was translated into English in 1579, and Appian, whose *Civil Wars* was translated in 1578 – as well as a more imaginatively conceived realization of the classical world in Samuel Daniel's *Tragedie of Cleopatra* (1593) and Robert Garnier's *Marc-Antoine* (1578, translated into English 1592).

Coriolanus is probably Shakespeare's most searching study of the ironies and paradoxes of the tensions between personal ambition and political necessity – a complex in constant evidence in contempotary Elizabethan politics. It is, however, to the classical world that Shakespeare turned for his examples, largely to Plutarch, also possibly to Livy, and consulting more fanciful works by William Averell and William Camden for the account of Menenius's fable of the belly, in the process.

Timon of Athens (c. 1607), *Pericles* (c. 1606/8) and *Cymbeline* (c. 1609/10) are not classical plays in the sense that *Antony and Cleopatra* and *Coriolanus* are. They do not exploit history in order to reflect dramatically upon the ironies of the political and the personal. They are, on the contrary, romances, whose sources, even when derived from what Shakespeare would have regarded as factual, are used to weave fable, to spin romance. Plutarch informed Shakespeare's *Timon*, as did the dialogue, *Timon Misanthropus*, by the Greek satirist Lucian, but it may have been an anonymous play written sometime between 1581 and 1590 which turned Shakespeare's mind in the direction less of 'history' than of 'legend'. *Pericles*, the last two acts of which contain some of the finest of Shakespeare's writing, comes ultimately from a very British source – John Gower's *Confessio Amantis* (1390–1393) – so it existed in romance form for Shakespeare from the first, although its environment, associations and character are classical. It is very much a play of the classical Mediterranean clime. And even *Cymbeline*, deriving partly from his most English of sources – Holinshed's *Chronicles* (1577–1587) – and pushed in the direction of romance and fable by Shakespeare's reading of Boccaccio's *Decameron* (1353), lies under the shadow of Rome. Cymbeline is a British ruler of Britain, but the country is under threat from Roman authority and the play is replete with Roman names, Roman references and associations. In fact, although *Cymbeline* belongs thematically to the later romances (indeed may well be seen as a first attempt in this genre new to Shakespeare) it also testifies to the hold on Shakespeare of the classical world.

During a very short period of years, then, at the beginning of the seventeenth century, Shakespeare's imagination concentrated on plays with a classical setting. The classical influence, in its wider sense, was present throughout his working life, and although he did not possess the meticulous intimacy with the classics of some of his contemporaries, his work is saturated with his own, often highly subjective evocations of its spirit.

Timon of Athens

Timon of Athens is, in many ways, one of Shakespeare's strangest plays. Doubts have frequently been voiced about the extent of Shakespeare's hand in it and indeed about whether he had anything to do with it at all. It can only be described as a tragedy, yet it seems conspicuously out of key with the other tragedies. Its inclusion in the first Folio between *Romeo and Juliet* and *Julius Caesar*, is surrounded with problems. It seems, however, that this position was originally reserved for *Troilus and Cressida* but because that play was unavailable for printing, a hurried substitution of a play roughly capable of fitting in the vacant space was made. The rough calculations were wrong and the printer found himself with the need to leave out a whole quire of paper. The result is that in the printed Folio there is a gap between pages 98 and 109, one completely blank page and another inserted which had originally been reserved for the names of the actors. The date of composition is also uncertain but a consensus of opinion would put it somewhere between 1605 and 1609 – certainly it seems to fall towards the end of the great period of tragic plays. These problems, however, pale into insignificance beside the textual inconsistencies, and the irregularities of verse, theme and character with which it abounds. Dr Johnson found that 'there are many passages perplexed, obscure, and probably corrupt',[1] and overall its acceptance by both critics and audiences has always been less than enthusiastic.

Yet no other play of Shakespeare's expresses with such directness a set of attitudes which seems so germane to many of the intellectual, emotional and moral preoccupations of many people today. So, ironically, while *Timon of Athens* is one of Shakespeare's apparently most uncharacteristic plays, it is also one of the most apposite to our times.

In several major respects the play differs from the four great tragedies. The most obvious may be described as one of genre. The other tragedies may be termed as essentially realistic – we believe as we experience them that their events and situations actually occur and that their characters are living human beings. This is not so with *Timon of Athens*, despite the fact that the protagonist was in fact a real historical figure mentioned in Plutarch's *Lives*. Perhaps the term most apparently applicable to this play is 'allegorical', not only because the reader or theatregoer has a persistent sense that personi-

318

fication is being used for the communication of abstract ideas, but also because of the symmetry of construction – of an imposed pattern – that is often to be found in allegorical work. The other tragedies move to their conclusions with relentless and realistic inevitability, but *Timon's* conclusion seems already intellectually established before the play begins and what we see is a demonstration of how that conclusion is reached. The personification may not be as absolute as in the highly-wrought *The Faerie Queene* of Spenser for example, but it is unmistakeably present. The play's 'idea', its central core, is concerned with enforcing a moral conclusion upon its readers or viewers, with a 'message' about what we are like, how we behave to each other, our sense of values. What happens in the play to the characters, and what is said by them, are fashioned for little more than the enforcing of this abstract message. Even Timon seems cabin'd, cribbed and confined when set alongside the free-ranging dramatic existence of the four great tragic heroes. Others, particularly the painter, the poet and the senators and, to a lesser extent, Alcibiades and Apemantus, are personifications of attitudes. Their place in the system can be clearly seen in the final act when Timon is visited by Alcibiades – the representative of the military, Apemantus representing philosophy, the Painter representing the visual arts, the Poet the verbal arts and two Senators the political world. The only significant absentees in this allegorical parade are the church and music – no priest to shrive and salve and no music (so often the balm of hurt minds in Shakespeare) to ease a broken spirit towards concord. Inexorably, these representatives who visit Timon are used as examples of man's inhumanity, his cupidity, his hypocrisy or his simple naïveté – for Alcibiades is less a villain than a well-meaning innocent in his brashly simple military way.

This allegorical basis upon which the play seems to have been built is reinforced by a consideration of its actual construction. It is one thing to condemn it, as many commentators have done, for its inconsistencies of characterization, for its lack of dramatic development, in terms both of incident and character, but quite another to ignore what seems, at the least, to be a strong pursuit by the author of symmetry. All the visitors to Timon (with the exception of Alcibiades) in Act V have already visited him, in his days of affluent but mindless generosity. In the early visits we experience a wry, satirical comment on social behaviour and are aware that we are far more conscious of the truth behind what is happening than some of the leading characters. In the later visits we experience the deliberately unambiguous fact of moral turpitude. Whereas, in the first instance, we may shake our heads sagely while we smile or laugh at Timon's gullibility in the face of the world's perfidy, in the second we are frozen into a recognition of the unalloyed hypocrisy of mankind.

Yet, these experiences, such is the force of the allegorical mode, are largely cerebral. The poet, the painter, even the senators, are not individualized and the frisson their presence gives is more of head than of heart. We are not asked to be engaged with them in a sense which is even approximately human.

It is this creation of an allegorical equation, as distinct from a dramatic reality, which marks this play off fundamentally from the four great tragedies. The isolation of Timon seems more of an artificial imposition than a natural outcome of event and personality. The society around Timon, although its rotted values can be taken as emblematic of mankind in general, does not have that quality of realism that is typical of the tragedies and not only is that at a premium, but also the whole relationship between the protagonist and his social context. Macbeth's perfidy becomes Scotland's ruin; Hamlet's and Elsinore's descent are inexorably connected; the darkness and chaos that come to inhabit Lear's mind have their intimates in the darkness and chaos that descend upon his country; what Iago works upon Othello's imagination and spirit affects the lives of others in the society about him. Yet what happens to Timon, both outwardly and inwardly, seems curiously insulated, self-contained. This play does not maintain and develop the rich theme of the interdependence of inner and outer order and disorder – begun in the early histories and reaching its peak in the great tragedies. The question therefore arises as to why this play should be of so different an order of tragedy from its fellows. The obvious answer is to attribute it to a persistent spirit of experimentation in Shakespeare.

At first sight the pursuit of symmetry might seem to provide the key to the argument that *Timon of Athens* is an experimental play. It could, however, very well argue for a quite different explanation.

Timon of Athens is believed by a few to be the work of someone other than Shakespeare, by some to be partly his and by more to be his entirely. There is a formidable weight of scholarship on the side of concluding that the text as printed in the first Folio is from Shakespeare's foul papers (i.e. a first uncorrected manuscript draft). If so this might account for the simple symmetry of the play and for the allegorical colouring. The tendency of the first 'blocking' of a play or a novel by an author is towards a balancing of forces, towards giving equal value to the constituent parts already decided upon. It is only in the later stages of writing that the more creatively fecund process of judicious unbalancing takes place – as a result the work's original mechanical format is fleshed over and the obvious constructional symmetry tends to disappear, to be replaced by a far more subtle architecture.

So far as allegorical writing is concerned, there is a tendency in creating character first to write down what a character represents. In a world demanding, as the Elizabethan theatre did, quick 'turnover' it is almost inevitable that characters, in a first draft, tend to be divided into 'good' and 'bad'; the subtleties come later. Clearly, if the characterization remains in this first state of creation, the emphasis will be less on individuality than on representativeness – a condition tending to the allegorical.

Some of the curiosities in the text of the play, however, may be due to the fact that Shakespeare's foul papers had, in part, been transcribed by a man who seems to have played a shadowy but important part in the preparation of the first Folio for printing. Ralph Crane was a scrivener who worked for the legal profession but is widely believed to have been responsible for transcribing *The Merry Wives of Windsor*, *The Two Gentlemen of Verona*, *Measure for Measure*, *The Winter's Tale* and *The Tempest* for the press. Crane's work may have gone beyond their transcribing, involving a deal of editing. The editor of a modern edition gives examples of Crane's work:[2]

'... "ha's" for both "he has" and "has" and "em" for "them", his curious use of apostrophes in phrases like "I'am" and "ye'have", and his fondness for hyphens colons and parentheses ...'

How far, then, an early draft, multiple authorship or scribal and editorial interferences are responsible for what seems like an unfinished play cannot be decided. *Timon of Athens* nevertheless lacks the sense of finish (even allowing for the exigencies of the Elizabethan printing trade) of the majority of Shakespeare's plays. The sub-plot is curiously separate from the main plot, not 'joining' with it until Act IV.3. The part played by women is minimal despite the hints that one or more were originally intended to be developed characters (particularly in IV.3 when Timon addresses one of Alcibiades' harlots by name). The language of the play, too, veers between able utterance and rough, uncut speech. The dramatic and psychological rightness of:

'They answer, in a joint and corporate voice,
That now they are at fall, want treasure, cannot

Do what they would, are sorry – you are honourable –
But yet they could have wish'd – they know not –
Something hath been amiss – a noble nature
May catch a wrench – would all were well! – tis pity –
And so, intending other serious matters,
After distasteful looks, and these hard fractions,
With certain half-caps, and cold-moving nods,
They froze me into silence.'   [II.2.204–213]

in which the Steward keenly impersonates the various excuses of
Timon's alleged friends, is counterbalanced by the thick-tongued
ineptitude of:

'They confess
Toward thee, forgetfulness too general, gross;
Which now the public body, which doth seldom
Play the recanter, feeling in itself
A lack of Timon's aid, hath sense withal
Of it own fail, restraining aid to Timon,
And send forth us to make their sorrowed render,
Together with a recompense more fruitful
Than their offence can weigh down by the dram;'   [V.1.142–9]

There are inconsistencies also in the character of Timon. We
become aware of him first less as a dramatic agent than as a kind of
emblem:

POET: Nay, sir, but hear me on.
All those which were his fellows but of late –
Some better than his value – on the moment
Follow his strides, his lobbies fill with tendance,
Rain sacrificial whisperings in his ear,
Make sacred even his stirrup, and through him
Drink the free air . . .
When Fortune in her shift and change of mood
Spurns down her late beloved, all his dependants,
Which labour'd after him to the mountain's top
Even on their knees and hands, let him sit down,
Not one accompanying his declining foot.   [I.1.80–91]

When Timon does take on a less emblematic guise what is dominant
in his character seems to be extravagance and gullibility. The scenes,
in which we meet the Athenian establishment of which he is a part,
first show us the sycophancy, expediency, calculated responses and
moral bankruptcy of that society, and then the self-indulgent, self-

deluding expense of wealth and spirit in 'a waste of shame' of Timon who, after all, is attempting to hold this society to him. Timon is tarred with the same brush that is found in such a society. He is defiled and his responses put him in a position to be defiled even more. His gullibility, for example, is stressed:

> I. LORD: Might but we have that happiness, my lord, that you would once use our hearts, whereby we might express some part of our zeal, we should think ourselves for ever perfect.
> TIMON: O, no doubt, my good friends, but the gods themselves have provided that I shall have much help from you. How had you been my friends else?' [I.2.80–6]

Apemantus is not fooled by the surrounding sycophancy –

> 'Would all those flatterers were thine enemies then, that then thou mightst kill'em . . .' [I.2.78–9]

Timon is, in fact, a long way from the mould out of which the great tragic heroes came. They all have a nobility at the outset or, at least, a justifiable proudness (as opposed to 'pride'). Their nobility is not a small thing; in Hamlet it rests upon moral complexity, intellectual and imaginative strength, in Lear it shows itself in will and mental courage, in Macbeth it is implicit in his military prowess. Timon is merely recklessly generous. It has been argued that the kind of largesse he displays would have been regarded as natural and desirable in a renaissance world. G.R. Hibbard amplifies this graphically:

> '. . . he goes in for the "conspicuous consumption" which became such a pronounced feature of upper-class life in England during the last twenty years or so of Elizabeth's reign and continued under her successor. There was a passion for building new and elaborate houses; men appeared at court with "whole manors on their backs" in the form of rich clothes; they put on lavish and spectacular shows for their sovereign;' and as a result 'the great frequently found themselves short of ready money, and proceeded to borrow it.'[3]

The fact that Timon is such a man does not, of course, render him noble nor does it mean that the majority of Elizabethans were prepared to condone behaviour which was meant to indicate to an astonished world that you had arrived. One of the reasons for the peculiarly contemporary tang to this play is the way in which it mirrors the headlong dash of Western civilization into the maw of materialism. Francis Bacon uttered warnings: 'Riches are for spending, and spending for honour and good actions – therefore extraordinary expense must be limited by the worth of the occasion',[4] and Timon suffers the fate which Bacon warns of – 'costly followers are not to be liked lest, while a man maketh his train longer, he make his wings shorter'.[5]

Timon of Athens is less a play than a kind of dramatized argument conducted by the protagonist with himself and with others. The outcome of the argument is unclear but it is certainly concerned with the despicable condition of man and the equivocal part played by wealth in man's life. The detritus of what might have been an unusual theme can be discerned in various parts of the play, and perhaps two particular elements are worth commenting upon. The first is to do with the attitudes taken up by Timon and others towards money and the second is the way in which the servant characters are presented.

The language of the play is full of references to buying and selling, to what is mercantile and assessable in material terms. Friendship is measured in terms of how it can be bought and kept by the giving of gifts. It is only when the means by which so-called friendship is thus obtained have disappeared that Timon begins to realize the falseness of the ground upon which he has stood. He rails, however, not about his own faults, but about mankind.

Behind this demonstration of the change in Timon there lies an attitude towards richness and poverty which, for Shakespeare, is given an unusual stress. At first, mainly through the servants, what is emphasized is the misery of poverty – 'Thus part we rich in sorrow, parting poor', but this shifts to an underlining of the misery of affluence. The Steward says,

'Who would not wish to be from wealth exempt,
Since riches point to misery and contempt?'   [IV.2.31–2]

The speech in which these lines occur is immediately followed by Timon's long harangue to himself in which he deplores the fact that it is mere chance which makes one man rich and another poor. These are curious sentiments to find written in an age when the acquisition of wealth and position was regarded as a most laudable ambition. Perhaps even more surprising is the sharp distinction made between the treatment of Timon by his alleged friends, and by his servants. The former are treacherous, the latter, particularly the Steward, are honourable. The distinction is almost mechanical in its appearance, as if the dramatist is bent on forcing a moral.

Indeed, the part played by servants in the play is unusually prominent. It would be very easy for a Marxist to read into this a justification of his own faith in the superior fidelity and honour of those who toil as opposed to those who merely acquire. Curiously, it would be equally easy for a Christian to regard the play as a demonstration of the words 'Blessed be the poor, for theirs is the kingdom of God'.

Its motivation and the precise meaning, its bitter, cynical, angry tone, uncharacteristically deep in pessimism, are discomforting, yet it is difficult to escape the feeling that Shakespeare's hand is in it. Perhaps the possessor of that hand had also been, for a time, weary of the world:

> '... My long sickness
> Of health and living now begins to mend,
> And nothing brings me all things.'   [V.1.184–186]

And such lines reflect, not only Timon's, but also the dramatist's own malaise of spirit.

Antony and Cleopatra

There is no play of Shakespeare's more effective in reducing considerations of dating, source, publication, to the status of annoying irritants than *Antony and Cleopatra*. To record that it very closely followed, some time in 1606/7, the writing of the great tragedies, that Shakespeare had clearly read Sir Thomas North's translation of the life of Marcus Antonius by Plutarch, that it was entered in the Stationers' Register in 1608 and first printed in the 1623 Folio seems curiously superfluous. The play, it can be claimed, hypnotizes the reader with its world of feeling, all else being either forgotten or seeming of no consequence. Certainly the miracle of transmutation that Shakespeare has effected with Plutarch's comparatively pedestrian narrative is a matter for wonder, and yet of Shakespeare's plays it is in some ways the least amenable to theatrical realization.

The dimensions of the geographical area which it covers, the variety of location, the number of characters of equally or almost equally strong dramatic potency, the particular qualities of its language, and the astonishing subtlety of its exploration of the 'psychology' of the two main characters – all these factors make its communication in theatrical terms extremely difficult. It is tempting to assert that there has never been a great or even very good performance of Cleopatra, and only rarely a satisfactory one of Antony. The imaginative power which has made her both physically beautiful but sometimes dowdy, overwhelming in passion but often petty in mind, utterly feminine both in the depth of her love and the width of her suspicions, guileful and self-indulgent, has, it might be suggested, created something too great for a mere actress to encompass. The irony is that Cleopatra is, of all Shakespeare's heroines, an extraordinarily faithful representation of what we call womankind, yet stage-history suggests that no actress has been capable of reaching the huge centre of the character.

To a lesser extent the same conclusion is true of Antony. In a sense there are two Antonys – one seen through Cleopatra's eyes and feelings, larger than ordinary life and beyond the reach of the human actor; the other we witness through Caesar's thoughts and words, who is very much within the range of realistic histrionic art. To present Shakespeare's Antony, both must exist, but they are basically incompatible.

Only a novel of the dimensions of *War and Peace* can give the sense of artistic elbow-room that is required by this story, in which the vastness of geography, the climacterics of great history, and the fathomless depths of great love are embodied and combined. The art of theatre which is the art of compression, and the art of acting which is the art of selection are, it may be claimed, inimical to the nature of the *Antony and Cleopatra* story. In *King Lear* Shakespeare carefully promotes a 'domesticity' of reference enabling the theatregoer to accommodate the huge areas of experience it encompasses; in *Macbeth* the relative restrictedness of location and a concentration on the protagonist suits dramatic communication well; again Hamlet's doubts and confusion, both mental and intuitive, find a startling counterpart in our own minds and feelings, and the traps into which the gullible Othello falls wait for any man. Needless to say, *Antony and Cleopatra* has scenes in which we almost painfully see the earth-bound feet of clay of the protagonists, but any attempt we might make to use this recognition in an effort to 'contain' the play is quite over-mastered by one overwhelming fact – the great mythical status of Cleopatra in the historical imagination of the Western world. Her image is far larger, more evocative, more tenacious than those of Julius Caesar, Antony, Richard III, and by her side Joan of Arc fades into mere human dimension, while Helen of Troy is a mere shadow. Henry V, alone, has something approaching Cleopatra's huge presence upon that stage in which reality is limelighted and turns into myth. So it may well be that J.B. Priestley's assertion that the only satisfactory realization of this play is in our individual imaginations is justified.[6]

While doubting whether the play is, ultimately, amenable to stage-production, one can but marvel at its psychological exactitide, its emotional subtlety, its verbal variety and its dramatic structure, and perhaps Shakespeare's greatest triumph is his close dove-tailing of language and character. This is noticeable on the first appearance of the two major characters, when an astonishingly large amount of information is given us about their personalities. Cleopatra in this mood is practical in a sense yet seeing beyond the immediate instant:

'Nay, hear them, Antony.
Fulvia perchance is angry.' [I.1.19–20]

She is calculating both about the larger matter which involves the possible return of Antony to Rome and about the quandary she intends putting him in – to stay or to leave. To a man drunk with love and lust there is nothing more exasperating than a cold peremptoriness in the face of his addresses. Her reply to his blandishments is like a cold douche. Antony says:

> 'Let's not confound the time with conference harsh;
> There's not a minute of our lives should stretch
> Without some pleasure now. What sport to-night?'   [I.1.45–7]

Cleopatra interjects:

> 'Hear the Ambassadors.'   [I.1.48]

There is in fact no scene in this play which does not give evidence of Shakespeare's most remarkable sense of the very close interdependence of character and language – what modern critical jargon calls 'psychological truth'. This kind of character-creation enables the reader or the audience to identify and recognize the smallest details of behaviour expressed in the speech, gesture, action of any character, either alone or with other characters. It is, in fact, a triumph of naturalistic writing, for it can only be identified by relating fictional character to what the reader or viewer of the play has experienced in actual life. That we should marvel at the 'psychological truth' of *Antony and Cleopatra* raises important considerations about the nature of the play, particularly in the context of Shakespeare's tragedies.

There is a sense in which, notably in plays like *King Lear*, *Macbeth*, and *Hamlet*, Shakespeare creates an imaginative truth rather than deriving one from actuality. We are convinced that, for example, Lear's or Hamlet's reactions and attitudes are 'truthful' because of the very potency with which they are communicated. It is only in the cool light of later appraisal that such-and-such an action or attitude seems, in fact, 'far-fetched', even ludicrous. In *Antony and Cleopatra*, however, the process is, in a way, reversed. Here it is the many small incidents of apparent actuality that catch at our imaginations, and examples of this fidelity to 'nature' abound. There is Cleopatra's interruption of Iras's and Charmian's speeches with the Soothsayer. She inquires for Antony, and her manner of address conjures up superbly an image of two lovers who have disagreed, so true is it to the beaten way of love where, in a quarrel, one partner seeks the other while pretending to want his or her absence:

CLEO: Saw you my lord?
ENOB: No lady.

328

CLEO: Was he not here?
ENOB: No, madam.
CLEO: He was disposed to mirth; but on the sudden
    A Roman thought hath struck him. Enobarbus!
ENOB: Madam?
CLEO: Seek him, and bring him hither. Where's Alexas?
ALEX: Here, at your service. My lord approaches.
CLEO: We will not look upon him.'   [I.2.75–84]

A little later in Act I, in the first scene of any length between the Egyptian Queen and the Roman general, Shakespeare offers a shrewd display of his knowledge of the female human heart. First, there is petulance – 'I am sick, and sullen'; then, a calculated avoidance of verbal contact with Antony – 'Help me away, dear Charmian'; then mockery and anger:

'None our parts so poor
But was a race of heaven. They are so still,
Or thou the greatest soldier of the world,
Art turn'd the greatest liar';

then assumed pride changing to a cold, wounding cynicism – 'Can Fulvia die?'. This is followed by an incitement to sympathy:

'Now I see, I see,
In Fulvia's death, how mine receiv'd shall be';

then a controlled contrition mixed with implied sexual passion;

'But Sir, forgive me,
Since my becomings kill me, when they do not
Eye well to you';

and finally, apparent acquiescence touched with dignity –

'Therefore be deaf to my unpitied folly,
And all the gods go with you'.   [I.3.36–99]

She has made her point and won.

This truth to human nature is by no means confined to the major characters. There is a notable example in Act II, in the meeting between Pompey, Antony and Lepidus, with Enobarbus present. Only in *Julius Caesar*, in the scenes between Cassius and Brutus, has Shakespeare rivalled this scene for its extraordinary fidelity to what we recognize instinctively as an imbalance between public faces and private hearts:

329

POM: No, Antony, take the lot:
  But first or last, your fine Egyptian cookery
  Shall have the fame. I have heard that Julius Caesar
  Grew fat with feasting there.
ANT: You have heard much.
POM: I have fair meanings, Sir.
ANT: And fair words to them.
POM: Then so much have I heard.   [II.6.62–8]

Can it be that Shakespeare's sense of naturalistic theatre was stirred more by his reading of Roman history than of Holinshed? Examples abound to suggest that he seemed to derive a sharper, starker, sense of actuality from Plutarch than from any other source. In the cautious meeting of the adversaries Enobarbus and Menas, the harsh direct language, the sly sounding-out of dispositions, the half-grudging mutual respect, are strongly reminiscent of the meeting between Martius and Aufidius in *Coriolanus*. Nothing in the English history plays is as graphically communicated except, perhaps, some of the battle scenes in the three parts of *Henry VI* – particularly those in which Queen Margaret appears.

This naturalness encompasses many verbal and emotional effects – anger, cynicism, wryness, duplicity, irony, and even, mainly through Enobarbus, a special kind of comedy. This comedy, however, has a bitter taste and comes from the soul of a man who has known better times and more faithful people, who has a sense of beauty and truth, but whose own warmth of personality (perhaps even at one time a kind of gaiety) has cooled.

ANT: Bear him ashore, I'll pledge it for him, Pompey.
ENO: Here's to thee, Menas!
MEN: Enobarbus, welcome.
POM: Fill till the cup be hid.
ENO: There's a strong fellow, Menas [*Pointing to the Servant who carries off Lepidus.*]
MEN: Why?
ENO: 'A bears the third part of the world, man; see'st not? [II.7.84–9]

The extent to which actual comment on the play, even when concerned with character, finds itself involved with language, is extraordinary. The truth is that the naturalism of the characters is in fact created by the kind of language used, with its short sharp phrases, conversational interruptions, interpolations, and questions. Yet the play is often written about as one of Shakespeare's most poetically expressed works. Granville Barker waxes eloquent on this:

> 'This is literally a sort of magic, by which the vibrations of emotion that the sound of the poetry sets up seem to enlarge its sense, and break the bounds of the theatre to carry us into the lost world of romantic history.'[7]

And even Shaw, though characteristically finding nothing of intellectual value in it, could not forbear to begin his review of a production in 1897 with the words, 'Shakespeare is so much the word-musician that mere practical intelligence ... cannot enable anybody to understand his works ... without the guidance of a fine ear.'[8]

Perhaps the most apt word to describe the effect of the poetic language of *Antony and Cleopatra* is 'unexpected'. We are, time and time again, surprised by joy at the lyrical splendour, the absolute rightness of so many phrases and the extent to which even single words seem to carry, even for Shakespeare, an unusual amount of lyric richness – '*plated* Mars', '*tawny* front', '*gilded* puddle', '*auguring* hope', '*waned* lip', '*discandy*', 'the rack *dislimns*', 'his *corrigible* neck', '*immoment*'. Words also frequently surprise with their reverberations as the variations upon the implications of the word 'Antony' testify. It is not so much that Antony is, at times, described as god-like by Cleopatra, bestriding oceans, cresting the world, dropping realms from his pockets like plates, or, less flatteringly, by Caesar as 'the abstract of all faults', but that at times 'Antony' seems to represent an entirely new, original, concept of creation.

> 'Sir, sometimes when he is not Antony,
> He comes too short of that great property
> Which still should go with Antony.' [I.1.57–8]

One speech in particular presents an unusual opportunity to catch a glimpse of the way in which Shakespeare's verbal imagination worked. His debt to Plutarch's lives has often been noted and discussed,[9] and the closeness of Enobarbus's description of Cleopatra to Thomas North's translation of Plutarch's own words has been commented upon. The specific details of this reworking, however, have received less attention.

Overall he attains two things. First, the speech is made viable for speaking and second, it is rendered into a superb embodiment of sensuous and sensual opulence. A sensitive actor will immediately recognize in the opening lines the remarkable imitation of the rhythmic movement of oars:

> '... the oars were silver,
> Which to the tune of flutes kept stroke, and made
> The water which they beat to follow faster,
> As amorous of their strokes.'   [II.2.198–200]

It is impossible to try to speak these lines without keeping in mind the rhythm of the oars. Yet at the same time the speech's movement and tone do not entirely ignore the realistic fact that it is spoken as a *reported* experience and phrases like 'it beggar'd all description' (not in Plutarch) and 'where we see' (not in Plutarch) give the speech a touch of colloquial immediacy.

Shakespeare's power over the sensual and sensuous effects is seen in his involvement of the five senses, applied with far greater concentration than in Plutarch/North. For example 'burnish'd', 'burn'd' (not in Plutarch), 'perfumed' (brought into much closer proximity with the sense of sight than in Plutarch), 'tune of flutes' (the half-rhyme is far more sensuous than Plutarch/North's 'music of flutes'), 'dimpled boys' (more sensuously evocative than Plutarch/North's 'pretty fair boys'), 'whose wind did seem/To glow the delicate cheeks which they did cool/And what they undid did', infinitely more vividly sensuous than 'with little fans in their hands, with the which they fanned wind upon her'. At the other end of the scale is the amount of hard, clipped naturalistic language; a mere wisp of a phrase from Plutarch sets Shakespeare off. 'There Cleopatra's women first brought Antoninus and Cleopatra to speak together and afterwards to sup and lie together' becomes:

> EROS: The Queen, my lord, the Queen!
> IRAS: Go to him, madam, speak to him.
>   Hers unqualified with very shame.
> CLEO: Well then, sustain me. O!
> EROS: Most noble sir, arise; the Queen approaches.
>   Her head's declin'd, and death will seize her but
>   Your comfort makes the rescue.
> ANT: I have offended reputation –
>   A most unnoble swerving.   [III.11.42–9]

In the case both of Enobarbus's speech and this – representative of the extremes of verbal manipulation in the play – the effect of the transmutation of Plutarch is to turn what seems reporting at a remove into much more direct communication, and what is verbally utilitarian into what is verbally evocative or active. In short, narrative prose becomes dramatic language.

The variation between extremes which is characteristic of the language is closely paralleled in the way in which Antony and Cleopatra are characterized. They veer, in their moods with each other, their relationships with others, and in the manner of their address, between the extremes of an almost raucous pettiness and a glorious magnificence; one moment they are slut and libertine, the next Empress and conqueror. This is of course a measure of their love – it is big enough, devious enough, too, to encompass both extremes, and even more, they come at times to stand for the whole concept of love itself. As observed, we have no doubt that they are obsessed by it, and we equally have no doubt that what we are witnessing is the total gamut of what love is and is capable of. Romeo and Juliet may convince us of the bitter-sweetness of romantic young love and its inevitable affiliations with tragedy or melodrama but it is Antony and Cleopatra who teach us not only what mature romantic love is but how it can be blind, mean, spiteful, generous, sad, passive, active, sexual, lyrical, physical and mental. This is no exaggeration – in fact, so vast are the implications that the modes both of tragedy and comedy are encompassed. There is, for example, something ludicrous about love's possessiveness as revealed in Cleopatra's silly pouting and there is something of comic pathos in Antony's precipitate following of Cleopatra from the naval battle.

The end, however, cannot be deemed anything but tragic – so much of human material that need not have been wasted is sacrificed. Croce says: 'The tragedy of *Antony and Cleopatra* is composed of the violent sense of pleasure, in its power to bind and to dominate, coupled with a shudder at its abject effects of dissolution and death'.[10] This is especially true if we recall Bradley's phrase – 'Its splendour dazzles us; but when the splendour vanishes, we do not mourn, as we mourn for the love of Othello or Romeo that a thing so bright and good should die. And the fact that we mourn so little saddens us'.[11] We cannot mourn for them, even admire them, for they have been wilfully prodigal, and

'The expense of Spirit in a waste of shame
Is lust in action . . .'

Yet in watching their downfall we are sad not only for their expense of spirit – but for all mankind's.

333

One of the most impressive qualities of the play is the manner in which it is able to show the 'guilt' of the two lovers without making them insignificant. Nothing could be further from the truth than Shaw's remark that 'Shakespeare gives us a faithful picture of the soldier broken down in debauchery, and the typical wanton in whose arms such men perish'.[12] If Cleopatra is merely wanton, what is Cressida, and if Antony is just a broken-down debauchee, what then is Thersites, or, indeed, Pandarus? There is, in fact, a remarkable consistency in the delineation of Antony from *Julius Caesar* to this play. In the former his greatness and his weakness are shown at source – he is courageous, wilful, politically unstable, intellectually and emotionally unsteady, but not without fidelity, decisiveness and nobility. These qualities are carefully disposed throughout *Antony and Cleopatra*, right through to the scene where he announces Fulvia's death to Enobarbus, a scene in which his will and dignity can be clearly seen. This scene is remarkable, too, for its demonstration of Shakespeare's superb ability to create dramatic tension with a ruthless economy of words:

ANT: Fulvia is dead.
ENO: Sir?
ANT: Fulvia is dead.
ENO: Fulvia?
ANT: Dead.   [I.2.151–5]

The Antony of yore who could use his tongue to effect in the funeral speech over Julius Caesar and in his dealings with Brutus, is still present in the older man. When he meets Pompey in the presence of Caesar there is a goading quality in the lines:

'The beds i'th'East are soft; and thanks to you,
That call'd me timelier than my purpose hither;
For I have gained by 't.'   [II.6.50–2]

and Pompey trying to emulate him seems awkward by comparison:

'But, first or last, your fine Egyptian cookery
Shall have the fame. I have heard that Julius Caesar
Grew fat with feasting there.'   [II.6.62–4]

The reply given by Antony is one of those which are typical of a dramatist able to give his actor both the hint and the freedom to accompany words with a look, a gesture, a nuance of tone, a pause even:

'You have heard much.'   [II.6.65]

And the reader is left to guess what accompanies it from Pompey's rightly apprehensive reply:

'I have fair meanings Sir.'   [II.6.66]

Such speeches and such language as this are constant reminders of the vivid reality of the political, military and personal background of the play. Indeed, it might be said that if the transports of the love of Antony and Cleopatra had been considerably muted, this play would still have been one of the most effective essays in political manoeuvring. Yet, time and again, our eyes are dazzled so that this sharp background has albeit the quality of a mirage. If in the end that love is judged as profligate, it is profligacy on a gigantic scale, accompanied by a music and a passion which the stage, after nearly four hundred years, has yet to recapture and which the imagination can only wonder at.

Pericles

In matters concerning what may be called the 'feel' of a text the instinct of the sensitive actor often seems (and sometimes can be shown to be) more reliable than that of the director or the critical commentator for he is in the long run more alive to changes of rhythm, of pace, of vocabulary. It is he who knows better than anyone else whether a text or part of a text is viable for stage-communication, whether it is built for the actor's mouth and is not just a literary attempt to be dramatic. The sensitive actor can in fact read the temperature of language with far greater accuracy than most.

It is because the actor's intuition (nourished by acquired skills) is so often seen to be correct in this respect that, faced with the kind of problem presented by Pericles, one is inclined to make doubly certain that the weight of the actor's evidence is placed squarely in the scales with what has been discovered or assumed or supposed or deviously constructed by scholars, commentators and directors.

Pericles is a suspect play because it does not appear in the first Folio (1623). Questions about the reasons for this are given extra point by the existence of a quarto text (in a very corrupt condition) printed in 1609 with Shakespeare's name on the title-page. Heminges and Condell, the begetters of the Folio, presumably had their reasons for omitting it. A natural conclusion would be that the ascription to Shakespeare of its authorship on the title-page of the quarto is a lie, or that there is insufficient of his hand in the play to merit putting it into a collection so lovingly dedicated to celebrating his genius. A lurking possibility that there was no room for it in the Folio has no evidence either way.

The quarto text is bad. It is mislineated, apparent verse appears as prose, some lines are almost impossible to understand. There is no doubt that a good deal of what is unsatisfactory about it is the result of rank bad workmanship by three known compositors. However, what is perhaps more interesting to students of Shakespeare's plays as dramas rather than as printer's copy, is the nature of one other unsatisfactory feature, that, bluntly, it is difficult to believe that Shakespeare wrote the first two acts of *Pericles*.[13] The construction is clumsy, the characterization is wayward, the language veers from the awkwardly convoluted to the banally pompous. However much it is necessary to beware of the traps of subjective impressionism it cannot be denied that the reaction of the majority of readers of Shakespeare's plays upon reading the first two acts is to declare that this does not sound like Shakespeare:

Antiochus from incest liv'd not free;
For which the most high gods not minding longer
to withhold the vengeance that they had in store,
due to his heinous capital offence,
even in the height and pride of all his glory,
when he was seated in a chariot
of inestimable value, and his daughter with him;
a fire from heaven came and shrivell'd up
those bodies, even to loathing ...   [II.4.2–10]

The various explanations for the state of the text may be briefly outlined: first, that it is an incomplete rewriting by Shakespeare of a play by some other dramatist; it is suggested that the last part kindled his imagination more than the first, so that he began at Act III, but, after completing up to and including Act V, he ran out of time and Acts I and II were left in their pristine mediocrity; second, that Shakespeare could not meet the director's deadline and a collaborator, George Wilkins, was engaged to work on the first two acts[14] (why Shakespeare should have reversed what is reasonably regarded as the normal process of writing is not explained); third, that the play is Shakespeare's half-completed version of the first draft of a play of his own composition – but again, why begin at the end?; fourth, in an ingenious and very plausible explanation, P.W. Edwards argues that two reporters attempted to reconstruct an original performance from memory, but that the reporter of Acts I and II was sketchy in recollection, while the reporter of Acts III, IV and V was familiar with the text. He concludes however that Shakespeare was the sole author.[15]

The possibility of another, less expert hand than Shakespeare's in the first two acts seems, however, to be an explanation closest to the actor's intuition about the play. A distinguished player of Pericles – Ian Richardson – recalls the jolting effect of the sudden transition from the generally banal verbal structure of Acts I and II to the infinitely superior last three acts. He suddenly found himself with language not only more compatible to his own experience of the true Shakespeare timbre but far more amenable to speaking.

The proponents of the idea that, at this time of his life, Shakespeare had already begun to be obsessed by the theme of reconciliation which, it is claimed, dominates the last plays, suggest that Shakespeare, perhaps overseeing Wilkins's work, saw the possibilities of the story of Pericles as an embodiment of the theme and persuaded Wilkins to allow him to finish the play.

Speculation, however, can become rife, and perhaps the more profitable course is to consider the kind of experience which the reader and the theatregoer receive from the play, for it can be, without question, very theatrically effective, and for three simple reasons. First, because it not only gives the opportunity for, but quite obviously demands the use of, spectacular visual effects. The stage-direction indicting masques or dumb-shows are copious, suggesting that the play was intended to cater for the new-discovered appetite of the early seventeenth century for the visually ornate. Indeed, it may be that some form of dumb-show is intended to be enacted even at times when it is not specifically designated in a stage-direction. The speeches of Gower – the rather quaint chronicler – with their occasional use of antique or quasi-antique words like 'killen', 'haps', 'ne' and 'perishen', could well have been accompanied by dumb-show which acted out the related narrative. There is testimony to this: for example (Act II) when Gower's speech is interrupted by a stage-direction specifying the details of a dumb-show:

'Enter at one door Pericles, talking with Cleon; all the Train with them. Enter, at another door, a Gentleman with a letter to Pericles; Pericles shows the letter to Cleon. Pericles gives the Messenger a reward, and knights him. Exit Pericles at one door, and Cleon at another.'   [II.1 between 15 and 20]

That this large amount of visual drama in the play was intended to exploit the resources for lighting effects possible (however crude by our standards) at the private Blackfriars theatre is contrary to the evidence on the title-page of the 1609 quarto, where it says the play:

'... hath been divers and sundry times acted by his Maiesty's Servants, at the Globe on the Bank-side.'

Its second theatrical quality, most noticeable in the first two Acts, is its language. Doubts about the presence of Shakespeare's hand must, surely, be at least a little shaken by the dramatic and poetic potency not only of a number of single lines but of whole speeches and scenes. The gold in this play, standing out in thin but unmistakeable bands amidst the dross, is not counterfeit:

'Must cast thee, scarcely coffin'd, in the ooze;
Where, for a monument upon thy bones,
The aye-remaining lamps, the belching whale

And humming water must overwhelm thy corpse,
Lying with simple shells . . .'   [III.1.61–4]

The language of the play is indeed a stange, heady mixture of the kind
of wry, almost fugitive lyricism of some speeches in *The Tempest*,
and the tight, inflexible, compressed, almost staccato language which
so characterizes *The Winter's Tale*. Such speeches as this, accompanied by music:

'The music there! I pray you give her air.
Gentlemen,
This Queen will live; nature awakes; a warmth
Breathes out of her. She hath not been entranc'd
Above five hours. See how she gins to blow
Into life's flower again.'   [III.2.96–100]

are counterpointed, dramatically and tonally, by the language of the
brothel-scenes. Stage-directions, in fact, indicating music either as
accompaniment to speeches or solo are as prevalent in the play as
those indicating masque or dumb-show, and the language is, for the
greater part of the play, attended most closely by either visual or
aural accompaniment. The very nature of the language plus this
accompaniment gives the whole action a particularly affecting
atmosphere of sadness – as if it were reaching out for something
affirmative, that is just out of grasp, fugitive.

The third theatrical merit of the play is the magnificent realism of
the brothel-scenes and the touching sensitivity with which the final
reconciliations are depicted. Perhaps nowhere else, with the possible
exception of *Measure for Measure*, has Shakespeare limned so vivid a
portrayal of the dark underbelly of society. The remarkable feature of
the brothel-scenes is that they are not only naturalistically stark in
detail but that they fulfil several subtle functions in the play's theme.
Whenever Shakespeare has the lower orders to deal with – and this is
particularly noticeable in the two parts of *Henry IV* and in *Measure
for Measure* – his language always acquires, to a degree, a kind of wry
wit. The malapropisms, the inventiveness, the sly conceits of the
language of the nether society are all grist to his mill. Here the verbal
texture of the brothel scenes is a marvellous series of variations upon
a comic naturalism of language and behaviour. Boult avers that one of
his customers is 'pouped', Pandar having assured him that 'The poor
Transilvanian is dead that lay with the little baggage'. The ghost of
the verbally tipsy Pistol struts once more, fleetingly, in Boult's
almost heroic assertion that once Marina's bodily details are known
to the populace 'performance shall follow'. There is a kind of

colourful splendour, like that of an oil slick on a wet muddy road, in Boult's description of how his account of Marina's attributes affected the brothel clientèle.

'Faith, they listened to me, as they would have hearkened to father's testament. There was a Spaniard's mouth so wat'red that he went to bed to her very description.' [IV.2.99–102]

And what infinite heart-ache lies behind his affronted cry:

'Worse and worse mistress, she has here spoken holy words to the Lord Lysimachus.' [IV.6.131–2]

The brothel-scenes minister very securely, if obliquely, to the play's theatrical development. Many critics and commentators who purport to find in the play a very determined preoccupation with the themes explored in the last plays – the concern with reconciliation, peace, concord, the compatibility, or otherwise, of artifice and reality, the healing virtue of youth, the wisdom of age – tend to overstress their presence in the Pericles/Marina relationship. In fact some of them are more strongly implied in the brothel-scenes. Certainly from *Pericles* onwards the plays have happy endings and virtue is seen explicitly rather than implicitly to be a more potent force than vice. Shakespeare is no longer so much concerned with showing our eyes and grieving our hearts, rather he seems intent to show that all manner of things shall be well. Symbolic or ritualistic embodiments of this (often claimed to be the dominant modes of communication of the last plays) are all very well, but the trouble with symbolism and ritualism on stage is that an audience is hardly ever prepared to take them as seriously as other modes of presentation – particularly naturalism. Mankind cannot bear very much unreality and, in the theatre, it is naturalism that elicits credibility. As a result, the implications of the brothel-scenes are much more likely to be taken to heart and head by an audience than the symbolic undertones of masque or dumb-show, and those implications are certain and clear. The chief one is that the power of virtue is immense. It is noticeable that Marina goes to the brothel still a virgin – the sailors testify to this and Shakespeare takes pains to assure us of her innocence in every sense of the word. The effect of this innocent presence in the brothel-scenes reveals naturalistically to us the power of virtue by showing us what happens to anyone who comes into Marina's presence. What is remarkable is that Marina is portrayed as being so virtuous without seeming priggish.

The other, and connected, implication of the brothel-scene concerns the pervasive quality of virtue – it spreads as swiftly, once its power is released, as the pox. There is no question but that Marina is the source of that power, that she is in a way a 'healing' agent, a kind of benediction, in this society, and presented any way other than naturalistic, that potency and persuasive force would have run the risk of seeming incredible. In the context of the raw brothel-world it becomes and remains truly natural, much more natural than Helena's.

Marina's triumph, both as character and chief embodiment of this theme of the play, in the brothel-scenes, makes what she is later to achieve for her father more easily acceptable. Her ability to transform his despair to exultation, to return a love he thought lost, and virtually to restore his life, is credible because the brothel-scenes have 'naturalized' both her and what she stands for.

So we are prepared for the play's astonishing final assault on any lingering doubts as to its truly, though intermittently, Shakespearean excellence. The recognition scene between Pericles and Marina is one of the most wonderful of this nature that Shakespeare ever wrote. It outdoes, in depth of feeling, the meeting and recognition of Sebastian and Viola, of Rosalind and Orlando, and its emanation of filial and paternal love has far more tenderness than is apparent between Prospero and Miranda. Tenderness, great joy, awe and total love are its hallmarks. Despite learned commentaries about symbolic meaning, the effect of this scene is *not* on the head; it does *not* cause us to speculate upon Shakespeare's 'theme of reconciliation', rather it makes us *feel* what it is to have loss amended and love restored, and that effect is gained by a calm mastery of technique. The questions and answers of the language are like an exercise in logic, but the quiet repetition of the name Marina, her own completely matter-of-fact statements counterpointed by Pericles's amazed and dawning realization, the musical subtlety of the language, make the quiet reasonableness of the scene into a sort of hymn of praise and joy:

> '... Oh come hither,
> Thou that beget'st him that did thee beget:
> Thou that wast born at sea, buried at Tharsus,
> And found at sea again. O Helicanus,
> Down on thy knees, thank the holy gods as loud
> As thunder threatens us. This is Marina' [V.1.193–8]

The 'theme' lies, in fact, buried inside this wonderful ceremony of recognition. Pericles's faith in the gods is restored and his belief in the eventual triumph of virtue is renewed. He hears the music of the spheres – the sounds of a higher order of reality. For if, indeed, there is anything which insistently, explicitly or obviously links this play with the last great play – *The Tempest* – it is the part played by music, and not just the verbal music which, very intermittently in Pericles and consistently in *The Tempest*, haunts our ears, but the indications of actual musical accompaniment to the action. Music not only gives us a sense of an 'otherness' but, as Shakespeare often recorded, soothes the savage breast of anger, hate, jealousy, envy. Perhaps, too, it may be suggested that he was coming also to realize that all art, finally, aspires to the condition of harmony.

Coriolanus

Coriolanus, written not long after *Antony and Cleopatra*, differs conspicuously from it in language, theme, attitude to character and focus on the political elements. Nevertheless, its genre as a Roman play and its dating (1607–8) suggest that it was written to exploit a success with the earlier play. T.J.B. Spencer in his edition of North's version of Plutarch remarks that 'we may assume from the evidence of his close following of Plutarch, that Shakespeare had a high estimate of his literary and historical merit'. It is, however, characteristic of Shakespeare that, having gained the solid basis of his play from the Roman chronicler, he bears down upon the mere shadow of a character in the original and creates Menenius.

The play has never been popular with audiences or actors, perhaps because its protagonist is, in Anne Barton's words, 'fundamentally imperceptive, even stupid, as no protagonist in Shakespeare's tragedies had been before'.[16] It is, however, not quite as starkly simple as this. It is not merely that actors are daunted by the unsympathetic role but that Coriolanus must be presented as both unattractive and sympathetic to an audience. He is obviously very blameworthy but neither the play nor the character can be easily borne unless they show some indications of approaching the tragic frontier for, indeed, both are very close to tragedy. The political chicanery, blindness, wisdom, courage, the personal stupidities, loves and hates, rise and fall with a huge rhythmic inevitability which has as its high point such scenes as the fable of the belly, the rejection and banishment of Coriolanus, the meeting with Aufidius, the curse on Rome, Coriolanus's meeting with his family, and his death. In these scenes we cannot but be aware of the way in which our responses are being called upon to waver between scorn and pity. The actor's problem is to enter into this rhythm and to be sensitive to the balance between the two contrary responses required of the audience. There is something else too which adds to his difficulties. Coriolanus has far more obviously than in any other great Shakespeare tragic protagonist, a flaw of character in the Aristotelian sense – that of mulish pride – which assures his downfall. A case can be made out for the existence of some kind of flaw in each of the tragic heroes, but in none of the other tragedies is it presented in so raw a manner, nor is it so graphically in evidence from the very first appearance of the character:

'... What's the matter, you dissentious rogues
That, rubbing the poor itch of your opinion,
Make yourselves scabs?'   [I.1.162–4]

The communication of this harsh simplicity is, in itself, not the
actor's greatest problem, although it does increase the problem of
credibility in the characterization, complicating the achievement of
balance between scorn and sympathy. Actors have differed in their
ways of facing up to the problems of the role but it is Laurence
Olivier's second and mature version, in 1959 at the Royal Shakespeare Theatre, that stands head and shoulders above all other
interpretations in the twentieth century. His triumph was the result
of his grasping firmly, without compromise, the simple fact of the
'flaw', without evading the attendant difficulties. This Coriolanus
was scorned by the audience for his arrogance, irony, conceit, but
pitied for his vulnerability, his self-knowledge, his brute courage,
and particularly for the agonizing gap between his own banal values
(patrician and raw) and those of most of his adversaries.

Coriolanus's flaw completely dominates both his character and
the action of the play – even the Volscian determination to make war
against Rome seems motivated more by Aufidius's violent and jealous
reaction to Coriolanus's insolent pride than by anything else. The
political and civil dissensions which grip Rome, although to some
extent attributable to plebeian under-privilege and patrician over-
privilege, are expressed as direct reactions to Coriolanus's personality
and when he leaves Rome the tribunes of the people stress the peace
that has resulted since his departure.

His pride is not simple, though its demonstration is stark. It has
four aspects of unequal force. First is his pride in his patrician status –
it is more this than anything else which incites the fierce reactions
from the plebs and their tribunes and which informs his attitude
towards them. It is pride in birth and blood – an inborn sense of
scutcheon – which makes him naturally believe that the plebs are of a
lesser order of being than him or his class. It governs his political
outlook, if indeed he can be said to have one that is stable enough to
be recognized – for of all the major characters in Shakespeare's
'political' plays, Coriolanus is the least given to, or capable of, the
formation of political principles. He acts upon passionate compulsion,
being 'ill-schooled in bolted language'. Menenius knows his measure:

'... His heart's in his mouth;
What his breast forges, his tongue must vent;

And being angry, does forget that ever
He heard the name of death.'   [III.1.257–60]

On one occasion, during the first campaign against the Volsci,
Coriolanus takes second place to another patrician – Cominius. The
reaction of the people's tribunes to this tends to suggest that
Coriolanus's pride is not only fierce, but shifty. He has, the tribunes
say, submitted to Cominius's command so that:

> '. . . what miscarries
> Shall be the general's fault . . .'   (I.1.263–4]

But there is no proof of this. Indeed Coriolanus accepts his place,
makes no aspersions on Cominius's generalship, only craving permission to set his wing of the army opposite Aufidius and his
Antiates.

Aufidius may complain, after Coriolanus's defection to the
Volsci, that:

> 'He bears himself more proudlier,
> Even to my person, than I thought he would
> When first I did embrace him;'   [IV.7.8–10]

but he has to admit that Coriolanus has never been otherwise, and
indeed it appears to be the sheer force of Coriolanus's personality
that accounts for his popularity with the Volscian forces:

> 'I do not know what withcraft's in him, but
> Your soldiers use him as the grace fore meat,'   [IV.7.2–3]

Coriolanus's patrician pride is, it would seem, in-built. There is no
evidence of its being deviously or slyly employed. If it were, surely
the innumerable imprecations he hurls at the despised plebs, his
simple sense of social and political superiority, would not be
expressed with such naive candour:

> 'You common cry of curs, whose breath I hate
> As reek o'th' rotten fens, whose loves I prize
> As the dead carcasses of unburied men
> That do corrupt my air ——'   [III.3.122–5]

Here the second factor of his pride must be noted. Coriolanus's
scorn for the plebs, his fierce berating of his own soldiers for faint-
heartedness outside Corioli, his ability to win Cominius's admiration

and that of the Volsci, the grudging admiration of Aufidius, are all the result of the scorching force of Coriolanus's martial courage and ability, and his indomitable pride in it. Martial valour excites his fidelity and praise:

> 'They have a leader,
> Tullus Aufidius, that will put you to't
> I sin in envying his nobility;
> And were I anything but what I am,
> I would wish me only he.' [I.1.226–30]

Martial cowardice arouses his anger. He regards military virtues and achievements as o'ertopping all others, and cannot abide those who have not experienced them. But he is not merely proud of military achievement, he is also courageous. All recognize this – there is nothing false about it. Its worst effect is to push him into self-dramatization:

> 'Sir, praise me not;
> My work hath yet not warm'd me. Fare you well;
> The blood I drop is rather physical
> Than dangerous to me.' [I.5.16–19]

Thus far, then, we have the portrait of a man of limited intelligence, immense pride, social arrogance, and physical bravery; his emotional responses are fierce but, on the whole, simple; his sense of what constitutes a fair and healthy society primitive. He is only happy when active and despises those who do not feel as he does. He is, in short, absolutely a military man, with all the virtues and vices that go along with the military mind. He could not be less than a leader and his knowledge of this increases his vices rather than nurturing his virtues, but, if he were less, he would probably be set down as a decent enough chap, a bit unpredictable, but reliable in a tight corner. It is the compounding of his worship of the martial and his pride in blood that makes Caius Martius so dangerous.

In this context the ritual needed for his election to a consulship obviously goes against the grain. A Pericles, a Cominius, a Brutus would not look ridiculous in the garb of humility. Coriolanus does and this, while it might not excite our pity, should uncover our sympathetic understanding. All the entreaties of his friends and his mother for him to bend with the wind a little and to be 'mild' (a word spoken by him, we may believe, as if it gave him toothache) in the brilliantly written, ironic and sardonic scenes of persuasion, are

346

against everything that he is. It is not so much that he is behaving like a petulant child, as that what he is being asked to do is totally inimical to his personality; he is reacting less by mood than by principle. It is in such situations that the actor's problem of balancing sympathy and scorn in the audience is at its most crucial.

It is in the light of the, for him, unnatural posture into which he is forced that the third element in Coriolanus's pride must be seen. He has tremendous, sometimes self-conscious pride in being regarded as a man of honour, of truth, and this, again, is military in expression. Indeed, Coriolanus may be said to be the living embodiment of another army man's constant preoccupation with a 'good' name – Iago – but where Iago's honesty is deliberate deception, Coriolanus cannot stand to have his word or his point of view doubted. It is rarely remembered by commentators how consistent Coriolanus is, unwavering in his attitude – any movement away from his own rigid standards appals him:

> 'It is a part
> That I shall blush in acting.' [II.2.143]

he says of the ritual preceding consulship; and when his mother asks him to relent, it is as if she had asked him to pay traitor to himself.

Finally he has the pride of a patrician born, fashioning himself upon what he believes his condition to be and becoming a complete copy of his mother. Volumnia's conception of the meaning of life and death is bounded by ideas of honour and shame – it is honourable, for example, to have progeny, shameful if they are not brave. Life is crowned in the possession of such sons as Martius, enhanced by the extent of his bravery, and death is acceptable provided honour has been satisfied. If Coriolanus is Shakespeare's clearest depiction of the military man, then Volumnia is his most penetrating study of the military wife and mother. Her pride in Martius is equalled by her hope for her grandson; she is accustomed to being obeyed; she makes war sound like the Olympic games:

> VOL: O, he is wounded, I thank the gods for't.
> MENEN: So do I too, if it be not too much. Brings 'a victory in his pocket? the wounds become him.
> VOL: On's brows, Menenius, he comes the third time home with the oaken garland. [II.1.113–17]

She is more cool-headed than her son and her dignity seems the greater because its expression is more controlled.

One of the most marked and affecting qualities of Coriolanus's immediate family environment is its human quality. Volumnia is not merely an element in the plot – she is very much a mother, and her kind of motherhood contrasts strongly with that of Valeria, who, with so little to say, bears witness to the sickening reality of her own situation. She has married into this family, but is incapable of responding to the mores which dominate her mother-in-law and husband, is fearful for his safety to the exclusion of admiration for his exploits and, a last straw, has a son whose destiny and character are, without a doubt, to be like those of his father. The glimpses of the father in the child are in themselves chillingly real:

> VAL: I saw him run after a gilded butterfly; and when he caught it he
> let it go again, and after it again, and over and over he comes, and
> up again, catch'd it again; or whether his fall enrag'd him, or how
> 'twas, he did so set his teeth and tear it. O, I warrant, how he
> mammock'd it!
> VOL: One on's father's moods.
> VAL: Indeed, la, 'tis a noble child.   [I.3.60–7]

The Volumnia/Coriolanus relationship is one of Shakespeare's most impressive and penetrating studies of mother/son relationship. His plays abound in father/daughter relationships, both where the father is still living and, as in the case of Olivia and Rosalind, where he is dead, and most end in reconciliation of some kind. However in both *Hamlet* and *Coriolanus* the impression given is of a potentially destructive tension between mother and son. If we think of Gertrude and Volumnia, we think of actual or potential destructive love:

> COR: O mother, mother!
> What have you done? Behold, the heavens do open,
> The gods look down, and this unnatural scene
> They laugh at.   [V.3.183–5]

In fact, even in a play where the mother/son relationship connection is not greatly developed, there is still a strong impression that the personality of a petulant, self-indulgent, headstrong son is the result of maternal care which is disastrously misguided. The Countess of Rosillion and Bertram in *All's Well That End's Well* are small but significant examples of this.

Because the personality of Coriolanus is all-pervading in dictating the action of the play, the other characters have only the status of isolated portraiture. No other character measures up to him dramatically, but although Menenius, Cominius, the Tribunes and Aufidius do not have Coriolanus's dramatic ubiquity, they are nevertheless superb portraiture.

Menenius, who is often played simply as a man of gentle honour, a wise statesman, liberal in his political and social views, a kind of cross-bencher, is so much more than this. In some ways he is the most devious of Rome's politicians. In his 'belly' speech he treats the plebs like recalcitrant children and seems like a father-figure, but he regards them with a contempt, chillier in expression and no less intense, than Coriolanus's. He is something of a back-biter:

'Nay, these are almost thoroughly persuaded;
For though abundantly they lack discretion,
Yet are they passing cowardly.'   [I.1.199–201]

He appears to be a man of peace, but like Volumnia, Cominius and other patricians, the bloodthirsty side of Roman 'virtus' means as much to him as it does to them and he is a good mediator, conducting negotiations with wit, even if his heart is wholly with Caius Martius Coriolanus. Coriolanus's treatment of him breaks him, and although he is curiously Janus-like, we cannot help but respect him, even like him a little. Like the Duke in *A Midsummer Night's Dream* and even, perhaps, somewhat like Prospero, he is basically a man of wisdom and in a city dominated by passion he seems like an enbodiment of civilized rational behaviour. Perhaps his presence is the more appealing to us because his weaknesses are so apparent, for he lacks the self-regard to be dangerous and, in a politician, whatever else his foibles may be, this can be most endearing.

The main opposition to him is represented by the two tribunes of the people, in that they stand for interests which are alien to both him and his class. They are not a mob in the sense that the plebs of *Julius Ceasar* are – mindless, ruthless, uncontrolled. They are similar to the plebs of that play only when passion seems to be governing them and to this extent they reflect one of Shakespeare's strongest antipathies – his hatred of social groupings motivated by unreason. But he makes a sharp distinction between the personality of a group, a mass, which he always depicts unfavourably, and that of its constituent parts. From the group in *Coriolanus* emerges a third citizen with shrewd aspirations for leadership, a first citizen burdened by an underde-veloped moral sense:

'For mine own part,
When I said banish him, I said 'twas pity.'   [IV.6.140–2]

and a second citizen who, when the emotional temperature is low, is not without some semblance of rational thinking:

> 'What he cannot help in his nature, you account a vice in him. You
> must in no way say he is covetous.'   [I.1.39–41]

It can scarcely be claimed as some have done that this play illustrates 'the wonderfully philosophic impartiality of Shakespeare's politics'.[17] What he is really depicting, in so far as he is here concerned with political faction, is the pathetic political naïveté, even primitiveness, of both parties. The patricians behave like the beleaguered headmasters or mistresses of a rebellious approved school, while the plebeians and their representatives act like recalcitrant children.

The existence of the two tribunes of the people however gives a deeper perspective to the scene. Not since his apprentice days, when he wrote *Henry VI*, had Shakespeare depicted individuals who had acquired, either by election or force, representative status. Jack Cade is admittedly an extreme case, but he speaks for those he represents – or at least they believe he does. The tribunes, on face value, are 'democratically' elected, but they are subtly shown as gradually detaching themselves from a strictly representative posture and adopting a policy of self-aggrandizement. The implications of this are deep. Shakespeare, though he may depict the patricians as politically effete, spares no pains in showing us one major virtue – their courage, Cominius, Volumnia and Menenius being adequate testimonies to this. On the other hand there is nothing mitigating in the characters of the tribunes – indeed their cowardice is dwelt upon. As the action proceeds, it seems to be suggested that there is something unnatural about plebeian representation – as though some law of political nature had been offended. Patrician rule, however effete, appears more natural and although individual patricians may be criticised, the principle of their superiority and status seems basically inviolate. Not so with the plebs, Shakespeare relentlessly stalks their leaders through a process of dramatic self-revelation, eventually reducing them to cowardly unprincipled self-seekers, and by the end, political representation by the plebs appears as a temporary aberration.

The covertness of their personalities is reflected in the number of times the tribunes are left alone on stage, speaking to one another – where a sense of frightened conspiracy is created:

> BRU: I do not like this news.
> SIC: Nor I.
> BRU: Let's to the Capitol.   [IV.6.158–60]

The old and prevailing notion of order, of the chain of being, of each element in the molecular structure of society having its ordained and unalterable place, is still hauntingly present. Shakespeare was probably throughout his life a believer in the idea of maintaining the status quo – though not necessarily an admirer of its specific representatives at any given time or place. The uniqueness, the quality and quantity of the attention he pays to the lower orders of society should not lead to the assumption that he believed a status quo should be altered to admit greater political power for the common people (either Roman or Elizabethan). Shakespeare may have been middle class by birth, plebeian by sympathy, but birth, instinct and sympathy were all at the behest of a dominating intellectual and moral certainty about the validity of the ordained pattern of the universe, and his stance in this matter is nowhere more firm than in this play.

Another aspect of the portraiture of the plebs and their tribunes is less evidence of the persistence of a major theme in Shakespeare's plays than of the exciting relevance of much of his vision to our own contemporary world, and the play, as we witness the shifty inefficiency of political leaders both high and low, comes to seem ironically reflective of what, in the latter part of the twentieth century, has emerged so starkly in the political life of so many countries – that the norms in political thought and action are *not* nobility, wisdom, fairness, imagination, but crabbed self-aggrandizement. It is because of this that Brutus (*Julius Ceasar*) seems such an odd man out in the vast array of Shakespeare's political portraits.

The graphic quality of the play's communication, reflected in the language which (for Shakespeare) is unusually functional, spareribbed, is given an additional sense of immediacy by the status of the stage directions in the text of this play in the first Folio. They are copious and fascinating in their possible implications. The Folio text is generally regarded as from an author's copy – in other words not a prompter's copy, but a fairly carefully prepared manuscript, or a fair copy of one, from Shakespeare's own hand. If this is so then the stage directions are Shakespeare's and not those of a prompter. Both W. W. Greg[18] and George Hibbard[19] suggest that the reason for the unusual amount of directions by the author in a manuscript is that Shakespeare was on the verge of retirement, may already have left London, and was therefore out of contact with the day-to-day affairs of the theatre; he consequently put into his copy an unusual amount of specific detail, which normally would have been conveyed by word of mouth in the theatre. Whether this is true or not – and it is very problematical considering our lack of knowledge about Shakespeare's retirement plans – what is amenable to consideration is Hibbard's claim that '*many* of the directions are too indefinite to serve for performance' and that some 'even have a distinct literary quality about them'.[20]

The sensitivity of scholars to Shakespeare's text is often not matched by any real awareness of its relevance in theatre terms. If the stage directions of Coriolanus are examined not by themselves in isolation, but as they exist *with the dialogue of the characters before and after them*, such conclusions emerge as quite erroneous. Very few of them are, in fact, 'indefinite'. In any case his example of 'indefiniteness' – 'enter seven or eight citizens' (II.3) – is itself unconvincing, for with crowd scenes this kind of notation is usual, even in theatre today, and even in a late stage of rehearsal, let alone in the author's manuscript. In fact, the majority of these directions seem precise to the point of being pernickety: 'Enter a messenger, hastily'; and the sense of a theatrical imagination being at work is revealed in such directions as: 'Exeunt patricians, Sicinius and Brutus stay behind,', and: 'Brutus and Sicinius stand aside', and 'Brutus and Sicinius come forward' and most graphically: 'Enter Coriolanus in mean apparel, disguised and muffled'. We are, so to speak, watching Shakespeare as he himself *sees* his own play unfolding on the stage of his imagination.

The other claim that some of the directions have 'a distinct literary quality about them' is no less doubtful. The example given: 'Titus Lartius, having set a guard upon Corioles, going with drum and trumpet towards Cominius and Caius Martius enters with a Leiutenant, other Soldiers and a Scout', is *theatrically* specific – action, stage business, sound effect, the overall visual impact are all here.

The important point about these stage directions, however, is that whether they were set down outside the theatre or not, they were written by a man who is realizing his play in theatrical not literary terms. There is a striking example of this. Despite the fact that the action takes place in I.9 out of doors the stage direction reads: 'Flourish. Alarum. A retreat is sounded. Enter, at one door, Cominius with the Romans; at another door, Martius, with his arm in a scarf.' This use of the word 'door' twice could hardly be designated non-theatrical!

The extent of Shakespeare's meticulous attention to theatrical realization is also clearly seen in his direction to the actors: 'He kneels'; 'Cominius and Lartius stand bare'; 'Holds her by the hand, silent'; and by the amount of care shown even in the disposition of the minor characters: 'Enter the first servingman': 'Enter the second servingman': 'Enter the third servingman': 'The first meets him': 'Enter second servingman': 'Enter Aufidius with the second serving-man'; 'Servingmen stand aside'. Such attention hardly seems to serve any literary aspirations, and far from being indefinite it is difficult to see how these directions could have been more specific.

It cannot be over-emphasized that the evidence provided by Shakespeare's plays always points to a man whose knowledge of the arts of theatre was as large and potent as his mastery of the arts of verbal creation. *Timon of Athens, Antony and Cleopatra*, and *Coriolanus*, in particular, provide us with a privileged and uncommon opportunity to witness the way in which he deployed his knowledge of theatre on the written page. In this context the word 'literary' is misleading. Shakespeare wrote plays to be dramatically and theatrically realized, and it may be salutary to remember this. For if Shakespeare can be as specific and as theatrically sensitive in a manuscript copy of a play, what must he have been like, in full vigour, in the Playhouse? Perhaps in this play we can catch a glimpse of him – on the wing as it were – in the stage directions to the capture of Corioli, the whole of the action being most carefully punctuated with carefully placed sound effects:

'Parley'; 'Drum afar off'; 'Alarum afar off'; 'Another alarum'; 'Alarum continues still afar off'; 'Alarum, as in battle'; 'Flourish. Alarum'; 'a long flourish. They all cry Martius! Martius!'

What could be more evocative of the rhythm of war, the aural ebb and flow of battle skirmish, the sharp short effect, the long finality? Here, we might say, is *Coriolanus* in production, on the stage – and it is William Shakespeare's own production.

NOTES

1 Samuel Johnson's edition of Shakespeare (1765).
2 Ralph Crane. 1550/60–c.1632. Scrivener. See also H.J. Oliver, (ed.) Arden edition of *Timon* (1959).
3 G.R. Hibbard, (ed.) Introduction to New Penguin edition of *Timon of Athens* (1970).
4 Francis Bacon, 'Of Followers and Friends', in *Essays* (1597), pp. 33–4.

5 *Ibid.*, 'Of Expense'.
6 In conversation with the author.
7 Granville Barker, op. cit., p. 51.
8 Edwin Wilson, (ed.) *Shaw on Shakespeare* (1969), p. 36.
9 See E.A.J. Honigman, 'Shakespeare's Plutarch', in *Shakespeare Quarterly*, X (1959).
10 Benedetto Croce, *Ariosto, Shakespeare and Corneille* (1920).
11 A.C. Bradley, op. cit.
12 Wilson, op. cit., p. 221.
13 See P.W. Edwards, 'An Approach to the Problems of Pericles', in *Shakespeare Survey*, 5 (1952), pp. 25–49.
14 George Wilkins. Author of a novel, *The Painful Adventures of Pericles Prince of Tyre*, 1608, based on Shakespeare's play.
15 P.W. Edwards, op. cit.
16 Anne Barton in C. Ricks, (ed.) *English Drama to 1710* (1971), p. 247.
17 G.R. Hibbard, (ed.) Introduction to New Penguin edition of *Coriolanus* (1967), p. 22.
18 W.W. Greg, *The Editorial Problem in Shakespeare* (1954), pp. 147–8.
19 Hibbard, op. cit.
20 *Ibid.*

8 Shakespeare the Experimenter

The three plays – *Cymbeline*, *The Winter's Tale* and *The Tempest* – when they are not given the emotive nomenclature of 'The Last Plays'[1] are often described in a manner no less associative. They are frequently called 'Romances' – a word fraught with overtones and undertones so dense in quantity and quality that precise definition is almost impossible. In so far as the word romance is used it is normally intended to imply a mode of play which, becoming popular in the early part of the seventeenth century, was exploited by a number of up-and-coming dramatists, and adopted by Shakespeare in an effort to keep pace with young dramatists like John Fletcher and Francis Beaumont.[2] Ben Jonson had already sensed a change in taste and reflected his ability to conform to it in his collaboration with Inigo Jones in the creation of masques.[3] Such entertainments had received a boost through the interest, almost obsession, of James I's wife, Queen Anne, in opulent and extravagant show. They were essentially court affairs and a good deal of money was spent, during James's reign, on preparing and mounting them.

The emphasis, in masque, is on show which is ingenious, beguiling and surprising and on sound both in music and in words which is haunting, pleasing and undemanding. The English masque vogue was fortunate in that Inigo Jones's ability at visual effect was untainted with vulgarity and Jonson's sense of verbal correctness was not compromised by emotional cheapness. These two men, in fact, raised the status of what was, in essence, an ephemeral entertainment, into true art. Yet it cannot be denied that the growing influence of masque heralded the end of the monopoly of pure drama in the London theatres. In able hands the masque reached a peak of sophistication, in lesser it contained the seeds of decadence – words, drama, character, plot, theme becoming subservient to the need to enchant the eye and ear. Beaumont and Fletcher, manipulating an older form of drama – the romance – and adapting it to new demands, were sweet poets, fertile inventors, arid creators of character and morally and thematically barren. There is a moral decadence in some of their tragi-comedies in effects which might in modern parlance be called sado-masochistic – where a young girl is exposed to humiliations, some no less indecent than the contemporary 'bondage' and 'sacrificial' sexual situations of pornographic writing. The audience has a series of vicarious experiences but is not called upon to exercise

intellectual thought, moral judgement or any deep emotional committal to what is being offered them. The least offensive elements in
their plays are equally profitless in strictly dramatic terms. Superb
lyric poetry, enchanting pastoral situations, fluid blank verse range
from the sentimental to the pathetic without ever brushing the
profound.

Apart from the growth in popularity of such entertainments other
factors contributed to the decline of pure drama. Most notable was
the success of the Children of the Chapel Royal, later the Queen's
Revels.[4] These juvenile troupes had performed at the private Blackfriars Theatre prior to 1608 when the King's Men (Shakespeare's
company) leased it only to face an audience, largely aristocratic,
conditioned to the kind of entertainment provided by the Boys'
Companies and obviously anxious for more. They expected, in fact,
plays largely garnished with dancing, singing and masques.

However, whether or not it is true that Shakespeare's 'romances'
were written in an attempt to keep up with the new popular trends, a
multiplicity of theories has been advanced to explain their nature.
They are a non-Christian exploration of reconciliation; a subtly-
disguised Christian exploration of reconciliation; an allegory of life
and art; disguised spiritual autobiographies; experiments in a new
kind of drama; inchoate – tired relics of a past genius; Prospero is
Shakespeare, Miranda is Susanna (Shakespeare's daughter), and so
on. The immense amount of critical haranguing about them can prove
daunting. However, there is one obvious general characteristic of
Cymbeline, *The Winter's Tale* and *The Tempest* that is acceptable
whatever interpretation is put upon their meaning. They *are* romances in the sense that they present events which are remarkably
strange, unusual, and which eventually lead to a pleasurable ending
for the spectators. The romance plays of the early part of the
seventeenth century contained, as did their predecessors of the 1580s
and 1590s, specific ingredients and Shakespeare did not change these
in any significant way. Briefly, the principal characters involved are
people of high degree; the events of the plays are affected, to a degree,
either by the supernatural or by chance often to an extent which
makes even chance seem ordained; the events are almost entirely
confined to a courtly and an Arcadian background; the movement of
the plot and theme involves the setting-up of barriers to the
consummation or continuation of true love; the events often seem up
to a late state in the action to be leading to a tragic or catastrophic
end, but, often, a sensational turn of events produces a pleasurable

conclusion; the emotional pattern is dominated by pathos and sentiment; there often seems to be an allegorical element to the disposition of events and characters – i.e. the romances may be said to be about the way in which evil is created by jealousy, hatred and treachery and then overcome by brave love, fidelity and integrity, strongly helped by Time and Fortune. Thus Virtue and Beauty triumph after heroic battle with the forces of ugliness and misery.

Shakespeare's three romances incorporate these ingredients – often modified. In *The Winter's Tale* for example the force of realism is as apparent as the flow of allegory – particularly in the creation of character – and the common ingredients of pathos and sentiment are rendered into something very near to tragedy and emotional complexity. In both *The Winter's Tale* and *The Tempest* the emphasis is equally disposed between the narrative line and thematic development – we feel that we are being not only told a story but being involved in a profound examination of something to do with what life and art and nature mean. In short, Shakespeare, yet again, takes the common dramatic and theatrical stock and enriches it immeasurably. The ability to do this, alone, should make us pause before accepting the idea that, in these plays, a tired man was writing them as a valediction.

There is also something more. Patrick Cruttwell defines it when he writes, 'They have many of the signs of an artist who is feeling his way towards a new use of his medium'.[5] To an extent, indeed, these plays show some evidence of experimentation, and even without deep critical examination some hints of its nature can be apprehended – for example, the extraordinarily subtle use of Time, both as a kind of *dramatis persona* (as in *The Winter's Tale*) and in a technical sense.[6] *The Tempest*'s construction is a marvel of the manipulation of, on the one hand, apparently real and, on the other, dramatic time. Then there is also the kind of language used. It eludes categorization – it is not like anything he wrote before. It can change from hard, gnarled naturalism to intellectual complexity to translucent lyricism as easily as water finds a quiet pool after its rush through rapids. These transformations mirror the way in which the moods of the plays change like light on a stormy day. The divisions between comedy and tragedy, naturalistic and symbolic, which, in Shakespeare's other plays were near a point of fusion are, in these plays, rendered meaningless. The plays are neither comic nor tragic – they seem to be a different breed of dramatic communication. No amount of theorizing about the reasons for this really helps. The truth is that we feel them to be different when we read them and when they are properly performed we are aware of the truth of our feelings.

It is, therefore, unwise to be too categorical about the use of the word 'experimentation' in describing Shakespeare's writing of these plays, yet such is the amount of surprise in their content and communication, that we should not lose sight of a possible conscious process of experimentation by Shakespeare. This is the more likely when it is recalled that, like all experimental procedures, not everything goes according to plan. Indeed, it may be that *Cymbeline* is a failure of extraordinary quality – the ingredients being right but the mixing art still being tentative and unsure.

Cymbeline

In view of the varied critical attitudes towards this play over the centuries it would have been enlightening to have accompanied Simon Forman,[7] the astrologer, who saw the play some time before 12 September 1611, at the Globe Theatre, or to have known what it was about it that the King liked when it was performed before him at Court on 1 January 1634. It had been written some time between 1609 and 1610 after Shakespeare had read or recalled a tale from Boccaccio's *Decameron* and turned back to a book he had long used – Holinshed's *Chronicles*. He may have had an eye on Beaumont and Fletcher's play *Philaster* but we cannot be sure that this was written before *Cymbeline*.

An acceptance of this play depends on how willing one's suspension of disbelief is, and perhaps any critical assessment of it is a subjective matter. Many people associate drama with realism of character and event, finding the whimsy of romance and allegory irritating, not to say boring. As a result the anti-romancers tend to condemn *Cymbeline* for the wrong reasons – because it does not fulfil their idea of what constitutes true drama. On the other hand, the pro-romancers tend to become over-ecstatic about deep layers of symbolism and allegory. Both tend to forget that the realization of a play upon the stage can confound both attitudes. *Cymbeline* can be a sheer delight on the stage though an inchoate bore in the study. Certainly Dr Johnson condemns:

> This play has many just sentiments, some natural dialogues, and some pleasing scenes, but they are obtained at the expense of much incongruity. To remark the folly of the fiction, the absurdity of the conduct, the confusion of the names, and manners of different times, and the impossibility of the events in any system of life, were to waste criticism upon faults too evident for detection and too gross for aggravation.[8]

J.M. Nosworthy exalts:

> There is, quite simply, something in this play which goes 'beyond beyond', and that which ultimately counts for more than the traffic of the stage is the Shakespearean vision, of unity certainly, perhaps of the Earthly Paradise, perhaps of the Elysian Fields, perhaps, even, the vision of the Saints. But whatever else, it is assuredly a vision of perfect tranquillity, a partial comprehension of that Peace which passeth all understanding, and a contemplation of the indestructible

essence in which Imogen, Iachimo, atonement, the national ideal have all ceased to have separate identity or individual meaning.[9]

Between these two extremes there are continents of contention, half-agreement, supposition, but perhaps Nosworthy's comments are the best starting-point to examine more closely the proposition that *Cymbeline* is not merely a romance, but a profound play.

His statement 'there is something in the play . . . which ultimately counts for more than the traffic of the stage', suggests that *Cymbeline* possesses qualities which can be separated from its dramatic and theatrical existence. The majority of the upholders of the play take up the same position – implicitly or explicitly. Even Harley Granville-Barker, the most hard-headed of critics, after declaring that 'It is not conceived greatly, it is full of imperfections', finally admits 'it has merits of its own' adding that one turns from *Othello* or *King Lear* or *Antony and Cleopatra* to it 'as one turns from a masterly painting to, say, a fine piece of tapestry'. He, too, has found 'something in the play . . . which ultimately accounts for more than the traffic of the stage'. This is as much as to say that the action, the events, the incidents, perhaps even the characters – all that traffic of the stage – are of secondary importance to the other thing, the 'beyond beyond', the 'Earthly Paradise' – or whatever.

If, indeed, we look at the 'traffic' of this play, there is no reason to disagree with this point of view. There is a good deal of the traffic that seems inappropriate, sometimes awkward, often apparently irrelevant. For example, the character who bears the title-name – Cymbeline – is curiously undeveloped, and it is difficult to see how one can satisfactorily explain him away either realistically or symbolically. As an interesting, vital, affecting, embodiment of human virtues or vices or frailties or loves or hates he is practically non-existent. He has been held up by some critics as a kind of Prospero figure capable of reconciling the apparently irreconcilable, healing old wounds and the last scene being seen as a splendid externalization of his inner power to reconcile. Yet, if we look at the scene closely, we will find that it is extremely difficult to cast him in this or any other symbolic role, for there is a verbal insufficiency in this language which makes us question any claim that Shakespeare intended King Cymbeline to embody or stand for some deep spiritual vision. He is unsatisfactory both as realistic character and as symbol. When he rediscovers his lost sons, his words are:

'O, what am I?
A mother to the birth of three? Ne'er mother

Rejoic'd deliverance more. Blest pray you be
That, after this strange starting from your orbs,
You may reign in them now!'   [V.5.368–72]

Pericles, a play from the same writing-period, which is treated with
far less patience by scholars and critics, also has a recognition scene.
The difference is astonishing. Where Cymbeline's reaction is singularly verbally arid, Pericles' expresses the grave, almost piteous,
happiness of the event, its meaning widening from the particular to
the universal:

'O Helicanus, strike me, honour'd sir;
Give me a gash, put me to present pain,
Lest this great sea of joys rushing upon me
O'erbear the shores of my mortality,
And drown me with their sweetness. O, come hither,
Thou that beget'st him that did thee beget;
Thou that wast born at sea, buried at Tharsus,
And found at sea again! O Helicanus,
Down on thy knees, thank the holy gods as loud
As thunder threatens us. This is Marina.'   [Pericles V.1.189–98]

If we enquire further into the stage-traffic – the dramatic means
and effects of *Cymbeline* as an acted entity – we find other characters
like Cymbeline whose dramatic status seems indecisively created.
The sub-plot involving Belarius, Guiderius and Arviragus has no
coherent relationship with the main plot involving Posthumus,
Iachimo and Imogen. Granville-Barker concludes that 'apart from
their use to the story, they have little life in them, and Cymbeline and
his Queen have less'.[10] Their use to the story is, indeed, difficult to
assess.

Belarius and Guiderius are, however, given a number of arias to
speak:

'What should we speak of
When we are old as you? When we shall hear
The rain and wind beat dark December, how,
In this our pinching cave, shall we discourse
The freezing hours away? We have seen nothing;
We are beastly; subtle as the fox for prey,
Like warlike as the wolf for what we eat.
Our valour is to chase what flies; our cage
We make a choir, as doth the prison'd bird,
And sing our bondage freely.'   [III.3.35–44]

and one of the most superb threnodies ever written is spoken over the apparently dead Imogen by Guiderius and Arviragus – 'Fear no more the heat of the sun'. Yet our admiration for this verbal felicity is tainted somewhat by their excessive virtue. They are really such *good* chaps; their goodness shines both through them and upon them and, in the long run, it is as priggish as Cymbeline's assumptions in Act V that his hasty peace treaty will work. It is not without some significance that the death of the doltish Cloten at the hands of the virtuous Guiderius is difficult to accept, either symbolically or naturalistically as the triumph of good over evil. Guiderius protests his virtue, and Belarius never seems to tire of commending the virtues of the two young men to the audience and to the gods, yet, as we watch the play, we feel some sorrow for Cloten. Cloten's chief fault is mindless folly, but its punishment is disproportionate to the crime and certainly does not deserve to be accompanied by the seemingly interminable catalogue of the virtues of the avengers and within the larger context of the play the distortion of human values is seen to be even greater. If the play is taken realistically, the distortion of justice in that Cloten is punished and Posthumus and Iachimo forgiven seems ludicrous; taken on a non-realistic level, regarded symbolically or allegorically, what kind of 'perfect' tranquillity or vision of the Earthly Paradise is it that will so cynically disregard the logic of what is meant by mercy, forgiveness and justice as we see them disposed in the characters of Cloten, the Queen, Iachimo and Posthumus? This is the only play in which Shakespeare makes the kind of unreasoned folly that Cloten is guilty of punishable by death and Shakespeare's lack of mercy here is curiously uncharacteristic.

Perhaps this play should be judged as a kind of fairy tale where often values may well be turned topsy-turvy. However, there are two reasons why such an interpretation might prove impossible for many people. First, it is against all that is known of Shakespeare's usage of romance to believe that he wants us merely to sit back and enjoy a fable, signifying nothing – certainly in these later plays. The second is that there are no means whatsoever of knowing, from the play, whether those critics who find some profound vision in it are right or wrong. Shakespeare may puzzle us as he does in *Hamlet* or disturb us as he does in *The Merchant of Venice* but in no other play of his are we left so relentlessly at the mercy of our own subjectivity.

A skilful theatre director may well be able to give the play an exciting visual effect and satisfy the imagination of some playgoers by an emphasis on fantasy and bizarre comedy, while ignoring the play's flaws of construction and characterization. But, as R.W. Chambers points out, 'So conventional a representation of life (i.e. in *Cymbeline*) can only maintain itself by being consistent. If it is brought into contact with the touchstone of real humanity, it ceases to persuade. This is an artistic principle which Shakespeare had not always grasped.' Certainly, early plays like *The Two Gentlemen of Verona*, a middle play like *The Merchant of Venice*, and *Cymbeline*, fail to persuade us because of the incompatibilities between those parts of the play stuck within a 'conventional' mode (in this case romantic comedy) and those which, transmuted by his imagination, derive from his own experience. Iachimo, Imogen, Cloten and to a degree Posthumous (though he has something of the conventional romance-figure) are conceived in too strongly human terms to be satisfying bedfellows for those relics of romance – Cymbeline, Belarius, Guiderius, and Arviragus. We have some pity for Cloten because his stupidities are only too recognizable; Imogen touches our sensibilities not as a symbol of eternal purity or any other 'beyond beyond' but because she is what we would wish fair ladies to be – faithful, beautiful, a little self-willed, intelligent, choosy but, above all, exquisitely vulnerable. It is the possibility of Imogen's being ravished which partly accounts for her attractiveness and what we experience in the theatre is not – 'ah! what a symbol of goodness and purity!' but 'oh! what is going to happen to her?'

We are also only too familiar – not only from Shakespeare's plays but from our observation of real life – with Iachimo. He has strong affiliations, admittedly, with the Machiavellian villain of Elizabethan drama but we know that he has a breathing contemporary existence. There is much of Iachimo in the pub-haunting cads, who drive fast cars with a certain punter's tip in one pocket and a dolly-bird's 'phone number in the other. But where can one meet Cymbeline, Belarius, Arviragus and Guiderius? Nowhere, unless one is an avid reader of Italian medieval novella or their Elizabethan versions and translations.

Cymbeline is a 'fractured' kind of play attempting, as it does, to unite the realistic mode which dominated Shakespeare's tragedies with the new 'poetic' mode, with its emphasis on myth and metaphor towards which he was moving.

The dissociation of modes within the play is graphically exemplified by its language. B.Ifor Evans has some trenchant comments to make on this, using Arviragus's speech over the apparently dead Imogen [IV.2.218–29] to support a very important generalization about the play's language: 'There is no urgency in this, no compelling emotion, for all is constructed as if it were the faded memory of a feeling rather than the feeling itself. This is a view which, I know, will not be accepted by those who have found elaborate and symbolical meanings for these plays'.[11] In fact, critical commentaries on the play's language show as much diversity as in the commentaries on its alleged symbolism. It is extraordinary to realize that the language has been called variously 'loose' and 'tight', 'slack' and 'tense', 'highly charged' and 'unemotional', 'image-packed' and 'metaphorically parsimonious'. Ifor Evans's remarks seem to get nearest to the truth of it especially in terms of the effect of language on a theatre audience. Even the highly ornamented verse of the early romantic plays and the complex verbal structuring of the last plays are characterized by what may be called a fidelity to the truth of character – what is said by characters seems to the ear to be inevitable to that character – so that we may say that language and personality are consanguineous. In *Cymbeline*, however, there are far too many occasions in the play when there is a tremendous and obvious gap between character and communication, when character is used merely to inform or explain some point in the plot. Belarius is perhaps the chief offender:

'Hark, the game is rous'd!
O Cymbeline, heaven and my conscience knows
Thou didst unjustly banish me! Whereon,
At three and two years old, I stole these babes,
Thinking to bar thee of succession as
Thou refts me of my lands. Euriphile,
Thou wast their nurse; they took thee for their mother,
And every day do honour to her grave.
Myself, Belarius, that am Morgan call'd,
They take for natural father. The game is up.'   [III.3.98–107]

There is much in this play that seems to mark it off from the vast majority of the plays in the canon. The crucial point, however, is – is it different because it is poorly written, or uncertain because Shakespeare was attempting something quite new and unfamiliar?

If he *was* attempting something new then it is a remarkable demonstration of his intellectual and imaginative tenacity, after the incalculably great amount of energy that he had recently expended on the great tragedies, that he was still in a mood to allow of experimentation. His genius lay not so much in the uniqueness of what he did but in the singular magnificence of the way in which he did incomparably better what other men stumbled after. It has been claimed that the nature of the experimentation in this play is an attempt to combine tragedy and comedy in the service of romance. Nosworthy says that Shakespeare 'was yet unpractised in the art of blending the two in the service of romance'. Yet Shakespeare was alreay supremely well practised in the art of combining comedy and tragedy (witness the *Henry IV* plays) and had already combined the two in the service of romance in *All's Well that Ends Well* and *Measure for Measure*. Neither should it be forgotten that *Twelfth Night* and *As You Like It* are romances and that, although the ingredient of comedy is the dominant one, both plays have dark traces in them. Indeed the happy affirmations at the end of the plays are made the more poignant simply because of the darker elements. If Shakespeare was experimenting in Cymbeline, then the direction was, though he may not have been aware of it, towards *The Tempest*. Perhaps, too, a certain amount of exhaustion after the writing of the tragedies accounts for what, is for him, a failure. He lacked the full imaginative freshness which was to enable him (in *The Winter's Tale* and *The Tempest*) to embark on an entirely new kind of dramatic writing and a re-focusing of his vision.

Finally it is necessary to say that if it is true that, in this play, Shakespeare shows signs of fatigue, modern Shakespearean production certainly does not. Actual performance allied to directorial ingenuity can provide an audience with an attractive, engaging fantasy.

The Winter's Tale

The Winter's Tale comes at the end of the section on comedies in the first Folio. The text is good and was possibly printed from a transcript of Ralph Crane, the scrivener, who seems to have done a good deal of copying work for Shakespeare's company. There is no quarto edition of the play but the ubiquitous Simon Forman saw the play performed at the Globe on Wednesday 15 May 1611. The description which Forman gives seems sufficient justification for the insertion of the play in the comedies section of the Folio:

> In the Winters Talle at the globe 1611 the 15 of maye. Observe ther howe Lyontes the kinge of Cicillia was overcom with Jelosy of his wife with the kinge of Bohemia his frind that came to see him. Remember also the Rog that cam in all tottered like coll pixci and howe he feyned him sicke and to have bin Robbed of all that he had and howe he cosened the por man of all his money, and after cam to the shep sher with a pedlers packe and there cosened them Again of all their money . . . [12]

The sense of 'happy ever after' is strong here as is the effect that Autolycus seems to have had on Forman. Shakespeare followed, at times very closely at others loosely, his source – *Pandosto* by Robert Greene (1588). Typically, the major changes are nearly all in the strengthening of character and the rendering more dramatic certain events and situation – Camillo is built-up, the effects of Leontes' jealousy are expanded and deepened in meaning, Autolycus is transformed from his position as a servant to a free-ranging scoundrel, Paulina is virtually a new character. Above all, however, it is Shakespeare's way with Time that, more than anything else, gives *The Winter's Tale* its peculiar and distinctive atmospheric quality. In Greene's prose romance Time is certainly consciously used as an agent in the plot. The full title of the book goes thus:

> Pandosto, The Triumph of Time. Wherein is discovered by a pleasant History, that although by the means of sinister fortune Truth may be concealed, yet by Time, in spite of Fortune, it is most manifestly revealed. Pleasant for age to avoid drowsy thoughts, profitable for youth to eschew other wanton pastimes.

It was of such tales as this that Philip Sidney was thinking when he wrote that the poet 'with a tale forsooth he cometh unto you, with a tale that holdeth children from play, and old men from the chimney

366

corner'.[13] Sidney was writing of the need for literary art to educate by beguiling, to improve the mind while delighting the imagination. Greene's statement in his title fits exactly the ideal demanded by Sidney. *Pandosto* is a moral tale about how Time heals and, in a very simplistic sense, so is Shakespeare's play. There is, however, no comparison in depth and subtlety of usage of Time. Firstly it is personified as a *dramatis persona* – the Chorus; secondly, its influence permeates the whole of the action, and thirdly, in the strictly theatrical sense, the manipulation of time is extremely subtle.

The Winter's Tale may be regarded as an innovation if only in the way in which the whole concept of Time is used. In a way, Shakespeare's notion of the role played by time in human affairs in his plays previous to this one, and in his sonnets, is unremarkable, simple, even if expressed with superb emotional effect. In the sonnets, for example, we find that Time is most often expressed as a destroyer – of beauty, power, rule, authority – but art is capable of preserving them. Much English lyric poetry derives a certain plangency from the tacit acceptance of the 'fallacy' that all experience of the physical world is transitory, mutable, but that the work itself, the enshriner of experience, is not:

> 'So long as men can breathe or eyes can see,
> So long lives this, and this gives life to thee.'   [Sonnet 18]

Shakespeare, particularly in his sonnets, faces up to the ravages of Time with his weapon of 'deathless' poesie, accepting its power on the physical world, but challenging it and taunting it with the 'metaphysical' force of poetry:

> 'Yet, do thy worst, old Time. Despite thy wrong,
> My love shall in my verse ever live young.'   [Sonnet 19]

The idea that art can, so to say, 'freeze' into perpetual suspended animation, a love, a beauty, which otherwise is doomed may in a curious sense be said to be a desperate kind of self-delusion. Perhaps what gives Shakespeare's sonnets their taut poignancy is the fact that we feel that any awakening from such a delusion can only sour us with despair. The remarkable fact about *The Winter's Tale* is that age seems not so much to have soured Shakespeare but to have enabled him to take up a stance towards time which is, in a sense, more mature, more rational, and, in no way, cynical. What once was sweet delusion becomes quietly joyful acceptance of the true facts of Time's influence on mankind.

As in Greene's tale, for Shakespeare the role of Time is to heal, to right wrong, to expunge evil, but it is never treated sentimentally. It is clearly recognized that Time will have, inevitably, its way with youth and beauty – a recognition that is foreshadowed in a small handful of the sonnets (notably 123, 124, 125) and expressed cogently in 123, in the lines, addressed to Time:

'Thy registers and thee I both defy,
Not wond'ring at the present nor the past,
For thy records, and what we see doth lie,
Made more or less by thy continual haste.'   [Sonnet 123]

There is no hint in the play of the earlier pathetic fallacy about the necessity for art, for almost the first reaction Leontes makes to the apparent statue of his wife is to comment on the way it has aged:

'But yet, Paulina,
Hermione was not so much wrinkled, nothing
So aged as this seemes.'   [V.3.27–8]

Yet ironically ageing is irrelevant to what, now, Leontes realizes with all his heart – that he loves Hermione and, after sixteen years the 'spirit' of her love shines through what he takes to be stone. The revelation scene [V.3] is rich in references which raise the level of human love high above mere matters of beauty, sex, social status and so on. In a magical way it is as if Time's sixteen years have released a spiritual beauty and, hence, a spiritual love, which transcends the physical. 'So much to my good comfort as it is/Now piercing to my soul'; 'You do awake your faith'; 'Her actions shall be as holy as you hear my spell is lawfull'.

This is a maturer conception of the relationship of Time to mankind and, indeed, of that of Time to art. In fact, art is, in a sense, relegated, the powers of nature operating through time replacing it. Hermione's actual physical existence, though aged, is, in fact, superior to any copy, any attempt at impersonation by a sculptor. There is something of a retraction from the artificial, the artificed, implicit in the whole play; one of the most affecting characteristics of Perdita is her quite unsullied simplicity, her 'natural' attitude towards life and experience:

'I'll not put
The dibble in earth to set one slip of them;
No more than were I painted I would wish
This youth would say 'twere well, and only therefore
Desire to breed by me.'   [IV.4.100–3]

Other Shakespearean romantic heroines are 'artificial' – not what they seem. Viola and Rosalind, for example, have to put on a disguise in order to achieve a real and natural consummation of love. Perdita, however, although she is thought to be shepherdess rather than princess, has not imposed this situation upon herself, and whether she be shepherdess or princess her essential quality is naturalness, a kind of glowing simplicity which is profound in its truth and in its spiritual beauty. It is possible to see how Shakespeare seems to have steadily proceeded towards the creation of the ultimate natural female – Miranda. From Imogen (*Cymbeline*) onwards the heroines progressively lose all remnants of the artificial, the sophisticated, the fabricated, as if there was a deliberate and curiously spiritual desire on the part of Shakespeare to create a total innocence, an unmatchable beauty which both partakes of and transcends the physical.

Thus, one aspect of Time's usage in this play is thematic. Whatever is natural is handmaiden to it, is subservient to it, but, in the end transcends in healing, in restoring. It may be said that concomitant to the triumph of Time is the triumph of nature – all things age but grow, within a larger rhythm, into reconciliation. The whole structure of the play is superbly made to accommodate this theme, for there is no scene or incident which does not in some way seem to have been constructed to emphasize some facet of Time. The play is starkly divided into two parts at III.3 with a speech by Time the Chorus, used conveniently to cover a gap of sixteen years, and achieving temporally what the Chorus in *Henry V* does spatially. Yet although in *Henry V* we happily accept the convention that we are being asked to exercise our imagination to step over boundaries, nothing in the play's structure helps us; we enjoy the Chorus's stirring words and leave it at that. The effect of the Chorus in *The Winter's Tale* is completely different. Despite the fact that his words are neither stirring, philosophical, memorable or lyrical, his actual intervention at this point has a powerful influence on our experience of the play. There is no other play which at any given point offers such a tremendcous sense that what has happened prior to the point is not only literally in the past but, as it were, both historically and dramatically so. Moreover, all the events up to the Chorus's speech suddenly seem not only to be in the past but also to embody everything we mean when we speak of 'things past'. Polixenes, Leontes, Hermione and the rest all seem not only dimly remembered but remembered with a dim regret. The events of Act IV have, however, an astonishing present-tense freshness about them. It is not just that the roguery of Autolycus or the gaiety of the sheep-shearing scene beguile us into this feeling but the play itself seems to swoop down from a far-away regretful memory to a starkly contemporary reality. Simultaneously with this experience we begin to apprehend that a new spirit has entered the play – it is joyous, raucous at times, but, dominated by Perdita, it is, above all, innocent and natural.

The extent to which the structure of the play is so built as to bring about this quite remarkable difference in pace, atmosphere, spirit was brilliantly demonstrated in Trevor Nunn's production at the Royal Shakespeare Theatre in 1969. This production amply showed that 'modern' interpretations and techniques when they grow from the text, rather than roughly impose themselves upon it, can illuminate a play with exciting clarity.

The interpretation and the technique adopted by Trevor Nunn seemed to take their source and form from the onset of Leontes' jealousy. Its suddenness has often been condemned as 'unnatural'; it seems unmotivated. Indeed the twentieth-century English audience often baulks at events which seem too sudden and flies against accepted canons of normal behaviour. Perhaps a less conventionalized audience, such as that of Shakespeare's day, would not make such demands, being able to take in its stride what we stumble over or for which we require explanations that seem rational – based upon the complex subconscious activities of infancy. There is ample evidence for a plainer sixteenth-century response – Elizabethan plays are crammed with 'unnatural' occurrences.

Today the customary way of 'naturalizing' Leontes' fit of jealousy is to make him somewhat odd in mien, gait, style of address, from the beginning his jealousy becoming a gradually mounting passion. This procedure, however, goes against the grain of the text for there is nothing, either implied or direct, in what Leontes actually says up to the point where he utters 'Too hot, too hot', to justify this. On the other hand it might be said that the text very cleverly gives the imaginative director a superb opportunity to 'naturalize' what happens – an opportunity implicit in the remarkable contrast between the amount of dialogue given to Leontes and that given to Hermione and Polixenes in I.2. A mere glance shows that Leontes' words are expressed in short sharp bursts whereas his wife and friend have more time, more leisure, to expand what they have to say. It is only *after* the sudden onset of the jealous passion with 'Too hot, too hot' that Leontes is given long speeches, although even then they are made up of short staccato phrases, hurried, rushed, precipitate. All of which adds up to an impression that Leontes seems to be living in a different 'time-reality' than those around him. Whereas the expansiveness of their dialogue (130 lines to his 19) suggests that what they are talking about – the continuation of Polixenes' visit in the context of his long friendship with Leontes – has a long time dimension to it, Leontes's suggests a bunched-up, immediate response to the situation. Whereas Polixenes and Hermione see a reality embracing Past, Present and Future, Leontes seems trapped in an abrasive Now.

Whether intentionally or not, Trevor Nunn's production reflected the two different, ultimately opposed, time-realities and, so 'naturalized' the jealousy. The interpretation suggested a modern explanation – the sudden appearance of a very severe psycho-neurotic condition. This was brought to our attention by Leontes' pallor, his maimed speech, his limping gait (as if he had suddenly had a minor stroke). The technique employed to convince us that Leontes had entered into a world of experience and judgement different from anyone else, was to use a flickering psychedelic lighting effect. Through this we, in the audience were, so to speak, put behind Leontes's eyes and saw events and experienced time through his mind. What we saw, *as audience*, was a Leontes in a sweat of immediate experience, almost excessively frenzied in his movements, watching a flickering, blue-lit, slow-motion mime of lust between Hermione and Polixenes. They danced slowly towards each other, undulated their bodies, kissed hotly, while Leontes panted out his words. We experienced, in fact, in a surrogate way, Leontes's acute psycho-neurotic condition in which judgement, sight, and the sense of time is maladjusted: in which he annihilates, in his condition, the real past and invents a present-tense fiction. The result, in this production, was an exciting emphasis on at least one aspect of the time-values implicit in the play. Certainly any production which ignores or minimizes the plays' absorption in and with Time is avoiding the heart of its theme and, indeed, as the Royal Shakespeare Theatre demonstrated, is missing an opportunity implicit in the way the play is constructed, to make what can seem fanciful have a natural and logical basis and movement.

All the older generation are immediately affected by Leontes's jealousy and so, eventually, are the younger generation. There is a very strong sense, in the play, of sacrifice by the older generation in order that two things may be achieved. First, a healing of scars and, second, a clearing-away, as it were, of the past, so that the new generation can step out, freshly, unsullied, to take its turn upon the wheel of Fortune, and this process is a quite new variant on that which informs the movement of the great tragedies. The equation is simply expressed: a wrong is committed, evil is let loose upon the land, the land and its people suffer; only after death and sacrifice is suffering abated and a new order established. Sometimes the emergence of peace, of a new order, is little more than implicit, as in *Othello* where we assume that Michael Cassio will restore amity and concord to the society amongst whom the events have been enacted. In *Hamlet* it is more explicit; the shining Fortinbras emerges to hear from a representative of the old order (Horatio) what has happened, and to cleanse the infected world of Elsinore. In the tragedies, in fact, the restoration of order, of reconciliation is, as it were, virtually a promissory note only. In *The Winter's Tale* and *The Tempest*, however, reconciliation is no mere promise, sacrifice itself has a kind of benediction upon it, the emergence of youth seems neither brash nor wry, but inevitable – not because of the ways of the political world, but because of the rhythms of Nature and the controlling demands of Time.

This mutation on the old theme and pattern of order and disorder, chaos and regeneration is sometimes expressed with a kind of muted harshness:

>   'I, an old turtle,
> Will wing me to some wither'd bough, and there
> My mate, that's never to be found again,
> Lament, till I am lost.'   [V.3.132–4]

sometimes with the hint of homespun philosophy:

> 'My lord, your sorrow was too sore laid on,
> Which sixteen winters cannot blow away,
> So many summers dry. Scarce any joy
> Did ever so long live; no sorrow
> But kill'd it self much sooner.'   [V.3.49–53]

occasionally with a hint of cynicism:

>   'What's gone and what's past help
> Should be past grief.'   [III.2.219–20]

But its most striking embodiment is in the so-called sheep-shearing episode preceded by the episodes involving Autolycus and the Clown. The regenerative power of Nature in its young spring-guise is given an unsentimental and virile communication in Autolycus's first song about the daffodils. Autolycus is virtually an original creation of Shakespeare's, bearing only slight resemblance to a character in Robert Greene's *Pandosto*. He has several functions in the play quite apart from introducing a harmless but necessarily abrasive virility to the season of the year. He is, very conspicuously, one of the most obvious examples of light comic relief in the whole of Shakespeare, being needed to prevent the play from falling into gloomy melodrama. More than this, however, he is an essential balancing element in the sense that he stands for a four-square naturalistic world in a play which is so subtly built upon non-naturalistic elements. He is Shakespeare's reminder to us that the world of commodity has not been and cannot be forgotten. In this respect he may represent the extent of Shakespeare's sensitivity to audience-reaction for only so much romance can be absorbed by an audience, and then we clamour for a touch of what we call the real. Autolycus provides us with it in a similar but less complicated sense as do the Fools in Shakespeare's earliest romantic plays. By the time we arrive at the sheep-shearing scene with its imagery rich in references to the rhythms of nature and life and its ritual in the dance of the Shepherds and Shepherdesses we have perhaps been the more conditioned to accept it because we know Autolycus is around the corner should matters come to too great a symbolic turn.

Yet, on the whole, it is for its non-naturalistic qualities that *The Winter's Tale* lodges in the imagination, sharing with both *Cymbeline* and *The Tempest* the pervasive qualities of a dream. The trial of Hermione and the scene of reconciliation, for example, powerful though they are in a purely dramatic sense, impress us, in the final analysis, less by their direct impact than by their curiously ritualistic movement – the one, sad, elegiac, hung with a pall of inevitability, the other autumnally beautiful in contour and verbal colouring. Even the sheep-shearing scene, despite the raucous presence of Autolycus, suggests more the realm of myth than the truly pastoral. Trevor Nunn indeed rightly conceived the appearance of Perdita in this scene through the eyes of Botticelli. Although Judi Dench did not have, nor indeed should she have as Perdita, the implied sensuality of La Primavera, her movements seemed to bring into actuality the natural physical sensuousness of the Botticelli figure, and her dress, in its floral splendour, made the still folds of La Primavera stream into motion:

'Come, take your flow'rs.
Methinks I play as I have seen them do

In Whitsun pastorals. Sure, this robe of mine
Does change my disposition.'   [IV.4.132–5]

The contrast between sophisticated court and natural pastoral reflects the interweaving theme – the superiority of nature over nurture and the way in which those who have been blinded, warped, by artifice, inimical as it is to true simple humanity, can be restored to a 'natural' state. The play becomes a testament of faith in mankind restored – aided by sacrifice and an acceptance of the rhythm of nature and the flow of time.

The Tempest

The last complete play that Shakespeare wrote is, in many ways, his most puzzling. *The Tempest* shows some obvious affiliations in theme with *The Winter's Tale* and its other immediate predecessors, but it has an atmosphere found in no other play, its meaning elusive, less amenable to rational argument. Anne Righter writes:

> Whole books have been written to prove that *The Tempest* is really an account of the purification and redemption of the soul as conceived of by Christian mystics, or in the mystery cults of the pagan world. It has been proclaimed as an allegory of Shakespeare's own development as an artist, or of the political situation in Europe at the beginning of the seventeenth century. Explanations of its peculiarities have been sought in a supposed dependence upon Neoplatonism, gnostic thought, the lore of the cabbala, the Old Testament, or the dramatist's private religious theories . . . At various times the play has been said to be about almost everything . . . [14]

This is an accurate summary of its mysteriousness. It is capable of being all things to all men in a spectrum of possibilities ranging from Samuel Pepys's claim that it was 'the most innocent play that ever I saw' to Victor Hugo's stern belief that '*The Tempest* is the supreme denouement, dreamed by Shakespeare, for the bloody drama of Genesis. It is the expiation of the primordial crime'.[15]

It is, however, not only the variety of its appeal to different people that makes it difficult to assess its meaning but the manner in which it is able to offer extreme variants of interpretation to the same person at different times. Pepys's bustling middle-of-the-road theatre criticism must not be lightly dismissed. By 'innocent' he presumably meant that the play can be experienced on a level which makes no demands on the intellect or disturbs the emotions unduly. This is true. Children find the play, like *The Merchant of Venice*, particularly attractive to them. They see a kind of innocence in the variety of episodes and characters, the element of fantasy or magic. They are prepared for the ultimate, willing suspension of disbelief. They believe in what happens, and their belief admits of no argument, puts no strain upon the mind or the emotions. In a certain state of mind many adults find themselves accepting the play on a fairy-tale level – a mixture of the grim and gay, the natural and magical, with the consequences half-guessed at, but sufficiently, beguilingly delayed to make expectation exciting. Prospero can be seen as a wise but sightly bored conjuror, Miranda as the enchanted and enchanting princess, with Ferdinand lacking only a white steed to complete his romantic image and Ariel the agent from the other world. The rest fall easily into place. No one, in the end, has been really hurt, although, like Fairy-Tale (or indeed, like Pantomime) the crimes committed earlier seem to merit punishment rather than forgiveness.

Yet there are other moods when Hugo's more severe attitude seems to fit the play more correctly. The strange atmosphere created by Shakespeare's language and his use of dramatic time suggest a greater significance, a deeper meaning, than that achieved in fairy-tale or pantomime. The atmosphere induces the sense that, from time to time the characters are in a trance – sometimes we witness the process by which it happens, and sometimes it seems to happen without conscious purpose on anybody's part, as when Miranda listens, at the beginning of the play, to her father's recounting of his and her earlier life. There also seems to be a distinct attempt to make groups of characters stand for, embody, certain ideas or concepts. It is difficult for example, not to see in the Trinculo-Stephano-Caliban relationship a sort of wryly comic allegory of political and social institutions as they are in deliberate contrast to the good Gonzalo's vision of how they ought to be:

> 'All things in common nature should produce
> Without sweat or endeavour. Treason, fellony,
> Sword, pike, knife, gun, or need of any engine
> Would I not have; but nature should bring forth,
> Of it own kind, all foison, all abundance,
> To feed my innocent people.' [II.1.153–8]

Further, there are occasions when Prospero's stage-managing of the events which occupy a few hours seems deliberately to have been contrived in order to fulfil what we may call a moral purpose – to reconcile and to heal; yet we puzzle at the apparent greyness of his mood when, after all is mended, he pleads for 'prayer' and says that his ending will be 'despair' unless prayer relieves it. We are conditioned by our education to regard the famous speech about cloud'capp'd towers as a magnificent piece of lyrical writing, but we often ignore the fact that it is curiously despondent – life is an 'insubstantial pageant', with the quality of 'dreams', and on each side of it lies the blackness of sleep. Modern 'absurd' dramatists could hardly go further, though they might do it with less grace.

So, the play intrigues, puzzles, enchants and infuriates. Its 'magic' is more pervading, less 'tricksy' than that of *A Midsummer Night's Dream*, the intellectual thought and argument it can incite is apt to start from even less common ground than is true of *Hamlet*; its moral and 'spiritual' preoccupations are less amenable to analysis than those of *Measure for Measure*.

Even in less esoteric respects the play stands apart. The proximity of its construction to the classical ideals of the unities of time and place is astonishing for a dramatist who had very rarely before shown much respect for them. The nature of its comedy is unusual – language being subservient to physical antics or movements, as if an appeal were being made to the eye rather than the ear. The shipwreck scene in I.1 takes an amazing theatrical risk. It is a scene which only the resources of the film camera and the sound recordist could adequately communicate and is always an embarrassing difficulty to directors easily becoming comic, or seeming pathetically inadequate. Shakespeare has, in fact, attempted a theatrical impossibility for what happens cries out for reported speech not naturalistic action. If the storm in *King Lear* is a problem, this one is a burden.

The stage-history of the play offers little aid in coming to an agreed consensus about the play. Prospero has been portrayed as tetchy, mild, very old, middle-aged, as a conjuror and as a prophet. Caliban has been depicted in ways ranging from brutally animal to the pathetically deformed. Ariel has been virtually naked, almost completely clothed, flying on wires, or emerging from holes in the ground. The theme of the play has been interpreted in forms as diverse as that of a comment on political organisation (particularly colonial) to an allegory of Shakespeare's own life. It has been presented visually as if Prospero were a kind of Alexander Selkirk,[16] and, again, as if the island had a quasi-lunar landscape upon which strange space-creatures roamed.[17]

Yet, for all this, which suggests both the uniqueness in the play and its baffling qualities, there are equally firm connections to be seen with other plays in this time-period of Shakespeare's life. *Cymbeline* has about it a strange, rarefied atmosphere; the events it communicates are, per se, even more contiguous to fairy-tale. It is, however, with *The Winter's Tale* that it has the deepest affiliations, and it is in the context of that play that it might be possible to throw some light on *The Tempest*:

'These are not natural events, they strengthen
From strange to stranger.'   [V.1.227–8]

There are two words which might seem to specify the thematic and dramatic ambience of the play – Time and Nature. Both of these, as has been shown in the previous chapter, relate very closely to *The Winter's Tale*.

Time is again used both in a structural sense and for certain emphasis. It has been commented on that Shakespeare clings very closely to the classical unities in the play, no more certainly than in the use of Time. The action covers a few hours, but it is interesting to observe how, even in a play which is so obviously based on a classical temporal construction, Shakespeare is not either entirely meticulous or forgetful. For example, Prospero (I.2) promises that Ariel shall be released 'after two days'. Some 125 lines later it has become 'within two days'. By V.1 it is expressed by Ariel in reply to Prospero's question 'How's the day?' as 'on the sixth hour, at which time, my lord,/you said our work should cease'.

Yet the occasional ambiguities are as nothing compared with the effects Shakespeare is able to achieve by manipulating Time. Perhaps the most affecting is described by Anne Righter as 'a sense of the enormous past bearing upon and almost overwhelming the pin-point of the present'.[18] The 'pin-point' is, of course, the few hours which Shakespeare has decreed for the action; but there are several reminders of the 'enormous past' – most notably in the long explanatory scene between Prospero and Miranda:

MIRA: Tis far off,
And rather like a dream than an assurance
That my remembrance warrants. Had I not
Four, or five, women once, that tended me?
PROS: Thou hadst, and more, Miranda. But how is it
That this lives in thy mind? What seest thou else
In the dark backward and abysm of time?'   (I.2.44–50]

and, certainly, the famous speech in which life is seen bounded by a sleep is, in effect, a description of the 'abysm of time'. Such huge implications as these are the contexts for minutiae like:

'I had forgot that foul conspiracy
Of the beast Calliban and his confederates
Against my life; the minute of their plot
Is almost come.'   [IV.1.139–42]

In fact here the unity of time has, unlike most plays based on classical construction, another dimension given to it and the play, as a result, is not isolated in its own unfolding immediacy but is seen as a particle of activity in a vast pattern of energy which stretches limitlessly before and after it.

Within the actual events of the play as they are unfolded to us another example of Shakespeare's clever manipulation is what may be called an impersonation of simultaneous action. It may be most graphically understood by imagining the existence of two television screens which are giving us two quite separate pictures of events that, in fact, are happening simultaneously, and in close physical proximity to one another. It is, of course, only an impersonation because Shakespeare was obviously obliged to present his play in the only way possible to him – in serial time. Yet there are occasions where one has the strange impression that although one scene literally *follows* another in the text, what it is communicating has happened during the same period of time as the preceding scene. The relationship of II.1 to I.2 is of this kind. Again, in II.2 Caliban enters to a noise of thunder which is surely the strange, frightening noise that the noble castaways have already heard some fifty lines *earlier* in II.1?

The placing of the ordinary serial time of the play's action against the awesome context of the abysm of past and future, combined with the unusual effect of the structural virtuosity just described, condition us to the acceptance of the 'magic' of the play. In fact, whatever necromancy is involved in Prospero's magical abilities, it is the haunting presence of time which convinces us of its efficacy and of its credibility, and at certain points time itself seems to be used in order to induce a trance-like condition in characters.

The most wonderful (in the literal sense of the word) example of this is I.2 in which Prospero recounts so much of the past to Miranda. Some theatre directors, finding this long scene an embarrassment, either cut it in order to avoid boring the audience, or persuade Prospero to so conduct it that he becomes a kind of quieter Polonius, half-comic in his stupendous ability to state the obvious. The comic effect is controlled by the reactions of Miranda to her father's speeches. The difficulty is that once you place a character as important as Prospero in a mould as recognizable as this, it is virtually impossible to change his shape – and there is nothing in the rest of the play to justify such an interpretation.

Read closely, however, the scene will be seen to contain what look like calculated effects. It begins with an incantation, of that sort which precedes hypnosis. Miranda's reactions throughout the scene have the terseness of the hypnotized; and Prospero's remarks to her have the peremptory commanding or questioning of the hypnotist. 'Obey and be attentive', 'Tis far off', 'Dost thou attend me?', 'Sir, most heedfully', 'Thou attend'st not', 'O good sir, I doe', 'Dost thou hear?' The effect is as if she were being induced into a state of trance, not of course, a complete one, neither is it being suggested that hypnosis is literally being exercised. Rather, it is a matter of tone, of atmosphere, of verbal response, of relationship between character – all of which induce the impression of swimming senses. It might be said that time-past is evoked both as the means of inducing Miranda's state and, in itself, a kind of dream into which she has entered – and certain figures come from this dark abyss, transformed as it were into reality. Miranda's later responses to Ferdinand and to the others have all the character of one who has had an inkling of what humans are like from a dream, and finds the reality startlingly wonderful.

The presence of a trance-inducing agent is, of course, obvious when Ariel appears in II.1 'playing solemn music' and putting all to sleep except Alonso, Sebastian and Antonio. It is usually assumed that the former then falls into a natural sleep while the other two plot to depose him, and most directors of the play interpret the plotting scene between Antonio and Sebastian in a brisk naturalistic way. In point of fact the text, in two respects, suggests that they have been put into a trance no less potent, if of a different depth, than that which has put their compatriots to sleep. The first evidence is the plain fact that they themselves are suspicious of their own waking state. There can surely be little question that this scene should be played as if they are in a waking dream:

SEB: What, art thou waking?
ANT: Do you not hear me speak?
SEB: I do; and surely
  It is a sleepy language, and thou speak'st
  Out of thy sleep. What is it thou didst say?
  This is a strange repose, to be asleep
  With eyes wide open;   [II.1.200–5]

The second evidence is the quality of the language. It has a languorous quality, it relies heavily, almost drowsily, upon vowels:

      'Ebbing men indeed,
  Most often, do so near the bottom run
  By their own fear or sloth.'   [II.1.217–19]

  'She that is Queene of Tunis; she that dwells
  Ten leagues beyond man's life;'   [II.1.237–8]

Significantly, too, so much of what passes between Sebastian and

Antonio has to do, directly or obliquely, with time and again it plays a dominant part in the creation of the unnatural state of the characters. In the first place, there is a strong impression given that the scene is isolated from time – perhaps, indeed, insulated. As it happens on stage, before us, it occupies perhaps eight minutes but its effect, largely because of the language, is of a 'timeless moment'. In the second place there are significant direct and oblique references to time. For example, Antonio says 'The'occasion speaks thee' which is to say – 'this moment of time is speaking to you'; then there are the strange references to the 'far away' in time where the Queen of Tunis dwells – 'Ten leagues beyond man's life'; and there is the reference to the fact that the past is a mere prologue to the deed they are about to commit decreed by destiny, but that the future is within their own hands:

> 'And by that destiny, to perform an act
> Whereof what's past is prologue, what to come
> In yours and my discharge.'   [II.1.243–5]

It should, incidentally, be noted that there are several puns here from a theatrical source – 'perform', 'act', 'prologue', 'discharge' (i.e. a theatrical performance). Moreover, the extent of 'trance' or 'dream' involved in this scene is fascinatingly re-inforced by Prospero's later words in which 'these our actors' are 'of such stuff as dreams are made on'.

The references to time undulate through this play and all seem calculated both to increase a sense of unreality –

> CAL: Hast thou not dropp'd from heaven?
> STE: Out o'th'moon, I do assure thee; I was the Man i'th' Moon,
>   when time was.   [II.2.127–9]

– and to emphasize Prospero's potent ability to use it, for it must be remembered that a good deal of his art consists of freezing action, stopping motion, so that all stands still, caught in a thicket of eternity for an instant.

The other word which describes much of the thematic material of this play is 'Nature' and its adjective 'natural'. It is the implications of this which binds *The Tempest* closely to the thematic material of *The Winter's Tale*. Frank Kermode indicates a starting-point for an examination of the 'natural' elements in this play when he writes: Caliban ... is the natural man against whom the cultivated man is measured.'[19] He suggests that Caliban occupies a quite distinct position in the play and that, thematically, he has a significant role in the development of a certain set of contrasts which are expressed both explicitly and implicitly. It is, however, misleading to assume that the sole basic contrast in which Caliban is involved is, simply, that he represents gross untutored nature, and that in varying degrees ranging from serene simplicity to sophisticated decadence all the rest represent tutored nature. Caliban, it must be recalled, has been taught language and he has the intelligence to conclude that his 'profit' is, ironically, that he has learnt how to curse. Further, Caliban is superbly articulate and is given one of the most haunting lyrical speeches in the play, where, as Robert Graves points out, 'it will be noticed that the illogical sequence of tenses creates a perfect suspension of time'.[20]

Caliban, it must be said, is not a gross and bestial thing, devoid of both reason and feeling. Indeed, the first contrast that is revealed to us is that between what has been made of him, by tutelage, by Prospero, and his own nostalgic memories of the truly natural state he was in when he was first discovered and subjected not to education, but to simple kindness:

> '... When thou cam'st first,
> Thou strok'st me, and made much of me, wouldst give me
> Water with berries in't, and teach me how
> To name the bigger light, and how the less,
> That burn by day and night; and then I lov'd thee,'   [I.2.332–6]

It is apparent that Prospero and Miranda together had 'de-naturalized' Caliban by attempting to educate him. The only reward they seem to have had for kindness and education is, first, an attempt to rape Miranda, and, second, Caliban's undying hatred. Caliban may be said to represent, like Perdita, an aspect of the natural, but whereas hers can be described as a plus state, his is minus. His 'natural' state has, in a way, been rudely forced by Prospero; he has been taken out of his proper environment. Perdita's, on the contrary, has been nurtured and has prospered. Caliban is no less sensitive to the realities of nature than Perdita, but he comes from the wrong 'seed', and the sophistications of civilization do not have any effect upon him except to make him grieve and to increase his hatred.

Although he can be contrasted with Perdita, it is with Miranda that the most wry and touching contrast is observed. They have much in common. Both have been tutored by Prospero, both have a sensitivity of spirit and, because of their isolation, hold much that they newly experience in awe. Most pertinent of all they both have a certain innocence about the nature of men. Miranda's exclamation about this 'brave new world' is echoed in Caliban's 'These be fine things, an if they be not sprites'. Miranda's completely frank declaration of love for Ferdinand has its complement in the touching and open-hearted invitation from Caliban to Stephano and Trinculo to allow him to be their slave and what he offers them is what we know he once offered Prospero – 'I do adore thee'.

It could be said that Miranda and Caliban are Prospero's children – the former by both nature and nurture, the latter by nurture. She is destined to retain a natural freshness, simplicity, grace of mind and spirit – all her breeding and her education have made of her something which tends always to express itself and to be expressible in spiritual terms. Caliban, on the other hand, is doomed to be impervious to the influence of nurture, of education. His breeding, the 'seed' from which he comes, is inimical to the beneficial effects of the education by which Prospero hopes to rescue him from his condition. Caliban is unhappy, grieves, is angry, for his 'nurture' has succeeded only in putting him in a kind of half-state of being. He has traces of the dignity of innocence which a basically natural condition endows, and there is a certain pathos engendered by the remnants of a totally natural sensitivity to natural responses, but the acquisitive, life-supporting predatoriness of the animal condition has been turned by 'education' into a cunning, self-indulgent materialism.

This essential contrast between the way in which one type of the natural (Miranda) responds productively to nurture, and the other (Caliban) responds destructively is a very important emblem of a fundamental opposition which appears in Shakespeare's plays and which, it can be argued, was basic to his vision of the nature of the organization of species in the world.

Shakespeare believed with all his mind and heart in an ultimate distinction between 'good seed' and 'bad seed'. No amount of nurture, of education, of tutelage was, for him, able to alter a predestined course of development from source to conclusion. True, from time to time, certainly in his early plays, the 'bad' makes a final conversion (as in *The Two Gentlemen of Verona*) but the most remarkable characteristic of such conversations is their convenience to the plot-line and their incompatibility with credibility. The separation of good from bad seed is, very obviously, in the plays, basic to Shakespeare's depictions of nature. The Duke of Burgundy's speech in *Henry V* is only the most specific example of this. He refers to both the naturally virtuous growth like the vine, the 'freckled cowslip', 'burnet', 'green clover' and the indigenously vicious but equally natural 'darnel', 'hemlock' and 'rank fumitory'; he is, in fact, talking of the difference between defective nature and effective nature. Just as 'rank fumitory' and the rest attempt to acquire and possess the gentler plants, so Caliban attempts to have Miranda; just as the 'hemlock' cannot be taught the gentler ways but can only await the coulter that 'should deracinate such savagery', so Caliban can only be controlled by punishment to deracinate his. There can be no reconciliation between hemlock and the freckled cowslip, it would seem. Yet, in *The Tempest*, Shakespeare performs an act of supreme charity to one of his creation, who has been chosen to represent a creature of bad seed. It is a sudden and peremptory suspension of sentence which, in no way, disturbs the basic contrast but lifts the heart with its access of mercy. Caliban's reply to Prospero's command, at the very end, that if he desires pardon he must go to the cell and 'trim it handsomely' is:

> 'Ay, that I will; and I'll be wise hereafter,
> And seek for grace.'   [V.1.294–5]

This, as Anne Righter points out, is 'in the direction of self-knowledge and understanding of the situation'.[21] Caliban, like so many of those characters whose 'seed' is their affliction, is blessed by that characteristic Shakespearean benevolence. If this makes Shakespeare seem authoritarian and élitist, then the descriptions are admissible. It is the last three decades of the twentieth century which have been ambiguous about discipline, authority, charity and mercy, and it is within that time span that more people have been wilfully destroyed than was imaginable to any era before.

Some of the most affecting moments of this play involve a character whose presence is passing strange. Ariel exhibits sudden accesses of human characteristics but for the most part he is either invisible or has taken some quite un-human form. His moodiness, which Prospero comments on, strikes us with the feeling that he is a kind of child. There are the two factors which give him sympathy: first, his sudden request to Prospero:

> AR: Do you love me Master? no?
> PRO: Dearly, my delicate Ariel. Do not approach
>   Till thou dost hear me call.
> AR: Well! I conceive.   [IV.1.48–51]

and his obvious desire to please:

AR: Was't well done?
PRO: Bravely, my diligence. Thou shalt be free. [V.1.240–1]

The first instance, together with Prospero's reply and the resigned response to it, suggests that love in the sense in which Prospero extends it to Miranda or Miranda to Prospero is not for him. He is, we feel, beyond love, and, for an instant our instinctive sympathies go out to one who, thereby, seems cut off, lonely. The other, only too human attribute – the desire for freedom from servitude – all too easily engages our sympathies for it begs the question as to whether service for the good master should truly be called slavery.

Yet, except in so far as they enrich our emotional experience of the play as a dramatic piece, they are misplaced. Ariel is not human, although it is one of the greatest problems of interpretation and, indeed, of presentation to decide what he is and how he should appear. We learn he has been a victim of Sycorax and was imprisoned by her because he, 'a spirit too delicate', refused to execute her 'abhorred commands'. He became Prospero's servant when he was rescued. He is, then, a 'spirit', but of what strain we cannot precisely tell, although we can make a quite certain contrast between his nature (which is good) and Caliban's. No one ever sees him except in some disguise or other, though he is present, invisibly in some scenes. No one human, except Prospero, reacts to Ariel, except in so far as they are stimulated to either fear, anger or awe by his ministrations. As a person, per se, he is non-existent, so how does Prospero see him? There is no clue whatsoever. He is not just air or water or something flighted that is now here, now there. As Derek Traversi has pointed out, one speech he makes – 'You are three men of sin . . .' [III.3.52] – is not only one of the most important in the play, but is delivered as if it came from one authority.[22] Yet the 'as if' is important. Immediately after the speech is made Prospero says:

'Bravely the figure of this harpy hast thou
Perform'd, my Ariel; a grace it had, devouring . . .' [III.3.85–6]

The tone is familiar; it is, yet again, an instance of theatrical words being used or a theatrical posture being implied. And, indeed, almost all that Ariel does in the play has the quality of performance, of impersonation or imitation. He is, we might believe, the ultimate actor since he seems capable of infinite improvisation and impersonation. He is asked to 'make thyself like' a water-nymph, he acts out the stern-sounding harpy, he is asked if he has 'performed to point the tempest . . .' (and it should be noted that like any staged tempest no harm really comes to anyone – 'not a hair perished'). Time after time Prospero uses the word 'perform' when he asks Ariel to enact something for him, and, as has been noted, Ariel shows examples of tantrums, the desire to be loved, the need for applause or praise, which is so characteristic of those whose job it is to be nothing unless they 'perform' or 'act' something else.

It may be suggested that Ariel is the ultimate example in Shakespeare's plays of that curious preoccupation he had with the nature of the actor-type. They appear in various forms throughout his plays, they appear – the Fools, Richard III, Hal, Hamlet – men who have a capacity not to be themselves and who, in some cases, have a desire to be nothing, lest they become vulnerable. Ariel, it may be said, encapsulates Shakespeare's final conception of the way in which the creative spirit may take up an infinite number of shapes and forms and disguises in order that some purpose may be achieved:

'Such shaping fantasies, that apprehend
More than cool reason ever comprehends.'
[*A Midsummer Night's Dream* V.1.5–6]

The Tempest has the quality of a dream or a trance and Prospero emphasizes the non-reality of the world and the universe, and yet through his manipulation of illusions he is able to convey a powerful sense of the necessity for a moral existence. An extraordinary number of examples of the ways in which such a moral world would or would not work in practice are given: treachery, duty, service, love, greed, hate are shown in action. Moreover, the world as a political entity is examined, even if comically, in the Stephano/Trinculo episodes with Caliban. In fact for all the trance-like and dream-like atmosphere it may be said that solid hard practicalities are dealt with. There still remains, however, at the end, a very strong sense that it is all an 'insubstantial pageant'. Shakespeare, in *The Tempest*, gets it, we may say, both ways. He communicates what turned out to be his final statement on life – a thing of bewildering contrasts yet, in the long run, wonderful to behold. At the same time he put on *his* stage a superb embodied distillation of the kind of being which had meant most to him throughout his life. Ariel is Shakespeare's most subtle and strange actor, the profoundest example of the theatre's world of shadows, illusions, tricks – a world of mystery and, in itself, a kind of mirror of the equally mysterious world in which we have to live from day to day.

NOTES

1 See E.M. Tillyard, *Shakespeare's Last Plays* (1938) and D.A. Traversi, *Shakespeare; The Last Phase* (1954).

2 John Fletcher (1579–1625) and Francis Beaumont (1584–1610) were dramatic collaborators, whose plays include *Philaster*, *The Maid's Tragedy*, and *Cupid's Revenge*.

3 Inigo Jones (1573–1651). Architect and stage designer. See Allardyce Nicholl, 'Shakespeare and the Court Masque', in *Shakespeare Jahrbuch*, 94 (1958).

4 The Children of the Chapel Royal were also known as the Queen's Revels, 1610–1616.

5 Patrick Cruttwell, *The Shakespearian Moment* (1954), p. 95.

6 See Inga-Stina Ewbank, 'The Triumph of Time in The Winter's Tale', in *A Review of English Literature*, 5 (1964), pp. 83–100.

7 Simon Forman (1552–1611). Astrologer and physician. His *The Bocke of Plaies* contains notes of his visits to three of Shakespeare's plays.

8 Johnson, op. cit.

9 J.M. Nosworthy, (ed.). Introduction to Arden edition of *Cymbeline* (1966).

10 Granville Barker, op. cit.

11 B. Ifor Evans, *The Language of Shakespeare's Plays*, op. cit., p. 204.

12 Forman, op. cit.

13 Sidney, *An Apologie for Poetrie* (1582).

14 Anne Righter, (ed.). Introduction to New Penguin edition of *The Tempest* (1968).

15 Victor Hugo, *Oeuvres Complètes de Shakespeare* (1859–1866); translated in New Variorum edition.

16 John Barton's production at the Royal Shakespeare Theatre 1971, with Ian Richardson as Pericles.

17 Peter Brook's production at the Royal Shakespeare Theatre, 1963.

18 Righter, op. cit., p. 15.

19 Frank Kermode, (ed.). Introduction to Arden edition of *The Tempest* (1970).

20 Robert Graves, *The White Goddess* (1961), p. 427.

21 Righter, op. cit., p. 32.

22 Traversi, op. cit., passim.

9 The Last Play?

Two of the most recent editors of *Henry VIII* exemplify in their different conclusions the abiding puzzles this play sets for readers, theatregoers, scholars and directors. Arthur Humphreys writes: '*Henry VIII* is not a deeply rewarding play to criticize (which is doubtless why it has inspired little good criticism) because it does not reveal layers of deep significance, an imaginatively stimulating sense of life, or a poetic style of rich or vivid challenge ... it does in fact reveal two hands, two poetic temperaments, and two creative procedures.'[1] On the other hand, R.A. Foakes writes: 'The play shows a unified, if special, conception and spirit.' And he further states that 'many of the peculiarities of style may well represent a further development of characters that had already appeared in Shakespeare's later plays.' Foakes concludes with a brave challenge: 'Throughout the remainder of this introduction Shakespeare is assumed to be the author.'[2]

The puzzles are – who wrote *Henry VIII*, and is it a play of any artistic consequence? The first question involves the possibility – some scholars would claim the strong possibility – that the hand of John Fletcher, Francis Beaumont's famous collaborator, played a large part in the writing of the play. Scholars have, however, been divided about the extent (if any) of his contribution, though there are some, like Foakes, whose inclination is to assign the play wholly to Shakespeare.

The second question obviously involves a good deal of subjective judgement. What Foakes sees as 'unified', Humphreys sees as the process of 'two creative procedures'. The arts and science of scholarly research do not always extend to reliable judgement upon that kind of dramatic and theatrical reality which makes a play viable for stage performance. The evidence of stage history is often more reliable. No recorded production of *Henry VIII* – and it was relatively popular in the nineteenth century – has ever revealed that it possesses more than a very superficial dramatic life. Equally no modern production has indicated more than that in Katharine and Wolsey it gives an alert actress and actor the chance to indulge in that kind of behavioural performance which, in the latter part of the twentieth century, is often mistaken for true acting.

At worst *Henry VIII* has the effect of a superior pageant, relying on spectacle and smooth but shallow dialogue. At best, as in the scene of the trial of Queen Katharine, it has a passionate verbal intensity and a theatrical intensity of incident of a kind to be found in the most effective dramatized historical chronicles – but no more than this. Of depth of characterization it has nothing; thematically it has no direction; its plot is mechanical. In fact, it is predictable in movement and direction, and blandly smooth in texture. Indeed, that smoothness is itself some evidence for Fletcher's having a share in its writing, for lacking Shakespeare's greater insight, he had a glib, sometimes plangent, fluency of his own.

It was written probably in 1613 and therefore has a claim to be among the last plays, perhaps *the* last one, written by Shakespeare. It has all the marks of having been composed for a special occasion – this may well have been the marriage, on 14 February 1613, of the Princess Elizabeth, King James's daughter, to Prince Frederick, the Elector Palatine.

But perhaps it seems even more fitting that it was during a performance of *Henry VIII* on 29 June 1613 that the Globe Theatre, at which Shakespeare had spent so much of his working life, and which history has indissolubly linked with his name, was burnt down to the ground when a cannonball, fired from a gun, lodged in the thatch of the theatre roof. The fact that such a play, having, whatever the minutiae of the disposition of authorship, only fugitive vestiges of Shakespeare's genius in it, should have been the last to be performed at the theatre with which, by now, his connections were becoming more and more tenuous, is both peculiarly dramatic – even, perhaps, symbolic.

NOTES

1 Arthur Humphreys, (ed.). Introduction to New Penguin edition of *Henry VIII* (1971).
2 R.A. Foakes, (ed.). Introduction to Arden edition of *Henry VIII* (1957).

Bibliography

A short selected list of material relating to Shakespeare, classified under subject headings and listed alphabetically by author.

1 Bibliographies

Berman, R., *A Reader's Guide to Shakespeare's Plays: A Discursive Bibliography* (1965)

Smith, G.R., *A Classified Shakespeare Bibliography, 1936–1958* (1963)

Wells, S., *Shakespeare: A Reading Guide* (1969)

2 Reference Works

Campbell, O.J. and Quinn, E.G., eds. *A Shakespeare Encyclopaedia* (1966)

Halliday, F.E., *A Shakespeare Companion: 1550–1950* (1952)

Lloyd Evans, Gareth and Barbara, *Everyman's Companion to Shakespeare* (1978)

3 Shakespeare's Life

Bentley, G.E., *Shakespeare: A Biographical Handbook* (1961)

Chambers, E.K., *William Shakespeare: A Study of Facts and Problems*, 2 vols (1930)

Eccles, M., *Shakespeare in Warwickshire* (1961)

Schoenbaum, S., *William Shakespeare: A Documentary Life* (1975)

4 Background to Shakespeare's Life and Works

Baldwin, T.W., *Shakespeare's Small Latine and Lesse Greeke*, 2 vols (1944)

Craig, Hardin, *The Enchanted Glass: The Elizabethan Mind in Literature* (1936)

Halliday, F.E., *Shakespeare in his Age* (1956)

Lee, Sir S. and Onions, C.T., *Shakespeare's England: An Account of the Life and Manners of his Age*, 2 vols (1916)

Reese, M.M., *Shakespeare: His World and His Work* (1953)

Tillyard, E.M.W., *The Elizabethan World Picture* (1943)

5 Shakespeare and the Theatre

Beckerman, B., *Shakespeare at the Globe: 1599–1609* (1962)

Brown, John Russell, *Shakespeare's Plays in Performance* (1966)

Campbell, Thomas, *Life of Mrs Siddons*, vol 2 (1834) (For Sarah Siddons: *Remarks on the Character of Lady Macbeth*)

Chambers, E.K., *The Elizabethan Stage*, 4 vols (1923)
Garrick, David, *An Essay on Acting* ... (1744)
Gielgud, John, *Early Stages* (1939)
Granville-Barker, H. *Prefaces to Shakespeare*, 1–5 (1963)
Harbage, A., *Shakespeare's Audience* (1941)
——, *Theatre for Shakespeare* (1955)
Hodges, C.W., *The Globe Restored* (1953)
——, *Shakespeare's Theatre* (1964)
Hotson, L., *Shakespeare's Wooden O* (1959)
Irving, Henry, *The Art of Acting* (1855)
Joseph, B., *Acting Shakespeare* (1964)
Lloyd Evans G., *Shakespeare in the Limelight* (1968)
Nagler, A.M., *Shakespeare's Stage* (1958)
Odell, G.C.D., *Shakespeare from Betterton to Irving* (1920)
Shaw, G.B., *Shaw in Shakespeare*, ed. Wilson (1962)
Spraque, A.C., *Shakespearian Players and Performances* (1954)
Terry, E., *Ellen Terry's Memoirs* (1932)
Trewin, J.C., *Shakespeare on the English Stage, 1900–1964* (1964)
Tynan, K. *Tynan on Theatre* (1964)
Wickham, G., *Early English Stages 1300–1600*, 2 vols (1959–72)

6 *Criticism and Textual Studies*

Anders, H.R.D., *Shakespeare's Books* (1904)
Barber, C.L., *Shakespeare's Festive Comedy* (1959)
Bradbrook, M.C., *Shakespeare and Elizabethan Poetry* (1951)
Bradley, A.C., *Shakespearean Tragedy* (1904)
Brooke, N., *Shakespeare's Early Tragedies* (1968)
Bullough, G., *Narrative and Dramatic Sources of Shakespeare*, 7 vols (1957–70)
Clemen, W.H., *The Development of Shakespeare's Imagery* (1951)
Evans, B. Ifor, *The Language of Shakespeare's Plays*, 2nd edn (1959)
Granville-Barker, H., *Prefaces to Shakespeare, 1–5* (1963)
Hartnoll, P. ed., *Shakespeare in Music* (1964)
Knight, G. Wilson, *The Wheel of Fire* (1930)
——, *The Imperial The* (1931)
——, *The Crown of Life* (1947)
Lever, J.W., *The Elizabethan Love Sonnet* (1956)
Reese, M.M., *The Cease of Majesty* (1961)
Ribner, I., *The English History in the Age of Shakespeare* (1965)
Spurgeon, C.F.E., *Shakespeare's Imagery and What It Tells Us* (1935)
Sternfield, F.W., *Music in Shakespeare*, 2nd impression (1967)
—— (ed.) *Songs from Shakespeare's Tragedies* (1964)
Tillyard, E.M.W., *Shakespeare's History Plays* (1944)

Wilson, F.P., *Marlowe and Early Shakespeare* (1953)
Wilson, J. Dover, *What Happens in Hamlet* (1935)
——, *The Fortunes of Falstaff* (1944)

7   *Journals and Anthologies*
    Lerner, L., ed. *Shakespeare's Comedies*. Critical anthology (1967)
    ——, *Shakespeare's Tragedies*. Critical anthology (1966)
    Palmer, D.J., ed. *Shakespeare's Later Comedies*. Critical anthology
        (1971)
    Stratford upon Avon Studies, vols 1, 2, 3, 5, 8, 9, (1959–   )
    Shakespeare Survey. Annual survey of Shakespearean study and pro-
        duction (1948–   )
    Theatre Quarterly (1970–   )
    Shakespeare Quarterly

Index